I0716380

After the End
Reckoning

RJ Lynch

Copyright © 2024 RJ Lynch

All rights reserved. No part of this book may be reproduced or transmitted in any form or by any means, electronic or mechanical, including photocopying, recording or by any information storage and retrieval system without permission in writing from the publisher.

Two Hands Media— Mukwonago, WI
ISBN: 978-1-7345323-4-0
eBook ISBN: 9798869365095
Library of Congress Control Number: 2024909050
Title: *After the End: Reckoning*
Author: RJ Lynch
Digital distribution | 2024
Paperback | 2024

This is a work of fiction. The characters, names, incidents, places, and dialogue are products of the author's imagination, and are not to be construed as real.

Cover Art: Shannon Unverrich

Acknowledgments

This trilogy has been a journey to write, and though I cannot thank everyone who has been a part of it, I want to thank those who have made the greatest impact in the chapters of my life. Some are still there with me every step, while others have gone their own way, but you are all important.

First, I want to thank my mother, Cindy, and father, Bob, for raising me to be who I am. I want to thank my cousin Shannon Unverrich for designing the cover for this last novel and the rest of my family for their support.

From there, I want to thank those who made high school better: Jarrett, Matt, Jeremy, and EJ. I remember only a few moments from High School, and the good ones involved one of you. Then, I want to show love to my Undergraduate friends who made college doable: Garrett, Tom, Ross, Courtney, Liz, Zak, Beth, Cy, Sav, and Payton. I had many difficulties in undergrad, and you all made my life better over those four years. I also need to show love to my Discount family: Chase, Brad, Dana, Matt, JoJo, and Frank. During my time there, I found out who I am. Last but certainly not least, my Graduate family. Though many people there helped me during COVID, there are a few that stick out above the rest: Anna, Jorge, Sam, Randi, Soley, Isa, Greta, Bailey, Tiff, Janne, and Megan. Our time together may have been short compared to the others, but your impact was what I needed. To all those I named here, I want you to know that I love you all. If you had not been in my life, I might not be here, and I know I would not be who I am. Thank you, and much love as we go through life.

Table of Contents

Part 1
Gathering Clouds

Chapter 1
Misty Visions

*W*aves crashed against a sandy shoreline. The beach was covered by a thick fog creating a dark shroud over the beachfront. Only, a few stars poked through the fog to provide light. In the starlight footsteps in the sand lead to a cloaked man. The cloaked man is Rob Doran, whom his city called a war hero and a drunk. Neither of those titles meant anything to him. Now, he was just a man with a single mission.

His cloak had holes and tears from nights when it was his only blanket. While his pants and shirt hung awkwardly off his body. In the past few months, he had thinned out heavily as all he would do was train and travel. But his eyes and mind were clear for the first time in many years. As he walked, his ears picked up the sound of feet stepping on seashells. He pulled out a compressed staff and extended it as another figure appeared. This man wears no cloak nor makes any effort to hide himself. Rob stares at the man who stands arrogantly in his path with a wicked grin that boils Rob's blood.

"Why are we here, John?" Rob asks at last. John does not respond at first. Instead, he turned his eyes to the water as the moonlight poked through the mist to shine on John's face. His pale, scale-like skin seems to reflect the moonlight. Rob could see the bags and circles under John's eyes.

"You're the one that followed me, so why are you here?" John never looked at Rob as he asked the question. He just looked towards the sea. He stood waiting for Rob to move.

"You killed the love of my life." When Rob answered, John finally turned to look at him.

"So? How many of those have we each killed? How many of those have we each lost? Are we really in a position to stand with moral authority?" John began to pace the beach. His movements appeared to be in slow motion as the sand shifted beneath him.

As Rob watched him, he could see John's condition. While Rob chased him through the country, John had not lost a step. His body was physically superior to Rob's. John had spent his weeks relishing in the lavish delicacy his influence provided him while Rob feasted on scraps like the rest of the world. John was superior to Rob, and the way his muscles stretched the suit made it clear that he was dangerous.

When Rob did not respond, John stopped and looked at his old brother-in-arms. "So, what are you going to do about it? I killed her, so what? Do something!"

Rob closed his eyes as John's words echoed in the night.

"I'm going to stop you."

"Stop me? I wouldn't be so sure about that but let us say you do. Will you kill me? Will you be the beast I know you are and avenge Iris, or will you be the weak child who refuses to do what is necessary?"

"I'm going to stop you," Rob said again. This time, his voice shook. His words were unable to not carry the same authority.

"Come now, Rob, you said the same thing at the bar at the end of the War. You were going to stop me from slaughtering that village. You were going to stop the squad from burning every man, woman, and child in it, but you know what happened. I put you through a table! Then, the rest of the team burned it all! So, how are you going to stop me now? How will you stop me from burning it all now that I have everything?!?" As John yelled, the wind blew and pushed the mist over the water. It revealed the beach they stood on and an army behind John. It stretched the entire length, with the most prominent figures standing in the front next to John.

John's most loyal soldier, the Executioner, stood next to their boss. The dark armor and mask still covered the mysterious figure. Emotionless and cold, the armored figure appeared to be a creature from a nightmare. On John's other side was Trisha, his niece with her blonde hair dyed dark ebony, nearly as dark as the armor of the Executioner. She was the opposite of Ex. Her beauty and light were every woman's envy while being every man's desire. She was a dream with an innocent smile that hid a twisted, psychotic darkness. Behind the three of them was a mass of faceless figures, all prepared to follow the command of their boss.

John's twisted grin grew as Trisha and Ex stepped closer to Rob. Pulling even with John, "What will you do, as you stand alone?"

Rob looked around him as he stood on the beach alone. Staring down John and his army, he refused to step back even after John's army approached. His heart raced faster and faster as they grew near. He took a deep breath and closed his eyes to calm him. John continued to come when he felt a light touch on his right shoulder. His eyes were jarred open, and he turned his eyes to where Dani was standing next to him. Her chocolate-colored eyes had a soothing effect on him. Her smile was soft as she carried herself proudly. Much like Rob, her muscles had started to decline from the traveling she had been doing in the previous few weeks, but she was still more than ready for battle. Once they locked eyes, they both looked ahead. John grimaced when he saw Rob was no longer alone. She was firm by his side, just as she promised in the swamps of northern Louisiana. As they looked at John, another hand touched his other shoulder.

Sam and Morgan stood to his left. Sam was uncharacteristically stoic. Unlike the other two, who had lost some of their muscle, Sam's lean figure had grown through her training with Rob. She had her dirty blonde hair tied back and was ready to fight. Morgan stood with Sam and was grinning with a certain excitement. She was still the more imposing figure between them and was prepared to show everyone that she could stand on her own two feet.

John was steaming as he stared at Rob and his new allies. His fist tightened as Rob stood defiant. "Your army might be larger, but I think you're the one that is truly alone." John's army slowly started to wither behind him until he was the only one left. The sand whipped around as John's forces turned to dust, creating another figure behind Rob. The first thing he felt was the arms wrapped around his shoulders and neck. Then he saw the blonde hair dripping down his chest as soft lips grazed his neck.

"You are never alone. I may be gone, but I'm with you too." Iris's soft and sweet voice whispered into his ears. Her voice breathed life into his tired body. At the same time, his heart broke hearing her voice and feeling her touch.

"Well, you win the battle in your mind, but what will happen when we meet again?" John laughed as the entire scene faded away until it was just him and Iris. The moonlight shined as he closed his eyes again to breathe.

∗∗∗

Rob opened his eyes and awoke from his meditation. There was peace in his eyes as they hung open. Despite the chaos in his meditation, he now felt a calm that for so long eluded him. While this feeling never lasted long it was a warm embrace that he treasured as his team prepared for the last leg of their journey.

The four-person team had found a small, abandoned cottage just a half-hour horse ride west of New Orleans to rest in before the final push. The cabin itself was falling apart as the old oak rotted in several spots and outside, there was a pair of graves with broken crosses. It was not an ideal spot, and the mosquitos made the meditations harder, but it was big enough for them to prepare for the final assault.

The long journey had exhausted them as they balanced training and traveling over the 300-mile horseback ride. While exhausting, the physical and mental training helped soothe some of Rob's concerns. Yet, something still bothered him. He had recently had the repeat vision of facing John and whatever army would stand behind him. Sometimes, he would stand firm, but his resolve would waver as he started to question himself. He had come so far, but there were still questions.

He looked out the cottage window and stared at the moon becoming visible as the sun set behind him. At the sight of the moon and stars, Rob whistled loudly. A clang came from a nearby room, along with several "ows" and other sounds as Morgan exited the room, followed closely by Sam, struggling to put her shoe on. From another room of the cottage, Dani joined them. There was a flow to how she glided across the floor compared to the chaotic mess that was Sam in particular.

"Time to go, ladies. The sun is finally setting," Rob explained.

"And what do we do when we get there?" Morgan asked as Sam used her to lean on as she put her shoe on.

"Yeah, what's the plan?" Sam followed as she tried to appear serious.

"Just outside the city, I have a contact with a stable for us to drop the horses off at, and he has a route to enter the city. I will warn you, girls. He said that it will not be pleasant," Dani explained while Rob rose from his seat.

"As if anything has been pleasant," Morgan commented. Rob chuckled at the bluntness.

"Come on, Morgan, it might be fun this time," Sam smiled, punching Morgan on the arm. Morgan shook her head as they grabbed their bags and left the cottage.

The quartet loaded the bare necessities and rode out on their horses. Using the night sky's darkness as cover, they plunged into enemy territory, unsure of what traps would lie before them. As they rode silently through the night, the wall that guarded the city came into view. The wall was unlike anything else left in the country. Due to the world's dangerous nature post-war, many cities put together a patchwork fence, but this was different. Standing somewhere between thirty-five and forty feet, it towered over the landscape. It had a firmer foundation and solid brick layers, making it nearly impossible to penetrate. Guards were dispersed all across the wall with few blind spots.

Their path diverted away from the wall as Dani took the lead. As Rob rode on, he started to think about the "plan." He was supposed to delay John until an army arrived, but he wondered how to get that army inside the wall. Even if it did come as he hoped, there was no obvious way for them to get past that wall without suffering mass casualties. He was lost in deep thought until a pine cone whizzed past him. At first, it didn't compute with him. Then, a second hit his shoulder. He turned to look at Sam, who was pointing at Morgan. Morgan just rolled her eyes.

"What do you need, squirt?" Rob asked as he slowed down to pull alongside her.

"Squirt? You never call me squirt, butthead," she answered back.

"Sorry, I was just trying something. So, what do you need?"

"Oh, I don't need anything, dude. You looked too serious, so I thought I'd help," she said as Rob laughed.

She was different, and Rob's demeanor had grown warmer since taking Sam and Morgan under his wing. Back in Memphis, when his blind mentor Mark and he had run into the pair, the ladies were raw. They had basic skills but were far from refined. Now, they still had a long way to go, but the impact he had made on them and them on him was undeniable. He wished Mark and his daughter Vicky had made it out of the city alive to see the growth.

As Sam and Rob spoke, the other two rode up front together. Dani smiled as she looked back at the grin across Rob's face. "Those two are something," she commented as she turned towards Morgan.

"That they are. Are you jealous?" Morgan asked.

"Morgan, I know what you are doing, and you know what the answer is. Besides, we both know you and Sam are sisters to Rob," Dani responded, staring Morgan down.

"I know, but one of these days, I'll get you to slip up," Morgan answered as they turned their attention toward the wall. Dani didn't answer. She just shook her head. Since Dani joined the trio, she and Morgan had grown increasingly close. Though Rob cared for Sam and Morgan, Morgan looked up to Dani more. Their personalities and habits clicked far easier, and Morgan had started to mimic Dani in several ways.

"Whatever you say," she started before calling back to the other two, "Hey, we are getting close. We should probably go quiet." Rob cut his conversation off as he moved up to pull even with Dani. They all knew not to argue as they grew closer to the stable and whatever entrance they would have to sneak through.

Chapter 2
Gatekeepers

Hidden against the backdrop of the night sky, guards stood upon the massive northwest gate. In the minds of many, these men protected the city from invasion. However, each guard on the wall knew that keeping people out was only part of the job. Their main goal was to ensure that no one left. They ensured that New Orleans remained a "paradise" in which people wanted to be. They could not allow the city to appear weak by allowing those who wanted to leave to leave. A paradise does not exist if those inside do not want to stay.

Walls have always served one of two purposes: keep people out or keep them in. The key to good leadership has been to convince their followers that those walls keep the danger out. Few people like the idea of being controlled or caged, but when tricked into believing that the wall fulfills their right to be safe, it becomes easier to gain control they are reluctant to give up. John was an expert at this deception. Like great kings before him, he had convinced his world that it was safe inside the walls while the outside was terrifying.

It was easy to do. Everyone inside still remembered the War, commonly referred to as Finis Temporis. The death and destruction were immeasurable. The fear it induced was untamable. John merely capitalized on this fear as he led Ascension to its position of power in the corporate world. Then, once he had the resources, he sheltered the people of New Orleans and "saved" them from the world falling apart outside the wall. He is now their king, but a better name would be prison warden.

On top of the gate, three guards patrol the borders. Their orders are strict, and they know that any failure could result in their deaths. John is not forgiving; if they let disruption enter the city, their heads would roll soon after. Despite the nature of their command, they are still light-hearted, standing above the city.

"I hope the rain holds off for the celebrations this week," one guard said as he leaned against his weapon. He tried his best not to yawn now that the sun had set.

"I'll second that one. The girls are never as fun if it is raining out. Except those wearing white, of course. Hahaha." The second laughed as he thought of the coming days.

"Joe, Fitz, shut up! If one of the bosses comes around, they will have our heads!" the third shouted as the other two just waved him off.

"Brett, ya butt licker. None of the bosses come up here because they have no reason to," Fitz responded.

"Didn't you hear about the unit from the south tower?" Brett asked as he turned to the others again.

"Ah, yes, the south tower. The three guards disemboweled and hung in the swamp for the gators," Joe began, "A myth made up by the captains or, at best, an exaggerated tale. Since Master Kore returned to the city, he has lost his edge."

"Is that so, gentlemen?" John's voice echoed from the shadows. The mere sound of it sent a shiver down everyone's spine. His shoes clicking against the floor made every man shrink as worry consumed them.

He emerged from the shadows as his emerald eyes peered from underneath the hood he had pulled over. Each step closer had the guards gripping their weapons tighter. John was never on the wall. That was reserved for the guard captains and, on rare occasions, one of the Executives, but never John. Whenever he traveled under cover of the night, every guard knew it meant one thing. Danger would be at their doorstep soon. He was the last person they wanted to see among all the guards. At least when the Executioner was sent to deal punishment, the unfortunate soul would be dead before they realized they were in trouble.

"Sir, I was only joking. We are just trying to keep things light with the festival coming." Joe quivered as he was trying to retract his comments. He had started to back away from his approaching boss, who said nothing. He just stepped closer to the trio until he could place his hands on the shoulders of Joe and Fitz. The pair shook hard as John just held his hands on them. It was not a tight hold. Merely resting, it seemed.

"Jokes are funny. You are not," John finally said, removing his hands and walking between them to overlook the swamps in front of the city. While John's back was turned, Fitz and Joe exhaled as they attempted to stay standing. Brett tried not to laugh at the two who had laughed at him moments prior.

John sat down on the edge with his legs hanging off. The guards stared at their boss. The silence of the moment just grew more menacing with every passing second. Each guard wanted to talk but was terrified to be the first to speak. There was a tension that gripped them, a particular atmosphere that surrounded John.

"Don't worry, gentlemen. I am in a good mood tonight. You will all make it to the festival, but for now, leave me be," John commanded at last.

"Yes, sir. When should we return?" Brett asked as the other two were still stunned.

"Just go patrolling the wall, and when you no longer see me here, you may return," John hissed. The tone of his response sent the guards skirring away.

Once they were gone, John pulled a small wristband from his pocket and started to play with it in his hand. The wristband was small and heavily worn from years of decay. All that could be made out of it was some cartoon bunny whose color no longer appeared and left nothing but an outline. His eyes were sullen as he looked at it. He kept rubbing it with his thumb and pointer finger. Then he brought it to his mouth for a gentle kiss. As he lowered it back to his lap, he began to cough violently. He needed to use his other hand to hold onto the wall in fear that the strength of the cough would throw him off the ledge. The cough continued for a few minutes before finally stopping as suddenly as it had begun. Once the cough had subsided, he turned his vision back to the world and the clouds that moved across the star-filled sky.

"Uncle, why are you up here alone?" Trisha asked as she stepped out of the shadows, reminiscent of her uncle. With each step she took, the sound of her knee-high boots clicked across the ground. Her movements were slow and deliberate as her words hung in the air. She wore skin-tight jeans tucked into her boots as a white tank top and leather jacket sat on her shoulders. Her eyes were distant and cold as she approached her uncle. His look nearly matched her own in the distaste for one another.

"Ah, Trisha. I see you've found my spot," John replied. His displeasure fully evident.

"Happy to see you too."

"Trish, what are you doing here? You know I do not want to be disturbed!" John stood to face his niece, who had strolled within a foot of him. His tone had grown to intimidate her, but she refused to give him the satisfaction of her being afraid.

"The Executives were worried about you. You just wandered off again."

"And since when do you care about what the Executives want?"

"Since you missed my training session. I can only beat up so many of your trainers. You know I need you." John sighed as Trisha answered him. His eyes rolled, and he sat back down. He did not want to yell or intimidate her, and he knew it would not work, so he tried to return to his peace.

"You are a stubborn girl. I will assist you with your training when I return. I need some time alone before the storm rolls in."

"Storm? I don't see any major clouds. So what type of storm are you referring to?"

"One that brings a man to his limits."

"Quite the storm; I guess I'll bring an umbrella then."

"Indeed, and I'd recommend a blade as well."

"Always, just as my uncle taught me," she replied, drawing a small dagger from her waistband. She spun the knife around a few times until, at last, she held it just inches from the back of his neck.

She kept it near his neck, saying nothing more. He smiled before twisting around and disarming her in a fluid spin. He wrapped his hand around her neck and hung her off the edge. Her toes barely clung to the edge.

"Come on, brat. You said you wanted training, yet you were easily overtaken."

"I was only joking, uncle," she pleaded as she tried to smile.

"Please, don't act innocent. I know you want me dead, but you cannot do it yourself." He smirked as he held her a little farther off the edge. She clung to his arm, but her smile had faded. She knew that Rob would be close and her uncle would not want to waste fighters, but did he value her enough to ignore the possibility of their being a betrayal? She wondered if she had played her hand too far with him.

"You're right. I can't kill you, but he can." She smirked just before John threw her back onto the gate. It was her only play. Rob was the only person her uncle would respond to, and they had been preparing her for him because of it.

"We'll see. He should be here soon."

"And what will you do when he arrives?" she asked as she brushed herself off and caught her breath.

"We will monitor him, and when the time comes, the storm will grow into a calamity that will consume everything." There was a look in his eyes that caused Trisha to shake. He was emotionless as he talked about the coming events.

"How can you say that so calmly? What if that storm consumes you and me? What if we lose everything that we have built? What if I lose everything you promised me?"

"You are whining again, dear. I have put every puzzle piece into place, and now fate will decide. Either I get what I want, you get what you want, or Rob gets whatever he wants. Now, is there anything else? Otherwise, leave me."

"Hmph…" She despised the phrasing of his answer but now was not the time to poke the bear further. Now, she needed to be a good niece. "Doc reported that a few more of Braden's guards have been harassing her and the nurses again," Trisha replied softer as she bit her tongue from saying more.

"That fool. I don't need more issues. Ex can administer justice as they see fit," he ordered with a scrunch of his nose.

"Ex will be happy. Now don't forget tonight's meeting. The Executives need to speak with you," she stated as she turned to walk away. She knew that any further conversation would do her no good.

"I won't. And Trisha…" John started hoping that she would pause.

"Yes."

"I know plans have changed in a way you do not appreciate, but I have prepared you to survive any storm, even if that means you turn on me," he said in the softest voice he had exhibited the whole night. Neither of them turned to look at the other. They both just stood silent while Trisha traced her hand along her neck.

Their relationship was complicated. It was not healthy by any stretch; neither treated the other well. John had tossed Trisha around, and Trisha had gone after him numerous times. It was unclear where the hostility started, but they were all they had. They were blood, and John at least loved Trisha. She may not return the feeling, but the issue is that they are both monsters who no longer understand love properly.

Trisha never responded. She walked off into the shadows, holding her neck and empty eyes. John sat looking upon the horizon as a few sprinkles began to fall. He looked at the sky and let himself feel the rain.

"Brother, I'm sorry I could not help your daughter more, but your actions created a monster that my brutish behavior could not help. But maybe, just maybe, Rob can do what I failed."

As John sat on top of his wall, a sewage pipe outside the city had become the entrance for Rob's crew. Rob now had to listen to Sam's critiques as they crawled through. "When you said this would be a tough route, I thought you meant physically, not…well, not this," she said with a choked-up voice as she was trying not to smell.

"You know, if you shut your mouth, you don't notice the taste of the air as much," Rob responded from the front of the pack.

"That would be a first," Morgan commented quickly to avoid having her mouth open for too long. Rob and Dani held back their laugh while Sam scrunched her nose. She tried to stick her tongue out but immediately gagged from the noxious odor.

"Are we at least close?" Sam asked after regaining her composure. Rob turned back to the group and nodded his head. Dani's contact had given him basic directions, but he was still guessing for most of the trip.

It took another ten minutes of crawling, and many complaints before Rob finally felt the grate. When he stopped, all of the talking stopped as well. He used his staff to pry the grate loose, then kicked it open. Squeezing out of the freshly opened hole, the group found themselves in an alley along the wall. They each took a moment to catch their breath.

"You've always taken ladies to the nicest places," Dani joked as she took a couple of deep breaths.

"You aren't helping," Rob responded.

"Wasn't trying to," She smiled as they started to chuckle. "So, what is the next step?"

"We should probably get off the streets before guards ask us questions. Let's start checking for any house that might be abandoned," Rob commanded as they spread out. Each person started to check house windows and jiggle door handles if they saw a building that appeared empty or abandoned.

Rob was growing nervous that their behavior would draw attention, but the street was barren. He had imagined that the city would be lively, yet only the sound of an owl echoed nearby. In the distance, he could hear some form of commotion and see the lights of the city lighting up the dark sky, but by them, there was nothing.

At last, Morgan found an open door, "Got one." The rest of the group joined her at the open house. Rob was the first to push the door open. He crept silently into the building, taking his time to look around. The house was in good shape, but everything was covered in dust or plastic. Rob motioned for the rest of them to come in.

They cleared each room before reporting back. The building had a creepy ambiance, with cobwebs in every corner, plastic on all the furniture, and every floorboard seemed to creak as they walked through the house. It was to the point that they felt a ghost would jump them before anything living appeared before them. The building Itself was relatively small and slender, with stairs in the back to take people to the main bedroom and bathroom. The bottom floor consisted of an old rustic kitchen, an ugly shagged carpeted living room, and a pantry under the staircase.

"The house is clear," Dani reported as she walked back down the stairs with Morgan. Rob just nodded his head as he made his way to the kitchen. He turned the handles on the sink. It seemed unresponsive, but then the water began to sputter out. It was scattered at first and cloudy until, at last, it turned into a solid stream. Cloudiness remained for a minute before finally growing clear.

"The water works."

"And what difference does that make?" Dani asked while Sam and Morgan took a seat on the plastic-covered couch.

"It means that you ladies can clean up after trudging through the sewers," Rob informed them. Sam jumped from her seat.

"You mean it, Rob?" Sam asked with her smile growing more prominent.

"I think you've earned it. It has been over a week since we have done more than a river bath. So I want you all to take turns cleaning up, and I will check the streets," Rob instructed. The younger girls appeared to be excited while Dani arched an eyebrow.

"Sam, you take the first shower. Morgan, I want you on the door. I will stay here and chat with Rob before he goes," Dani ordered. Both of them hurried up the steps without hesitation as Dani approached Rob.

"I take it that this won't be an enjoyable chat," he started. She just shook her head with a scowl on her face.

"What do you mean you are going to explore? Did you forget that everybody in this city wants you dead?"

"Not all of them…just the important ones."

"That doesn't help your case."

"I know, but I've learned not to lie to you."

"Smartest decision you've made so far, but circling back. Why do you want to go out there without us?" Dani asked, finally cutting to the point.

"I just want to make sure that we are secure. I promise that I won't go too far from where we are. There was a light off in the distance that piqued my interest. We need to make sure it isn't coming closer," he explained as he put his hand on her shoulder and flashed that dumb grin of his. She just sighed.

"We could explore together, or I could do it since they don't know my face either."

"You need to be here in case anyone shows up here."

"You said you wouldn't lie."

"I'm not lying."

"Well, I wouldn't call this the truth. You know we could wait and make a plan, but you're getting antsy."

Rob exhaled loudly, "Everything's going to be fine. I do this all the time." She looked at his eyes as he replied, and they held her for a moment before she caught herself and shook the look off.

"Fine, there is no point in arguing. You'll go when I'm showering anyway. But promise you'll come back in one piece," she finally said, yielding to his suggestion.

"I promise." He smiled back just as yelling started coming from the bathroom above them. They both turned their heads to listen, and Dani brought hers down first to look at him.

"If you die and leave me alone with those two, I will kill you," she said, poking him in the chest. He winked and slinked out the door.

Dani marched upstairs to figure out what all the commotion was about and put an end to it.

Once Rob was outside, he started to stroll down the street, looking for anything that could threaten his crew. As he walked by the houses on the street, he noticed a few lights on the upstairs of each place but nothing on the lower floors. Each house he passed looked reasonably similar to the one they had found, though some were a little wider, most had four windows and were scrunched up tight to their neighbor. The buildings were made of brick, stone, and whatever scraps could be found when the city was rebuilt. These homes may have been tiny, but there was some character, unlike in other towns John ruled where ruin or uniformity were the only two options.

He cut through a few alleys and traced out a decent perimeter. Just before turning back, he heard a commotion from one of the alleyways. He peered around a corner to see a young woman cornered by a pair of men. Three brutalized dead bodies surrounded them. Rob couldn't see clearly, but the one near him had its throat pulled out and chest gashed. Rob's stomach churned at the sight. He wondered if these men or the woman had done it, but just by their appearance, he could tell none of them had the heart to gut people like that. The person who killed the dead men had to be a demon of some kind with an emotionless core. It reminded him of the Executioner's work back in St. Louis. That masked figure that had bested Rob twice was something he did not want to run into now, but Rob decided to take a chance. He stepped over the bodies, which were ripped to pieces, until he could finally overhear the conversation.

"You say someone else did this but can't give us any details, darling," one of the men said. He put one hand against the wall to pin her and crept into her personal space.

"These men were going to rape me. I was terrified and didn't memorize the face of my savior," she barked back. Whoever she was, she didn't waver.

"These men were our fellow boa guards. You better come up with a better explanation than that girl," the other guard bellowed. Despite her strong convictions, his voice did cause her to shake.

"Yo, what's going on here?" Rob asked as he finally approached them. The two guards turned to the approaching figure as the young lady kept her eyes on the guards.

"Move along, citizen, and head back to the festival," the first guard barked, trying to keep his voice down.

"Festival…" Rob whispered to himself.

"Move along! Are ye deaf!" the second yelled, not keeping the composure of his mate.

"Oh, I heard you. I was just thinking of something. Like how two people can be so dumb to believe that a woman like her could do this."

"What did ya say?" the guard asked.

"You heard me. Or are you two actually the deaf ones?" Rob didn't know why these men were harassing the woman, nor did he understand why he had to involve himself, but once again, here he was. In the middle of something, he could have just left. Maybe he was doing it to make an ally in the city. No, he knew this wasn't the case. He just had an itch to take on John, and these two were the nearest thing right now.

"Watch her! I'll take care of mister smart mouth," the first guard ordered as he started to approach Rob. Rob took a step back and raised his hands. He shook his open palms at the guard, trying to wave the man off.

"Yo, I was just trying to help the girl out. I didn't mean nothing by it." While backing up, Rob started formulating a plan to take out the other guard without the woman being in danger. The first guard was only carrying a club and knife. He had hoped the guard was carrying something to throw, but he was out of luck. His eyes turned to the woman, who still had her back against the wall, but despite how things looked for her, there was still a bit of defiance in her eyes. He wondered if she just needed a chance to do something.

"It is too late now. You should know people who defy the guards end up in hell or the sewers." The guard withdrew his knife and lunged towards Rob's gut. In an instant, Rob dropped his defenseless act and used his hand to deflect the guard's arm away. He grabbed the man's wrist with one hand and drove his other hand into the guard's elbow. The man screeched as he let go of the knife. Rob twisted his arm and tossed the man to the ground.

The woman kicked the other guard in the groin when his eyes turned. The guard dropped to his knees as she ran to hide further down the alley. Seeing that the woman was free, Rob picked up the first guard's knife. He charged into the guard and drove the blade into his heart before he could fully stand. The second man pulled out his club once he returned to his feet and approached Rob as his mate dropped to the ground to bleed out. Rob drew his staff from the back of his waist and extended the staff to meet the club. The weapons clashed as the man's momentum sent Rob back. Rob rolled himself back into a standing position as the guard swung wildly. Rob slinked around each blow until the guard fell off balance.

As the guard stumbled, Rob kicked the club from his hand and wrapped his staff around the man's throat. He began to choke the man. The man thrashed, but Rob had complete control until the man was choked out. Once the man was done struggling, Rob threw him to the ground and sprinted out of the alley toward the safe house. The same direction the woman had run.

He reached the end of the alley and found her leaning against a house wall, curled tight with her head pressed against her knees.

"You're going to be alright," he said softly as he bent down next to her.

"Those assholes!" she yelled into her legs. He looked at her thoroughly and saw the blood splattered on her clothes. He wondered momentarily if she killed those other men but quickly shook the thought off. She was there when they died or walked up on the scene but was not covered in enough blood to have done it.

"We need to get you off the streets," he said again, being careful not to place a hand on her. Whatever occurred before the guards was terrible. He didn't need to do any more harm. However, he now felt responsible for helping her.

She raised her head and placed it against the wall. Her arms curled around her legs, and her knees were pulled tight to her chest, but now her eyes looked up at the sky. "I know, but if I cross these streets in blood. It'll just happen again. Hell, if I walk home alone, it might happen."

"Then come back with me. I can help." She turned to him with a deadness in her hazel eyes. He took a more extended look at her as she stared at him. Her skin had a caramel tone, while her hair was a dirty blonde. She was not a very tall woman, but there was plenty of muscle that helped fill out her frame. Age was starting to show on her face, but he was not one to talk. A life consumed by a world war and the chaos left in its wake leaves anyone feeling a decade older than their body.

"Yes, an even better idea. Go home with a random stranger who stabbed a man and choked another out!" He could see her tense up as she spoke. He scratched the back of his head to think. Just leave her there, he thought. It would simplify life, and he wouldn't have to explain it to Dani, but his inner voice wouldn't let him leave.

"I get that it sounds like a terrible idea, and it probably would be in most cases. But you can trust me. Do you think I would go through all that trouble just to kill or rape you now?"

"Maybe…" He saw the fear in her eyes as they sat together.

He exhaled, "Don't trust me then. Walk behind me if you want, but I cannot leave you covered in blood, and staying out here does neither of us any good. So please." As he sat next to her and spoke, she could feel a certain relaxation come over her. She didn't know or trust this man, but something in her gut told her that he would not harm her.

"Okay," she said after a minute, "but you lead, and I follow so I can watch you." He slapped his hands on his legs and rose. His hand stretched out to help her up as well.

"Deal, now let's go, and you can tell me what happened as we walk." Rob started off back towards the safe house. The woman stood for a moment in her blood-stained shirt and pants. She looked at her other options before finally following him. At first, they moved cautiously, unsure if any other guards would be around the corner, but just like his trip out, there was nothing in sight.

When he thought it was safe, he finally asked her the question that had been burning in his mind, "So, what happened back there? That blood doesn't appear to be yours." She paused for a moment and looked back again. Rob stopped a few paces ahead of her but never turned around. If she ran, she ran, but he wouldn't be the one to push her.

"Those three…those three have been harassing my friends and me for a few days. They arrived from some town in Illinois and had a God complex…Then, they followed me home from work tonight and jumped me in the alley. But this time…" Her voice trailed off as her eyes faded down to the side.

"This time, they wanted more." She just nodded her head. Though he could not see it, he didn't need the confirmation. "So, what happened to them?"

"One was on top of me, trying to rip at my clothes, but I held him off for a minute. I only needed that minute because that is when the screams started." Her voice got quiet as her body started to shake. Her eyes closed as she tried to compose herself. "The men were screaming, and something ripped the man off of me. I didn't look. I just curled up in a ball to hide. Then I heard a woman yell, 'Get off her, Dad! Get off her!' One of the guards was sliced and gutted brutally, blood sprayed everywhere. I only saw a raven-haired figure running as those other two arrived." She ended her story and just stood shaking. He turned back to her and stood a few feet in front of her.

"I'm sorry." She just shook her head and hands. She looked back up to him and started to walk again.

"It doesn't matter. That's our world now, and I've accepted that." She brushed past him and continued to walk before stopping. Neither had to say a word.

They were nearing the house when he asked one last question, "So, what is your name anyway?"

"It's quite rude to ask for a name before giving your own." She tried to crack a half smile.

"You're right. My name is Rob; pleased to meet you."

"You can call me Clarissa."

"That's a name I haven't heard in years. It's quite beautiful."

"Thank you."

"Of course. We're almost there." Clarissa looked at the houses nearby, and her eyes grew large. She jogged slightly to pull up next to him. She placed her hand on his shoulder. When he turned to look, her eyebrows were drawn back, and color had started to leave her face.

"I figured you were an out-of-towner, but you can't be at these houses," she said rapidly as he grew concerned.

"Why?"

"These houses belonged to people who are enemies of the city. The house burns or gets shot if people are seen in these."

"Well, that is a problem…I still have to go in and get my people." She just shook her head as she thought about what to do now.

Finally, after biting her lip, she said, "Fine, grab them and help me get back home. You saved my life. I save yours. Then we are square." She reached her hand out to shake his. He paused to think it through and wondered how Dani would respond. He knew she would doubt this woman's story, but a betrayal at this point didn't make sense. He doubted she would know his face if those guards did not, and up until now, she had trusted him, but he had to be sure.

"I trust you, but my people won't. Tell me what you mean by enemies of the city." She put her hands to her face and tightened them into fists when she pulled them away. She was struggling to find the right words.

"I can't, not here. We are too far in the open."

"Why does that matter?"

"Because the truth will get a person killed. I shouldn't even know about this."

"You're afraid of John," he said. When he spoke the name, her face went pale, and he could see the goosebumps on her arms. This woman was terrified just by the name. They may not be on the same side, but they did have a common enemy or at least a target for their despair.

"Who…who isn't." Her voice shook as she spoke.

"I'll convince them to return to your place, but I'll want answers when we arrive." His voice, on the other hand, had more conviction than before. When John was mentioned, she watched him move with confidence that did not exist in this city. She did not fully grasp who this man could be or be capable of, but she realized there was something special about him.

Rob approached the door as he thought about what Dani, Sam, and Morgan would think. This was the exact thing that he would lecture them about and lambast them over constantly. However, if she was telling the truth, staying in this location would be even more disastrous. His eyes moved to the windows that were darkened. The bathroom on the second floor had its windows blacked out. They had done their best to hide their presence and hoped they would be prepared for someone to enter unannounced. He slowly turned the doorknob and opened the door. As he stepped through the threshold, he immediately felt Morgan's sai pressed against his neck while Sam grabbed his right wrist.

"Nicely done." He grinned while Morgan hit the light switch. After seeing Rob, Morgan dropped her weapon. He entered the room with Clarissa following close behind. Seeing how these young women greeted him, her face was scrunched and confused. Morgan and Sam instantly readied to fight when they saw the new person. Morgan's eyes kept shifting between Rob and Clarissa. She could not believe that Rob had brought someone back to the hideout. It was against every instinct he had instilled in them, yet he was standing next to some women. Sam looked the lady up and down with concern. She noticed the blood on Clarissa's clothing while Morgan recognized the look in Clarissa's eyes. They could tell this woman was not an immediate threat, but were still concerned.

"Who is this?" Morgan asked with her hand tight around her sai.

"This is Clarissa. I helped her out of a tight spot, and she said we are in danger here."

"And you believe her?"

"I do. You would also if you saw what I saw in that alley." As Rob finished explaining to Morgan, Dani strolled down the stairs. Her hair was still wet as she tied it back into a ponytail. Her eyes locked with his, and she communicated her displeasure without a single word.

"Well, I made you promise not to die. Next time, I'll be more specific on not being stupid either." She approached the pair at the door. Her hand was on her hip, her head tilted, and her eyes studied the new girl. Instantly, the blood spattered across her jeans, and a helpless look in her eyes caught her attention. "So, what is her story?"

"My story is that I was attacked twice in an alleyway, and Rob saved me." Clarissa stepped in, tired of Rob answering for her.

"That sounds like him. So why are we in danger?"

"These houses belonged to traitors and are marked as so. If you are caught here, there will be no arrest. Just a death squad," she explained. Clarissa was becoming more comfortable now that the others were around and started to use her hands as she spoke.

"And why should we believe you?"

"Because I've trusted Rob this far."

"I don't like this." Dani looked at Rob for a moment.

"But if she is right, we are in trouble," Rob added. Dani looked at the woman and then the house they were staying in.

"Do you have some food?" Dani asked as she started to think about the options.

"Plenty." Clarissa smiled.

"Alright, but if you turn on us. I will put an end to you," Dani explained as she got within a foot of Clarissa's face.

"Calm down, Dani. If anything happens, I will take care of it." For the first time since she met him, Clarissa felt a shiver down her spine when Rob spoke. She had felt his kindness in every other interaction, but these words carried a different weight.

"I won't."

"I figured, but what do you two think?" Rob asked as he looked towards Sam, who had taken a seat on the plastic-covered couch, and Morgan, who stood with her hand near her weapon.

"You haven't led us wrong yet," Sam said with a shrug of her shoulder.

"Her eyes don't look like those of a traitor. They remind me of how mine were for a while," Morgan added, finally relaxing and walking to the couch to sit next to Sam.

"Good, then let's head out," Rob said as everyone collected their bags.

"Before you all come, I want to clarify one thing," Clarissa started as she looked at the group she was taking home. "I know you don't trust me, and I don't trust you either, but I think all of us have some sense that this will be best for all of us." With that, the group headed out. Rob through a hood over his head to hide his face as they crossed the streets.

This time, Clarissa led as Sam and Morgan walked next to her. Rob and Dani kept themselves a few steps behind in case there was trouble. This also allowed them to talk as they watched her lead.

"We have taken several turns to keep us off the main roads," Dani whispered as they each noticed Clarissa's odd pathing. Rarely did the group walk in a straight line, and at several points, they seemed to double back onto the same roads. The only noticeable thing was that she was keeping them away from the city's center.

"We have indeed. She is either scared or leading us into a trap," he replied as his hand stayed near his collapsed staff, and her hand rested on a knife on her belt.

"Reminds me of someone trying to lose a tail." Rob just nodded as he looked toward the city's center, where the lights and sound came from.

"What is special about this time of year?" When he asked the question, her eyes also turned to the lights before returning to him.

"I don't know. I've been trying to remember myself. Fighting alongside Pan rarely allows a person to celebrate."

As Dani and Rob trailed, Morgan had questions for Clarissa. "The people that Rob saved you from. Were they trying to rape you?" Clarissa clenched her left hand as Morgan asked the question so bluntly.

"They tried indeed, but that isn't the worst part."

"How so?"

"What makes it worse is the fact that they were guards. Men that are supposed to keep law and order in this city, but one of their leaders promotes their behavior."

"That's horrible, but it reminds us of our old home." Sam gasped as she looked at Morgan, who was lost in her thoughts. She looked at the ground and remembered the day she was nearly assaulted and how it cost her the man she loved.

"I'm not surprised. John is a man who loves law and order, but at the same time, his evil only allows for other vile individuals to rule with him. His Executives are the perfect example, and the pure misogyny the one boasts makes the city nearly unbearable for people who remember how things used to be."

"Then why do you stay?" Sam asked.

It took Clarissa a moment to think. It was a question she often struggled with but had at least some answer to, "Well, at first, it was love for a man. He was sweet, strong, and had a kindness from the brokenness he experienced. That was until that brokenness became all he is, then I decided to stay for the people of this city."

"For the people?"

"Yeah, it sounds dumb, but there are so many good people here, and I thought that if I could do a little good, maybe that would be enough," she explained. Her voice had gotten just loud enough for Rob and Dani to hear.

"Maybe you were right to help her," Dani said as Sam continued her conversation with Clarissa. Morgan had removed herself from the conversation, and Sam did her best to keep Clarissa from asking why. Luckily, talking about nonsense to distract people was a superpower of hers.

"Maybe I did. Let's hope she keeps that belief when she learns more about us."

"I hope so, too. We need all the help we can get. I fear Pan won't have enough people to siege the city." Her voice grew quieter when talking about Pan as she stayed mindful of her surroundings.

"I've worried the same thing." Clarissa cleared a smile from her face after Sam's jokes as she pointed to a relatively large house. Compared to most homes they had passed, this one was two stories tall and much more expansive than the others. It was twice the size of a typical house and looked like an old wooden lodge. The rustic wooden exterior was well maintained. There were no bullet holes in the siding or any clear sign of decay. Clarissa pulled out a key and opened the maple door. She waved to hurry everyone inside before locking it the instant they were inside.

As the lights flashed on, Rob was instantly impressed and more curious. It was an open floor plan with the stairs on the right side, a kitchen in the back, and a bathroom in the right corner. The living room blended in with the kitchen to create an open space. The wooden floors were well maintained, and a sizeable reddish-green shag carpet was under the sofa, chair, and coffee table. The lights were made from scrap metal and hung just off the ceiling. To their right was a bookshelf filled with old tales and medical textbooks. Back in Despartian, Rob had one of the nicest houses in the city outside of those who worked for Ascension because he was a war hero in the eyes of the citizens, which made him wonder who this woman was. New Orleans might be John's crown jewel, but he saw the other houses battered from the War and the rebuild. This house belonged to someone special with the kind of influence to know about Rob.

Rob stood more on guard now than he had the entire walk as Dani explored the four rooms and bathroom upstairs. She did not investigate deeply but shook her head as she walked down the steps. A pit in her stomach grew as she took in the lavishness. All the struggles and pain that people were facing. All the nights she had spent sleeping in the mud to fight for Pan, and here was this woman with a home that looked like it was out of a time capsule from before the War. It stood utterly untouched by the ugliness of the world.

"So, do you live here alone?" Dani asked from the bottom of the stairs.

"I do. I am one of the lucky ones who works in the medical district. I was blessed with this lovely home and my kitty, who will probably show up eventually," Clarissa responded as she made her way to the kitchen. The kitchen had an old refrigerator, stove, sink, and two open counters, with an island between it and the rest of the living room. She reached into one of the cabinets and pulled out a teakettle.

"A cat? That is even rarer than dogs these days," Rob remarked as he made his way towards the kitchen. He sat at the island's barstool while Sam and Morgan sat on the couch. Dani leaned on the other chair as she watched Clarissa prepare the tea.

"They are, but my former…well, former doesn't feel right either. This guy I have this thing with got it for me. He is powerful, so he has those privileges," Clarissa explained with hesitancy in her voice. Dani returned to the main area with everyone else and sat beside Rob. They both looked at each other when Clarissa mentioned this man.

"Sounds like a piece of work. Maybe Rob and he would get along," Dani suggested as she turned her eyes to look at Clarissa's back.

"No, I think that would be a bad move. He is quite the hothead." Clarissa turned to look at the two as the water started to boil.

"Hot heads and bad moves seem to be the norm," Rob said as the teakettle blew.

"I've noticed." Clarissa pulled the kettle off the stove and poured a glass for them. Sam was leaning against Morgan's shoulder as they started to doze off. Clarissa, Rob, and Dani were staring at each other as they appeared to play a game to see if they could trust each other.

"So, speaking of hot heads, who were the men that attacked you?" Dani asked, trying to keep the conversation moving.

"As I was telling the girls earlier, those men were guards. Specifically, men from Braden's Boa Division."

"Boa division? What does that mean?" Rob asked.

Clarissa stayed silent for a moment as she drank her tea. Just like earlier, she was holding back on information. "The boas are the basic troops. They are a standard group of slackers who think they can get away with things because Braden is one of the Executives," she explained.

"Basic troops and Executives?" Dani chimed in.

"Yes, the boas make up a majority of the troops. They are just average people who signed up to fight for John as soldiers and guards. They can fight, but their training is not great. Based on how he fought, they are not a concern. Instead, the mutated komodos and the vipers are the most concerning," Clarissa further explained.

"Boas, komodos, and vipers. John does enjoy cold-blooded things like himself," Rob pointed out.

"Once again, you used that name so casually and with no regard to the weight it carries." Clarissa's face pulled back, and Dani shook her head as she looked at Rob.

"She's right. You do speak of him too easily. He is feared by most people or respected enough that they do not call him by his first name," Dani assessed as she looked at Clarissa's reaction.

"Bah, he is just a man," he started, but Dani's eyes grew more intense. "But I see your point. In the future, I'll try to be more cautious."

"How do you know him?" Clarissa asked, more confused by his statements. He just sat silent as he sipped his tea and thought about the best answer.

"Well, in simple terms, he's punched me a couple of times, I punched him a few times, and then there was some other stuff," he explained.

"So, not one of his underlings?"

"Definitely not."

"Well, I hope you aren't lying."

"And we hope we can trust you," Dani interjected. "So now that he told you how he knew him, can you tell us more about the other units?"

"If you insist. The komodos are special units led by Kenneth, a large, brutish man who makes most people look like ants. They are rarely seen, and only rumors exist to inform us about them. Meanwhile, the vipers are special assassins controlled by the final Executive..." Clarissa paused for a moment before speaking. Her lips began to quiver, and her hand shook. "They are commanded by the Executioner. A terrifying being that is John's blade." Even as she spoke, she was terrified. When speaking of John, she was quiet but composed. However, the Executioner was a different story. The mere name seemed to provoke a terrifying memory.

"So the Executioner has a full squad. That is a dangerous development but narrows down our first target," Rob stated as he turned to Dani and the others. Just as he spoke John's name so casually, he did the same with the Executioner. Clarissa's eyes grew larger than before. She was shaking talking about them, but this man spoke without fear or hesitancy. He was unlike anyone else in the city, but that recklessness is dangerous.

"You know the Executioner as well…what kind of trouble have I gotten myself into?" she asked, still stupefied.

"The worst kind," Dani replied as she turned to Rob.

"Let's put it this way, Clarissa. We will be out of your hair as soon as possible for your own sake, but before we do, I want to investigate that commotion you were steering us away from," Rob stated as he finished his tea.

"Alone?" Both Dani and Clarissa asked.

"Yes, alone. Despite how it looks, it's how I work best," Rob stated as he rose from his chair. Before he could go anywhere, Dani had cut him off. Their commotion awoke Morgan and Sam.

"Really?" Dani asked this time.

"Please, I don't want to fight again. We've had enough of that tonight," Rob pleaded.

"Then don't argue. I've given in twice already. This time, I get the say," Dani demanded as she got into Rob's face.

He twisted his face around a few times as he tried to figure out a response. She was right, and he knew it.

"I was keeping you away from the celebrations. Peace Week just draws a lot of guards, and my bloody clothing would not have done us any good," Clarissa explained as she tried to defuse whatever was going on with the two of them. Rob turned to her after she spoke with a smile on his face.

"That's what this week is. I should have put it together sooner," he said with his hand to his face. Dani still appeared confused.

"Peace Week?"

"Come on, Dani. Don't tell me you've never got to celebrate in all these years," Rob commented, shocked by her question.

"No, I haven't."

"Alright, who are you? I thought everyone outside of the Revolutionaries celebrated this week. I mean, it is the celebration to commemorate the end of the War." Clarissa, who had been so confused by Rob and his closeness to John, almost appeared more concerned about Dani.

"I'm just someone who has lived a hard life, and peace hasn't been a word I've heard often. So, please, Rob, can you tell me more."

"Sure…" He paused momentarily as he realized how hard the years had been on Dani. She had spoken about it briefly, but this made him reflect on all the years he had spent drunk while she was battling. "Peace Week is an event once a year to commemorate the end of the War. They celebrate for a full week because of how long it took for the news to spread. It is meant to remember the lives lost as the word of the treaty spread on deaf ears." Rob explained as he recalled his own team and battles. Remembering the lives ended by them as they waited to hear the news. He realized why he didn't recognize the celebration earlier; whenever it reached this time of year, he grew his most drunk. He had to drink to drown the memories, and now the realization that it was this week brought several of the memories back in an instant. He sat back down as he thought.

He took a few breaths as his world started to spin. Dani placed her hand on his shoulders as she recognized the sight. He grabbed the table with one hand and steadied himself as he shifted his thoughts.

As Clarissa had said, Peace Week would draw a heavy guard presence. Still, they would also be occupied by many other events taking place. He no longer needed to investigate the commotion but wondered if he could still use the event as cover.

"Are you alright?" Clarissa asked as she handed him some ice water. He waved the water off.

"I'm fine."

"Well, at least you don't have to go out now to investigate."

"No, but this will make the perfect cover for Dani and me to explore." He smiled as he stood himself back up. His legs shook briefly as he rose but gathered them quickly.

"But why?" Clarissa asked.

"Because we need to know more about this city," Rob explained.

"And Rob is right. It will be the perfect cover. If it is the event you claim it to be," Dani interjected as she started to formulate her own plan.

"But we will need a pair of masks for the first night," Rob stated. Clarissa raised her hand sheepishly.

"Go on," Dani said.

"I may have a pair, but you two cannot bring me more trouble," she offered.

"I promise I won't let Rob cause more trouble," Dani said.

"What about us?" Morgan asked just before Clarissa could leave to get the masks.

"You are going to stay here and get some rest," Rob ordered. Morgan bit her lip at the order. She wanted to say something, but Sam placed her hand on Morgan's shoulder before she could. Sam understood how Morgan was feeling, but this was not their time. Besides, they had both already dozed off once.

"Okay, but stay safe out there," Sam smiled, trying to hide her disappointment.

"We will, don't worry," Rob replied.

"I'll go grab those masks now," Clarissa slipped out of the room. A few minutes later, she returned with the two masks and extra clothes. They changed into their disguises and made their way onto the streets. Clarissa also loaned them a small amount of currency to help with their efforts.

"Thank you, we will be back." Rob handed Dani a mask and then turned to the girls. "Both of you behave. And treat Clarissa with respect while we're gone."

"I'll keep Sam in line," Morgan answered as Sam turned to her, offended. After saying their goodbyes, the pair left for the festival. They wore green and yellow masks as they trekked through the streets.

Once they were a distance away, Dani turned to Rob. "She is hiding something."

"Probably, but so are we, and I think she wants to be on our side."

"For now anyways, but you were reckless back there. And not your usual self."

"What does that mean?"

"Well, you've always been one to act on emotion, but stupidly trusting is not your game. I partially expected you to jump into someone else's battle, but then you bring her to us," Dani replied as she turned to look at Rob. They were nearing the source of the commotion, so she wanted to finish this conversation before more ears could hear them.

"You think I'm stupid now?"

"No, I never said you were stupid, but trusting someone so easily isn't like you. Something feels off here, and I need to ensure you have your head straight before we face him."

"My head is perfectly straight."

"So, you say, but just look at what happened at her home. I saw your nightmares flashing as you sat on that stool. You are distracted and unsure."

"That had nothing to do with John. That was just me realizing what this week signified. And when it comes to trusting her, some people would call that growth, rather than arguing about it."

"I'm happy that you are learning to trust people. Just in the short time from when we reunited in St. Louis to when I saw you again in the swamps, there was growth, but still..." Her words trailed off for a moment as she bit her lower lip.

"But still, what? What is the issue?" Rob tried to look Dani in the eyes, but she refused to raise them to meet his. She cast her gaze to the side.

"But still, you don't trust me. You've already tried to exclude me twice since we arrived, and I let you get away with it once." Her voice cracked as she spoke. This was not the anger he was used to seeing from her. This was genuine hurt. "You told me back in the swamps that you wanted me to stand with you and fight. You wanted to go to war together, and now it feels like you want me to be protected like something fragile."

This time, Rob bowed his head as her eyes searched for his. He rubbed his face and felt the unusual prickle of his facial hair. This distraction allowed him to pull away for a moment. Still, he recognized he was trying to run from the conversation again.

"No, I trust you, Dani, and I want you to stand with me. I needed someone to protect Sam and Morgan if something went wrong...no, that's not entirely true."

"Then what is the full truth." She stepped closer to him as he leaned back to keep some of the space between them.

"The truth is, I'm afraid. People close to me keep dying, and I can't lose you three." She responded to his sentiment with a light slap to his face. Followed by a gentle caress.

"One day, you will learn to stop trying to protect me and instead work with me. I'm not that young girl you knew anymore."

"I know, but..."

"But nothing, and as for the other two, you have trained them well."

"I know they can do this, but if I lose you all, what is this all for."

"Who knows? All we can do is do our best and hope," she assured him as her hand rested on his shoulder. It had been carrying large amounts of tension as they talked but relaxed slightly.

He sighed and shook his head, "Are we alright?"

"Of course, just stop trying to exclude me from the dangerous stuff. Now, come on, it has been ages since I had a chance to celebrate." Dani answered as she shifted the conversation and started walking away again.

The main streets were packed with people. Moving through the crowd was a difficult and annoying task that Rob did not miss from his younger days. It took him a minute to catch up with her, grabbing her arm once he did. She just smiled as she grabbed his hand and pulled him along. They cut through the crowds, observing all the sights. People were hanging on street poles and off of buildings. Groups played cards and dice in the street. All while alcohol was flying freely.

The men and women were dancing while draping themselves over one another. Occasionally, they would pass a small brawl breaking out, but guards quickly separated each one. Some citizens wore ornate and flashy outfits, while others were nearly naked, streaking down the streets. Now that the children were put to bed, there were no rules as long as people stayed safe. The sounds of sex came from alleyways and bathroom stalls but were mostly ignored except by those too curious for their own good.

Not every moment of Peace Week was like this or the same everywhere. Though there were similarities across the globe, the debauchery of New Orleans still rang louder, especially on the first night, considered the second largest night of celebration only behind the last night. This is often when fireworks would fill the sky, and cities would put on grand displays to help the citizens forget the pits many of them lived in.

While observing the celebration, the pair was also gathering intel. Each time they passed a guard, Rob made note of them and what styles of weapons they had. He paid attention to any differences that he deemed relevant. Dani was doing the same, but she also focused on the citizens. She wanted to see how the guards and ordinary people interacted with one another.

Dani may have hesitated with Clarissa, but she was friendlier with the everyday folks. Despite Rob's attempts to stop her, she bought food from street vendors and rolled a hand of dice. Meanwhile, each one had their own way of dealing with the drunks that tried to throw themselves into their arms. Both men and women tried to grab at them and pull them into dances and other acts. Rob had to stay with his breath as he kept from returning to his old habits. Dani, on the other hand, indulged the drunks a little longer as she tried to fit in and talk with them.

After some coaxing, she got Rob to play a few hands of poker. Though he was better at it than the drunks, he was uncomfortable letting his guard down. Once he had won a few hands, he dismissed himself so they could continue.

"Now, was that so bad?" she asked him with a little more pep in her step than before.

"No, but it was a waste of our time. Something we do not have a lot of, remember?" Rob responded, annoyed by the stop they had made.

"Oh, I remember, but I talked to people while you gambled. Braden, the Executive, will be at one of the local bars up ahead." She smiled as she pointed to a bar a block ahead of them.

"So there was a plan."

"No, I just wanted you out of my hair for a minute, and I made a fun little discovery."

"Hmph, well, at least the bar will get us out of the eyes of the guards for a bit and away from the men and women who keep begging you to take off your shirt," Rob replied as they crossed another street and ignored some hollering on their left.

They slid into the bar, almost as busy as the streets but more controlled. People sat at tables telling stories and jokes while more liquor than Rob had seen in years was exchanged. Eventually, they made their way over to a corner booth where they could watch the comings and goings of the patrons as they waited for Braden to arrive.

"Can I get you two love birds anything?" the waiter asked as he came over to them. He was a mess as he tried to keep up with all the patrons who filled the place and coworkers who were just as flirtatious as the people drinking. The only people who looked worse were the bartender and cook, sweating profusely.

"A glass of the house gin," he ordered.

"Just a beer for me." Once the waiter was gone, she asked Rob, "When did you start drinking gin?"

"I don't, so I'll be less likely to drink it too fast," he explained as he continued to scan the room.

She just shook her head as she turned to do the same. They listened for anything important, but just a few myths that made good stories were told. They spoke about El Cazador, the bounty hunter who was creating a name for himself as the best shot in the West. Then they talked about the Tokyo Dragon, a killer who supposedly left only fire in its wake. There were also the German Amazons, a group of women that would raid cities in Germany, terrorizing Ascension in particular. At the same time, others talked about how they were from New York and that the city would soon rival any led by Ascension. All stories that made for a good time but were just as accurate as old-school dragons or the Kraken.

Nothing useful was being shared. The drinks were brought to the table after a few minutes, which broke their concentration on surveillance.

"How is it?" Rob asked as they each took their first sips.

"Not bad. I'd guess it is some type of lager. Quite impressive for today's world. How about yours?" she asked as she took another drink.

"It's fine, definitely homemade," he said with a slight cringe at the harshness behind the drink.

While enjoying their drinks, Rob finally noticed a man sitting in the back corner alone. There was something off about him. At first glance, he didn't seem out of place as his clothing was every day by Peace Week standards with a mask covering his upper face, but just like Rob's eyes, he was scanning the room. Meanwhile, all the other patrons were avoiding him. Even the guards that were stationed inside wouldn't make eye contact.

"Did you see the man in the corner?" he asked as he used the drink to hide his mouth.

"Oh, you mean tall, dark, and creepy over there. Yeah, I saw. Do you think he is one of the vipers?" she asked, adjusting her hair to hide her mouth.

"It would make sense. There isn't a boa stitched on his clothing like the off-duty guards here, but his actions speak of someone on duty. A trained assassin."

"So, what are you thinking?"

"Well, I don't think he has us marked yet. The masks cover our eyes enough that I don't think he see us scanning, so if we keep a low profile, we should be fine," he instructed, hoping Braden would arrive soon to make the whole journey worth it.

A half-hour passed without sign of him, and they started losing faith in the lead. They ordered some Cajun food to buy themselves time, but if they stayed too long, the viper would surely make them out as something suspicious. At this time, a large group of guards burst into the restaurant. They were escorting a tiny man who was causing quite the scene.

"Bartender! Bartender, pop your best champagne! It is time for the real celebration to start! Then have the cook send me something as tantalizing as some of your waitresses!" the small man called as the guards kicked a group of people out to clear a table for him.

The man was about five foot five and a hundred thirty pounds but carried himself like a giant. He wore a bright purple suit with gold splashes on the shoulders. The suit was accompanied and styled with gold and silver gloves bedazzled to shine like diamonds. Everything flashed except for his brown bowl cut that bounced as he snorted with each laugh. His nose was slightly crooked, and his eyebrows were far bushier than anything Rob had seen, especially for a man whose face was bare of any beard. The most striking feature was a twisted grin.

The man leaned over the bar counter to grab a bottle of champagne that he quickly popped for himself. The cork bounced off the ceiling and into one patron's head. He acted rashly as if the place was his with all the maturity of a ten-year-old. The bottle sprayed in the air, dousing a few waitresses, and then he drank straight from the bottle. His guards took a few more bottles to pour for themselves and the other patrons who occupied the room.

"It is the first day of Peace Week, everyone! That means it is time to revel in mind-altering drugs, barrels of liquor, and euphoric sex!" he yelled while chugging from the bottle and kissing a nearby woman. Initially, she seemed to lean into it, but her face told a different story once she disengaged.

While this was occurring, the guards passed out glasses to everyone. The only one who refused was the viper, who was rolling their eyes at the display. Even Rob and Dani took their drinks to maintain the image they were attempting to hold.

"Think that is our guy?" Dani asked.

"Most definitely, but he doesn't appear to be the normal company I would expect John to keep," Rob replied. At the same time, he continued to watch the antics unfolding in front of him. There was no doubt that it had to be Braden between the escort and the silence from the viper. However, something was different about this man. He was telling stories about sex and drugs while trying his best to impress any nearby women. Most of them indulged his attempts to flirt, but none looked comfortable around him. They would turn from him when he was not looking and fake smiles when he looked at them. He was often handsy, ensuring he fully grasped the situation before him. Eventually, Dani caught his eye.

"He has been looking at you for a few minutes now," Rob noted as he finished the glass of champagne.

"Trust me, I've noticed. You can usually feel when creeps are undressing you with their eyes," she replied as she tried avoiding his gaze. Despite her avoidance, Braden rose from his seat to head towards their table, only to be cut off by some man.

"Your guards raped and killed my wife!" the new man yelled as he stood in front of Braden's procession. The guards reached for their weapons until Braden waved them off for the moment.

"That is quite the accusation, considering there hasn't been a murder here in over a year," Braden responded as his voice leveled off and turned icy.

"They raped and killed her!" he yelled again with zero exposition. Braden sat back down and with zero emotion on his face. As he hesitated to speak, he snapped, and one of the women who had been happy to see him leave a moment earlier was brought to him. She sat on his lap with a fake smile as his hand ran up and down her leg. It made its way up her skirt as she tried to ignore it.

"I'm sorry to hear about your wife's suicide and extramarital discretions, but blaming my men won't change the fact that your wife was a slut who couldn't live with herself. Now, you are lucky that I have no intention to punish anyone today," he claimed as he grabbed a nearly empty bottle with his other hand. He paused and looked like he would cheer just before he swung and smashed the bottle across the man's face. "My, my, you are a clumsy fella. Falling face first onto a bottle is quite dangerous." He pushed the woman off him and gloated as he stood over the man whose tears and blood mixed as he squirmed on the floor.

Braden waved his hand. A pair of guards dragged the man out the door as Braden took another bottle from the bar and popped it open again. The cork fell to the floor as the spray doused the room. Despite the earlier shows, what John saw in this man was apparent. A ruthlessness that cannot be taught but comes naturally to those who are truly heartless.

"Not going to help him?" Dani asked as she turned away from the scene that Rob's eyes were still locked onto.

"Not this time. We are too exposed," he replied while his hand tightened around his glass. He would have broken it had Dani not put her hand on him in time.

"What if I say I want you to help him?"

"I'd say you're crazy, and there are more important things," he replied as he started to bite his lip slightly.

"How about this? He has been eyeing me pretty well, so I'll distract him while you run and help. Maybe I'll even get some intel," she whispered.

"How are we going to do that?"

Without answering, Dani rose and threw her drink in his face.

"How could you?!? Out of all weeks, you drop this on me!" she yelled as the whole restaurant turned to them. Rob sat in shock as his hair was now drenched in beer. His mouth hung open as he looked up at her. "I mean with my sister, of all people!" After this comment, she winked at him. Seeing the woman he had already had eyes on grow emotional, Braden walked himself over to the table.

"Is there something I can help with?" he asked as he stood as close to Dani without touching her.

"Not until this cheater leaves the bar!"

"That can be arranged." Braden snapped his fingers, but Rob rose before the guards could grab him and backed away.

"No need for that, I'm going." Rob started to leave but turned back to them just before he was out of earshot. "Your sister was more fun anyway." Dani instinctively grabbed a bottle and threw it at Rob, missing high. Braden, at this point, had put his arm around her. She reciprocated the gesture by putting her hands on his chest.

"Well, hello there, darling." Braden smiled as his attention turned from all the other girls to solely focus on her.

"Thank you," she sniffed, wiping her eyes with her free hand. She had managed to create a few tears during the encounter.

"You are more than welcome. Now, please take a seat."

"Sure thing, this could make for some good revenge," she said as her hand moved to his face and traced it softly.

"I like that spirit," he whispered as he pulled her in close. She did her best to fake a flirtatious smile and keep her eyes from rolling at his comment.

"Oh, you are a brash one."

"That I am, but don't be mistaken. I can be gentle when I need to be," he insisted as she pulled herself close.

"Who says you'd need to be?" she whispered, pulling herself as tight as she could.

While Dani worked Braden over and distracted his guards, Rob searched for the man beaten inside. The guards at least had the decency to not punish him in plain sight. Rob found them in a back alley, still kicking the broken man. Checking to see if anyone else was around, Rob saw no one. He grabbed the lid of a metal trash can and drove it into one of the guards' heads, knocking him down. Then he followed this with a slam to the other's gut and drove the lid upwards through the second's chin. With both men rolling in pain, Rob helped the innocent man up.

Once they were a safe distance away, Rob helped the man pick the last few pieces of glass out of his face and patched up the wounds the best they could. While using some gutter runoff to wash the blood away.

"Thank you, sir," the man said as tears ran down his face.

"Thanks are not needed here. It was the human thing to do." Rob smiled back.

"Maybe so, but it is no longer normal, and I promise to pay you back," the man guaranteed.

"Just stay safe, and don't be reckless until that face heals," Rob stated as he patted the man on the shoulder. The man just nodded before running away. With his cover partially blown, Rob headed to Clarissa's, hoping Dani could care for herself.

Chapter 3
The Executives

An hour after Rob's confrontation in the alleyway, a meeting was being held in the mansion estate overlooking the city from the water's edge. The mansion is a large two-story building with a distinct iron balcony wrapping around the outside. The black metal acts as a steep contrast to the white marble that forms the base of the estate. A quarter of a mile of brick-laid road leads up to the building as it is decorated with fountains and greenery. The green tiled roof is by far its most distinct feature. A work of craftsmanship that overlooks the water on one side and is guarded by iron gates on the other. A half mile of field sits between the gate and the rest of the city. Littered by the remains of the old city, the mansion feels like it is in a different world compared to everything else. The beauty of the outside almost masks the vileness of the individuals gathering inside.

One of the main meeting room chairs was turned to overlook the water. As a bloodied knife was continually tossed into the air from the chair. To the right of this chair sat a monster of a man who barely fit in the oversized chair. His jaw was square, his face was covered in scars from hundreds of battles, and the top of his head had recently been shaved and polished. He wore plated armor that made him look like a walking tank and a five-foot claymore leaned against the table. The man's muscles twitched whenever the knife was thrown from the other chair.

"Enough with that stupid knife play," the monster growled with his entire seven-foot, 400-pound frame. After he gave the order, the blade was thrown one last time. It was tossed into the ceiling this time, where it became lodged.

"Better?" A muffled voice asked as the chair turned. Sitting in the spot was the Executioner, covered in black robes and armor their body blended into the chair. Though their mask hid their face, the large man could feel their eyes peering through them as they sat relaxed and calm with their head leaning against their hands.

"You are an arrogant ass, Ex," the man replied, looking up at the blade hanging from the ceiling.

"It isn't arrogance when I'm just better than you, Kenneth," Ex gloated.

"I could cut you in half with a single swing," Ken proclaimed as he leaned forward in his seat.

"You can try and get embarrassed," Ex mocked. Without hesitation, the beast swung his mighty blade with a single hand, slicing the chair in half easily, but Ex was gone. They had jumped and were now balancing on the sword, staring Ken in the eyes. The knife they had stuck in the ceiling fell. Ex snatched it from the sky and pressed the edge against Ken's neck. Though Ken was at a distinct disadvantage, his strength was fully displayed. Not only was he holding a two-handed weapon at full extension with one hand, but an entire human was also balancing on it without a single tremor in his grip.

"How?" Ken asked as a small amount of sweat started to fall from his brow.

"We are simply on different levels, and there is nothing you can do about it," Ex explained as they withdrew their blade and jumped off. It was then that the door creaked open. Ex threw the knife at the door, which caused a high-pitched scream to ring out from the other side.

"You are late, Braden!" Ken yelled as the third executive crept in with a face now drained of all color.

"I would have been more late had that hit me!" Braden yelled back as he tried to pull the knife out of the door. He struggled to pull it out as the other two rolled their eyes.

"Maybe, but it would have been a quiet meeting," Ex announced as they found another chair to sit in.

"Bah," Braden called out with tongue out as he reached for a bottle of wine on the counter in the back of the room.

"You are late, drunk, and drinking more," Ex pointed out as Braden draped himself across one of the chairs.

"Oh, blow me, Ex. The boss isn't even here yet. If I wanted someone on my dick, it certainly would be someone much prettier than your masked ass."

"Language Braden. Otherwise, Ex will cut your tongue out, and I will not stop them this time," John said as he emerged from the shadows. Braden spit the wine out as he straightened up immediately.

"Sir, I didn't mean to..." Braden started begging before John raised his hand.

"Oh, you did, but more troublesome is that with you being late, we have to waste time on the small things my Executives should be in charge of without me," John lectured as he pulled up a seat for himself.

"Yes, sir."

As soon as John's presence was known, he commanded the room. The squabbling from before was squashed and would no longer be tolerated. Even the drunk sobered up the best he could. This command did not arise from respect. He ruled by fear and intimidation.

"What's first?" Ex asked as they were the first to be brave enough to talk.

"Let's start with basic updates from each division, and in that, I want to know how the fireworks are coming," John instructed.

"On my front, the first round of the new implants have been installed, and the komodos are responding well to the treatments. We should be good to expand on schedule. Then the R+D team reported that the base form of the internet should be rebuilt by the end of the month," Ken reported.

"Perfect. Start the expansion as soon as possible. Pan will not sit around much longer now that St. Louis and Memphis have fallen. Ex," John commanded as he turned to the masked figure.

"Only three people needed to disappear this week, and we are working overtime during the festivities. There was even a report on a fellow Executive tonight." The group turned to look at Braden collectively as his eyes grew large.

"My apologies, but a man made a baseless claim and had to be taught respect."

"Sure, just don't do it again; my forces have enough to do. Sniffing out rebels and figuring out who the leak is in R+D has been enough," Ex explained as they turned to Ken this time.

"Don't you dare accuse my people!"

"Sit and be quiet," Ex commanded.

"You…" Ken started as John raised his hand again.

"That is enough! I ignored the mangled 19th-century chair, but don't test me tonight." His emerald eyes burned through Ken, "Now, is there anything else from you?"

"Yes, we would have had one of the sewer rebels had Braden not smashed his face with a bottle."

"Alright, my turn," Braden muttered as he tried to ignore Ex's comments. He wanted to retaliate but stayed quiet after watching his fellow Executive being silenced.

"Could you first tell us why you were late?" Ex asked.

"Why?"

"Just curious, as I'm sure we all are," Ex replied as they put their head on their steepled hands.

"Fine, my usual antics. Now, can we move on?"

"Not until you answer the question," John commanded, annoyed by the conversation's direction.

"Yes sir…" he quivered as he tried to figure out what to say to his boss. "Well, there was a beautiful woman I was going to make honest."

"Honest for thirty seconds, sure," Ex joked, unraveling Braden, who was gaining some composure.

"Ha ha. I was trying to seal the deal when your guards graciously reminded me of the meeting long after when they should have," Braden snarled, knowing what a fool he had just made of himself.

"So, you chose…" Ex began.

"Enough Ex!" John shouted. "I let you run with your questions because I thought there would be a point, but you wasted more time. All you've accomplished is gaining your own punishment along with his." Ex dropped their head and cast their glare to the side.

"Ooo…Okay, I guess I will finally begin. Peace Week started as planned, with only small complaints and no incidents from the wall. Now, the fireworks are a different story. It has been a slow progress as the people in the Sewer District are not fond of our men hanging around, and I will advise one last time that the fireworks should be moved to avoid an inevitable disaster."

"Braden, don't you worry. Everything will be…" John paused to cough into a tissue before beginning again, "Everything will be fine. The three divisions will put any rebellion to rest before we need to be worried." John placed the tissue on the desk, and Ex noticed specks of blood in it.

"But sir," Braden pleaded.

"Just follow your orders unless you cannot handle it," John offered as he rose and placed a hand on Braden's shoulder.

"No, no, I can handle it."

"Good!" John announced as he let go. "Now, is there anything else worth noting tonight?"

He looked around momentarily as the Executives looked at each other. "Well, Pan's forces hit another decoy supply caravan this morning," Ken reported.

"Which one?"

"KL-2B was hit at the tri-state border of Texas, Arkansas, and Oklahoma," Ken answered after he found the right piece of paper.

"KL-2B…KL-2B. That is one of Serge's lines and the fourth on his line this month." John paused to rub his chin. "It seems we have our spies."

"Oh, Serge is a lovely guy…a little too fond of vodka, but a good time nonetheless. I sure hope it isn't him," Braden commented as he started to relax again.

"Does it matter either way? Once the komodos have their implants, no one can resist us. It will take us one move to obliterate them all," Ken proclaimed.

After Ken spoke, the room fell silent. John paced around the wooden floors. An eerie feeling was in the air as he walked to the window. He tapped his fingers on the window thrice before returning to them. His eyes narrowed as the three Executives, who would be the largest monsters in any room, shrank away. Even Ken, who stood over seven feet tall, appeared as a toddler when John imposed his presence.

"Those abominations I approved will change this fight, but do not underestimate Rob," John began before Ken interjected.

"I fear no mortal man outside of you, sir. Not anymore." Ken looked at his twitching muscles, which appeared to grow as he spoke.

"And I only fear him, Ken. Remember that." John crept closer to the tank of a man.

"As if he will even get into the city. It is impossible!" Braden claimed.

"Oh, he is already inside the walls, Braden." John turned back to the window and stared into the darkness. The lights from the city were finally darkening as even the heartiest party-goers were beginning to call it a night.

"How do you know this, sir?" Braden asked.

"Because I can feel his presence…I know he's here," John answered without looking back. Once again, the room went quiet as things were closing. "Now, is there anything else we need to talk about?"

"No, but how should we handle the spy?" Ex asked.

"Eliminate the whole division."

"Yes, sir. I will send word to the closest vipers immediately after the meeting." The eyes of the room looked for any final words, and Braden raised his hand.

"Sir, there has been some word from the Sewer District that the rebels will attack during one of the speeches during Peace Week, but nothing has been confirmed yet."

"Don't worry, sir. I added more vipers to the daily rounds. Those people won't cause any issue," Ex told the group.

"No, pull back your guards, but boost the gun deactivation switches. Let's lure them out. Now, if that is all, you are all dismissed."

"They can go, but can I talk to you alone?" Ex insisted.

"Lead the way," John instructed, motioning his hand back towards his office. The pair left the room and closed the door behind them.

"What do you think they talk about in their secret meetings?" Braden asked as he rose from his chair to go hunting again.

"I don't want to know."

"I do if it is about us," Braden commented, his face drained of color.

"They would just kill us if they wanted."

As the Executives left the room, John settled into his main chair. His office was nothing remarkable, with a pair of chairs and a rarely used desk.

"Rob snuck in through a drainage pipe," Ex explained as they paced around the room.

"Excellent, so the farmer did make contact. Pan may use it later, so leave it open," John replied, unfazed by the statement.

"More importantly, he is not alone. According to our spy within Pan's organization, he is traveling with three women." For some reason, this statement seemed to irritate John. His fist tightened, and his face scrunched.

"Who? I knew he and Pan would team up, but this seems different."

"Does it matter?"

"It does. I wanted to break him. I wanted him to be in my position." John's voice trailed off as he spoke. "What are the names?"

"Well, the younger two are no-names from Memphis he adopted when Dave killed their leader. The third is Pan's second division commander, who knew Rob before the War. I believe her name is Danielle." John started to rub his head. He could feel the headache slowly moving in but stopped as he heard the name. It was as if a ghost had arrived to haunt him.

"It can't be," he muttered, "It can't be her. She is supposed to be dead." Ex saw concern written on John's face for the first time in years.

"Why are you worried about some woman?"

"Because despite all my attempts to break him, she can keep him together. Her name is Dani Noone, Iris's best friend. On top of being connected with Rob, she is a formidable warrior who can likely match you," John explained as the realization set in.

"She is, but one woman, sir. She may be able to match me, but that is still one fighter," Ex pointed out.

"And it only takes one weak link. We need to draw them out as well," John lectured. He threw his head back as he tried to calculate what adjustments would need to be made. "Trisha will be giving the speech tomorrow instead of Braden. Then we'll figure the rest out."

"Why will Trisha's presence make a difference? I don't understand?"

"We need to take care of our rebel problem quickly, and Trisha's presence will draw them out without question."

"So, you are using her as bait?"

"Of course. Now, go and make the preparations. With any luck, we'll kill two birds with one stone." With that order, Ex left the room and left John to think. He paced around the room, muttering to himself for a few moments.

"How did you find them, Rob? You should have been broken like me, yet here you are with new friends and old...Will this change your answer? Was all of this pointless?"

Chapter 4
Who is He?

While John assembled his Executives, Dani was sneaking back to Clarissa's. She had escaped Braden's creepy clutches when a guard came to collect him for the meeting. His hands had continued to creep up on her, and she had grown afraid that she would have to submit to something to keep her cover. The timing of the guard worked out perfectly and allowed her to sneak away.

As she snuck into the house, the first thing she saw was Rob passed out on the couch. He had taken his traditional meditative seat but had not stayed upright for long. She figured he would wait for her, but his body had a different idea. There was a smile on her face, seeing him actually resting. Since they had started traveling together, he rarely slept more than one or two hours at a time. Even when he did sleep, his restlessness would wake him up far too soon.

She knelt next to his sleeping body and placed a blanket over him. His hand reached out and pulled it to him tight. As she watched him pull the blanket tight, her eyes teared as she studied his face and body. They were the same age, but War and everything that had happened since had aged him heavily. He was only in his early thirties, but the wear on his body made him look closer to fifty. Gray stubble now appeared mixed in with his chestnut hair. She noticed the wrinkles on his forehead as she wiped a tear stain from his cheek. She had asked him before about the tears during his meditation and despite his denial of their existence she knew it was about Iris.

When Dani first heard of Iris's fate, she cried for a week straight. It nearly derailed her mission; disaster would have followed if it had not been for her partner at the time. Yet, Rob went straight into the fire. He began training and hunting as soon as she was gone. The pain for the woman who was his perfect match had to be unbearable now that they could not be together again.

She wished there was something she could do, but there was nothing. Instead, Dani climbed the stairs to look for a bed as Braden's wine started to catch up to her. The first door she opened led to Sam and Morgan. Sam had pulled the sheets completely to her side while Morgan nearly fell off the bed thanks to Sam's pushy feet.

She closed the door behind her with a smile and moved on. The next room was not empty either. Clarissa was lying on her bed, staring out the window.

"What are you looking at?" Dani asked as she crept into the room. Usually, she would have just moved on, but the wine was doing some of the talking for her now. Clarissa didn't say anything at first. She just sat up and motioned for Dani to come closer. Her finger was at her lip, knowing the rest of her house was asleep. After a moment of hesitancy, Dani joined on the bed with her legs crossed beneath her.

"Just the city. I never visited it before the War and sometimes marvel at how beautiful it must have been," Clarissa whispered back. As she answered, Dani followed her gaze. She was right.

However, the most prominent feature that remained was the most terrifying. As the moonlight shined down, the wall glistened in the background. It towered over the buildings that remained, holding the people inside captive and the rest of the world at bay. Dani looked up to the sky, where the clouds covered some of the stars, and the moon only shone through. It looked peaceful up there and close. Yet, it felt more unattainable inside those walls than at any point during Dani's travels.

As the idea of freedom and peace faded, Dani turned back to Clarissa, "So, if you're not from here, how did you end up on this side of the wall?"

"You know your girl Morgan already asked me that. She is quite the interrogator. Sam, not as much." Clarissa laughed as she recalled her evening.

"Sorry about that. Rob has taught them to be curious, and Morgan has always been untrusting. However, I am also curious," Dani responded as she shook her head. She could only imagine what the girls were like. It did comfort her that they did not just accept the new woman without question.

"Don't apologize. We already went over the whole trusting thing. I get it, but if you must know, John brought me here personally," she replied, saying his name as calmly as Dani had seen. This statement did worry Dani. Being hand-picked by John is usually a sign of psychopathy. Yet, everything Dani had seen so far pointed to Clarissa being someone they could trust.

"Why you?"

"Well, I was studying to be an oncologist when the War broke out," Clarissa replied.

"Okay, but there had to be other options. I know the War killed many doctors, but there had to be someone with more… experience. No offense."

"None taken. I was just as shocked. However, John knew of my father, a leading cancer researcher. His specialty was radiation poisoning, and I may have only been a student, but I knew more than some of my professors thanks to him."

"Well, that is something. What was his name?" Dani asked, growing closer.

"Dr. Fletcher Wright, a hysterical man who connected and loved his patients. He was weird but brilliant in a way that even if he couldn't cure you, you died at peace." Clarissa smiled as she reminisced about her father.

"Sounds like a wonderful man. Wish I could have met him, but glad we got you." Dani placed her hand on Clarissa's lap. As Rob had said earlier, there was a feeling about Clarissa that made Dani trust her.

"He was," she started, clearing a tear, "but that is enough about me. What is the deal with you and Rob?"

"We were friends before the War and only just found each other again," Dani replied, trying to figure out what Clarissa was getting at.

"So you are going with just friends?"

"Yes."

"Sure…*cough*…bull…*cough*."

"It's complicated," Dani replied as she lay on the bed. Replaying the thoughts she had only a few minutes prior.

"Girls like us, in a world like this, are too old for complicated things."

"Hahaha. Oh, I know, but he is complicated. Plus, I don't know if that is what I want. I enjoy being friends, but he is…well, he's him."

"Pray tell, I know he is a cute little number, but what else is there?"

"Well, his biggest, most annoying flaw is he is the most overprotective and arrogant man I have ever met."

"Trouble."

"Yeah, sort of. The arrogance is, but the overprotective comes from the people he has lost. More importantly, he is still the sweetest man I have ever met. That's why I was shocked when we reunited. He was bitter and cold, something I had never seen. There was a brokenness that those girls changed. I've seen more smiles in the past week than ever. And everything he does, no matter how dumb, comes from a place of helping."

"Sounds charming, so what is complicated about it all?"

"Well, right now, the biggest thing is that he is hunting the man who killed my best friend and his fiancé a few months ago," Dani answered as her voice trailed off near the end.

"Well, shit. That's heavy."

"It isn't light, and on top of that, he is hesitant with feelings. He will tell you he likes you or enjoys you being around, but I've rarely heard him use the word love, even when it came to Iris, his fiancé. I only heard him say it a few times, though you knew it by the things he did for her and the look he gave her, but...well, like I said, it's complicated, and I've said too much already," she said as she started to shake her head. Hours previously, she threatened this woman, and now she talked about her love life. She had to get herself to bed.

"Sorry to pry. It was lovely talking to you," Clarissa said as Dani left the room without a response. Clarissa rubbed her face as Dani passed out in the only empty room left.

Chapter 5
Introductions

Despite the late night, Rob was the first to rise. He removed the blanket that Dani draped across him and placed it nicely on the couch. From there, he started to unfold from his seated position. Every movement caused aches and creaks in his bones. An ankle barely healed, ribs beaten to Hell, and a million other pains. His limit was fast approaching, though he would never admit it to anyone. His body needed rest more than anything, but until he found John, his mind wouldn't let him. The hunt possessed him even if his mission had grown larger than just one of revenge.

As his body slowly woke up, he strolled gingerly through Clarissa's house. Joints creaked with every step. He winced in ways that he would never have if everyone else had been around. He tried to stretch out using the counter to support his body, but in the end, he just laid his head on it gently to breathe. Several coughs followed after one inhale aggravated a rib he damaged back in Despartian months prior.

He was still unsure how to fight John, but for now, he settled on a brisk morning walk to wake his body up. Morning mist covered the streets that were now empty of the life he had seen pack them last night. Only a few people were as ambitious as him, rising this early in the morning, and most of those were assisting in the clean-up. A few boas passed him, but none paid attention to him. The only other people he saw were the fishermen heading to sea to feed the city.

No one was interested in him, as his morning tidings were met only with grunts and groans. Only a few hellos were returned to him. Eventually, he went to the nearest cemetery, where he sat beside a large stone in its center.

Stones like this were common across the globe as they were used to replace the millions of headstones smashed during the War and to account for the astronomical death total. They were meant to be a sign of shared suffering where anyone could go to feel heard by the ones they lost. Each monument has an inscription on it. In Despartian, it read, "Death leaves a heartache no one can heal, love leaves a memory no one can steal." While this one read, "Death is inevitable, memories are eternal."

Rob sat silent for a few moments. Speaking softly after a time, "I meant to bring flowers, but no one was in a chatting mood today," he said with eyes rested on the wilted flowers.

"I miss you, Iris. I miss that smile that could always put me at ease. I miss the kind soul that saved mine. I miss lying next to you and knowing that no matter what, the most important thing in my world was in my arms," Rob began as his head sunk into his hands. The echo of the fall wind, as it blew through the graveyard, was the only sound to be heard.

He wrapped his arms around his body as his eyes tightened. Picturing Iris with him, he gave into emotions he had been bottling up for weeks. His mentor, Mark, and his daughter, Vicky, would appear every few weeps, but the focus was Iris. It has always been Iris deep down.

"Why was I so stupid? Why did I hold you at bay for so long? When I needed you most, I pushed you away and made you miserable. Then, just like that, you were taken from me. And now I don't know what to do. You told me to let it go, but I defied that for too long, and now I'm stuck. The people who stand at my side will expect me to lead them against John, but I don't know if I'm strong enough. My body is breaking down, and I find myself reluctant to do what they need of me.

"I thought my hate for him would be enough, but now he has revealed so much I don't know if I can. He is more alone than I am and has fallen so deep into darkness that no one can truly get close like I can. Am I supposed to save him or kill him? Am I supposed to be the one who doesn't betray or get taken from him? You were the psychologist who always told me anyone could be saved from darkness if there was the right glimmer of light, but am I that glimmer? I just don't know.

"I just don't know a lot anymore, Iris. Months ago, I knew it all. John was evil and deserved to die, but after reading his letters and piecing them together, I don't know if he was ever given a chance. In those letters, he wrote about a brother who helped him kill someone at an age too young. In those letters, he told me about a love taken from him. He spoke of a world that used him to start a war and then betrayed him. It makes me wonder if he is right and this world is sick. Maybe we weren't supposed to survive that war…Iris I…I don't know if I will see you again as I don't think I will end up in the same place as you, but I want you to know…I need you to know…that I will love you forever." As Rob finished, a tear ran down his face. Turmoil consumed him as his stomach churned.

An hour passed, and he sat in silence. Unable to move or say anything, he just wished he could hear an answer. Nothing came, so he finally rose from his seat and returned to the city. This time, the streets were awakening. The food market was opening. While everyone else either headed to breakfast or work.

Not wishing to return to Clarissa's, he ducked into a clothing shop to look around for a moment. He thought about replacing the tattered and smelly clothes, but at the same time, money was tight. His decision was almost made for him when the shop owner asked how the fish were biting that morning.

"Oh good! You did find a way into the city. I should have known that my uncle was right," Trisha's voice called from behind him. He stood frozen with a shirt hanging from his hand.

"Out of everywhere in the city, you are here," he muttered as he turned to look at Trisha. She stood leaning on a clothing table with her icy grin.

"Don't be so negative, Rob. You know our fates are intertwined. Just be happy he isn't with me," she replied, growing closer to him despite his efforts to create space.

"The answer is still no," Rob expressed in an attempt to get her to back down.

"Oh, I knew you would be stubborn, but it is because you don't know what I can do for you yet," she replied as her grin grew more prominent.

"And what is that?"

"Well, first off, I can tell you that my uncle knows you are here and brought friends. Specifically, he knows about Dani." As she spoke, she crawled her pointer and middle finger up his chest like a spider. Rob tried to remain unfazed. He knew Trisha's game now, but the mention of Dani did cause him to react enough for her to notice.

"Also, you should know it is because of her that he has assigned me to give today's address instead of hungover Braden," she added, handing him a poster with her and Braden's faces. Rob took the poster and placed it in his back pocket.

"That should be nice, but it sounds like a trap."

"Oh, it probably is, but you know the best way to deal with a trap isn't always to avoid it..."

"Sometimes it's best to spring it with intention." Rob finished, knowing she was stealing a quote Gene had taught the team.

"Exactly!" she exclaimed, patting him on his chest with her palm. "Now, since you will attend, you will need better clothes. I think your girls will enjoy these," Trisha claimed as she held up a couple of outfits.

"I can't afford any of them," he snarled.

"Oh, they are on the house. I'm screwing the owner's daughter, so he won't give you any trouble. Ciao." She kissed him on the cheek and slinked away as quickly as she had arrived.

"Take whatever you want. I do not want any trouble, sir. That woman is the devil." The shop owner quivered as soon as Trisha was out of sight.

"You have no idea," he muttered as he picked out a few outfits, including the ones that Trisha had suggested. The only way for him to pay back the shop owner was to save the city; this would hopefully be the first step. The question was how he would explain the clothing and the speech?

He reflected on different ways to explain the new clothes the whole trip back but could not figure out what to say. Inside, Clarissa was in the kitchen making pancakes. She was dressed in her lab coat and slacks. As soon as Rob entered, she turned and smiled.

"You look like you should be retired on the beach somewhere," she remarked, noticing the new attire, before turning back to the stove.

"That would be my preference right now, but here I am."

"But here you are. Would you mind grabbing the syrup? It's on the top right shelf of the cupboard," she asked, pointing to the door to her left.

"You know that you don't have to make us breakfast," he commented as he grabbed the syrup.

"I know, but after talking with the ladies last night, I decided I like y'all. Sam is a bottle of sunshine, and I think I made a breakthrough with Dani."

"You forgot Morgan."

"That's because she still doesn't trust me," Clarissa replied as she flipped a few more pancakes.

"Don't mind that. Morgan isn't the trusting type. Even with me, I feel her keeping me at arm's length."

"I haven't paid it any mind. It is nice to see someone in this house with some common sense."

"What do you mean by that?"

"Well, I let a band of strangers into my house, and you all have trusted me. Not exactly a common thing these days," she answered as she pulled the last few pancakes off the stovetop. The plate next to the stove was filled with twenty pancakes.

"You have a point, but sometimes you just need faith. That's a lesson that took me a while to learn." Clarissa just paused for a moment after his answer. It appeared to Rob that she wanted to say something but seemed to hold back.

"Go wake everyone. Breakfast is ready." Rob headed upstairs to wake up his compatriots. He knocked on each door. First, he heard the crash and cussing coming from Sam and Morgan's room while Dani grumbled at the wake-up call.

Back downstairs, Clarissa had set the table for everyone. Rob's mouth drooled at the sight of the pancake piles. The ladies dragged themselves down the steps and were immediately revitalized when they saw the food. However, Dani was still holding her head and groaned all the way down the steps.

The five of them dug into the feast, making quick work of the batches of food. The four strangers thanked Clarissa profusely in between the mouthfuls. Despite the happiness, Dani could sense that there was something up with Rob.

"What is up with you today?" Dani asked as she finished her third pancake.

"Nothing."

"Liar," she accused as the rest of the table turned their eyes to him. He looked to his left for a moment, still trying to come up with a cover, but nothing was coming to him.

"I may have run into Trisha," he finally admitted as the eyes that were locked on him suddenly grew large.

"The devil girl!" Clarissa yelled.

"Devil girl is…well, actually, it's accurate," he started before biting his lip.

"You ran into that evil princess! And didn't immediately tell me!" Dani yelled as she rose from her seat. Rob just nodded.

"Isn't she the one we saw in Memphis when the buildings started to blow up?" Sam whispered to Morgan, who answered with a nod of her own. Though they were quiet, Dani heard them and latched onto the words.

"She was in Memphis?" Dani asked as she was finally starting to put the missing pieces together.

"Hold up. You all were in Memphis when it was ruined?" Clarissa asked now that she was aware of the company she was keeping.

"Well, we were, she wasn't," Rob indicated as he singled out Dani as the lone difference.

"Two young ladies and an older man. You three are the terrorists," Clarissa accused.

"Older man? And, technically, we were just accused of that. Trisha and the Executioner were the ones to hit the button that blew everything up," Rob defended.

"And you didn't tell me any of this or Pan's forces we encountered!" Dani yelled.

"It wasn't relevant," Rob claimed as he tried to remain calm through all the yelling.

"I should kick you in that pretty mouth of yours! Trisha and the Executioner were in the same spot blowing up their own city, and you thought that wasn't relevant! When were you going to tell us about today?" Dani was infuriated in a way that Sam and Morgan had never seen.

"Probably when you asked about the clothes she secured for us," he muttered as he motioned toward the bags near the door.

"Rob, whose side are you on here?" Dani asked as she tried to calm her voice.

"Iris's," Rob rebutted. "I didn't start my journey to fight a war or to lead men into battle. I agreed to help because Mark helped me see that I could accomplish my goal and help people. But in the end, there is one man I care about." Dani and Rob stared each other down after his comments. It felt like it lasted forever and was only interrupted by Clarissa, who was finally starting to question her decisions.

"Alright, who are you four, and what have I gotten into?" Clarissa asked, nearly choking on her own words. Dani dropped her hostilities momentarily as she realized how much of a scene she had just made. Both she and Rob had revealed a lot without actually saying anything to comfort her.

"Well, you've heard this much, so what is a little more? I am Danielle Noone, a fighter in Pan's revolutionary army," Dani answered first.

"And I'm Samantha Wojcik, that's it. Dani is a lot cooler," Sam smiled. After this, Clarissa's eyes turned to Morgan, who lowered her head to answer.

"Morgan Willard." Then, all eyes turned to Rob, still sitting and mulling things over in his head.

"And I am Rob Doran. Former member of Shadow Squad along with John Kore," he reported. Clarissa stood overwhelmed.

"So, I have two of John's most wanted enemies in my kitchen eating pancakes," she summarized slowly. Her mouth was barely able to make out what she was saying.

"Pretty much, so what now?" Rob asked as he slowly reached for his staff. Dani was doing the same with her knife.

"We celebrate. You are exactly what they are looking for!" Clarissa proclaimed as she reached across the table to hug each of them. "John may employ me, but I know this city is sick, and a doctor's duty is to cure. I didn't think the treatment for it would work until today." The group was confused as Clarissa continued to ramble, "I have people that will help you with your plan, but it will have to wait until after work. If I am late, the vipers will come and make a mess of everything. Just wait here." As she spoke, there was a rejuvenating look on her face. Each of her words was quick and full of excitement. She started to pace around the room, picking up her gear.

"Wait a minute, you have to tell us more. We just exposed a lot of details," Rob replied. "And now you are going to make us wait for more."

"I know, I know, but I need some time to explain everything. You've trusted me with this information, so please give me some time."

"No, we need answers now, or we're gone," Dani said. Clarissa looked at a clock she had on the wall and then outside. She needed to leave but did not want them gone.

"Okay, okay. So, a group in the city resists John, and I think I can help smooth introductions."

"Smooth over?" Rob asked.

"Yeah, they're a bit rough and untrusting. The last outsider they trusted ended up ruling the city, so there is that."

"Well, that is pretty par for the course, but how do we know you're not lying?" Clarissa looked at the clock again, but Rob stood firm while waiting for an answer.

"If you go to the speech today, there will be a commotion. I cannot say anything else, but those are your people. Now, I have to go. If I am too late, questions get asked. Please."

Rob looked at Dani and nodded his head slightly. "Thank you. I'm sorry that we kept you late." With that, Clarissa left in a hurry; as she hurried out the door, Morgan approached Rob and Dani.

"Are we about to be ambushed?" Morgan asked as they all turned to each other.

"You know. I'm not sure, but she is telling the truth about some speech happening," Rob replied as he reached for the paper in his back pocket.

"Care to elaborate and tell us about Trisha?"

"Trisha bought us these clothes to spring a trap that John is setting at a speech she will give today," he answered, handing her the slip of paper first.

"How about no? I don't like springing traps on purpose," she responded, handing the paper off to Morgan and Sam.

"But sometimes avoiding a trap is more treacherous. Besides, Trisha is not fully on John's side. She is scheming something that might end up helping us," Rob told her without going into the deeper details.

"So, you made a deal with the devil. The one that Pan's army believes is more dangerous than John himself."

"I did not make a deal, but now that we know other rebels are going to be there, this could be an opportunity to cause chaos." Dani was unhappy, but Morgan let out a gut-wrenching scream before they could talk more. She began to cry and ran out of the house, dropping the poster. Dani and Rob looked at each other and then at Sam, who was just as confused.

"I'll go see," Rob said. He headed out after her.

Outside, Morgan was sitting against the side of the building. She was hugging her knees to her chest with her face buried. He could hear her crying as he sat beside her. Even though he volunteered, he wasn't sure what to say to her. This was the first time she had acted this way, and his concern grew as her wails continued.

"What happened in there, Morgan?" She just shook her head and buried it deeper. He put his arm around her and pulled her close. At first, she resisted and attempted to push him away. Until, at last, she gave in and snugged herself tightly into his arms. There, she began to cry harder and harder.

"It's…it's…it's him Rob," she cried, her words barely audible as her face was still tight against his body.

"Who?"

"Braden…that is the man who killed…he's the freak that tried to rape me!" Now, her voice was turning from sadness to anger. Her hand gripped Rob's shirt tight.

"So, he's the one who killed your boyfriend," Rob clarified. She finally pulled her face away from his chest and wiped her eyes while nodding.

"He was a soldier assigned to transport us to safety, but he tried to attack me. I trusted him, Rob. Then the love of my life died because of it." Rob could feel the hurt in her voice and the anger that reminded him of his own. Braden was her John. Braden was the face that haunted her the nights Rob woke to find her curled up tight, shaking.

"Don't worry, Morgan. He won't hurt you, and he will be stopped." She shook the answer off and looked him deep in his eyes.

"He won't hurt any of you because he is mine."

Chapter 6
The Doctor

While Morgan fell apart, Clarissa biked to the research and treatment facility where she worked. She smiled and waved at the people she passed as she cut through the streets, avoiding the hungover masses that tried to stumble home before their nights of revelry restarted. Most of them returned the wave, even some guards who had grown used to seeing her on her morning route. Many of the children who played in the streets or headed off to school were the happiest to see her and would chase the bike for a few feet, cheering and calling her name. Every one of them hoped that she could stop a minute to play with them or that she would have a treat to share, but today was not the day for them. The goodies she usually shared were left with Rob's team.

She arrived at what was once the largest hospital in New Orleans but was now a shell of itself. Though the hospital would never be the size it once was or treat as many as possible, it now contained some of the greatest minds in the medical field. John had tracked down the world's greatest doctors covering many areas and housed them inside. John claimed that he had 23 of the top 25 doctors in the world in this building. All of them completed research, trained the next generation, or treated the people of New Orleans. However, the two that escaped him were ones he prized highly. The first was Dr. Anna Galen of Despartian. After the War was concluded, legends were told about all the soldiers she saved with little equipment. This led to many considering her the best field surgeon still alive. However, this title was challenged by an older doctor named Dr. Rafal Hakimi. Dr. Hakimi was known as a great trauma surgeon before the War. During it, his ability to perform as a field surgeon garnered him even greater fame. Unlike Dr. Galen, his location is unknown. Many believe that he works with Pan and the rest of the revolutionaries.

She strolled through the halls, passing all the other departments to her own on the top floor. She brought energy and vibrancy to the building like the streets she biked through. She said hello to everyone who passed her, whether they were one of the best doctors in the world or a young child who would not see adulthood; everyone was treated the same by her. She stopped to play with the kids in the pediatric ward. Danced with those in the rehabilitation center. Joked with those who had been waiting too long for their appointments. Everything she did was an attempt to emulate the actions of her father.

She was an exceptional doctor, but her personality made her unique. This personality shined even brighter when compared to the other doctors working inside the building. To survive the War and prosper after they had hardened their souls. They had been robbed of their practice and forced into intense battlegrounds where they had to focus on efficiency. Many of these doctors had to care for twenty to thirty patients at a time at the height of the War. There had been no time for bedside manners, and they lost that part of themselves. On the other hand, Clarissa was still young when the War broke out and had time to grow into her role. She still had a spark that the grizzled old masters had lost.

When she arrived, the other full-time doctor and two medical students were working hard in her lab. The four mainly focused on treating and researching cancers that had become frequent due to the War's after-effects. The occurrence rates had multiplied exponentially between drug testing, nuclear leaks, and at least one explosion.

"You're late again," the male doctor announced without turning away from his work.

"Sorry, I had a guest over this morning. And besides, you're not allowed to give me crap when you are still using my notes from last week, Dr. Maki," she quipped back with her tongue sticking out at him. His head shook while she put her gloves on.

"Good to see you, Dr. Wright," the male student remarked with a bright smile across his face. While the female made hand gestures expressing the same thing.

"And good morning to you, Thomas," she called while hand signing '*Morning Jackie.*'

Dr. Maki is a fifty-year-old man of Japanese descent who had come to the US five years before the start of the War. He had already established a reputation as a cancer research prodigy in his home country but was propelled into a legendary status when he came to the US. Unfortunately, his bedside manner was coarse. He preferred to live in his lab, but a man of his talent could not exist solely in theory.

Thomas and Jackie were refugees snuck into the country as the War escalated. Their parents were doctors in their home country of Burma. They ensured the best for their kids, especially Jackie, who was born deaf due to a genetic disorder. Even before the War, the plan was to immigrate to the US for better opportunities.

At first, their parents held off on the move when the US plunged into their civil war. However, when China made its move by invading the desecrated Los Angeles, their parents had to make a rash decision. Asia and the rest of the world would soon be plunged into conflict and hoped that sending their kids to the war-stricken but stabilizing US would be the safest move. Eventually, the children separated from their parents and remained orphans. Clarissa was the first to engage them in the slums of New Orleans and created a position for them in her lab.

"So, Maki, did you make any discoveries while I ran behind?" she asked now that she was set up. Even before asking the question, she knew he hadn't. He would have boasted about it the moment she walked in. No, she asked him to get under his skin, as irritating the arrogant man was one of her favorite pastimes.

"No, but the results came back on Ken's project. They are exactly what we anticipated," he reported as he slid a folder labeled "Classified" over to her.

"Big surprise. You inject people with something that creates uncontrollable cell growth and cancer becomes probable," she commented while flipping through the charts. Stopping on one page that caught her attention. "It didn't just increase the likelihood. It increased the chance by 23% for those whose bodies accepted the serum. While those who did not saw a mortality rate of nearly 90%." Clarissa sat down after she read the numbers. She covered her mouth as her body trembled seeing the data. Given the sample size, that level of mortality was disastrous.

"Yes, yes, sad stuff, but don't lose track of the objective. John and Ken only want cures for those whose bodies accepted the serum. The failed experiments are nothing to them," Maki responded in his monotone and coarse tone.

Clarissa just rolled her eyes. "I will treat anyone who comes through those doors, failed experiment or not."

"*Huff*...your pride will ruin us, but fine. Just be here on time. Starting today, John is sending fifty men over from the original batch and needs cures tested," Maki explained as life drained from the room.

The two lab assistants sat in the corner as Thomas relayed the conversation to his sister. His hands became unsettled when Maki mentioned fifty men. Jackie did not have a full grasp because of her brother's pauses, but she understood something major was happening. Clarissa put the file down and blinked repeatedly, hoping she had misheard him.

"Fifty men...we will have fifty new patients on top of everyone already coming in here. That is insanity, and I don't even think we have enough resources for that much chemo," she explained, just barely able to talk.

"I think John is just trying to keep you out of trouble," Maki suggested as he finally turned away from his work.

"I'm too busy for trouble already!" She defended, "And that reminds me...I need to look at another case's results. Thomas, can you retrieve the test results for Patient 184RD." Thomas nodded as his sister, and he left to go fetch the documents.

Once they were gone, Clarissa approached Maki, who sneered at the sound of her shoes approaching.

"You say that, but here you are late for work. Bossing around sewer rats who are just as likely to undo us as they are to help us," he criticized drawing disdain from her.

"Don't call them sewer rats. That district is crucial and should be treated better than it is," she defended as she tied her hair into a ponytail. "Especially when you're the only rat here."

"Careful now, calling traitors, racists, and killers crucial to this city is traitor talk. And if you keep defending them, you will lose this job."

"And if you really believe that John only puts nasty people in that district, you'll be amazed when you find yourself there for saying something his people don't like."

"Bah, you'll be there long before me. You'll be curled next to those rats."

"Careful, your bitterness is showing."

"Arguing with you is like talking to a rock with a smile painted on it, pointless." He smirked.

"And yet you have the personality of one." She smirked back as she returned to her work. He grew red but turned to his work to hide it.

"And who 184RD?" he asked after a few moments.

"Just a special case that John asked me to handle personally and wants kept confidential, hence the ID," she answered without stopping her work.

"Ooh, top secret. Can I at least see the charts?" She knew that mentioning a top-secret patient would make him pleasant. Despite the proof, he still thought he was the most intelligent person in the room. He felt he could make some discoveries to prove he was better than her, even with just the charts.

"Since you asked nicely. He is terminal anyway, so I think he'll be done within the next two weeks, if not sooner," she explained just as the two assistants returned with a large file.

They handed her the file, and she looked it over in detail. Her expressions made it seem like the newest findings were insignificant. Once done, she handed Maki the folder, who took it gratefully. He scanned through the documents, memorizing every detail and line. His eyes grew as he hovered over a few critical points.

"This is one of the most interesting charts I have ever seen…Why did he start taking the Leopard Skin…and what are all these readings? The dates are inconsistent and all over the place," he asked, digging deeper.

"He was in remission and left for a few months. While he was away, he felt the cancer returning, so he injected himself, hoping to ease the pain…It worked…it worked for a time, but as you can see, the results were disastrous. It took him from a two to three-year window and changed it to a six-month one, which is nearly up. Most notably, it caused it to spread to the brain, which has caused him to become erratic." She kept her back to Maki as she explained. Despite her voice's confidence and strength, a tear formed in her eye.

"Quite unfortunate. What are you going to tell him?"

"The same thing I've been telling him since he had a psychologist send me the blood test results. The Leopard Skin makes his case unpredictable."

"Terrible waste. Based on the rest of these numbers, he would be 10x greater than any of the current komodos and dominate Ken if it wasn't for the cancer but no reason to worry about a dead man; back to the ones that can save our lives. They will be here at noon," Maki said as he slid the file back to Clarissa.

"A waste indeed. Could have been an amazing man, but the stupid male ego," she whispered with a deep exhale.

She tried to attend to her work from there, but her mind kept drifting elsewhere. At first, it drifted to RD, but the thought of him faded after some time. Soon replaced by Rob and the ladies. She kept thinking about how improbable it was that such people stayed in her house, especially during Peace Week when the rumblings of civil unrest began to spike. All the makings of something big were coming together with her in the center.

Her dream of making the city a better place for people like Thomas and Jackie was becoming a reality. Yet, she still needed to figure out her role in the coming storm. Her direct access to all the players was invaluable, but it also put her in contradiction to her core values. A fight was coming, and that was the only reasonable outcome. However, all she wanted to do was save, which would soon be impossible.

She tried to focus on her work, but it was hard to motivate herself. Every idea that came to her was impossible in their current world. Either the technology had been lost during the War, or they did not have the people to put anything into practice. As her mind wandered through the options, time escaped her, and soon, a knock came at the door to the lab. Noon had snuck up on her. She approached the door, wondering which of the thugs John would send. She prayed that it would not be Braden with his insufferable attempts at flirting. Her jaw dropped when she opened the door and saw who stood on the other side.

"Good afternoon, Doc," John announced as he kissed her hand upon entering. The whole room turned to see the man who had walked in. His cold green eyes had a hint of fire as he smiled at the doctor.

"Why are you here?" she stuttered, still in awe.

"Sir," the rest of the office bowed as Jackie signed her response.

"Afternoon," he responded as he signed to the young lady.

"Afternoon, but why are you here? Shouldn't you be at the festival?" Clarissa repeated as she felt slightly insulted by his lack of answer.

"I will head there in a bit, but I thought I would drop off my men while I was on my way. Plus, I wanted to inspect the hospital since Ken does not give me sufficient updates as you do, Ris," he answered at last, replying in sign language at the same time. His focus stayed on Clarissa until, out of the corner of his eye, he saw the file labeled 184RD. Without hesitation or objection, he began to finger through the file. Focusing on the latest data that had been run.

"I would say that he only has a week or two left, but given Leopard Skin injections, they will probably not show signs of it until they die. Though I wouldn't be surprised if a cough begins given what is in their lungs," she assessed. It appeared that his eyes were growing watery for a moment, but he quickly threw the file down and moved on.

"Well, we now know what happens when Leopard Skin is added to a patient with early onset cancer and radiation poisoning, death. Now let's see what can be done for those to whom Leopard Skin gives cancer," he ordered as he trekked through the office.

"Yes, sir, we shall begin immediately," Maki groveled, almost kissing the floor that John walked on. Meanwhile, Clarissa just rolled her eyes, and John stood with arms crossed. Neither enjoyed the actions of the man, but outside of Clarissa, there was no one better, making the man irreplaceable.

"Let's go," he commanded, leading all four of them downstairs. Once in the operating room, the doctors let the assistants prepare the room as they set up the chemo treatments. They took 10 of the 50 men for the first round to create a decent sample size.

They led each giant, standing nearly 7 feet tall and likely north of 350lbs, into the room. With their assistants' help, the doctors hooked them all up. However, this was a nearly impossible task. The Leopard Skin had hardened their skin to the point that most needles snapped with any amount of pressure. Clarissa had to order the men to cut small incisions into each other to hook them up. Once they passed this step, things began to go smoothly.

"So, what is the plan?" John asked while they observed the patients from the observation room.

"Given the odd nature of your monsters' bodies, we would have wanted to cut out some of the tumors first to test them for any reactions, but given their steel hides, we are forced to start with a slow drip and low dosage treatment to minimize any poor reactions. Hopefully, we can catch anything before it kills them, and then we can adjust to new treatments as we see fit," she explained as she watched each drip fall into the tubing. She swayed side-to-side and bit her nails as they waited. The unknown with these men frightened her, especially after seeing RD's results. Adding to her nerves was John's presence. She had no idea what would happen or what he would do if it went wrong.

At first, her worries seemed unfounded as things progressed as they usually would with any patient, but this did not last long. One of the men began to shriek at the top of his lungs, which launched the doctors into action. They burst into the room just as the rest started to yell. They stopped the treatment immediately, but it was too late.

Moments after they had begun their screams, each man was dead. Clarissa slammed her hand into one man's chest, expecting to hit a wall, but it gave like gelatin. They removed the shirt of the man. Across his body, the leopard marks, a side effect of the drug, had grown, and his blue veins had turned into a sludge-like black color. Where his heart should have been, a giant black mark was growing inside of him. At the same time, the sludge began to pour from his tear duct.

"I don't think chemo is our route," John stated once he entered the room.

"No, it's not."

"Let's talk in private, Ris. These three can handle the clean-up," John ordered as he made his way out of the room. She dragged her feet as she made her way out of the room. The other three kept their heads down as they unhooked the corpses.

Once alone, he violently closed the door behind them and cornered her. His eyes were filled with anger and fire. Despite his presence, Clarissa did not back down. She stood tall and proud before him. "So, what do you want to talk about?" she asked, making the first move.

He stood snarling momentarily before finally answering, "A battle is coming to our footsteps, Ris, and I need to know if you can save my soldiers."

"I will try."

"Try isn't good enough. Pan, Rob, and the city's rebels are coming. I need to be at full power!" he yelled as he slammed his fist into the wall. He panted for a few moments as his fist sat on the concrete that he had cracked.

"You will never be at full power, and you know it, but I will do what I can for these men. You know that, so calm down," she demanded, not wavering at his attempts at intimidation. He huffed for a few more moments before finally taking a deep breath.

"I know, Ris, but the end is coming faster than I thought, and I just need things to be set," he said as his head lowered. He began to cough. Nearly dropping him to his knee, but Clarissa caught him.

"John, when did it get this bad?" she asked as her voice softened.

"Just before I left Despartian but there is no time to worry about that. I have to win. I need to do it for him and for her," he said as his cough subsided. A few drops of blood dripped from his mouth and Clarissa wiped them away.

"John…there is still time. We can still run away," she begged as he gained the strength to stand on his own again.

"No, it is too late for that. Soon, the world will be reborn, and the sins of the people who broke me will be washed away for eternity."

"John, don't do anything rash. Not in your current mind state. Stick to the plan you had before it all started," she begged one more time, but her words fell on deaf ears.

"I will do what I must. Now fix my soldiers," he ordered before slipping out of the room. He did not want to be seen again by Maki and the assistants.

Chapter 7
The Revolutionaries

As the storm of change started to brew in New Orleans, the heads of revolution gathered in a bayou just north of the city. Pan, the world's most wanted criminal and hero, stands in a shack looking south towards New Orleans. He is considered the only international threat left in the world and is not safe anywhere. However, those loyal to him will quickly point out that his title was given to him by Ascension and those that are underneath John's thumb. He is the man that Ascension hunts like a wild animal but is protected by the people who have nothing. He is a symbol to the world that a future still exists.

He is slightly above average in stature, but to most, he appears larger than life. He speaks with purpose when he talks. A certain aura surrounds him that calls hundreds to his cause. It takes one interaction for people to be engulfed by this aura and plead their loyalty. His spirit had touched them all, from Dani to the lowest soldier in his rebellion.

As he stared out the window, his hand hovered around his face while a cigarette hung from his mouth. His hand partially covered the Japanese kanji inked upon his skin. The lines had been tattooed to compliment and finish the scars on the left side of his face—all elements combined to represent the kanji for sunset.

A bell rang as he stood watching the birds fly through the swamp. The sound resonated throughout the facility. After the final bell tolled, he turned from the window and headed towards the door of the small room he had been in. On his way to the meeting room, he strolled through an old creaky wooden hall. It was poorly lit, and the walls were thin. He could hear the troops in the basement as they ran to make preparations. Those not running, he could hear laughing as they finished their meal breaks.

He took long, slow strides as he paced the halls until he reached a large oak door. He pushed it open to the sight of cheers and laughter that immediately went silent.

The lower-ranked soldiers exited the room. The contents of the meeting were only for the highest-ranked officers, and any disturbance would not be tolerated. Four commanders were seated in their chairs, and another man stood behind an empty chair. Pan approached his seat at the head of the table and sat down instantly, leaning to his right as his eyes scanned the room. Upon sitting, a young red-headed woman ran to his side and filled a glass of water for him. He nodded as a sign of appreciation, and she pulled out a notepad.

"Good afternoon, everyone. This is the third commanders' meeting," she announced with a clear and crisp voice that fit the momentous event. "I will now ask everyone to state their name and division for my records."

"I will go first. From the Southern region, I am Dirk Mattson, the 1st division commander," Dirk declared from his seat that he was leaning on the right arm of. Dirk is a tall, dirty blonde who always has a smirk on his face. He was also one of the most muscular revolutionaries. A man in charge of training recruits before they were dispersed to the other regions.

After Dirk was done, the room turned to the empty chair and the man behind it. The man was the second largest in the room after Dirk, but unlike Dirk, his body was a mix of muscle and fat. His towering mocha skin was a sight, but he said nothing. Dirk just shook his head.

"And for those who don't know, this is Khalil "No Voice" Thomas, the second division's captain. He is here for that bum Dani since she is in New Orleans relaxing. And as you can see, he ain't much of a talker," Khalil grunted at the explanation. Pan eyed Dirk and stopped any other comments.

"Cool it, Dirk. We're all allies here," the man across from Dirk stated in a loud, boisterous voice. "We are all here to kick John's ass. And if you are going to be a prick, then my 3rd Division will be doing all the work. Bahaha." The tallest man in the room laughed. He had broad shoulders, a slender frame, and a beard so bushy that he would often lose parts of his dinner in it.

"Ugh, Tank, if you're going to be loud and annoying, at least state your name as instructed," Dirk commented, rubbing his fingers against his eyebrows.

"Oh…yeah. I am Tank Hoppell, the 3rd division commander."

Dirk put his head on the table and hit it softly. "Next," he called.

"Yes, I think it's time to move on. I am Gina Mack. The oldest commander and 4th commander, North Region," the oldest woman in the room declared. Gina had met Rob when he rolled into a deserted town, and at that time, she was skeletal from weeks of suffering with the townspeople. She regained some of her muscle in the time since her return to the revolutionaries. However, she was still the most diminutive of all the commanders. The bones of her cheeks protruded slightly, and her movements were gentle.

"It is good to see ya, Grandma Mack. We were worried about you. We weren't sure you'd be alright when we heard about what had happened," Tank said.

"Don't you worry about me, you bloody fool. I'm going to outlive all of you idiots. Hehehe," the old lady joked as she patted Tank on the hands.

"You probably will, but we still love you." The last woman in the room smiled. She had a gentle yet firm voice. "My name is Catori Prairie. I am the 5th division commander in charge of the West Region and our international communications." Catori hails from the Hopi tribe. Her raven hair trailed down to her butt and was tied at the end. Her hands were beaten from the years spent fighting and surviving. After announcing her name, she reached for her water, nearly knocking the glass over. She barely caught it as her body moved in a flurry to stop the spill. Pan muttered to himself before he turned to the woman beside him instead of commenting.

"Yes, first, thank you all for your patience. It has been a while since we gathered, and I wanted to ensure we all remembered each other. These meetings are rare, and our interactions are sparse to keep the revolution healthy. Now, for those who have not met me, I am Brooke Hugh. I do not have a rank like the rest of you, but I am Pan's special assistant," the petite and fiery redhead explained as she finished writing down all the names.

With all the introductions complete, it was time for the meeting to begin. The issue was no one was quite sure how to run the meeting. In the revolutionaries' existence, a meeting like this had never occurred. They first gathered when the organization was founded, and Pan elected his commanders. Of that group, only three commanders and a handful of the captains are still alive. They replaced the 2nd division commander and the 5th during the second meeting. Of those who attended that meeting, several captains had been killed and had since been replaced. This meeting was something entirely different.

Across the different divisions, the commanders were given free rein to do as they pleased. They may have communicated if a problem crossed multiple regions, but there were never strategic meetings like this. So, the idea of having a war meeting where all the commanders were brought in to discuss a singular strategy made many of them nervous. Several commanders did not trust the other divisions' captains or had grudges kept at bay because of Pan's leadership. However, they could easily be exposed here. They all looked at each other with watchful eyes while holding their hands near their weapons.

Pan sat in his chair, leaning back and observing his leadership group. The mix of men and women he had elected were the strongest in his army, but not all were leaders. As the silence continued, he leaned forward in his chair, put out his cigarette, and spoke, "You all know what is at stake, so what are you all willing to wager in New Orleans?"

"As it is my territory, all of my forces will be available along with equipment. That should total 328 soldiers and various amounts of weapons," Dirk reported with his head held high. Pan nodded as Brooke wrote the number down.

Khalil took out a notepad and wrote down a number he passed to Brooke. "Khalil says that 242 will be available. Which is fair considering St. Louis and Memphis are still in chaos," Brooke reported.

"That is good to hear. Unfortunately, the East can only supply 135 in the timeframe given. Seventy-five of our forces were stranded by a sudden snowstorm. That said, our 135 will fight as if they are 300," Tank informed the group as he pounded his chest. Dirk's eyes rolled as he heard the report.

"Well, it is a good thing that the North is compensating. Our forces in North Dakota were prepared for their storm. Then they recruited twenty-seven volunteers from Despartian and twenty-four more from the factory city I stayed in to add to the 293 already on their way." Gina smiled as she turned to Tank, who was pouting over her wording.

"Lastly, the West has 113 that will arrive as scheduled, with another 100 within striking distance. They are my cavalry units and will make up the time as we travel. Meanwhile, some of our European allies are delaying boats that John sent for," Catori assured. After each commander had reported, Brooke began calculating the total force at their disposal.

"Given what has been said, we will likely have 1,262 soldiers, along with the commanders and the group Dani travels with. That will make this the largest assault since the last year of the War, but we do not know how many fight for John behind his wall. Reports indicate the city's population is around 15,000. Given what John has done in other cities, it is safe to say that he will keep nearly 15% of that population in guards and soldiers, which puts us at a disadvantage of nearly 700, not factoring in others loyal to him in the city," Brooke calculated as she turned back to the table in front of her.

"Bah, 700 is nothing if you consider the heart our forces will show. A warrior's passion will always outweigh a hired gun fighting for his skin," Dirk boasted.

"Don't let your hubris undo us all, Dirk. Your calculations don't account for losses during the trip, and the fight needed to take the wall, nor do you consider that some of our forces are just medics," Catori lectured back, clearly annoyed by Dirk's arrogance.

"There's 'Chicken Heart' Catori," Dirk taunted.

"You say that, but I think the group would rather be led by a chicken heart than old 'Kicked in the head by Bull' Dirk," she responded. Tank laughed as Dirk's smirk vanished.

"Remember your place, Catori. You are still a junior in my presence."

"I may be your junior, but that doesn't make me wrong," Catori retorted. Both of the commanders reached for their weapons when Gina stood at last.

"Enough both of you! You are commanders, not children! Pan gave you that title; don't mock it!" she scolded as both commanders looked ashamed of their bickering. Once both calmed down, Gina sat and motioned her hand towards Brooke.

"Thank you for settling things," Brooke bowed, "Now that we know the numbers, we must discuss transportation. Once our forces are gathered, we must sail quickly, so are things ready, Dirk?"

"Based on the numbers that you all reported, we should be. Our ships are hidden in the swamps and will be ready to sail the Mississippi," he assured.

"Perfect, we should be able to begin the assault in seven days," Brooke informed them as she set her papers down. They all looked around and choked up for a moment. A week to prepare for the fight of their lives and the world's fate. They could feel the pressure mounting by the moment, and the air grew thick.

All the commanders looked around, waiting for someone to say something. No one knew what it would be, but something was in the air.

Then, at last, Catori asked the question that they were all thinking, "Is this the right move, Pan? This army was not designed for a full-scale battle."

Once she asked the question, there was relief in the room. The fear was starting to subside as they turned to their leader.

"Only fate knows…Ladies and gentlemen, this meeting was inevitable. Either John hunts us down one region at a time, or we would bring the fight to him. It is up to destiny to choose what is meant to happen, and we must have faith that when we act for humankind's good, all of our gods will be in our favor," he replied in a deep, stoic voice. Though it did not contain many assurances, something about his voice calmed his forces down.

"Once we reach the walls, what is the plan?" Gina asked. "We have discussed going after New Orleans a hundred times, and we always stop because of those gates?"

"We will set up camp just outside and wait for word from Dani. I should be receiving a message from her soon. In that message, she will provide intel on John's forces and how to sneak in the commanders," Pan answered.

"That is not much of a plan, sir," Gina stated with a shake.

"No, it isn't, but the plan will reveal itself once we have intel. I know that all of you have thrived planning out your strikes carefully and meticulously, but in this one instance, I need you to trust in me, and I need you to trust your people."

"I'll be ready," Tank proclaimed.

"Hmph, we know you will be. What about the rest of you?" Pan scanned the room to see where his commanders stood.

"Sir, my people have grown tired of attacking trains and small skirmishes. They are ready for this fight, and I am ready to drive our cause home," Dirk stated as he slammed his fist on the table.

"And I am tired of watching mine starve while John grows fat. The West will be strong," Catori assured. Eyes turned to Gina, who had leaned back in her chair.

"In all my years alive, I have done many things. I fell in love, became a mother, fought in a war, and led many to victory in battle, but one thing I haven't done yet is die...I think I can wait a few more weeks to see what that is like. I will be ready," Gina's statement brought a slight grin to Pan.

"It is good to hear that you are all ready. In a week, we take down the world's last great evil. Then we will build a unified republic from the ashes."

"Is there anything else you need from us?" Dirk asked. Pan just looked at Brooke as he rose from his chair.

"Yes, Pan wants a full update on the regions and our progress in cutting off John's supply chains. Specifically, we want to hear about opportunities to unite our forces with those overseas," Brooke answered as Pan headed for the door.

"Is he not staying?" Dirk questioned.

"No, Pan has other matters to attend to. So, he has given me full control over any manner he would normally handle." The four commanders and Khalil looked at each other as Pan exited the room. While the commanders did not trust Brooke's ability to handle matters of war, Pan walked out of the room confidently as she took over.

Once he had left the room, he strolled down the halls of the old museum and sanctuary they called a base. As he wandered, he listened to the soldiers from the different regions talk about their families and life they missed. He lit another cigarette as he continued to roam, shaking the hands of his revolutionaries.

Usually, he knew every fighter's name and would try to learn it if he didn't. These names rested heavily on his mind. Especially now that he was preparing to send 1200 to their death, this would be a Hail Mary and most likely a failure. He had spent most of the morning smoking, hoping his migraine was from withdrawal, but deep down, he knew guilt was eating him.

After shaking a few more hands he strolled into a room marked "Toy Room." Inside the room, Pan just stared at hundreds of destroyed toys. They covered shelves and the floor, from teddy bears to toy trains to electronics. Each item represented a childhood ruined by war. His body gravitated to one action figure. A toy soldier whose left side had been melted and crushed.

He raised the soldier to his temple and placed his head against the toy. His face wrinkled, and his eyes twitched as the plastic rested against his skin. Every part of him wanted to cry, but his tear ducts had dried years ago. His grip tightened as he pressed his head against the toy. Ensuring that he did not damage it further in the process.

"I hate to interrupt, sir, but you need to take your medication while I check your recent wounds," a stocky middle-aged Arab man in a white coat explained, breaking Pan's concentration. After taking a moment to refocus Pan placed the toy back on the shelf.

"I know Raf." Pan turned to the esteemed doctor of the revolution, Dr. Rafal Hakimi.

Dr. Hakimi was considered the perfect doctor by most who understood the field. His genius matched both Clarissa's and Maki's. His bedside manner was on par with Clarissa's. At the same time, his technical ability and efficiency surpassed that of Anna's. It has been argued that Dr. Hakimi adds over twenty soldiers to your side in a battle due to his ability to save lives and return them to action. Years of experience completing humanitarian efforts in war-torn countries had prepared him for everything the War offered. Now, he stood next to Pan and did so faithfully.

"I know you know. But you are still late, Pan," he insisted, giving his boss a cup filled with medication.

"I had to be sharp for today's meeting. The morphine messes with my head and the others, my gut," he explained taking the pills with a few quick gulps. All while they headed to Hakimi's office.

"Unfortunately, that is the price you have to pay."

"We just have a few more battles to survive, then I can rest."

"Sir, I have treated soldiers my whole life, and somehow, they always have a few more battles to fight no matter how many times they see me," the doctor lectured as he started to prepare the IV for the morphine. Pan said nothing as he watched the doctor work. "Now remove your clothes so I can check your wounds."

Without hesitation, Pan started with his shoes. Revealing the seven toes that remained and the aftermath of frostbite that took the other three. He unbuttoned his shirt to reveal skin grafts along his back and a chest littered with bullet wounds. Scars from different edged blades outlined several areas. Both shoulders had been operated on numerous times with large scars. His shoulder-length blonde hair was tied up to show the surgery scar on the back of his neck that repaired some vertebrae. Lastly, he undid his pants. Screws were littered across his knees, dog bites had taken chunks from his right calf, and a scar was still healing from his new right hip. None of these scars showed the psychological damage he had incurred over time. No matter the cost, he continued to sacrifice.

Chapter 8
Local Help

Back in New Orleans, Rob, Dani, Morgan, and Sam had dispersed through a crowd gathering for Trisha's speech. Despite Dani's hesitancy, she agreed to help Rob spring the trap. Rob kept his hat low to hide his face from any guard who might recognize him or the Executives who would know his face. Meanwhile, Dani, Sam, and Morgan were able to move freely. Dani's name was known, but only John would know her face, while the girls were completely anonymous.

Sam and Morgan stayed together to protect one another. In contrast, the other two stayed far away during their patrols. Unaware of all the details, Morgan focused on the crowd while Sam's attention was split. Rob had instructed her to keep an eye on her friend in case Braden made an appearance while also looking for anything that would be important.

As the crowd waited, a band played various tunes to maintain the party atmosphere. The good times continued until, at last, Trisha arrived at the stage. She was met by thunderous applause, but the crowd's face did not match the excitement their cheers would indicate. Some were enthusiastic, but most stared blankly into space as they clapped. Upon further inspection, Rob noted that those who clapped happily carried blades hidden under their garments or showed signs of drinking since early morning.

Trisha raised her hand, and the crowd fell silent until Braden appeared. He was then met by loud cheering as well. Morgan's reaction was far more violent. Sam had to grab her arm to restrain her from storming the stage. Morgan's fist tightened, and she shook at the sight of the man she wanted to see dead.

"Morg," Sam whispered as she held her friend's arm.

"That's him, Sam…that's him," Morgan snarled as she tried to pull her arm free.

"I know, but you have to be patient. Rob wouldn't want us to rush like this," Sam stated as her grip tightened. Morgan was still stronger than her, but she would give everything she could.

"Don't…"

"Don't what?"

"Don't you bring Rob into this. Just because you're his favorite doesn't mean you have to be his lap dog. Remember, we are here for his revenge. Now I want mine," Morgan replied as she stepped closer to her friend.

"I'm not his lap dog. I'm your friend, and this is not the right time."

While Sam held Morgan back, Dani watched them from a distance. She didn't want to intervene, but simultaneously, she doubted Sam's ability to hold Morgan back. After a minute of going back and forth in her mind, she started to cut through the crowd to them. Still, the people were too tightly compacted for her to make her way through without drawing attention. As Dani worried about the others, Rob was oblivious to the situation.

His eyes were too focused on watching the guards and looking for the hidden blades. A pedestrian bumped into him and stumbled, revealing a concealed weapon imprinted in his pants as the man gathered himself. Rob watched this man scurrying through the crowd toward a nearby rooftop. His eyes never turned to Rob as they focused on the guards and scanned the area. At this point, he could feel a certain tension in the air. It was a familiar feeling to him, and he grew excited by it, but at the same time, he knew the feeling meant trouble. He slunk his way to a clearing where no blades or weapons surrounded him. He needed air to think about what to do when the powder keg blew.

As he cleared his mind, Trisha began her speech, "Good afternoon. I hope you all enjoyed the first night of Peace Week. The numbers make it look like you did… It would seem that liquor flowed like water, and sex was rampant across most homes and some streets…I'm proud of you all." As she spoke, Braden poured her a glass of wine that she raised for a toast.

"I was too young when the War started to truly understand what was happening around me. All I knew was that everything was changing, and I would have no say in it; none of us had a say. It was a tragedy we could never have imagined, but now…now we have a choice again. We can choose to live freely and enjoy every moment of it. If we don't, then what have we learned? If we don't live, then why did we survive?" She let her question hang on the air as her words gripped the crowd. She was not the most elegant speaker, but there was something about how she worked the crowd that held their attention.

"We survived all that tragedy so that we could learn to do this life thing right, and that is what Peace Week represents: freedom and a second chance. Now drink, screw around, and enjoy your second chance. Ascension will continue to protect you all and bring prosperity to those who live within its walls!" She toasted and the crowd cheered at her words.

As Trisha began to speak again, Rob noticed a man next to him who was acting restless. He appeared to be twitching and unnerved. When Rob looked closer, he saw that it was the patron he had saved the night before. His face was still damaged, but he had a gun on his hip pocket. The man reached for it, but Rob intercepted him before he could pull it and make a mistake. As Rob grabbed the man's arm, he caught a glimpse of a second man lying prone on a nearby rooftop, pointing a rifle at Trisha. The building was a few hundred feet from Rob, and there was no time to stop them.

The angle was perfect, and the man's shot was lined up. Rob watched the man pull the trigger…but there was nothing. It was a misfire. The man looked at his gun, stunned, but tried to calm himself to line the shot again. He pulled it again, but nothing. Rob could see the panic on the man's face. He rose to his knees and threw the gun to the rooftop. Before he could rise fully, a pair of guards had grabbed him and slit his throat. No sound was made, and outside of Rob, no one knew what had happened. The two cloaked guards pulled the body away past a third man who stayed on the roof to watch the speech. A hood and high pulled collar mostly hid the man's face, but the face turned slightly towards Rob. He did not have to see everything to know who it was. The eyes gave John away in an instant.

They made eye contact, and their worlds became empty at that moment. To the two of them, there were no other sounds or sights. Rob was not standing next to another man, Trisha's voice could not be heard, and there was no crowd around. Their stares said everything in that moment. The pain, the hate, the love, and everything else they felt was shared in their eyes. Rob's fist tightened as he held himself back. He wanted to end the fight now, but he couldn't. At this moment, he wondered who the trap was for. Did he plan for him, or was it these people he was trapping? He thought as he remembered the man's arm he was holding.

As the man looked at John, his body shook. He whipped his arm free from Rob and started to run. Rob was tempted to let him go, but at the same time, being in John's eye was not where he wanted to be. They locked eyes one more time before Rob went to chase the man.

While Rob ran, John's eyes went scanning the crowd. "So, you did come. And if you came, where is she?" he asked himself as he looked around. At last, he caught a glimpse of her raven hair and eyes looking for Rob.

"There she is. You are as beautiful as ever." He paused to look at the rest of the crowd. "Now, where are the new ladies?" It took him only a moment more to find two young women acting odd in the crowd.

"That must be them. They seem like a quirky pair. I wonder why Rob chose to keep them around." He turned to his niece, finishing her speech, then to another rooftop to his right. A mirror flashed a light at him, and he nodded. "Good, one dead, one captured, and the other leads Rob to the Sewers. Things went better than expected." With that, he turned to leave the rooftop and disappeared like a mirage that was never there.

With his cover blown, Rob exited quickly, but the man he was chasing was making a big scene. Rob snagged one of the hidden blades to seem more legitimate, but it did not help him build trust with the stranger.

As they pushed through civilians, Rob continued to yell that he had him, which appeared to be enough for the undercovers. Once they were free of the crowd, they continued the cat-and-mouse chase down the alleys. The man tried to knock over trash cans and debris to slow down his pursuer but to no avail. Rob was both faster and more athletic. He closed the ground quickly until, at last, he tackled the man. Pinning him to the wall after a brief scuffle.

"Enough!" Rob ordered as the man attempted to weasel out of the hold. The man was not about to take orders, so Rob tried to bargain. "If you stop struggling, I will let you go, but know if you run, the next time I break your legs." At first, the man hesitated, confused about what was happening. The guards of the city usually start with the bone breaking. Then, he began to recognize the familiar face from the night before. Finally, he stopped struggling, and Rob kept his word.

"You're the man from last night," he stated once he was free.

"Yeah, the one that told you to lay low."

"You did, but that was not the plan."

"Clearly, but a quick tip that plan sucked." The man's face scrunched as Rob's words cut deep.

"It was not stupid. We had three guns in case of a misfire, but you stopped me!"

"It wouldn't have been that simple. And you would have been dead like your partner."

"What do you mean?"

"I'm assuming you all had weapons made by Ascension, correct?"

"Indeed, as they almost all are, why does that matter?" The man was growing more confused by Rob, who was trying to figure out the right way to break the news to the man.

"Well, it matters because they all have a mechanism installed that makes them malfunction when they are near Trisha, John, and the Executioner. That is why every guard was holding a blade," he explained.

The man held his gun up to Rob's head as he was shaking, "How do you know this?"

"I had a run-in with the Executioner a few months back and saw the same thing happen to another man," Rob explained as he looked through the gun. Rob's focus never wavered as the man held it momentarily before dropping his hands.

"But that means...that means our weapons are useless," he stuttered as he was starting to wonder how truthful the stranger was being.

"Not completely. They still work against the regular guards, but you have to face him straight up to beat John. And any large-scale fight will be decided by those without them," Rob said it just as much for himself as the other man.

"I don't know if we have a man that can do it." The man rubbed his face.

"There you repeated it, 'we' and 'our.' Who are you referring to?" Rob asked as the man realized how loose he had been with his tongue to a man he barely knew. He threw his hands over his mouth.

"Sorry, I misspoke. I was still thinking my friend was alive," the man said with his voice growing pitchy. Rob looked at the man's eyes as they darted around and watched his mouth shift to the side.

"I understand you don't trust me, but that might have been the worst attempt at lying I have ever seen…that was just…bad. Never try that again." Rob's face was dumbstruck as the man rubbed the back of his head. "No, let's start with your name and what is happening."

"I ain't tellin' you shit! That better?" the man shouted back.

"Yes, but this isn't going to get us anywhere. I saved your life twice, but I never told you my name. So I will start there. I am Rob, the man who can stop John," Rob replied, trying a more polite approach.

"Big talk. I've seen it many times," the man snapped back before Rob punched him in the gut, sensing that polite wouldn't work.

"My name is Rob; what is yours?" he asked as the man stood bent over from the swift and punishing punch.

"My name is Eduardo."

"Good start. Based on what I saw, we have a similar goal, but that should not be discussed in these alleys," Rob suggested as he motioned for Ed to lead them somewhere else.

"I take it you will not let me go without that discussion."

"You're catching on. Now, I'll let you choose the location." He patted Ed on the shoulder as he started to walk. Ed hesitated for a minute but shook his head and led Rob elsewhere.

Rob was wary of Ed but had not proven competent enough to be a threat. Just as he did with Clarissa, the pair stuck to the alleyways and shadows as much as they could. From the alleys, Rob saw the newly constructed New Orleans transform into run-down shacks with siding falling off and broken windows littering every building. An odor was also growing stronger as it stung his nose.

When Ed darted into one of the abandoned buildings. Rob held the guard's blade firmly and hovered his free hand towards his staff as he followed. He slowed his breathing and listened for anything that should not have been there or anyone who was not Ed. He may have saved the man twice, but Ed's loyalties were still unclear.

The decrepit building was as empty on the inside as the outside appeared. The furniture and lighting were gone. Even the spiders had abandoned their cobwebs for more promising homes. Unable to see, Rob called out for the man, but there was nothing but a faint plodding. He continued to stumble through the darkness towards the sound until he found the basement door unlocked.

The door was barely open, but he could see light illuminating the steps down. He crept down the stairs as carefully as possible, avoiding unnecessary noise, but a few steps creaked under his weight. At the bottom of the steps, Rob found Ed standing behind a counter with a pair of stools in front of it.

"So, what is your pleasure?" Ed asked.

"Tequila, but what are we doing?" Rob asked as he sat on one of the old leather bar stools, breaking at the seams.

"Ah, tequila. A man after my father's heart." Ed grabbed an unmarked bottle and a few glasses into which he poured a drink. The worm in the bottom floated on each poor. Growing closer and closer to the glasses.

"Your father must have had good taste."

"Good taste in liquor. Horrible taste in women and work."

"I feel that is common for us tequila lovers." Rob took a sip, and his face scrunched at the taste. He shook his head before looking back at Ed, "Now that the niceties are over, are you ready to talk?"

"Not particularly, but do I have a choice?"

"No. So, will you tell me who 'we' is?"

"Not until you tell me why you care. I'd rather die than give them up to the wrong person." Ed took a sip of his glass as he stared at Rob. Rob leaned against the counter and looked deep into Ed's eyes. He could see the pain in his eyes and the recent hurt. The physical beating from the day before had barely phased this man, but the deep wound he had experienced had cut him. It was a look Rob had seen in the mirror a thousand times and one that had plagued hundreds of others he had met.

"I can understand that, especially with what John has done to this city. How about this: you can ask me a series of questions, and if you like my answers, you take me to this 'we' if you don't, I kill you."

"Doesn't sound like much of a deal for me."

"No, but it is the only fair one. You see, I will tell you the truth, and if you cannot believe that after saving you twice, you leave me no option. I can't risk my goals either." Ed leaned away as he took a sip. Goosebumps were appearing on his arm as his body shook. The way Rob stared at him was unnerving. It was similar to that of John yet entirely different. The way he stared captivated him, and had a certain peace but a deadness that also terrified him.

"If I have no other choice, I will play. So, why would you come here?"

"A good first question and a long story. Simply put, I let John kill people precious to me, and now I need to stop him before he hurts more people." Rob took another sip.

"Revenge then, that is something I can relate with, and many people can rally to."

Rob stood swirling his glass for a moment, thinking about that word 'revenge.' it had been his goal for so long, but it was an ugly word to him now. He wished there was something else he could say, but nothing would suffice.

"Yeah, revenge…next question?"

"This is the big one. Why can you stop him?" Ed leaned in closer to hear this answer.

"That is even more complicated, but he wants to fight me, and I have known him long enough to understand his weaknesses," Rob explained, sipping the drink. As he spoke, he thought about John. Internally, he could feel happiness and anger fighting with each other. They had been inseparable for a long time, and some moments they shared were precious memories of Rob. Whether it was long nights in a forest where they were alone telling stories, exchanging whiskey in blizzards, or pulling leeches off one another, they were memories that he would never give up. However, there was Iris and what John did to her. There was everything he had seen done in the name of Ascension.

"What do you mean by 'he wants to fight' you?"

"After he killed someone I knew, I followed him down the Mississippi. At least, I thought I was following him, but he left me clues at every step. At every turn, I played into his plan, and now he won't let anyone else close until he has me."

"And why would he want that if you can beat him?"

"I don't know…" Rob answered with hesitancy in his voice.

"Then it has to be a trap for you. Why would that be an advantage?" Ed placed his empty glass on the counter and leaned closer to Rob. His fears had slowly turned into intrigue.

"It could be, but I understand that and am planning for it. On the other hand, your people knew nothing, so I have to ask, why set a trap for you today?" Rob's voice had raised slightly as he spoke, backing Ed up until a lightbulb clicked.

"There was a third man there. He…he is one of our best fighters." Ed's head dropped, and he placed his hands on the counter to steady his body.

Rob pushed his drink aside and started pacing around the room as Ed thought, "You were worried about me betraying you, but you already have a traitor. John knew this. He had to, so what are you going to do?" Rob stared at Ed, who was still thinking about what had happened. "And they let one person get away, maybe the rat." Ed raised his head and pointed a finger at Rob.

"Don't you call me a rat! I have been beaten and lost my wife because of them! I would never be their rat!" Ed steamed as Rob questioned his loyalty.

"I believe you, but will your friends?"

"I'm…I'm not sure. And if I bring a stranger back, they won't."

"True, but I can bring them intel that might keep us both alive. I've already saved your life twice. Let me see if I can do it again." Rob reached his hand out, hoping that Ed would extend his own.

"I don't know if I can."

"Do you have a choice?" Ed shook his head. "Then let's find out if my offer is good enough." Ed sighed before pressing a brick in the wall behind him. Rob listened as metal started to click, and the wall scraped across the floor, opening a small space in the wall for them to walk through.

As Ed led Rob into the tunnel, Rob noticed that it was much older than most of the city. The hard stone had been hand-cut and dug through. The gears that moved the door had been restored over the years, but most of it dated back to a world Rob could not have imagined. It might have been used during Prohibition or as an escape tunnel for slaves. So many years had passed, and while modern technology faltered during the War, this system remained strong.

Rob tried to memorize the path Ed led him down, but with all the turns and extra tunnels, it was impossible for Rob to know where he was. He tried to leave marks on the wall to track his steps, but Ed led him in several circles, repeatedly causing him to see his marks.

Eventually, Ed took him down a straight path without lighting. As they walked, Rob's hand would graze the walls and feel a dampness from condensation that had built up. Then he started to step in puddles while barely keeping his footing in mud patches where the ground had worn away. Rats scurried past them, and Rob was struck by a sudden odor, nearly knocking him off his feet. The smell brought tears to his eyes while his guide seemed unfazed. He recognized the smell as human waste, decaying trash, and dead fish, but never had he experienced the smell to this degree.

At last, there was a glimmer of light behind an old wooden door. Ed approached it slowly, looking back at Rob and taking a deep breath. He opened the door, and Rob was instantly blinded by the light.

Chapter 9
The Sewer District

Rob had to blink several times as he stepped out of the pitch-black tunnel and into the open air. He cleared water from his eyes as he fought through the smell that had only intensified now that they were outside. The first thing he heard and saw was the seagulls flying above, headed to the open water.

"We are here," Ed claimed as Rob continued to collect himself and let his eyes readjust. Once he had, he looked at the area around him. They were in an open basement much like the one they had just left, but the floor above them and the house that once hid the tunnel had been burned down, leaving nothing but the tunnel and a brick staircase. The rest of the hole they stood in had deteriorated away and was nothing more than dirt.

At the top of the steps, Rob took in what appeared to be an old wharf turned into a place for people to live. Wooden docks and concrete stretched onto the water attached to the couple-mile stretch of land they stood on. All around them were tents and shacks that barely stood. A strong storm would collapse many of them. Each building had been set up close to the others, creating a city within the city. Lake Pontchartrain was no more than two hundred meters from them, and the breeze that came off of it did help soothe the smell slightly.

Rob started to search the wharf and shack houses to find the source of the smell. In the distance, piles of trash towered over the huts and slid right up to them. Then, there were pipes that moved sewage to their doorsteps. Some pipes extended from the wall a few hundred feet away, while others came from the ground raised just before the area.

As he had been looking for the source of the smells, he saw the saddest part: men and women dressed in rags as they tried to keep their children out of the runoff and keep the runoff out of their homes. Several of their bodies had succumbed to the sicknesses that the sewage had given them. While those who were still healthy enough to do anything sat on the docks fishing or cooking food for the others. A few of them noticed Rob and just stared at him with contempt. He could feel a vile hatred in them.

Rob was beginning to understand why Ed hated John and why Clarissa had spoken about the suffering in the city. John had learned from the cruelties of those that existed before the War and built slums.

The hardest thing for Rob was that this was John's city. During the War, John had always been a fighter for equality. He came from slums like this, and John showed his soft side anytime they were in a city. Even in Despartian, John worked hard to ensure there weren't areas this bad. Yes, there were poorer areas compared to his stars that worked for him, but no one lived in the trash. Rob wondered why New Orleans was so different and what made him change.

"What is this place?" Rob asked, at last, turning to Ed.

"This…this is the Sewer District. A name well earned as you can imagine," Ed began as the drains continued to rumble and shoot debris out. "But the name also stems from John's hatred for this area. We are trash to him and the Executives." They started walking through the district as Ed showed Rob what was happening. Rob tried not to make eye contact as they passed the kids, coughing and crying.

"Was it always like this?" Rob asked.

"No, it wasn't, and that makes it worse. Everyone in the city let this happen and even promoted it." Ed's eyes teared slightly as he spoke.

"What do you mean by that?"

"Well, at first, John moved criminals to his prison. If laws were broken, John quickly threw them away, and we cheered because it made us safe. We didn't object to the lack of trials, and then he created this district for those deemed a 'threat' but not criminal. He threw people in here that were considered racist, sexist, and bigoted. They were allowed to live free, but they had to sleep here. Life was great and almost like a utopia where peace was inevitable." Ed paused to look at some of the oldest huts and the occupants dying from infections that could not be treated.

"But it did not stop there." Ed just shook his head.

"No, from there, he started to make the case that they could not access the limited hospital beds as their hatred would be best off dead, and to keep them alive would threaten war again. Most of the city was still at his side, but rumblings were growing. About that time, runaway and suicide numbers began to skyrocket across the city." His tears grew more consistent as the memory of his wife, who had recently 'committed suicide' came to his mind.

"He was making people disappear."

"Yes, and the people who said this were sent to this district as they became 'threats' to the city and a danger to peace. He started big with those who made threats and spoke like the others we had already accepted as people belonging in the sewers."

"And then he changed it to whoever opposed him." Ed closed his eyes as he stood for a moment, eventually nodding.

"You say this as if you have seen it before."

"I trained and fought with John and know him well. One of the lessons we learned when we were sent to destabilize an area was that it is impossible to topple a united front, but if you can slowly turn people against each other, the moment the last survivors look for help, they realize they have already turned on their allies. At that moment, they realize the people, their friends, were the ones they turned on first," Rob explained, pacing through the district, avoiding the streams of waste that ran across the ground.

"That is what I found. When they came for me, I realized I had turned in the neighbors that would aid me, and the others were willing to throw me under the bus to save their skins."

"And unfortunately, the time will come for them unless they completely sell their soul to his corruption and words."

"That is where we are at. When I turned in neighbors for being horrible people, I thought I was doing the moral and righteous thing," Ed began to cry fully this time as he dropped to his knees. Rob stood beside him briefly before bending over to comfort him.

"It is alright. This is not the first time this has been done, but we must focus on stopping it from worsening. We need to stop John and correct the mistakes made." Ed wiped his tears and rose to his feet with the help of Rob's outstretched arm.

"Indeed, come on, we are almost there." Ed motioned for Rob to follow him. They began to approach a shed no bigger than 20x20 feet. Its right side was falling apart, and a chimney rose from the back. The door was covered by an old black curtain. As they approached the shack, Rob could hear faint footsteps behind him, but is was too late to worry as they reached the shed.

The ground in front of it had been worn down from high foot traffic, and Rob could see scuff marks on the ground from nearby logs and rocks that had been pushed around a small campfire. Ed pushed the black curtain to the side, and dust fell from the fabric. He led Rob inside, where an old man sat cross-legged on the floor. The man's skin drooped, and age spots were scattered across his body. He was missing his right leg and barely raised his eyes to meet them. Ed stood just off-center while Rob went to sit across from the old man. He sat crisscrossed and stared at the ancient and shaggy man before him. The old man picked up a pipe and took a deep puff that filled the room with smoke. The haze lingered momentarily as Rob tried to gain a better look.

As he looked closely, he saw the man's right ear had been burned heavily, and his right eye was glazed. He may have had some sight, but it was limited. The man's skin was dark with a permanent tan, and he had long, scraggly gray hair draping down his back.

"Eduardo…how are you here?" The man paused as every syllable was long and drawn out with a deep voice. "And who is this man?"

"His name is unimportant, but he shares our purpose, Sir Mancio," Ed reported. The old man's brow raised as he grabbed his pipe again.

"An unimportant name, you say…," he began as smoke filled the air again, "If it is unimportant, then you should have no problem giving it." Rob silently sat for a second as he observed the man before him. He was different and gave off this aura that filled the room like smoke. It was calming yet powerful.

"Rob Doran," Rob answered after his long pause.

"Robert means bright fame, and Doran, a Gaelic name that means wanderer or exile…quite an interesting combo. What brings you to our city?" Mancio asked as he pulled a small marinet from a bag behind him. Rob sat silent as he turned to Ed for a moment. The marinet was almost as old as Mancio. The wood had started to decay but had been repaired several times. The strings that were attached to the puppet had been rethreaded as well. Rob looked closer at the puppet and saw the face of a young man smiling with blue eyes painted on it.

"I am here to stop John," Rob said plainly, no longer wanting to waste time. Mancio smiled as his puppet began to dance.

"Stop… an interesting word to use rather than kill… May I ask, do you meditate?"

"I do," Rob answered as his head tilted. Unsure of what the question's purpose was.

"Ed, leave us for a second. I wish to sit with this man and read his soul," Mancio ordered as he shooed Ed away. Ed bowed and exited promptly. Leaving the two men alone. "Now exile, will you meditate with me for a second? I wish to feel your spirit and destiny." Rob's head tilted again as he blinked a few times.

"I guess…if you promise there will be more answers," Rob stated, and Mancio nodded.

"Of course…And then I will also have questions, like why my son did not come back, but you and our bait did."

With no other alternative, Rob watched the old man close his eyes, and Rob did the same. He started to breathe and relax just as Mark had taught him. He let himself feel the moment and the presence around him. The men sat silently for nearly a half-hour before Mancio finally opened his eyes.

He snapped his fingers to wake Rob up. He blinked a few times to return, and as he did so, the old man was attaching a prosthetic leg. The man rose and started searching the shed.

"So what now?" Rob asked as he watched the man.

"Now we talk and see what destiny has in store for you."

"I don't think I need that. I already had an old woman tell me I was destined for life while John was destined for death."

Mancio stopped and turned to Rob, who was still sitting in silence. He moved his tongue around in his mouth as he contemplated. Then, at last, he spoke, "Interesting, so your destiny's motivation has already been read, but you say it was done with John?"

"Yes, it was, and what do you mean destiny's motivation?"

"Well, first for motivation. No one can truly read another's future, but we can sense their souls and see what will drive it. When one walks for life, everything they do will be motivated by the love of life and living. They may have lost people, but act for those who still exist. While those who are destined by death will act to avoid death or create it. They are controlled by losses they have experienced and act because of them. Unfortunately, if your destiny is read with another, you will forever be intertwined on your journey. A mistake that should always be avoided," he explained as he grabbed a small bag and sat down again.

"So, it does not mean we are destined for life or death, only that we are motivated by it."

"Correct, and I have not known you, but I know John's is accurate. His actions are motivated by the deaths that haunt him and the one that scares him," Mancio answered as he began to pour a powder from his bag around a candle in the center of the shed. Saving a little in his hand.

"But then mine must be wrong. For I am here because of a death," Rob replied, thinking about his destiny and what brought him to New Orleans.

"No, it is right. I sensed it when we meditated. Let me ask you: when you act, are you protecting people who still live? Do you attempt to give them a better life, or do you act to avoid your death?"

Rob took a moment to think and reflect on the past few months. He started to avenge a death, but now he wanted Dani, Sam, and Morgan to have a better life. He wanted people to live and stop John for them as much as Iris.

"I guess it is the former."

"This is known." Rob rolled his eyes as he watched Mancio.

"What are you doing?"

"Creating an omen."

"Creating an omen?"

"Yes, I do not adhere to any faith because they are all conduits for the true destiny of the universe, love, and life. This leads me to watch the world, waiting for omens to appear before me, but on occasion, I have to create a moment for the omen to appear. For instance, this powder mixes different chemicals that change the fire's colors. When I throw it, the order and lasting nature of the colors will tell me what to expect. Then the embers will burn the circle around the candle to give me the final destiny and whether I should trust you," Mancio explained as he took the powder and threw it at the candle.

In a burst of color, the fire turned an intense purple, a majestic red, a floral pink, and a calming blue. Then the circle of powder ignited, dominated by pinks and blue, until all was consumed in red. Mancio watched in awe as the colors danced. He was memorizing the order and intensity. Meanwhile, Rob sat with his hands clenched on his knees. Unsure of what was happening, he grew nervous about what it meant.

Once done, Mancio sat momentarily and smoked his pipe. "You are dangerous." Those were the only words he said. Rob went searching for his staff, unsure of what would happen now.

"I'm sorry to hear that. We could have been allies. I thought you were the people Clarissa spoke of." Rob sighed as he extended his staff and rose to his feet. Mancio's eye grew big momentarily when he mentioned Clarissa but then settled back into his seat.

"The doctor always has big dreams but has not seen what I did."

"And what did you see?" Rob gripped his staff tight as he waited for Mancio's next move.

"I saw war and the death of my people. I cannot allow this. Now go, or I will force you to leave."

"No, I need allies to stop him. He won't be stopped if we don't join together."

"I am sorry, but you are a threat." As he spoke, his voice grew more steady. He pulled a string to the puppet, and it released a smoke cloud that filled the shack. Rob jumped through the curtain into the open only to have two men descend from the roof on top of him. They came crashing in with steel pipes and pinned him on his back. Laying on the ground and resisting them with all his might, Rob had to think fast. He kicked the one on his right, which provided a slight amount of space. Rob pushed the staff up on his left side, allowing the right to lower while still keeping it off of him. With the slickness of the pipes and staff, the man on his left slid down and crashed into his partner. Rob kicked up to his feet to capitalize, but before he could, two more men with knives came charging from behind. One was able to catch a piece of Rob's shirt but nothing else. Rob retreated, but now the four men had regrouped.

They charged at Rob in a coordinated manner. He, in turn, did his best to create space and used the entire length of his staff to keep them away from him. The four men charged in. Rob countered with a swing that broke one man's jaw, but another slipped past the block and struck Rob in his ribs, aggravating his older injuries. From there, the three men restrained him.

"What should we do with him, Father?" One of them asked.

"I want him removed. The fire talks of a man who is torn and restless. His passion and hate will bring more suffering and war to our doorsteps. Then he will either be salvation or peace at the expense of my family," Mancio explained as Rob knelt in the dirt.

"You are making a mistake," Rob pleaded one last time.

"I may be, but I ignored my visions of John, which have cost many people in this city their lives. I will not do so again." Mancio turned to head back into his shack.

"But I can kill him!" Rob yelled as the men began to drag him. Mancio paused for a moment before turning back to Rob.

"You can, but you won't. Many deaths lay in your wake and on your path, but not his. And I will not risk my sons and daughters in your war."

"Then you will lose yours," Rob said at last before the men knocked him out. Those words hung in the air briefly, and the men looked at Mancio for their next order. The old man stood staring at Rob, unconscious on the ground. The old man put his hands behind his back and thought with his pipe hanging from his mouth.

"Dump him near the hospital. If he truly knows Clarissa, she will take care of him." Mancio reentered his shack. His eyes stared at the fire, which returned to its normal color, for a long time as he sat back down. "Maybe I was too harsh on him, but he is dangerous to keep around. He needs to settle his destiny before I can allow him around my family," Mancio whispered to the sky with another giant puff of his pipe.

Chapter 10
Those Who Heal Us

After Rob disappeared from the speech, Dani made her way over to Sam and Morgan. She assisted Sam in restraining Morgan, and they made their exit before the speech had fully finished. Dani decided it would be best for them to explore the city, hoping it would distract them from the missing Rob. Sam and Morgan had asked about him, but Dani assured them that Rob could handle himself, and they needed to do their part to ensure they succeeded.

As they walked through the streets, Dani acted like a mother with her daughters. Meanwhile, both Sam and Morgan remained anxious. Morgan, in particular, was on guard the whole time. Her eyes scanned every corner as if a monster would jump out and attack them. Dani picked up on her friend's anxiety and placed one hand on Morgan's shoulder to comfort her. Morgan turned to see Dani's calm and smiling face.

"How are you so calm?" Morgan asked once they were far enough away from the crowd. Dani wrapped her arms around both women and pulled them in tighter.

"Simple, Rob is a survivor. I've seen him shot, stabbed, burned, and so much more. Yet, every time, he finds a way back. And now that he has you two, I know nothing will stop him from coming home again," she responded with a side hug.

"What do you mean by that?" Sam asked, tilting her head and raising an eyebrow. Dani took a moment to think and then noticed a food stand not far from them.

"How about we get some food, and then I'll tell you," Dani suggested as she could feel her stomach rumbling.

"Hey, if I ever say no to food. It's code for 'I'm in trouble,'" Morgan said, still holding her eyes on Dani, wanting the question answered.

"But I'm not sure you can afford us," Sam giggled.

"Oh, I'm sure Clarissa left me enough," Dani replied, pulling out a small pouch left on her nightstand that morning.

The three of them headed to the nearby food stand. It was a small stand operated by a tiny Indian man with a thick accent and a glowing smile. Morgan was simple and ordered noodles and chicken. Sam took longer ordering her dessert first and then some pork and rice. Finally, Dani ordered a spicy bowl of curry. They took their food to the nearest bench, where Sam allowed Dani to take a few bites before asking a question.

"So what did you mean back there about him not being stopped now that he has us?" she asked.

"I guess it's because when he is around you two, I see the old Rob again." Dani smiled as she took another bite.

"And what does that mean?" Both of the girls asked this time.

"When I saw him in St. Louis, the loss of Iris was still heavy on him. He was possessed by a lot of anger, and he wasn't him. But since I've seen him with you two, I see him smiling and laughing more. There is still a lot of hurt in him, but in the short time he has known you, he has found something else to drive him." Dani smiled while the other two listened intently.

"Something else?" Morgan asked.

"Yeah, instead of fighting to avenge Iris, I think he has started to fight for you two."

"Why would he do that? We have only known him for a few weeks," Sam asked. Dani looked to the sky as she thought about answering the question. She thought deeply about Rob and wondered what she should share. Her mind twisted over what Rob would want the ladies to know about him. All the while, Sam and Morgan waited patiently for her reply.

"Well, to answer that you must understand the old Rob. The one that I've started to see again," Dani said with eyes that rested on the horizon. Her gaze was tender as she thought about Rob. Sam poked Dani in the arm to bring her back down.

"So, are you going to tell us about the old Rob?"

Dani bopped her head back and forth a few times before answering, "He was a complicated but straightforward man. He was a guy that I learned lost a lot early in his life and was alone for many of the losses. This led him to be annoyingly overprotective…"

"Well, some things never change," Morgan said, looking at Sam, who raised her eyebrows. Dani chuckled, listening to the ladies confirm what she already knew.

"No, that is one fight I still have with him, and I don't see it changing after Iris was killed. His loneliness and the scared boy inside drive many of his flaws, but in the few weeks with you two, he has found something that reminds him of Iris. I think the hole she left in his heart has started filling," Dani explained as she looked at the girls and thought of Iris. Morgan and Sam just sat for a moment. When Dani mentioned Iris, they both lowered their eyes to the ground as if something taboo had just been said.

"What…what was she like? I've heard him say her name in his sleep before, but he rarely talks about her," Morgan asked once she lifted her head. Dani's face scrunched at the question. It was not one she felt ready to answer, but she wanted to find the right words.

"Iris was," Dani paused again. She thought she had the words, but as she began to speak, the words no longer felt like enough. "She was…an angel that walked among us. In all my years, I have never met someone so pure of heart, so kind and giving, so happy even when she shouldn't have been. She was my best friend and someone Rob believed he didn't deserve. He thought he was too weird and annoying. He was, but they were also perfect for each other. Each had their damage, and they helped each other repair it. They didn't 'complete' each other but were the right people to help the other heal. Her kindness and patience allowed him to grow into a man who could be more than his traumas. At the same time, his stubbornness, confidence, and motivating nature pushed her to be more than she believed she could be." Her eyes watered as the last words left her lips. It was the first time since her death that she had talked about Iris besides conversations with Rob. The ladies hugged her instantly.

"She sounds amazing," Sam said as she held Dani tight.

"She was, and that is why he was so hurt. He had lost so much when he was younger that he had walled off his heart until she broke through. Then the War hurt him, and John tried to break him."

"So, why do you think we have been able to fill that hole?" Morgan asked.

"That is complicated, but we'll start with this: how has he helped the two of you? I mean, each of you has lost people precious to you, and you seem to face it well." The two looked at each other as they thought on this question.

Morgan became the first to answer, "Well, he showed me the love of a brother that I never had and protected me when I was weak. Then he taught me to protect myself and others." She turned to look at Sam, whose mind was swirling in thought before she spoke at last.

"Yeah, he became the family I lost during the War and in Memphis. He never tried to replace my real family but did his best to remind us that we are not alone."

"And you two did that for him by opening your hearts and letting him be who he is. You could have left and went your own way. You could have called him a weirdo like many people did early in his life, but you stayed. You let him be just as she did, but you never tried to replace her or fill that hole. All you have done for each other is helped one another face the pain inside. It may have been a quick turnaround for this to happen, but those weeks were tough. They made you choose to stay or leave, and all of you stayed."

"I wish it wasn't like this," Morgan mumbled as she held her heart. This talk of loss had made her think of all the loved ones she had lost with the War and otherwise, causing the pain to tear at her heart.

"Neither do I. But Rob's mentor, Mark, told me something that has stuck for some time now. He said, '*Suffering is human. Our muscles must be torn to grow strong, and our food acts as building blocks. So, our heart, a muscle in its own right, must be broken before it can be stronger. But it is not actual food that is used for growth. It is a connection that fuels the healing; this is why Rob will grow again.*'" Dani recited, thinking back to when Rob was unconscious after meeting the Executioner.

Morgan momentarily pulled her knees to her chest and thought about Dani's words. Morgan spoke before Dani could ask what was wrong, "Are you sure? I mean, what you say makes sense, but then there are those days when he is distant. He leaves us to do something, like today or that first night here."

"Yeah, those times…you remember when I said he was alone when he was younger?"

"I do."

"Well, part of that was his fault. He has this habit of self-isolating and growing cold. I've never asked him directly, but I think it is a bit of depression he struggles with. I talked to Iris about it once, and as a therapist, she explained that he had this thought pattern where he believes he does not deserve the love people give him, so he isolates himself until people are sick of his BS. Then he is right. That is why you two staying has been so important. It shows him that he doesn't belong alone. It helps him see that he is worthy of love," Dani responded as she placed her hand on Morgan's shoulder.

"I hope he is happy again soon," Sam muttered as she turned her eyes to the sky.

"He is getting there." Dani set her other hand on Sam's shoulder and held the ladies tight.

All three sat silent for a moment. There was a lot of information for the young ladies to digest. It also led to a slight change in their perspective because they had never known the peace on the other side of tragedy. They did not understand how Rob had to bury parts of himself so that he could be the soldier he was.

On the other hand, Rob had a past beyond the War that tore at his mind as he prepared to face John again. Killing a man, you hate is one thing, but to kill one who was once a brother is a burden of a different kind, especially for someone who had longed for connection as long as Rob had. However, it gave them both solace to know they were helping him.

"Well, we are just about done, so let's check the gates," Dani ordered after the silence had hung for a few minutes. They threw out the food packaging and made their way north.

The gate was about a half-hour walk from the food stand. During this walk, Dani kept her eyes moving, looking for any disturbances. Unlike Rob, their faces were unknown, yet she still had this itch that made her feel they were being followed. She led the other two through every maneuver she could muster for losing a tail, but it still did not feel like enough.

"Is there something we need to know?" Morgan asked after looking back enough times.

"Not sure…I just have this feeling and want to ensure we stay safe," she explained, leading them down an alley. Just before exiting, a couple of men stepped out in front of them. The leader of the pack grabbed Dani by the wrist.

"So what are you pretty little things doing out here without strong men like us?" the man holding Dani asked as his compatriots surrounded the ladies.

"Oh, just trying to avoid creeps like you." She winked at both Sam and Morgan. Dani could smell the liquor on the man's breath and assumed his friends were in the same spot. Had they encountered other ladies, they might have gotten what they sought. However, these three were the wrong women to test.

"That's not very nice…I just wanted to play a ten-minute game with y'all." He smiled while withdrawing a knife from his waistband. He twirled it around in his hand to intimidate, but Dani fought back a yawn.

"Don't give yourself that much credit," Morgan smirked as she and Sam adjusted their footing.

The man in charge went to hold the knife against Dani's neck, but she blocked his knife with her free hand and then broke free of his grip before kicking him back. Sam and Morgan went on the offensive as soon as she moved. They struck fast and hard, sending the other two men flying towards the alley wall. All three men looked at each other, trying to understand what had happened.

The women had positioned themselves so that each could strike at one of the men. The men charged in. Morgan blocked one's wild swings while diverting the swings that had a smidge of aim. As he struck, she moved closer until he finally took a big swing that she diverted. She hit the back of the man's shoulder with her elbow and then grabbed his other arm to flip him. Once on the ground, he grabbed her foot, but she stomped down on his arm and then dropped her knee on his chest before a quick chop to the throat.

Meanwhile, Sam employed different tactics as she spun around and avoided the man's strikes. She could not absorb blows like Morgan, but she was agile, and the drunk man grew dizzy quickly. When it became clear that he could barely stand, she kicked the back of his knees and struck his head with the lid of a nearby trash can.

Dani was a mixture of both as she fought. She might not be as clean of a fighter as Rob is, but she is methodical. She mocked the man the whole time they fought. Like a cat toying with its food, she would jab and avoid. She exerted as little energy as possible while he grew enraged. Then, she finally surprised him by getting in close and striking his arm. She hit with such precision and velocity that it popped out of the socket. This was followed with a punch to the throat and a kick in the balls.

The women left the alley quickly to avoid the eyes of all the guards. Dani hoped the feeling of being watched would subside, but it still lingered. Sam and Morgan boasted to each other about the beatdown they had just delivered as Dani led them away. After a ten-minute walk, they arrived at the large stone gate. Dani saw the sinister nature of the fifty-foot gate and forty-foot walls.

Five men were standing on either side of the gate. One group stood just outside, and the others stood just inside. Everyone that entered and left the city had to be checked and rechecked on each side. Meanwhile, four more guards stood by the gate switch. Fourteen men were alone in that close space, and at least twenty more were walking around the plaza with their hands on their weapons. As Dani continued to scan, she saw a door inside the gate and another inside the wall that likely acted as a passage for the guards if the gate had to be closed suddenly.

It was not impenetrable, but there were only four of them, and they would have to open that gate on their own. If they do not, Pan's forces never enter the city, leaving any rebellion dead before it could even start.

The job was a critical one that they could not fail, but she wasn't sure how to do it with just them. Sure, the four of them could cut through the fodder currently, but if an army approached the gate, then John's entire forces, including himself, would be there to fight. She ran every calculation she could as they roamed the plaza for about an hour. She memorized guard movement patterns and looked for gaps. However, they could not stay long as she could feel the eyes of the undercover vipers taking note. They couldn't risk getting caught, so the ladies retreated back to the home.

The ladies returned to the house just after the sun had set. Clarissa was sitting on the couch, drinking tea and looking through some old, beaten medical books. Several notebooks were lying on the table, and a pile of used sticky notes was next to them. Her hair was in a mess from her left hand, that she ran through it.

When they entered the house, Clarissa barely reacted. Her eyes just turned to them momentarily before returning to the book and notes. The ladies walked in and sat around Clarissa. Morgan and

Sam sat on the floor while Dani sat on the couch beside Clarissa. As Sam looked at the notes, her eyes grew big as she became increasingly confused.

"What is all this stuff?"

"It's just some old data on cancer and performance-enhancing drugs. Most of it is outdated, but I've been stumped all day," Clarissa admitted, setting the book down and turning to Sam.

"Why, what's the issue?"

"Well, I have some clients with a rare form of cancer, and the drugs in their system are reacting poorly." Dani sat listening and tried to deduce what Clarissa was working on. She did not know much about medical needs, but what she did see was troubling her. What she saw made her stomach churn.

"These patients…are they soldiers?" Clarissa leaned back and had a long sigh before replying.

"These are not, but the goal was to make them soldiers. John has been messing with Leopard Skin, and the results have been mixed. He has some behemoths like his Executive Kenneth, but more are dying like my current clients."

"Leopard Skin is not a pretty death in any form," Dani commented, recalling her experiences watching people fall apart from the withdrawal.

"It is ugly. Today, I had the internal organs of these men melt inside their bodies and rot in a matter of minutes." She rubbed her eyes as she tried to clear the memory from her mind while Morgan and Sam were both taken aback by the statement.

"That's horrible."

"It was, but let's talk about something else. I have been looking at numbers for hours and need distractions. How was your day?"

"It was good. We went to the speech and then did some surveying. The gate is a masterpiece."

"It's quite something. Where is Rob?"

"We're hoping he is on his way," Dani informed her with a slight quiver of unsureness.

"Did he go missing, or did you all talk about it?" Clarissa leaned in close as her right hand began to twitch. Sam and Morgan kept out of the conversation as their faces tried to hide their worry, but nothing helped. Clarissa knew the answer before Dani even spoke.

"Missing, I guess. We covered different areas during the speech, and I think I saw him chasing after someone." Dani's eyes were closed, and she rubbed the back of her neck as she tried to remember what she saw.

Clarissa started to pace around the room. Her hands twitched every step, and her face scrunched while she thought. She leaned against her kitchen counters as she bit her nails. "And nothing happened at the speech that was out of the ordinary?"

"Not that we saw."

"Then they failed. I wonder if he followed them," she muttered under her breath. She thought she was quiet enough, but Dani started to approach her.

"What didn't succeed, and who would he have followed?" Clarissa threw her head to the sky when she realized she had been too loud.

"Mancio's forces were supposed to disrupt the speech. How? I don't know." Her face was still pointed towards the sky as she spoke with a pain in her voice.

"And who is Mancio?"

"He leads the local rebels and is the person I talked about this morning."

"The one you wanted us to meet."

"Yes, but I fear that things might get complicated if Rob met him alone." Now Clarissa started to rub her hands against her face as her head throbbed.

"Why is that? If he is a rebel like us, he should love Rob and any offer for help." Sam and Morgan had approached the kitchen and were standing behind Dani now. Clarissa finally lowered her hands and head to look at the women.

"It's complicated because Mancio is overprotective of his region and superstitious. Depending on his 'visions,' Rob and he are planning to overthrow John, or Mancio is having Rob thrown off a bridge. There usually isn't much in-between." Hearing this, the two younger women started to head towards the door, but Clarissa called out to them. "It would be pointless to go now. Whatever happened with Mancio has already settled. If you go now, you just put yourselves at risk."

Morgan turned to Clarissa first, "Then what are we supposed to do about it?"

"You wait until tomorrow. I work with two siblings that live in the Sewer District. They will know what happened to him if he was there. Once we have an answer, you can act, and if he chased someone else, we can go to Mancio for help."

"Why wait?" Dani asked.

"Because the District is off limits at this time of night. Only people who want to stay in the district are allowed in. That said, Mancio gives kill-on-sight commands for anyone unknown entering the district with weapons, especially at night." Dani looked at Sam and Morgan, who did not care about the danger. If Dani gave the order, all three would go after him. She turned back to Clarissa, who had eyes that pleaded for them not to go. Deep down, she knew Rob would risk everything for his friends, but then she remembered this was a mission. Pan had strict rules never to jeopardize the mission for a single soldier.

"Sam, Morgan, stand down. We will wait until Clarissa provides us with intel tomorrow. Until then, grab some food and get some rest."

"But…" Sam began.

"No, buts! If we rush in recklessly, we won't do Rob any good; instead, we might hurt more people. Now, go to bed." Dani had only raised her voice slightly, but it was to the surprise of the others. Sam stood her ground, but now Morgan was grabbing at her arm. She yanked on Sam and dragged her upstairs for the night. Both of them had tears in their eyes. Clarissa put her hand on Dani's shoulders and stood beside her.

"That couldn't have been easy, but you did the right thing."

"I hope so. That idiot better not die on me."

Chapter 11
The Komodos

*R*ob *found himself walking around an open field. The grass gently swayed in the wind as the cool breeze flowed through. As he looked in front of him, the bluffs of Despartian stood over the landscape, and the sun just barely peaked over. The sun warmed his cold skin as his body felt at ease while he walked. His eyes lowered to the field, and standing a few yards in front of him was Iris in a pair of blue jeans and a white blouse. A wildflower sat in her flowing blonde hair as they slowly approached one another.*

"Iris," Rob whispered as they embraced. He held her tight and with all his might. They stood in silent embrace with only the chirp of the robins around them filling the air.

"I missed you too, Rob." After letting him hold on for a few moments, she let go and grabbed him by the hand. Their fingers interlocked as they started to walk through the field.

"Am I dead?"

"No, they just knocked you out. But it has been a while since you rested well," Iris assured him. She leaned her body against his as they continued to walk.

"It has been a few nights."

"It has been weeks, Rob." Her hand gripped his tighter as she said it.

"It has, but whenever I close my eyes, I see him or you lying there, just out of reach and bleeding out." He stopped in his tracks as he tried to keep himself from crying. When she felt his hand pull, she turned to him and snuggled her head against his chest."

"You need to find peace again, or he will destroy you," she whispered with her head still tight to his body. He squeezed her again with his other arm and allowed Iris to lead him to a small park bench under a tall maple tree. The squirrels and birds jumped around in the branches that seemed to stretch farther and farther every time he looked.

"I have tried, but I just haven't found it since losing you. Not in the same way."

"It will never be the same, Rob. There is only one me, and if you spend your whole life looking for what I was, you will never find peace. You have to find something else to make the loss hurt less. Like your companions." Iris's arm hung over the side of the bench, and her legs were tucked under her as his gazed was filled by her beauty.

"They are great, but they can be frustrating."

"And I wasn't?"

"Oh, you were the worst, but those were the things I loved about you deep down."

"Sooo, what's different?"

"I don't know."

"I think you are stuck in your past, Rob. You may not always remember it, but you were the same way with me at first."

"Was I?"

"You were horrible. I could get you to tell me all these things one day, and then you would just shut down the next, and I could never understand it. That was until we talked about your past, and I think it's your past in the way again."

"John..."

"Why would you say that?"

"Because I have let him control me. You told me to let go and move on. Instead, I let him bring me down to New Orleans." She just sat as he thought about what he was saying.

"And I guess I really haven't come to terms with why. At first, it was anger, but I think a part of me was afraid to lose him too. Outside of my parents, no one was in my life as consistently as he was. Yes, you and I were lovers, but John and I were somehow closer. Then, he tried to destroy everything in my life. How do you reconcile two opposing realities like that."

"Granted, killing your fiancé is unnatural, but the rest is. Whether you like it or not, John became part of your identity, and losing that has caused you a lot of distress. It has made you question who you are, and when you think you are only half a man, how can you give yourself to others."

"Is there a way to fix it?"

"Yes, and you know how."

"Are you sure?"

"Definitely. You can be a stubborn idiot, but you are not dumb. So, what do you have to do?"

It took Rob a few moments of silence to think through the answer. When it finally came, his voice was low and soft. "I have to accept that he was a part of my past, but he doesn't have to be my future."

"I knew I was going to marry a smart one. Leave the past where it belongs and stop carrying it with you," Iris concluded as she placed her hand against his cheek. He kissed it softly as his eyes closed.

***

Rob woke up on a stiff medical bed surrounded by about twenty others in various states. The beds were thin as could be with porcelain white sheets. A majority of his bunkmates laid on their sides, puking excess liquor into buckets, while some had elevated limbs in casks. There was one unfortunate fellow who had nothing but a bandaged nub for a right arm.

A single nursing assistant was in charge of changing out the buckets and caring for all the people in the room. They were rushing around the room, exhausted. Rob's eyes followed them for a few minutes as he waited to get up. They ran out of the room with several buckets, and Rob took the opportunity to escape.

He gingerly rose from the bed. Each movement aggravated the bandage wrapped around his ribs and stitches on the back of his head. The dressing on his head was still drying from whatever amount of blood he had lost. Mancio's men had hit him harder than he thought, but at least they had dropped him off at the hospital. He assessed his situation once he was standing upright. He was still fully clothed, but his staff was missing.

He crept out of the room, looking for anything to help him. There was a severe lack of people in the hallways, that shocked Rob. Outside of the nurse who had run off to change the buckets, the halls appeared silent. He strolled to his left first and, as he passed a window, realized that the sun was rising and that most of the city was likely still asleep. Some of the birds chirped outside, but that was all the life he had heard.

While walking around, he saw a men's room that he entered to assess his damages better. He stood before the mirror and looked at the bandage around his head. He unwrapped them and felt his head looking for the stitches. There was no blood leaking out, so he left the bandage off and was glad when the wound was smaller than he thought. After taking a sip of water, he headed back down the corridor until he reached a sign on the wall that gave directions to the different areas. He followed an arrow labeled storage room, but just as he reached the next three-way, he heard voices coming from the left direction. He hugged the wall and waited. The voices grew closer until they reached the intersection and continued straight. Once the voices were gone, he headed back down the hall.

Just before the hall became a larger opening, he stopped to listen and watch. There were a series of doors in front of him, but a guard in front of a single room. Intrigued Rob ran through a few plans before at last approaching the guard. The guard immediately pulled out a knife and pointed it at Rob.

"Stop! Why are you here?" Rob did not answer. The guard raised the knife, and Rob still said nothing. The man lunged at Rob, who avoided the blow and drove his knee into the guard's stomach. From there, he patted the guard down until he found the key. Once the door was unlocked, he pulled the unconscious guard into the room.

It was a dark, damp closet filled with boxes and weapons. He used some rope in the room to tie up the guard and then searched for his staff. After a few minutes of quiet searching, he found it in a barrel with several clubs. His elbow flared and knocked over a box as he pulled it out. The box hit the floor hard, and a plethora of papers flew out. As he cleaned up the mess, he looked to see what they were.

They were all handwritten notes that started with one of the following lines: "I was invited to be a Komodo; John and Kenneth have bestowed a great honor on me; I love you, and when this works, you will be taken care of for life." Then, they would tell tales about how they were recruited and how this would benefit their families significantly. They were personal and heart-filled, not something that should be stowed away in a back closet.

Each note started to paint a picture of the lie John had been spewing. Hoping they would be helpful, he stuffed a few of them into his pockets and returned the box to where it belonged. Before exiting, he heard voices crossing through the storage room.

"You didn't tell us you were coming, Sir Kenneth," a woman's voice quivered.

"You should always be expecting me," Ken responded.

"Of course, sir. But what brings you here today?"

"I have come to expect the newest batch of komodos. John believes a battle is upon us, and I want them to be perfect," Ken answered. His footsteps grew louder as they passed by the room. Once the footsteps faded, Rob slid the door open just enough to see the massive Executive marching away. A trail of guards followed, but Ken towered over all of them. Rob knew now would be the perfect time to escape. Still, it was his only opportunity to uncover more about the mysterious komodos, so he had to investigate.

Rob snaked his way down the hallway, staying far enough away so that they could not see him but close enough that he could hear what they were saying when he focused. Unfortunately, they did not give him anything overly useful. Most of the conversation was quivering, accompanied by scientific babble that meant nothing to Rob. They talked about different ingredients and how they were nearly perfecting the drug. At first, Rob was unsure which serum they spoke of, but then they said Leopard Skin.

The idea of them perfecting the super soldier version of the drug terrified Rob. He had enough run-ins with people on the drug to know that no good would come from it. That is why he was happy to destroy the factory in St. Louis. Yet, it was not enough to stop John.

Rob still remembered the first time he ran into the super soldiers during the War.

***

It was early in the second half of the War, and his team went to investigate another drug that was making its rounds in Southeast Asia. A typhoon had ravaged the area days before their arrival, and heavy rain still fell in droves. They used this rain to mask their arrival in the territory.

Once the team landed, Gene divided them into groups to follow the rumors. Rob, Dave, and Jackson tracked a rumor to an abandoned village where stories of a man with the power of an elephant had driven away the population. When they arrived, the town was desolate. The huts were collapsing, the animals slaughtered, and a constant primal scream echoed through the ghostly roads.

The three men moved together with their weapons drawn. Covering one another's blind spots, they crept down the streets. They stepped through the muddy roads as they followed the scream's source. Searching the village, they found soldiers ripped in half and dead villagers lined up with bullet wounds on the edge of the village. By the smell, they had rotted since before the rain had washed many of them down a hill. When they reached the edge of the town, the scream stopped.

A boulder crashed through the nearby hut and scattered the men. Before they could react, the source had grabbed Rob and tossed him through another hut. Rob had to pop his shoulder back into place before he could return to his squad mates, who were giving the beast trouble. Once all three were able to unite again, they put the monster down. Later, they would discover that this was one of the original versions of Leopard Skin that caused the user to grow rapidly and triple their strength at the cost of their humanity.

***

Since he was thrown through that wall, Rob had come across other users of Leopard Skin. Still, none had resulted in the strength gains of the original without the cost of the mind. The idea of a perfected form was a nightmare he didn't want to believe. After several minutes of pacing down the cold hallways, Ken entered a room heavily guarded on the outside.

Knowing there was no way forward, he sat and thought. He let his mind concentrate on creating a plan when he heard a slight humming from the hallway beside him. He approached the sound, not believing his ears at first. Then he found a rattling air duct, just large enough for him.

Rob looked for a platform to boost himself up to the vent. When he found nothing, he opened one of the nearby rooms and searched for a chair. Another pair of footsteps approached as he grabbed the chair. A stray guard had wandered down the hallways. Rob glued himself to the wall again.

As his mind quieted, he could distinguish the man's breathing and the sound of the vent, which allowed him to track how far away the man was. The guard's breathing was uneven and labored.

The guard began to open the door to Rob's room. As the man did this, Rob jumped into action and kicked the door back into the man's face. Rob heard the door break the guard's nose. As the guard stumbled to the ground, stunned and confused with blood gushing, Rob threw him into a chokehold. The guard struggled, but Rob was in complete control.

"Be silent. I do not intend to kill you, but I need your uniform," Rob whispered as the man fell unconscious. Rob dragged the guard into the room and tied him down with his belt. Then, he stole the uniform and stuffed a sock in the man's mouth. For a moment, he wondered if the uniform would be enough to get past the door but decided to stick to the original plan.

Rob placed a chair under the vent and used his staff to prop the vent cover off. He then contorted to push the chair away with his staff and grab the vent cover. Though the chair was still left as evidence, he hoped he had moved it far enough that most people would not pay it any mind.

He crawled through the tight ventilation system, zig-zagging more than he would have liked. This left him questioning his direction, but his internal compass claimed he was on the right path. After several minutes had passed, he began to hear the sniveling scientist Ken was speaking with. He peered through the nearest grate and gazed at his targets far away. Guards were all over the room, but nearly all were looking at Ken and the head scientist. Using this moment of distraction, Rob popped the vent off silently and slunk to the floor. Once he landed, he was quick to reset the cover.

He patroled the floor to keep up his guard disguise. He slowly edged himself closer and closer to a pit in the center of the room with every step. Ken and the group of scientists around him stared deep into the hole.

"How many accepted yesterday's treatment?" Ken asked as he leaned over the pit.

"Twenty were administered the treatment, and so far, fifteen have shown no complications with the eye mechanism," the scientist reported.

"Excellent and quite unexpected. John will be happy to hear that. Now, how long before we hit our battle-ready target?" Ken asked as he turned with a grin that terrified Rob. Rob walked closer to the pit and could almost see inside of it.

"Based on the results from yesterday. We should be good by the end of the week." Rob barely heard the answer as he had to restrain himself from letting out a gasp. Inside the pit was a nightmare.

Sprawled across the floor were nearly a hundred soldiers. All had taken a Leopard Skin treatment and had some form of mechanical alteration similar to what Rick had done to the Despartian board members. Their muscles were rippling from the drug while mechanical eyes, feet, and hands gave John control of them. Rob had seen enough of these mind-controlled eyes on ordinary humans and how far they could push them past their limits. The mere thought of it attached to a super soldier was beyond what Rob had imagined.

They were perfect monsters. They had the strength to rip a man in half. Yet, someone else completely controlled them and would act without conscience. Then, the eye and mechanical parts mixed with Leopard Skin acted as a pain dampener, allowing these soldiers to push beyond their limits. If a few abominations without Leopard Skin could push Rob to the brink, these men alone could flatten a city. At the same time, a thousand of them could control an entire country.

"I am pleased with the progress, but you will need to move the lab and experiments to Prison Island," Ken ordered.

"But, sir, a move like that with all this equipment will set us back. Why would we do that?" the scientist asked as she backed away from Ken slowly. She knew the consequence of questioning an Executive, and only after she had spoken did she realize how much of a mistake that was.

"John's old friend Rob has been spotted in the city, and your facility is too exposed," Ken clarified with a scowl. His hand slowly moved towards his gigantic blade.

"We are moving for one man? That is absurd and disastrous to our deadline," she argued, grasping her mouth at the last moment. Ken had forgiven her insolence once, but he would not allow her to question him twice. In a single swing, he drew his blade and cleaved her left leg clean off. The scream and the gruesome mess shocked the entire room. Even Rob, who had grown entranced by the pit, was flung back into the present moment.

Before anyone could rush to her side to stop the bleeding, Ken had wrapped his paw around her throat and pressed her against the railing.

"Find a way, or I will find someone who can!" he snarled as he threw her across the room toward the medics coming to her aide. "Now, back to work! War is coming, and John demands that his soldiers be ready!"

Ken's focus broadened, and Rob realized he was in danger. Not every guard would recognize Rob's face, but an Executive would. Ken's eyes circled the room until they finally fell on Rob, who was trying to turn his face to hide it. Ken recognized that something was off, but another guard came running in before he could approach Rob.

"Sir, one of our men has been found unconscious and stripped in an office," the new guard reported.

"We have an intruder! Fan out and find him!" Ken snarled. Ken turned back to where Rob had been standing but found no one there. It only took a moment for the stranger to disappear.

When Ken's attention split, Rob hot-tailed his way to the vent; he did not take time to hide his exit or have a route in mind. His focus was exiting as soon as the coast was clear. He snuck down the halls on the other side of the guarded door, slowly stripping out of the uniform. They were looking for someone in a guard uniform, and street clothes would make a better disguise. However, the alarm was ringing, and guards were flooding the halls. They were stopping everyone not escorted by a doctor, including each other.

The guards had him trapped like a rat. He wanted to fight, but after seeing the beast in the other room, fighting through the circles of Hell would be a more straightforward task. He hid in a corner and was preparing for anything when a hand pulled him into a nearby room. Shocked by the jolt he reached for his staff, but before he could move, the figure spoke.

"What are you doing here?" Clarissa's familiar voice whispered? He turned to look at her and saw her caramel tan skin accentuated against a porcelain robe draped around her body. Her hair was damp and curled from the humidity. Looking around, he realized she had pulled him into the women's locker room.

"Someone brought me here while I was unconscious," he informed her once after registering her question. He could tell that the term unconscious did not ease her anxiety as the alarm continued to ring.

"Well, at least that answers that. Sam and Morgan were worried about you, but why do I feel this alarm is your doing."

"Well, about that...I may not have lain in my bed like a good patient when I woke up." Clarissa's tongue was pressed against her cheek, and he felt her irritation as she refused to speak. "Then I may have knocked out a guard and snuck into Ken's secret lab." Clarissa's eyes rolled back momentarily as she heaved a heavy sigh.

"Why does every man I know have to complicate my life?" she whispered to herself as her eyes looked towards the ceiling, and her fingers rubbed her forehead, "Alright, I cannot change what you did, but we can get you out of here safe. I need your weapons and clothes. We will turn you into a nurse and sneak you out." As she laid out the plan, Rob could hear giggles from around the corner.

"I think someone heard you," Rob commented as he peered around the corner at the bay of women in towels and fresh scrubs.

"Oh, don't worry about them. They are more mine than John's. Now change," she ordered again.

"Any other ideas?"

"Oh, come now. Stripping in the nurses' locker room seems like it would be a fantasy of yours. So, come on, mister tough guy," she mocked in a baby voice. As he removed his garments, he could hear the gasps from the others in the room.

Even Clarissa, who had worked with many patients, was taken aback by the sight of Rob's body. Yes, it was in good condition, but the years of difficulty were hard to look at. The scars, the holes, and the missing flesh were a haunting sight. She could only wonder how he was still up and walking with a body this damaged. Then, underneath the old wounds, she saw the bruising from the night before and the stitches on the back of his head.

As he finished disrobing, he could feel the eyes looking at every inch. "That's okay, just stare and don't get me new clothes," Rob said as he tried to distract himself from his discomfort.

"Sorry," Clarissa stuttered as she snapped back. She ran towards the lockers, searching for anything that might fit him. Meanwhile, the others acted like they hadn't just been staring.

Clarissa produced a semi-suitable disguise that she threw at Rob. The shoulders were a tad tight, and the pants a bit short; he could pass for the first day at the office. He took a moment to look at himself in the mirror.

"At least this time, I'll look like a doctor while impersonating one," he commented as he tried to loosen the shoulder.

"This time?"

"Yeah, there was this time in Beijing, but I'll tell you later. What about my staff and clothes? I have some letters in my pockets that are important."

"If I can get you out, the rest will not be a problem." It took him a moment to give his staff to her. It felt like a betrayal to hand it over after Gene entrusted him with it, but his trust would mean nothing if John caught him now.

"Don't lose it." He sighed as he finally handed it over.

"What now?" he asked.

"Turn around. I let you keep your underwear, but I have to change fully," she instructed as she twirled her finger. He rolled his eyes and followed orders. A part of him wanted to peek, but she threw the towel at his face.

Afterward, she went to check outside the room. With the coast clear Clarissa led him down the hallways as swiftly as possible, trying not to talk much as they hid from guards. Clarissa had earned enough respect from the guards that most dared not stop her. The few that did were satisfied with her quick and straightforward answers.

Unfortunately, it wasn't just guards lurking in the corridors. "Hey, I know we had that spill, but you went to change ages ago. Where are you going?" Maki hollered from down the halls. Clarissa turned to her partner, who was followed by Thomas and Jackie. The assistants were happy to see her while Maki stared at her disgustingly.

"Oh, I'm just escorting a new recruit to the exit. He hasn't gotten his pass yet, and there seems to be a ruckus," Clarissa answered as Rob stood with his back to them.

"I told you no more recruits. I already regret these two," he scolded as if he was the boss.

"He isn't for our department, you uptight prick. He's from pediatrics. They just asked me to show him around when I was passing by earlier. They wanted to ask you but figured your work was too important to interrupt." She smirked.

"Thomas, I want your sister and you to finish the tour. Clarissa and I have work to do," he ordered as Thomas made the hand signs for his sister. As the pair approached, Clarissa signed something else to Jackie.

"You heard what he said, Ben. Follow these two for the rest of the tour," she said as she passed him off to the siblings.

Once the three were gone, Maki had one final snide comment, "I wonder if John will expand experimentation to children. It is the only reason I can see him hiring for pediatrics, plus it would solve two of my issues." Clarissa just bit her tongue as she walked back to her office. She did not want to dignify Maki with a response.

The three could navigate the facility with a fair amount of ease. Most guards were acquainted with the siblings and knew she was deaf. None of them wanted to deal with the hassle of sign language. On top of that, several guards still held bitterness toward the skin color that Thomas and Jackie had. Despite their Americanized names, their home country had been home to enemy soldiers during the War.

Thomas and Jackie could feel the hate for them, but it worked in Rob's favor. They were able to exit the facility without incident.

"Thank you," Rob both said and signed as he recalled the sign language Gene had taught him.

The pair just signed back to him and headed back inside. Guards patrolled the outside circle, and Rob was still out of place. He did his best to blend in as he weaved through the crowd. In an attempt to change his disguise again, Rob tore up his shirt and tied it around his waist. Then, he stole a hat from one of the passed-out drunks. From there, he wobbled through the streets like a stumbling drunk. With the festival going on, none of the guards noticed him as he disappeared. The only problem was that he had no idea how to reach Clarissa's house.

Once he had snuck down the alleyways clear of guards, he stopped stumbling and began climbing. It was not an ideal option, as the fire escape he chose was rustier than he would have liked. One step he took sent his leg through the step. His pants tore, and there was now superficial damage to his lower leg. It was not much, but he still released a small yelp. He continued his climb as he tried to pull wood and metal splinters out of his calf every few steps.

After climbing two flights with a slight limp, he could finally rest on the roof of the building. He leaned against the ledge and evaluated his position in the city.

Once he had his bearing, he started yanking the remaining splinters out. He figured the wall was about nine miles from where he was sitting. This meant that Clarissa's house was around four miles away. It was doable, but not a walk he wanted to make in his current condition. He sat against the roof's ledge and leaned against it with a grimace across his face.

His body started to fade as he lay against the rooftop's edge. The wound in his head was aching, and his sore ribs made it hard for him to breathe. Altogether, the exhaustion pushed him to pass out for some time.

Chapter 12
Afraid and Unsure

While Rob rested on a nearby rooftop, Thomas and Jackie returned to Clarissa. Inside, the hospital was still on high alert as they trekked through the halls. Though no one said it to them directly, Thomas could hear the whispers as guards called them "sewer trash" and other slurs. His blood boiled listening to them, and he hated every moment. Still, their family and Clarissa sacrificed greatly for them to have this opportunity. He kept his tongue silent and headed for Clarissa, pulling his sister along faster to avoid the guards' words.

When they arrived, Clarissa and Maki were bickering about ideas that Clarissa had for healing the komodos who rejected the Leopard Skin. Clarissa smiled at the return of the twins while Maki's eyes rolled. Yet, he was the first to speak.

"I see you two found your way back…unfortunate. Anyways, your Ideas are flawed and will require testing on samples we do not have. I still say we try a second dose to see what happens first."

"A second dose won't work. It will only accelerate the cancer."

"You don't know that, we've never tested it."

"I told you that was what 184RD did, and it's killing him."

"Bah, that was one man and, more importantly, one who had cancer before injections. His sample doesn't count." Clarissa just stared at Maki with her jaw hanging open. She knew how cold Maki was, but this was bad even for him.

"Doesn't count? How can you say that? These are real people, dammit!"

"Your heart is too big for this deadline we are on. We don't have time for all the ethical testing you want to do. Either we start pumping drugs, or we can expect to die before they do."

"You can't be…" As she started her argument, the door to their lab opened. On the other side of it was Ken.

"Maki, come with me," he ordered.

"Yes, sir. May I ask what you need?"

"I am moving the komodos to the Prison Lab and need someone competent to monitor their health."

"That is me. I will be right with you," Maki assured as his legs shook slightly. He hurried after the Executive without another word.

Once the door was closed and the pair were out of earshot, Clarissa signed to Jackie and Thomas, asking them how Rob's exit went.

"It went smoothly. No one suspected anything, but who was that man?"

"That was Rob, a new friend of mine who came to help this city. I hoped he had met Mancio last night and had a good conversation, but now I fear I was wrong. What have you two heard from the district?"

"I did not hear anything. When I returned home, I was too tired to see what was up in the district," Thomas told her as both turned to Jackie, who had bowed her head slightly to think. Then she began to weave a series of signs almost too fast for Clarissa to keep up with, but she caught the crucial parts of the story.

Jackie's hands weaved a tale about a strange man being dragged out of the territory with a staff on his hip and blood coming from the back of his head. Then she watched a meeting with Mancio and some of his other fighters, but one of the leaders, Teche, was missing. She could tell the rest of the group was distressed and angered by the absence. Mancio had spent much of the time pacing around on his prosthetic foot as smoke from his pipe filled the air. Soon after the start of the meeting, a newer man that Thomas had called Ed was brought before Mancio. Ed had gotten down on his hands and knees to bow or beg. She could not tell from where she stood watching. Meanwhile, Mancio stood emotionless as he listened to the words of this man who was stabbed from behind by a tall, muscular man wearing a leather vest and pants. Afraid of what she had seen, she fled and did not tell a soul until now.

"That is terrible news, but it all makes sense now. I bet Ed brought Rob back to the camp, but when Mancio saw his beloved Teche missing and this outsider, he became afraid and overreacted. This is not good for any of us," Clarissa summarized. She started to walk around the room with her right fingers at her chin. She fell into deep thought as the twins wondered what was going on.

"Why is it so bad?" Thomas asked, breaking her concentration for a moment.

"Well, Rob and his friends want to help our city, but I fear Mancio's actions may have ruined diplomacy."

"But there must be something we can do. If this Rob guy can help our city, we have to do something."

"I'm not sure if we can. Mancio likes me because of the medical supplies I sneak out with you two, but if he has already made his mind up, then I don't know." Jackie weaved signs asking about 'The Women.'

"The women? Do you mean The Asters?" Jackie nodded her head once Clarissa made the proper signs. "I mean, the head Mother does know Mancio better than I do, but last time I checked, they were not talking. Besides, that is a harder group for Rob to befriend." Jackie's head hung low after the explanation. Clarissa bent down to look her in the eyes and signed 'thank you.'

"So, what can we do?" Thomas asked again.

"For now, see if Mancio will meet with me to discuss Rob, and if not, ask him why Rob was treated that way. Hopefully, that will help us out."

"Is that it?"

Clarissa put her hands on each twin's shoulder. "I know you want to help and do more, but you must be patient. Your time will come, and I'll need you to be ready when it does." She smiled before turning back to her work. Mancio would have to wait. She needed a solution for the sick komodos that did not involve a quickened death sentence.

Rob woke again around midday as the sun's heat beat down on him. Sweat was soaking through his clothes, sticking him to the rooftop. After peeling away from the roof, he stood up with a few breaths and a deep stretch. Wishing he could stay down longer but had to return to the others. They needed to be prepared for the komodos, so he carefully crawled down the streets and headed toward Clarissa's home.

He started the long hike back as he continued to look for other alternatives. Men and women gambled in the streets as the children played various games. Rob kicked a ball back to some children who had let their soccer ball get past and said hello to the others he passed. He even helped a drunk man to a couch in the street and watched him pass out, hugging his bottle. As he watched guards patrol, people would head inside their homes or walk away. The few that did not found themselves harassed physically and verbally.

There was a brake carriage on one of the main streets. He approached the carriage to talk to the men driving it as people jumped in the back.

"Excuse me, sir. Where is this carriage heading?"

"We are going downtown," the driver answered in a spirited tone.

"Is there one that heads in the direction of the gate?"

The driver looked down at his pocket watch, "Yes, that one should be here in about twenty minutes, sir."

"Is there a cost?" Rob's face had started to brighten when he realized he might not need to walk the rest of the way, but he feared this could stop him.

"Not during Peace Week. We are here to ensure everyone returns home as safely as possible. Anything else?"

"No, that is all I needed to know. Thank you." The driver nodded. His partner tapped him on the shoulder, and they left with their carriage filled. Rob headed to a group of men and women playing dice at a nearby table, where Rob played with them for the next twenty minutes and made some silver. When the carriage arrived, he climbed in and let them take him to a spot about a block from Clarissa's.

At the house, he opened the door slowly, anticipating the girls to be on guard as he had always taught them. Unfortunately, his anticipation was not met as he found both girls napping on the living room couch. He sighed loudly and then threw a pillow at each girl.

"What the Hell!" Morgan screamed first while Sam fell off the couch with an oomph.

"Come on now, girls. Always on guard and always vigilant when we are in enemy territory!" Rob criticized them as they collected themselves. The girls came to their feet, ashamed, as they tried to formulate an apology.

"We're sorry. We were up late worrying about you and just passed out," Morgan said with her gaze resting on the ground. His anger was mitigated when he saw circles had formed under their eyes.

He bit his lip as he thought. "I appreciate the concern." He did his best to breathe and realize that this was partially on him this time. Both of the women looked at him with raised eyebrows.

"Aren't you upset?" Sam asked before Morgan could.

"Oh, I'm furious, but I missed you two more than I'm angry." The women looked at each other, still trying to figure it out, and communicated something to one another without a word.

"Rob, we missed you too. When you didn't come back last night, we were scared," Sam started. "Especially after Clarissa told us what might have happened to you."

"You were scared? For my lousy butt. I appreciate that, but I need to tell you I was also scared in the last few hours."

"Of what?" Morgan asked.

"The monsters that John has been creating. They were unlike anything I have ever seen."

"Clarissa mentioned something about soldiers…were they that bad?" As Morgan asked this question, they could see Rob's body tighten.

"They are, and I don't think you two are ready for them."

"Don't make us sit out, Rob, we can do this," both Sam and Morgan pleaded.

"No, you can't, but there isn't time for you to sit out anymore. Instead, we are going to train like never before. The intensity will be higher, and I will push you both. I will be here with you at every step because I refuse to lose you two, but if you are not ready, you can leave with no shame." Rob's face was emotionless as he gazed into their souls. He wasn't sure what they would say, but he knew they had to be committed. That was the only way they could win.

The two looked at each other and turned back to Rob, "We aren't leaving you."

"Then let's get started. I will grab a new set of clothes while you grab your nunchaku and Sai," he ordered as he walked to his bag and picked out an older pair of clothes.

After he had changed, he met the women outside. He stood opposite them and stared at them with a stern look. His eyes shifted from one to the other every few moments. Sam and Morgan stood tentatively with the weapons in their hands. Morgan had practiced with her Sai a few times in Pan's hideout in Northern Louisiana, and Sam had used her nunchaku twice. However, neither of them was comfortable holding the items. In Memphis, they had pipes, fists, and other scraps as their only weapons.

"I had hoped that you two would never need these weapons, and part of me did not want to teach you because I knew that if I did, it meant you would fight in this battle. I had hoped to spare you because I was afraid to lose you, but now I'm even more afraid of what those monsters would do if I don't teach you. So, let us begin. Morgan, hand me one of your sai first." She walked over and handed him the blade.

"The Sai is a unique weapon you can hold in three different positions, like a normal sword, with two fingers around the blade's body, and reversed for defensive maneuvers. It is a quick weapon best used to disarm opponents, bash them, and stab them, as these have sharpened tips. The pronged guards are perfect for stopping other weapons but never rely on its block. Avoid contacts when you are at a disadvantage." Before handing the blade back to Morgan, he demonstrated the different grip patterns and basic moves. "Your nunchaku, Sam." She handed him her weapon now.

"Sam, yours are a bit different. The first thing is don't whack yourself in the face. Now, I need you to hold towards the top to learn how to spin. Once you master the spin, I want you to bring it over your shoulder and swing down. From there, most of our movements are built from the spins to strikes. Once you master this, I'll move you down on the handle for increased power and range that you can work in either hold." Rob spun the nunchaku around several times and taught her to strike from different positions. Then he handed it back. She hit herself a few times in the back and other body parts but did manage to avoid her face.

After half an hour of practicing and correcting, the ladies started understanding their weapons. They were still far from proficient but could stand comfortably holding them. Once Rob recognized this, he stepped away from them and stood opposite.

"Alright, now it is time for fighting with them. Ready up and come after me," he commanded. He shifted his feet and planted himself in a ready position. Both women knew their training goals. They had to knock him off the lawn. The ladies positioned themselves on each side of him, prepared to move together. He smiled as he watched them position themselves perfectly and corner him. Their bases were stable but quick to react to the first movements. It was a good start but meant nothing if they could not act on it.

As they readied themselves, he darted his eyes back and forth, trying to calculate who would make the first move. They had moved the weapons to their hips, which was another good sign to him. They had used the weapons but were still unfamiliar. He would have been concerned with their choices if they had charged wildly. Morgan inched closer while Sam crouched into her fighting stance.

He had practiced with them enough to know what the plan was. Now, he just had to foil it. Morgan locked horns with Rob first. She was the stronger of the two and usually acted as the distraction. She moved with a grace that Rob lacked, which complimented her ferocity. The first few strikes were all about feeling out their opponents, but Rob was toying with her. He deflected each blow without moving. He was honed into every movement Morgan made but saved his intensity for Sam, who was still lurking. She was patiently waiting for the perfect moment.

Rob made a motion that made it appear that he had lost focus, which was all Sam needed. She scooped dirt off the ground in a quick sweep and threw it towards Rob's eyes. However, he anticipated her movements. It was a single motion to grab Morgan's arm and pull her in front of the dirt. With her temporarily blinded, he kicked her in the rear and sent her tumbling away.

"Good maneuver, but you telegraphed it. Easy to bait," Rob instructed as he shifted to an offensive position.

He lunged at the recovering Morgan, driving his kick through her block and sending her flying again. The ferocity shocked Sam, leaving her open for an attack as well. As soon as his kicking leg landed, he spun around on it to build momentum for his next kick. Sam dodged the kick by a hair, but had it landed. She would have been knocked out cold. She wanted to counter but knew she could not match his intensity without Morgan. She rolled to her friend's aid.

"I was not expecting a kick that hard," Morgan admitted as she licked her busted lip.

"I told you the intensity is up. I have been going easy as you learned to master the basics, but now I need to see that killer instinct."

"We'll be ready," Morgan claimed as Sam helped her back to her feet.

"Will you? I've taught you to defend and fight off thugs without killing, but now I need you to fight monsters. I need to see a drive to send your hand into their chest and crush their beating hearts." Sam's eyes turned to the ground as Rob described the scenario. In contrast, Morgan's gaze just grew more intense.

"Don't worry, put me in a room with Braden, and I will," she snarled as he looked at the hate in her eyes. Regret filled him as he thought about his words carefully.

"That anger is only useful if you can control it. If you become too aggressive, then your enemies will use that. I need a killer who is focused, Morgan. Now, try again and see if you can use those weapons this time," Rob explained as the two women prepared.

Over the next two hours, Rob pushed them hard. Mixing mental and physical training together in a manner that exhausted all three of them. Rob specifically focused on teaching Morgan to be aware of her anger towards Braden. He taught her the lessons Mark taught him while riding down the river. He did not want her to give in to the rage or restrict it but to become aware of it.

During the first hour, when they were fresher, he focused on teaching them techniques for their weapons. Then, they were conditioned through intense fighting bouts during the second half. All three were growing weary but refused to be the first ones to stop. Rob was beginning another onslaught when a hand grabbed his leg while going for a kick.

"Are you nuts?" Dani yelled before releasing his leg. He set it down softly before turning to her.

"They need training," he stated as they all caught their breath. Sam and Morgan were gasping for air as Rob needed a few deep breaths to settle himself.

"Fine, but you are outside. That's reckless."

"Normally, I would agree, but John is not trying to catch me yet. He knows I'm in the city; Trisha knows I'm here. Yet the patrols have been all but nonexistent. He is waiting for something," Rob explained as he justified his moves.

"I understand that. Things have been light, but still, it is reckless," Dani conceded. She knew that John was not a fool, so the lack of guards in their area had to mean there was another plan.

Her eyes turned to the girls panting from the training. Then, when she turned to Rob, something in his glare worried her.

"What happened, Rob?" she asked. He said nothing until he led them back into the house.

Once inside, Rob told them about everything he saw inside the hospital and his interaction with Mancio. As he described the rebel camp, Dani had a slight glimmer of hope for the reinforcement, but this hope was quickly dashed when he told her how he ended up in the hospital. His voice shook as he described the monsters inside the pit, causing an uneasiness in the room. To help them understand his fear, he told them about Despartian and how 80-year-old men were modified with similar electronics without Leopard Skin, and they pushed him to his limits.

"We need to warn the others," Dani said as she approached a nearby window.

"And how will we do that?" Rob asked as she whistled several times. The whistles called a pigeon to the window sill. She proceeded to write down some details and tied the paper to its leg before releasing it with three more whistles.

"So, you have been messaging him."

"Of course, this is part of the job, Rob. Unlike you, I do not have the luxury to act alone." Her words had a venom in them.

"Sam, Morgan, head upstairs for a moment. I want to talk to Dani alone." The pair left without an argument. Rob's body had tightened as he told them to leave, and neither had interest in staying.

"Problem?" Dani asked with a scowl.

"I hope not, but I need some answers."

"What kind of answers?"

"What have you been telling him?"

"Just notes on our progress, what we have seen, and intel that can help Pan's cause."

"Anything about me?"

"Yes, you are a part of the plan, and he needs to know what he is working with."

"You should have told me Dani."

"I didn't think it mattered. I figured you'd understand that I am his second commander and loyal to his cause."

"I understand Dani, but we're friends, and you have told me nothing about him or his plan." Rob's voice rose slightly as he talked, and her eyes rolled at the comment.

"If there was something to tell you, I would, but my duty is bigger than anyone in this house. My intel will determine the fate of hundreds." Rob paced around the room as her words set in. In contrast, Dani stood with her hands on her hips, waiting for him to reply.

"Is there anything you can tell me? Is there a plan? Do we know what he will do if he wins?"

"I'm sure there is a plan, but pigeons only go to their home. The ones I've sent have been following us as I feed them each night. And no, I don't know what he will do because it doesn't matter." Rob was shocked by the nonchalance of her answer. His mouth just hung open as he tried to understand.

"So, we don't know anything. And worse, you don't even know what you are fighting for…you could be fighting to put the next tyrant in charge, and that doesn't bother you?"

Dani bit her lip as she thought about the response. Unable to make eye contact with Rob, she looked outside the window. "He isn't a tyrant. I follow him to stabilize the world, which he will do. Isn't that enough?

"No, because I don't trust him. Throughout my life, I have seen 'good' people promise stability and create disaster. For all I know, when this is over, he will turn on all of us, and now he knows things about me because my friend chose duty over me." Rob didn't allow his voice to rise, knowing that Sam and Morgan would hear, but Dani could see the look in his eyes and the vein in his forehead popping.

"You're right. I should have talked to you about what I was telling him, but it was what was asked of me before I joined the team. He wouldn't allow me to help if I didn't send reports." Once again, Rob looked at her with a lost look.

"So, what now, Dani?"

"I don't know, that is up to you. I can't take back what was written, so you can trust that I am here for you as much as I am for him, or you don't." With his arms crossed, Rob leaned against the kitchen island and gazed at the floor. His mind raced as Dani approached him.

"I understand, and I'm going to trust that you did not tell him anything he doesn't need to know."

"I didn't I…" she started to explain.

"But, when the moment comes to decide who leads this fight, I need your support. I will need you to push for my command of the main battle." She gazed deeply into his eyes, looking for anything hidden behind his words, but all she saw was his vulnerability. She saw his heart on display fully as the conflict raged within him.

"I will support you," she said, putting her hand on his shoulder.

"Thank you."

"Of course, any other questions?" Rob bit his lip for a moment. "Yeeesss."

"Why didn't he recruit me?"

She took a long breath. "That wasn't his fault. He asked about you."

"What do you mean?" His eyebrows had raised, and his mouth hung open slightly.

"He asked me to recruit you, but when I got to Despartian, you were a drunk lying in the street. You were not fit for battle, and Iris was working for John. So I told him that you were unfit and unneeded." As she admitted this, she could see the light in his eyes dimmer. His body slouched as his knees weakened, and he grabbed at his heart.

"You were in Despartian…and didn't tell us you were alive. You didn't tell Iris?" As his words echoed, she closed her eyes, and her jaw tightened.

"I wanted to talk to you, Rob, but I couldn't look at you, and I was afraid you wouldn't recognize me in that state. As for Iris, I couldn't risk John seeing me," she said with choked words that barely escaped her lips. He could not tell if he was mad at himself or Dani. All he knew was that his heart was torn hearing that his drunkenness had driven Dani away and kept him out of Pan's forces.

"I…you…no, I cannot think about it anymore. We've come so far, and I cannot dwell on it," he choked out as he gritted his teeth. Iris and Mark's words whispered to him to let go. He had to redirect to the present again. "Okay. You don't know his plan, so what can you tell me."

She could see the hurt in his eyes and wanted to know more, but she could not ask, so she stayed with his question. "He will bring the other commanders, captains, and hopefully a few hundred to a thousand revolutionaries."

"That may be enough, but we need help inside the walls, and we must drop the gate for it to matter."

"The gates are heavily guarded, but I think we can sneak some of the commanders in like we did and then strike from the inside." Rob nodded his head as he ran the scenarios through his mind. He assumed that the other commanders would be near Dani's level. Still, it wasn't enough, no matter how many times he ran the numbers. He needed to convince Mancio or some other force in the city.

"Thank you. That gives me a lot to think about."

"You're welcome. Now, what is your next move?"

"Well, tomorrow, I want to train the girls while you do more surveillance. We are better off if you can find a weak spot that isn't the gate. Then, I need you to train them the day after while I investigate another lead."

"And what is this lead?" she asked.

"Just searching for some flowers."

"What?"

"Don't worry about it. I do not want to get your hopes up if the lead turns into nothing." She tried to investigate his words further, but he stayed silent as he called the girls back downstairs.

"Are you two done fighting?" Sam asked in a soft and frail tone.

"We weren't fighting, but yes," Rob answered as they joined the living room.

"So, what now?" Morgan asked.

"We prepare for war. Training and preparation are key. Are you all ready?" Rob said.

"That's why I'm here," Dani said.

"You aren't going to scare me off that easy." Sam smiled, and Rob messed with her hair until she backed up to fix it.

"Until Braden falls and you all are safe, I can handle anything you got," Morgan answered with fire in her eyes. Rob could still see the anger in her eyes, but there was also a desire to protect that he admired.

"Let's go then."

They spent the rest of the afternoon working on the basics behind the weapons. They stayed inside under Dani's orders and kept training lighter. Both Rob and Dani would take one of the girls through drills. Then, Rob would work on his mental skills.

When working with Sam, Rob sprinkled in some blade training. In case she needed to use something sharper than the nunchaku. Her training focused on turning the weapon into an extension of herself, using her natural shiftiness to create a flow an opponent couldn't handle.

His training with Morgan was focused on control and moving with proper intensity. He pushed buttons to throw her off and would go after her with ferocity. This was done to sharpen her ability to counter her opponent's aggression while channeling her own. His training of her was particularly draining for both of them and required a lot of pauses.

The training day had exhausted the entire group, and all three women had passed out before Clarissa had returned. Rob was barely hanging on when she walked in and only stayed awake because he was determined to talk with her. She handed him his staff, clothing, and the letters. After she changed, she grabbed two glasses of wine and joined Rob outside in the back of her house.

"So, I heard that meeting Mancio didn't go well," Clarissa said as she sipped her glass.

"I've had worse conversations. John put me through a table once." He chuckled, trying not to think about losing the first impression with Mancio. He just swirled his glass, looking at the red blend she gave him.

"I was hoping you two would be allies."

"It may still happen," he said, sipping on his glass while looking at the rising moon. The stars were not easy to see, with the lights from the city glowing, but the moon had a glow that still captured his eye.

"Didn't expect optimism from you based on how Dani described you."

"Hmph, I have my moments but need some right now. I need allies to fight those komodos."

"So, you saw them?"

"I did, but it sounded like they were being moved."

"It is already done. As soon as the alarm was sprung, Ken hurried the move. They are now at Prison Island, but I think he lost a few during the transition."

"What do you mean lost a few?"

"I don't know how much you know about Leopard Skin, but it is dangerous. I treat failed experiments daily now and have seen things go wrong when they are forced to move too soon," she explained while staring at her trembling hands. He saw her shaking but chose not to dive deeper.

"Well, that helps us slightly, but we are still outnumbered, outmatched, and out everything."

"That instills a lot of hope."

"You don't need a lot of hope, just some. We will find a way, Clarissa. Somehow..." His voice trailed off as drums and cheers started in the distance. The third day of celebrations had begun. Thousands of people were dancing, blissfully ignorant of what was forming in the city and what was to come. All while they finished their glasses of wine.

Chapter 13
Broken Hearts

As was typical, the festivities around night three of Peace Week stretched the guards thin. They were working overtime to deal with the heavy drinking, fights, and sex in the streets. However, there was still peace as the opposing sides of the coming battle stayed silent. Mancio had kept his freedom fighters in their territory after the debacle from the speech, Rob's team was catching up on sleep, and John kept his elite forces in for the night. The average citizen would never have known the heavy minds that slept in the city.

The following morning came faster than usual. While guards swept the drunks off the streets, Rob began training the girls again. He did not wake Dani or Clarissa but was rough on the other two.

While Rob began training, John stirred from his bed. Never one to sleep easily, he crawled from his bed before anyone else in the mansion could wake up. After a quick shave and wash, he dismissed his watch guards. Then headed out for his walk.

Every morning, he ensured the city's people saw him strutting through the streets, unafraid and cloaked in power. Early in his rule, a few tried to attack him but quickly learned what true strength looks like. The bodies of the fools who struck at him were left on display, brutalized, and unrecognizable. Each one was left alive, but only enough to tell what had happened to them. Since then, no one has been foolish enough to test his power face-to-face.

He stayed reasonably casual this morning with black sweats and a plain blue t-shirt to blend in. His route was nearly identical every day as he started his stroll on Lake Pontchartrain, where the mansion sat on the banks of the ruins of the old university. Then, he headed west towards the edge of the Sewer District. He would come close enough to taunt Mancio's rebels but still far enough away that they dared not leave their territory's safety. Then he headed southeast towards this small flower stand worked by an old, frail Creole woman.

"The usual today?" she asked John as she had already begun to wrap a series of flowers.

"Of course, Sweets." He smiled as he handed her several coins. "And what is Pops cooking up today?"

"He should be finishing the calas, and the coffee should be ready if you are hungry," she replied as she handed him two bouquets, one of red roses and lilies, the other of white roses, daisies, and white carnations.

"You know I would never survive without Pops' cooking," he added, already on his way into the house. Once inside, John was greeted by every wonderful smell that could be mustered. They stimulated him and woke him from any remaining tiredness. The aromas were accompanied by the brightest smile in New Orleans, which belonged to a tall, dark-skinned gentleman whose flowing hair and emerald eyes were taken straight from a classical painting. When John was within arms reach, the man lifted him with a giant hug.

"Good morning, John," the man's baritone voice echoed while setting John down.

"Good Morning to you too, Pops." Sweets brought everyone coffee as John was the first to sit. Pops added the calas to the table. It was not much, but it was something they could share and enjoy.

It was a peaceful meal filled with jokes, several of the vulgar variety that pleased John and Pops while infuriating Sweets. No one knew about this part of John's routine. Despite being the same daily, he was sure to lose any tails before arriving at the shop and ensured no one knew of their connection to him. This was his treasure and the small piece of normalcy he had while running the city.

"Another delicious meal, Pops!" John proclaimed as he leaned back in his chair to stretch his stomach.

"I appreciate it. So are you off to see Bunny then?" Pops asked while rubbing his own belly.

"Call Violet by her real name," Sweets ordered as she slapped the old man on his belly before John could reply.

"Everyone called her Bunny, so that is what I call her." He steamed over the hit.

"Enough, you two!" John commanded. The pair stopped bickering instantly. John would never hurt them, nor did he lose his temper often when they were around, but they knew not to challenge him when he gave an order. They understood how dangerous he was, particularly in the past few months. "I hate it when you two argue in front of me. It reminds me of my parents."

"I'm sorry, John," Sweets whimpered out.

"No, don't apologize. I'm not mad at you. I have a lot going on and have not spoken to Bunny or Lawrence yet today."

"We understand. And I can empathize knowing how close it is to Lawrence's birthday," Pops said as he mumbled the second part.

"Yes, three days after Peace Week ends. I am well aware of that and will celebrate like never before," he claimed with a slight twitch that worried both Pops and Sweets.

"And what about your health, John? Has there been any change?" Pops asked as he tried to divert the conversation.

"Unfortunately not."

"Well, we are here if you need anything, son," Sweets stated as she put her hands on one of his. He did not react to her comment. He just rose from the chair, grabbed the flowers, and said his goodbyes.

Throughout the rest of the walk, he would shake his guards' hands, greet the shop owners as their days started, and played soccer with a few of the kids in the streets. Wherever he walked, the reactions would be mixed. Some would welcome him openly, while others hid and kept out of sight. John walked a thin line between ruling with fear and love, which was reflected in all of New Orleans's citizens. What worried people the most was the erratic behavior that had increased in the last few months. He would send Kenneth to burn down the house of opposition. The next day, John would be a part of the construction crew, rebuilding the spot for travelers with nowhere else to go. He would play catch with children, and then their parents would disappear.

His walk ended at a small cemetery where only a few mausoleums stood in the patch of grass. The first one belonged to Jeffery Irons, the civil reform leader. A man John shot and unknowingly started the entire civil war. As John passed the grave, he placed his hand on it and bowed. John was not regretful, but this grave weighed heavy on his mind. He continued his stroll until he finally reached two graves at the very back.

He cleared the dried day-old flowers, wiped off the grass clippings and leaves that had blown on, and then placed a bouquet in front of each. The graves read *Violet "Bunny" Nicole Kore* and *Lawrence John Kore.*

"Life is a precious gift. And one taken away from those most deserving," John whispered as a single tear streamed from his right eye. He remembered the last day he saw them and when he heard the news.

***

"Dad, where are you going?" A young boy asked as he ran towards a young John standing in the doorway of his home. The young boy has his father's green eyes and his mother's reddish-brown skin with cool undertones. The boy is around seven years old, stumbling around in pants that are a little too big for him.

"I've got called on an assignment, Lawrence. It is my last one, I promise." John smiled. His eyes were kind and loving as they sparkled like emeralds looking at his son.

"But Daddy, you said we were going to go fishing this weekend."

"I know, buddy, we'll go next weekend."

"But..."

"Your Dad said he'll be back. Besides, you have homework to do," a young woman with chocolate eyes, flowing raven hair, and soft reddish brown skin said as she entered the hallway. Lawrence turned to John, who had bent down to his son's height.

"Listen to your mother. And if you have everything done next weekend, we might even go camping." Lawrence's face lit up when his father mentioned camping. He leaned into his father's arms with a big hug.

"Bye, Daddy."

"Bye, buddy." John kissed his son on the forehead, then rose to look at his wife while his son ran to his room to work on his homework.

"You are supposed to be sitting at a desk. Why are they sending you on this mission?" Bunny asked.

"They needed the best, but don't worry. I have clearances, and the mission should go off without a hitch," he assured her. Her eyes just looked up into his, and he could see their fear.

"I'm afraid, John. Something doesn't feel right."

"Things are going to be fine, I promise. I will be fine and back here to protect you both."

"Don't go."

"I have to."

"No, you don't. Stay with me, please."

"This is my life, Bunny. We've talked about this before. I am a soldier. My life is a battle."

"It doesn't have to be."

"Yes...Yes, it does. Even if I were to stay, I'd probably be fighting those racist idiots who left the note in our mailbox." Bunny rested her head against John's chest, and he wrapped his arms around her. He kissed her, and they said their goodbyes.

He never made it home. After his assassination mission, he was arrested by those who approved it. The people who ordered the killing put him in jail so that he would not reveal they ordered Irons's death. Not long after, he discovered that the men who had left the note in their mailbox raped Bunny and killed both of them. This sent him spiraling, unable to eat, speak, or interact for a week. His body wasted away as Bunny's last words plagued him every day.

***

His mind continued to run through those days over and over again as he sat. The pain intensified, but he never let a second tear fall. His body had grown numb even if his mind still raged. After an hour passed, he rose to his feet, leaned over the graves, and whispered, "I love you, Bunny. I love you, LJ, and soon there will be a reckoning." A few people passed the cemetery as John sat with his thoughts, but no one approached him. They all kept their distance and allowed John to do whatever he was doing.

Once this was done, he returned to the mansion, where Trisha met him at the door in sweatpants and an old t-shirt. "Your messenger hawk returned." He ignored her existence as he walked to his main chamber, where the hawk sat just outside the window.

The bird rushed in as soon as he opened the window pane. It rested itself on top of his hand-carved oak desk. There, it began pecking at a container on top of the desk. John removed the note from the bird's leg while fetching a chilled mouse from the container to feed his pet. He unfurled the letter:

Peter's lost boys multiply by the day. There are 200 times as many as the tale speaks of, and they will dream for five days and four nights more. Then a wet ride will ensue, but be wary they now know how Hook is using the fairy dust,
Your Confidant,
D

John memorized the meaning of the message before burning it. He clasped his hands and rested them behind his head while he sat in his chair. After a few moments of thinking, a smirk appeared along with Trisha, who had changed since meeting her uncle at the door. Instead of her sweats, she wore slacks and a vest.

"So what is the note about?" she asked, sitting across from him.

"Nothing important or groundbreaking. Just some logistical things and confirmation that the end of Peace Week will go uninterrupted," John replied as he placed his feet on the desk.

"You do remember that Rob is here, right?"

"I do, but he has played his part perfectly and will continue to do so."

"He does not seem like the type of man that will just go along with your plan, Uncle."

"Oh, you worry too much, Trisha."

"Then please elaborate for me." As he remained relaxed, her body had begun to tense. Her forehead had scrunched, and her hands tightened.

"Well, he 'saved' you, met with Mancio's forces, and is leading Pan's forces to slaughter," John summarized, giving her no actual details.

"That is not elaborating. That is stating facts, you prick." John just laughed off her comment.

"Fine, fine. I had heard Mancio's forces wanted to attack during the speech, so I threw you in as extra bait to lure them in and entice Rob. Knowing he would stay back to survey the area, I lowered the guards in a few spots. This created an overlap between him and Mancio. Then I let one live to give Rob a possible "ally" while capturing another for intel. Once that happened, I knew Rob would feel secure enough in green lighting Pan's march. This means all three of my enemies will work together and act as a unified front to be crushed in a single strike. Pan thinks he is leading forces to war, but the shepherds are merely bringing the lambs to slaughter," John revealed as he wove through the tale.

"And what is the next step?"

"Well, tomorrow, I will activate the city-wide disarmament array so that any firearm processed by Ascension will be useless. Pan will be unaware and unprepared for arrows and spears to cut through his forces. Meanwhile, I will burn the Sewer District and capture Rob as he defends it."

"Why is he going to defend them? We don't even know if they are allied."

"Why? That is simple: it is Rob. He is born to protect the lost causes. Plus, they are the only force in the city big enough to help him take the wall from the inside."

"And we are *capturing* him?" she asked.

"Unless he gets himself killed, but I'm hoping he doesn't so I can ask him a question."

"A question?"

"Yes, a question, but that is not your concern. I need you to prepare to lead after this battle."

"So, I am still going to get the world. You are going to let me lead the forces across the globe?" John hesitated to answer. Instead, he leaned deeply into his chair and looked at the ceiling above.

"I have ships coming from our Tokyo and Berlin locations with orders to take legions of komodos who survive the battle with Pan. Once they are battle-tested, I will give you the passcodes needed to guide them and the rest of Ascension across the globe. With Pan out of our way, no one will be strong enough to stop our spread."

"And if Rob wins?"

"Then I will give you a world of ashes to rule," he growled as he brought his feet back to the floor. She clenched her hand into a fist. In response, his eyes grew large, and she could feel his demon nature. She wanted to talk back but stormed out of the room instead. Nearly taking Braden out while moving past him.

Braden meandered into the room, making faces at Trisha behind her back, but was terrified when he looked into John's eyes. All pettiness was put to rest as soon as he saw the intensity. Braden even stepped back, but his loudmouth nature overpowered the fear.

"I have yesterday's report," Braden declared as he threw a file on the desk. John just ignored the file as he looked at Braden.

"I do not care how many drunks were arrested, orgies were broken up, or how many women rejected you last night," John hissed as his eyes rolled back. Braden merely laughed at the insult.

"I'm sure you do not care, so I will tell you the big news: we identified the man we captured at the rally as one of Mancio's main sons." Braden grinned as he knew that would catch John's attention. John's contempt for Braden was pushed aside momentarily when he talked about Mancio's son.

"Has he been placed inside Prison Island?" John asked as he rose from his chair.

"He is, and I have already given the guards orders to prepare for your arrival," Braden explained. John patted Braden on the shoulder and went to change.

Once in one of his velvet black suits and blood-red undershirts, he met Braden outside. They jumped into one of his carriages and were on their way. The carriage was close topped and only big enough for four inside. Their driver was an older gentleman who knew New Orleans's streets better than anyone and had the horse moving as fast as he could. The crowds scattered as they saw the ebony horse and the even darker-colored carriage tearing through the streets.

Inside the carriage, Braden attempted to talk to him. John on the other hand, paid little attention to the gibbering nonsense that Braden spewed. Braden's conversation usually involved women or liquor, two topics that John had no interest in. He enjoyed his drink but did not care to discuss it. Only a few women since Bunny's death have caught his eye enough to mention in conversation.

After some time, Braden finally had a question that John would answer. "By the way, Sir, why has Trisha been such a pain this week?"

"Why don't you ask her yourself?" John smirked as he tuned into the conversation.

"Because the only people I fear are you, her, and Ex."

"Smart man, and if you must know, this is the anniversary of when she escaped her monster and came into my care."

"You are not the monster?"

"No, there was one worse than me, and the things he did to her psyche are unrepairable. And I think you remind her of him," John explained with his cold green eyes. When Braden heard John say this, he gulped.

"What do you mean by that?" Braden gripped the seat as he leaned in close to hear the answer.

"I mean her father, my brother, was a rapist who often boasted about his 'underage conquest.' In a way, much like how you speak about 'conquest.' Well, my brother spoke that way until the day that she stabbed him forty-three times." Braden shrunk when he heard those words. John spoke them with no emotion and a callousness that frightened him. As Braden shook, John turned his eyes towards the sky and enjoyed the peace and quiet that came now that Braden was terrified.

Back at the mansion, Trisha knelt on the basement floor. It was a dark, musty space with dull lighting and blood stains splattered across the brick walls and concrete floor. She yawned as a plethora of guards surrounded her. All of them were unconscious and barely breathing with blood dripping from their bodies. One was a komodo monster still trying to move despite all of its tendons being cut and its spine stabbed.

Against the walls, two men were pinned by knives and needles. Next to them, straw dummies hung with weapons piercing their hearts, the middle of their eyes, and several pressure points. It was an efficient display, yet Trisha seemed bored by her handiwork. The only blood on her hands was someone else's.

"Next time, use more komodos! The rest of them are useless to train with!" she yelled at her trainer standing in the doorway.

"Then be faster next time. You were thirty seconds slower this time and missed a dummy on the first attempt," the trainer insisted. His answer drew a twitch from just above Trisha's eye.

"Maybe if you were a better teacher, I would be faster," she responded, not holding any of her contempt back.

"You pompous little princess. I am the best!" he boasted.

"Don't ever call me princess!"

"Oh, did I hurt your feelings? I'm sorry, princess, but I will call you princess if you act like a princess. Get it!" he mocked her with a grin.

"I'm going to need a new trainer," she snarled as she rose from her seat.

"Oh, really. Who is it going to be? Ken won't do it, Ex won't, the idiot in Despartian blew himself up, and you hate your uncle. I'm all that is left," he gloated as if it was from a position of power.

She pulled out one of her small hidden blades and lunged at him so fast he could barely track it. The trainer narrowly avoided the blow but could not draw his blade before she slithered around him. She was ferocious as she went for all of his tendons and muscles, dropping him almost instantly. She knelt beside him as he lay motionless with the knife hovering centimeters from the trainer's eye.

"Say princess again!" she ordered as she held the blade close. He refused to speak. She grabbed a throwing needle and stuck it into the trainer's cornea. Then, she commanded him to repeat it.

"Princ…ugh," he started as she grabbed his tongue. From there, she began to cut it out. He tried to squirm but accomplished nothing. Once she was done, she stood over him and laughed.

"Princess is what my father called me." She chucked the tongue to the side and then finished him with a knife to his throat. Once the man was dead, she screamed with anger. The only thing that had caused her strain the whole day was that scream.

Her body was still twitching when she entered the basement's bathroom to wash up. Inside the bathroom, she started washing her hands, but when she looked in the mirror to find any blood still on her face, she saw his face. Her father's face stared back at her as her heart began to pump rapidly.

Then she heard his voice, "Morning Princess, your friend was cute." His voice echoed in her mind as she slouched to the floor with her knees tight to her chest. She did not blink as her eyes stared at the floor. His voice and laugh echoed in her mind the entire time. She hugged her legs and put her face in her knees to hide from him. Then she screamed like she did after killing her trainer, but the noise became muffled by her legs.

"But I loved her, Dad," she whispered with each syllable, barely leaving her tongue. Minutes passed as she collected her breathe enough to finally stand up. Once her legs were underneath her, she smashed the bathroom mirror. Then, headed upstairs with a staggered walk. Each step was uneasy as her body shifted from side to side. At the top of the steps, a pair of guards stood by the door.

"Grab some others and clean up the mess down there," she ordered. Her voice was uneven and slow, with hesitation in it. There was no command to it, which worried both guards. They had heard the scream and noticed the trainer was missing as well. Both of them shook as they headed to grab others to clean up.

Trisha dragged herself back to her room, stopping at several points to lean against one of the walls or the sofa tables that scattered the path. Her eyes were glazed over as she ignored any guard that passed her. She reached her quarters, the second largest bedroom in the mansion after John's and Inside the room, a guard's uniform and a dress were pilled on a nearby dresser.

She crossed the room towards her bed, a mess of sheets and two bodies underneath them. "I see you two are still sleeping," Trisha pointed out as she sat on her bed. As she did, one of the bodies started to moan, and the other began to mumble under their breath.

"Well, now that you are both awake, you need to leave. You can do it now with your clothes and dignity, or wait until I pull you out and force you to run the streets naked." It took the ladies a minute to register Trisha's threat, but they rolled out and ran to their clothes once they did. Trisha just watched as the two women panicked to put their clothes on. Once they were dressed, Trisha approached them.

"Take this girl home, guard, and if you find any other beauties like this, bring them back tonight. Unless you want to return to that inept husband of yours." Trisha smiled while slapping the ass of the other girl, who was blushing.

"Yes, ma'am," the guard replied as she guided the girl out.

Once both were gone, Trisha paced around her room and tidied it up. She opened her walk-in closet and armory. One wall was dedicated to her outfits, while the others were filled with knives, swords, needles, and weaponry. She hung up the weapons she used during training and grabbed a few others that she could hide in the dress she had for the day. A scarlet darling that had hidden stitching for her blades. Once dressed, she sat on the bed and looked out the window. Her eyes just watched the seagulls flying over the lake as her mind started to find peace from her father again.

As Trisha sat in her room calculating her next moves, the carriage carrying John and Braden rolled into a dock where a boat was parked to take them both to Couba Island, once a wildlife area that became a prison during the War. Now that it was his prison, he had filled the water surrounding it with explosives. The only way that people could reach the island was if they took the path through the Bayou Segnette. An approach lined with snipers and outposts, each man had shoot-to-kill orders unless a flag on the boat was flown at the proper height. Beyond the guards, the bayou is protected by the gators and other wildlife that populate the space.

The trip does not get easier when visitors arrive on the island. Of the 2,000 acres, much of it was still a marshland, but a circle with a diameter of a half mile contains the colossal prison. The walls stand thirty feet high and just outside of the central building. As John and Braden exited their boat, they were greeted by a group of vipers and boas who scanned every ship, even John's. The island is the only place John still has protocols he must follow without question.

Once he passed these guards and entered the gate, he entered the multi-layered prison that extends down to the bottom of the lakes surrounding. Built at the start of the War, the engineers of the time were given everything to construct an innovative prison that descended eighty feet into the ground and grew wider at each level. All without a single leak from the water pressure surrounding it. The prison engineers accomplished what had never been done in the area: a below-ground structure immune to the wicked weather that plagues the south. The engineers who built it created an inescapable hellscape that required every prisoner to climb through the levels above before seeing daylight. There was no human decency or ethical rights for the individuals contained within, and the farther down they were, the more dangerous the inmates became.

The first level was used for reception, torture, and the lowest-level threats. John used this first floor and the screams that echoed from the floors below to scare many prisoners into joining his side. If they refused, they were sent to the proper level where they worked or rotted for the rest of their lives.

Occasionally, a rumor would surface that John himself was once a prisoner within the walls and improved it after his exit. Legend says he inhabited a hidden sixth layer designed to extinguish all hope and erase the inmate from history. After taking over the prison, John added komodos to crucial points and destroyed extra staircases so there was only one route. The stairwell to the next floor is always on the opposite end as the one the person is climbing. They would have to cross the quarter of a mile hallway with guards waiting at every stop if they wanted to escape. The only exception was the guard elevator that went through the guard station of each floor and sat attached to the staircase.

John marched through the reception to the torture chamber that housed Mancio's son Teche, a young man in his late twenties with Chitimacha heritage. Close behind John, Braden followed uneasily. Each time a prisoner yelled, Braden would jump, and John would have to pull him back in line. When they arrived at Teche's cell, the man snarled at John.

"You will not get anything out of me. I am Teche, and my loyalty is everything you pig!" he proclaimed as his shackles shook.

"Now, now save your voice. I want you to listen, not talk." John smiled as he opened a small bag in his coat pocket. He pulled out a vile and several needles. The vial was forced down the struggling man's throat, and John slowly inserted the needles.

Part 2
The Storm

Chapter 14
Northern Troubles

A storm rages through the swamps in the northern part of the state, delaying the Pan and his rebels. In the storm, rebels are working to load their ships with food and equipment as they prepare to sail down the waterways to New Orleans. The insurgents are screaming as they try to hear one another over the wind and thunder that fill the air.

"Keep any extra packing light! We are off to battle and need all the room for food and weapons!" Pan yelled as Dirk helped him carry a chest filled with weapons onto the lead boat.

"You heard him! Keep it light!" Old Lady Gina yelled from the top of the second ship. Her eyes searched the area for problems and saw a group of soldiers dragging a crate up a ramp with a fraying rope. "Khalil, the ropes breaking!" she called to the large, silent man on the shore. Khalil looked at the ramp and ran to the crate. Just before the rope snapped, Khalil applied enough pressure to relax the rope. The other soldiers breathed easily once Khalil was pushing. Once they were at the top, Gina approached Khalil and patted him on the shoulder.

"Good work, Khalil. Now, gather a crew to pull on the last ship. It has run ashore, and we need to move it while the ground is soft," she ordered. He nodded before heading towards the back of the convoy with a group of individuals to see if they could budge the craft. As Khalil went to handle the ship, Dirk and Tank ran to help clear a tree that had fallen in the water.

Pan watched from the top of the main ship as his forces struggled to load and prepare for the journey. Boxes of supplies had to be left as they broke from drops, soldiers suffered minor injuries as the storm caused them to lose grips and footing, and his top commanders were forced to exert large amounts of energy to keep everything on schedule.

He looked to the sky as lighting flashed across it, "Why have you done this to us? Is John your chosen victor?" he whispered to himself. He closed his eyes and prayed for something to change. They had to head out soon to make the deadline he had set for himself, but where there should have been order, there was nothing but chaos and confusion.

While he prayed, Catori approached him from behind, "Sir, the last of the forces from the North have arrived," she reported as her body shook. Pan turned to her and saw that she was covered in mud.

"Good, there should be room on my boat and the last one if they can pull it back into the water." Catori headed to the group to report their positions, but before she could leave, he called her again, "And Catori, get yourself changed. I don't need a cold to undermine one of my best warriors." She had a soft smile as she bowed and left. Pan headed into his cabin, where Brooke stood against a table with a map.

"I told you, you are not coming." He brushed past her to grab a dry shirt. She just turned to him with a scowl.

"Yes, I am. You need all the soldiers you can get. Especially with one of the captains missing."

"That loss will be difficult on us, but you are not a soldier."

"I could be. Khalil has been helping me with blades and firearms." Pan just shook his head as he put it through his new shirt.

"Sir, I feel like…"

"I don't care." Brooke was taken aback by the statement. She stood with her mouth hung open slightly, and her eyes appeared to be looking for another response.

"But Pan."

"Brooke, I need you here for when we are victorious. If you fight, you could die, and if we lose, I will have no one left to lead us; if we win and you die, then I will not have anyone to help me transition this world to a unified peace," he said as he approached her.

"I…I guess I understand, but you will have Dirk or Dani in that case," she begged putting her hand on his chest softly.

"Once this battle ends, I don't want soldiers to lead us. I need reasonable people like you. I want them to retire or move into other roles that aren't policy related." Pan grabbed her hand and kissed it softly.

As he held her hand, she shuddered at the thought of not being by his side. "I understand but come back to me," she said after a few moments of thought.

"Go summon the commanders, then start prepping for the transition. I want a strategy in place right after the battle. One where we create the Holy Utopia that we dream of," he ordered letting go of her after another kiss of her finger. Once she was gone, he turned to the map on the table. He started to outline the wall and several other locations Dani had detailed for him, including the drainage tunnel exit, the house the group had first found, and the estimated position of John's estate. Pan stood with a blank piece of paper and tried to devise a strategy but would erase every attempt he made. Until his commanders and Khalil arrived. Each of them was dripping wet and doing their best not to pant, but Pan could see the tiredness in their eyes and bodies.

"Is the last boat usable?" Khalil nodded his head. "Good, now I want you all to come here. This is a map of New Orleans with some landmarks Dani gave me, including a safehouse that a few of us can stay in. She will check it every night to see if we have arrived." The commanders looked at the map, and their jaws clenched as they noticed where John's mansion sat.

"Sir, do we have the manpower for this? I mean, that's the whole city we have to cross," Dirk pointed out.

"We have what we have. Hopefully, there are allies within the city, but this is the fight. He will run everything if we cannot stop him here, before his 'komodos' are fully operational. With his known and unknown strongholds across the globe, a few hundred of those things could take everything in months," Pan explained as he rubbed his chin.

"He is right. If those things are as strong as Dani described, no one can stand against him. I have talked to an old friend from before the War who is working across Europe, and they say there are small towns across the continent begging for Ascension to open shop. If they are reinforced with these komodos, they will destroy the little opposition over there," Catori explained with a long look in her eyes.

"Any other concerns?" Pan asked as he scanned the commanders for any dissension. No one showed any signs, "Good, so all of you will be in separate ships to monitor the soldiers. This morning, I saw a non-native hawk that I fear was a messenger from a traitor to John."

"Are we sure it is just one?" Dirk asked. The question left the room silent as they all thought about the implications. They could hear the rain hitting the boat hard, and the lightning flashed in the windows.

"No, that is why I am telling you all. Each of you has shown the greatest devotion to the cause, and I need you to remain vigilant. Understood?"

"Yes, sir." They all agreed in unison except for Khalil, who bowed his head.

"Good. I will give you more orders when we arrive. You are dismissed." The group left one by one, and Pan stood alone in his chambers. The ships were finally loaded, and now that the commanders were gone, each ship had its leader. Dirk stood at the ship's helms, providing instructions and guiding his boat. Catori and Tank each helped the crew as another steered. Both of them dived into the work as the rain pelted them. Gina sat near the helm and offered advice as needed but couldn't tolerate any more work on her body.

Khalil took a detour back to the boat, stopping in his room to grab a bloodied knife. The knife had a name engraved on it. He slid the knife onto his belt and hid it under his coat before heading to the last ship, where he joined the other division captains. On the boat, he wrote a note that was handed to the other captains. Then, he slipped to his quarters. All the while, Pan looked out his window as the ships' soldiers began to lift anchor and sail out.

Chapter 15
The Asters

Rob started his day out early on the morning of the fifth day of celebrations. After a day of training with Sam and Morgan, he hoped to sneak out without disrupting the others, but Dani and Clarissa came down the stairs before he could leave. Initially, they had been whispering, but both stopped to look at Rob, who was nearly at the door.

"Where are you off to?" Dani asked as they reached the bottom of the stairs. Her arms were crossed, and there was a slight scowl of disappointment. He rolled his eyes before motioning for them to join him outside.

Once outside, he showed them the tattoo he received when fighting alongside Gina in Illinois. "Have either of you heard of the Asters?" Dani looked at him with raised eyebrows as Clarissa's face glowed with a smile.

"You know, I heard that when you were a drunk, you were a man-whore, but I did not expect this kind of commitment. What was your going rate? She joked with a clear understanding of the primary business of the Asters.

"Depended on how cute they were, so it would be more than you can afford." She just glared at him as he chuckled at his joke.

"One day, you'll be funny. Now, what is your plan exactly?"

"Well, I'm hoping they'll talk more than Mancio did and assist us."

"That is a lot of faith in people who sell their bodies and secrets for a living," Dani replied as Clarissa waited to chime in. Her eyes going back and forth to each speaker.

"It is, but it is our last chance unless Clarissa has a better idea." They both turned to her.

"No, I don't," she started, shaking her head. "And I wasn't even going to suggest the Asters. They are generally unkind to non-clients and have been quite difficult."

"So, you know them?" Dani asked.

"I do. The Mother down here is very cautious, and her three main guards are brutal, with the leader being particularly skilled."

"How skilled?" Rob asked.

"Well, let's put it this way. John's orders state that guards in this city can engage anyone except for three people. The first is me because of the value I bring him, the second is Mancio's 1st son and the main fighter for him, and the third is the captain of the Asters guards. Both require a squad of vipers, a komodo, or an Executive. If none of those are present, the guards are to flee on sight."

"Hmmm," Rob started as Dani turned back to him. His eyes were looking up as he sat in deep thought. She raised her finger at him.

"Don't 'hmmm' do you realize what that means if you piss them off."

"Of course I do, but that's why I'm going. I am the people person between us." Dani rolled her eyes and brought her left hand to her face to rub it.

"You're going to get yourself killed."

"I'll be fine. Now, do you know where the Asters are located?"

"Umm, if I remember right, they are just east of downtown. If you ask around, some wife will tell you where she dragged her husband out, or a boy will tell you where he became a 'man' the first time. But I wouldn't go to their main entrance. A lot of off-duty guards are patrons," she explained but paused before revealing anything more. She could see that Dani was just shaking her head.

"You said the main entrance. Is there another way in?"

"Yeah, I mean, I think so. There are rumors of an underground entrance, but I don't know where. They've never invited me in, and I only met them when I talked with Mancio."

"Well, that at least gives me a heading. I appreciate it, Clarissa, and if you can talk to Mancio again, please give it your best."

"You're welcome, and I will."

"Thank you. Now, could you give Dani and me a minute to chat?" he asked, looking at Dani, who stood with crossed arms.

"Sure." Clarissa returned to the house to prepare breakfast for herself and the group staying.

"Do you not approve of the idea?"

"No, I do, but I'm worried."

"Worried? Why?" he asked with raised eyebrows and shoulders.

"Because I thought I lost you the other day, and the girls thought they lost you too. And now you're running off into another hornet's nest with a group that may not accept the tattoo on your shoulder.

"Very valid points, but we have to do something."

"Then let me go."

"You know I can't."

"Why not? Are you just superior or something?"

"Of course not, Dani."

"Then why are you excluding me again? Is it because of the messages I sent Pan?"

"No, it isn't that, but if something happens, you will be the one that connects with Pan. You are the one that Mancio hasn't met yet and might favor, and I have the tattoo. This actually makes strategic sense."

Dani thought on this for a moment as she stuffed her tongue to her cheek to think, "So, you aren't trying to protect us this time."

"No, I realized I can't keep you out of the fight anymore. Now I have to do what makes sense."

"And you're sure that more factions is the right move?"

"No, I barely trust the intentions of what we have, but numbers don't lie. John has enough support here and globally to rule everything by spring if we don't give everything," he pleaded, knowing his current plan was a million to one and that what lay ahead was impossible.

"Alright, but I have two conditions." She held up two fingers as she spoke.

"What do you have in mind?" he asked as he crept closer.

"First, you do not make any deals without me present. Second, don't sleep with any of them, you bimbo." She laughed as she pushed his chest and him away.

"I accept your terms, but what is behind that second condition...jealousy?" he pondered with a wide grin. She blushed ever so slightly and then hit him on the arm.

"No, you just make bad calls when thinking with your second head. Now get out of here so I can train the girls," she ordered, pushing him down the street.

Until now, Peace Week had enjoyed perfect fall weather for outdoor celebrations, but a storm from the northwest had brought in dark clouds and light rain. The light rain was not enough to scare away all the partygoers. However, as it grew heavier, more people headed inside the local bars. Some even headed home to use the day for rest so that they could prepare for the last two days.

With the crowds slimming out, Rob had to be extra cautious. While he did not believe John wanted to capture him, it would only take one guard to change that. He made his way east using several back alleys to avoid guard patrols. Once there, he started to talk to a couple of the locals. They were not as open as Clarissa made it seem, but a few were able to narrow down the location for him.

By late morning, he finally arrived at an old wooden building that had been redone. Standing a few yards away, there were some off-duty guards and others entering the building while others left with a grin on their faces. He figured this was likely the place, and it had every marker of being a brothel, especially as he picked up the scent of perfume being washed away by the rain.

Once he had the location picked out, he wandered around, looking for where the secret entrance could be. He paced around the building and the nearby alleyways, but nothing stuck out. He returned to the main entrance to watch for anything that could help him. After studying the area in front of the building for an hour, he noticed a pattern. About every ten minutes, a young woman would walk out of an alley, bump into an off-duty guard, and then make her way to an alley a block over. After ten more minutes, a new woman would arrive, bump her way through the new group, and repeat.

During the most recent attempt, he watched the woman closely. Not only did she bump her way through the crowd, but he saw her divert her walk to head towards specific individuals. After noticing this, Rob counted in his head and waited for the next opportunity. He approached the crowd as the time drew close, and without fail, one of the first women he saw approached from the nearest alley. He watched her closely as she bumped into the crowd. She was skilled in making contact at the perfect time to pick their pockets without them noticing. Rob stood in the crowd for a minute before following her.

When she reached the alley, he paused before turning down it himself. He looked for her once he entered the alley, but she was already gone. She could not have exited the other side without going into a dead sprint. He searched the alley for any entrances, but none of the buildings opened to it directly. The windows were too high to climb into, and no sewer entrance existed.

"Where did she go?" he asked as he paced up and down the alley, knowing that he only had a brief time before the next runner would be through and catch him, but there was nothing extra in the alley. As he stood there, he realized something was missing. There should have been an opening to the sewers like every other alley Clarissa had taken him through. He looked closer at the building edges and noticed that most trash cans were filled to the brim with food waste and liquor containers, but two appeared empty. He approached the cans and pushed his foot against them. They did not budge an inch. Both of them were attached to the ground. Then he noticed the Aster flower etched into one of the lids. He opened it and found a ladder down into the sewers.

"Clever," he started to descend cautiously. At the bottom of the ladder, he stood in an extensive underground network. He wondered if it was a sewer or some other tunnel system from the city's history. He closed his eyes briefly and breathed slowly, allowing his mind to focus and attention to jump from one sound to the next. As sounds echoed, he tried to label them and find what did not belong.

The water flowing past him was the first sound, and he followed it as it merged with other streams to create a large open flow. Then, the rats could be heard with the pitter-patter of their paws on the concrete. Their squeaks grew loud as they approached Rob and drifted away as they scurried past him. He continued to follow the near and distant sounds until there was something he could not identify. It was a faint sound that did not belong in the putrid sewers, and it gave him a heading.

He pursued the echo, hoping it would lead him to whatever he sought. At every intersection, he would stop to listen again. Each time, it grew louder and more precise. The source was still a mystery to him, but there was a series of clicking and clacking sounds.

Finally, he was close enough to hear laughter and voices echoing with the repetitive clacking. Once he was near enough, he finally recognized the sound. It was not one he had heard in a decade, not since his mother showed him the device when he was young. The sound was a series of typewriters working in unison.

Arriving just short of the sound, he peered around a corner where fifty women worked on typewriters, ten ran papers, five organized notes, and one roamed around just observing. As he watched, he saw a few other women come in and out of the room with their own messages. They would drop a note at one of five desks and then leave up a stairwell. On the main desk was a collection of wallets and other pickpocketed items. The room was twenty feet high, and all their desks sat on an elevated platform, keeping them out of the water. As he continued to search the room, a woman descended the stairwell and whispered to the main foreman, who whistled three times.

At the sound of the whistle, two burly men came clunking down the stairs along with three athletically built women. The men were covered in leather armor, while the women wore various outfits. The one in the middle wore a leather breastplate with broad shoulders, while the other two wore regular clothing.

The three women scattered down the other connecting tunnels while the men charged at Rob's position. He had to hope the tattoo would help him now. He stepped out of his hiding spot with his arms raised, ready to declare his intentions, when the first man started swinging. His swings were faster than Rob expected but were still too slow to connect.

Rob could tell after a few swings that the man had trained as a boxer and responded accordingly. It was a style that Rob could counter easily as he flowed from side to side and drew him in for blows. The second man came and grabbed a hold of him like a wrestler. It's not a style of fighting Rob enjoyed, especially when dealing with a brawler. He resorted to straight street fighting as soon as he could. He focused on kicks to keep the wrestler away, then would draw himself in close to strike the boxer's ribs.

At last, when they were tired, Rob connected with a hook to the boxer's chin, and a kick to the wrestler's knee knocked the fight out of both of them. He felt victorious until a set of legs were on his shoulders and crossed around his neck. Whoever had him spun their body and slammed him down. The leg toss sent him rolling, but he used the momentum to help himself back to his feet. Once readjusted, he saw the three women from before. On his left was the smallest of the three. She wore a blue and pink outfit that hid the darkness of her deep natural tan. In the center was the one who wore the leather blood-soaked armor. She had fairer skin tones and long black hair that went with her armor. The last woman had skin the color of the night and a gray robe concealing most of her outside of the brown eyes.

"You bested the idiots, but now you are outmatched," the center one explained with her dagger eyes.

"I don't want to fight at all," Rob argued.

"Funny way of showing it," she responded as she turned her eyes toward the men on the ground. As she looked at the downed men, the one to Rob's left giggled.

"You know he is kind of cute, Liesh," the giggling one stated as she looked towards the center woman.

"He is also kind of stupid," the one in the gray spoke at last. Rob was unsure if he should interject, but Aliesha spoke again.

"Kya, Tia, that is enough. It is time to put him down and bring him to Mother!" she commanded.

Rob knew talking would be meaningless now, but he refused to use his staff. These had to be the main guards Clarissa warned him about. They would not be easy, but he had to balance his fighting to keep himself safe without hurting them. In the gray, Tia threw two knives at him that moved him off his spot right into Kya, who delivered a spin kick that he barely blocked. As she was closest, he engaged Kya first. She reminded him of what Sam could do when she is refined. A snake in the grass that combines martial arts with gymnastics. He thought he had mastered Sam's style, but she took it to a place he could never. Even when he thought he made contact, she brushed it off as she moved with his force. As he started to catch up, Aliesha called her off and joined the battle herself.

Rob recognized her Muay Thai style as she moved through every technique in the book. It was a perfect match for Rob, but he grew sluggish from the other fights. She dropped below his guard, rolled onto her shoulders, and drove both legs into his gut. He hit the wall behind him with a gasp. But before he could hit the ground, a series of knives had pinned his body against the wall.

"Can we kill him, Mother?" Aliesha asked with a slight snarl at the word mother.

"No, Liesha, we will hear Mr. Doran out," the older woman who had initially whistled for them announced, leaving the ladies on the typewriters at last. Aliesha huffed as she returned to a single file line with the smiling Kya and bored Tia.

The woman they called Mother approached and looked him over a few times. Then, she took one of Tia's knives and cut his shirt open. Kya and Tia were shocked by the scars stretched across his body, but Aliesha appeared unimpressed. Mother traced the knife along his body and pulled his shoulder down slightly to see the aster. Once she saw it, she groaned.

"That idiot whore of a younger sister," Mother mumbled.

"I take it you know Mother Althea," he commented from his powerless position.

"I do, unfortunately. She was the one that created the Asters, but I am the one that has made them great." She groaned as she signaled for Tia to collect her knives.

"Why are you releasing him? We do not need him," Aliesha pleaded as she stepped between Rob and Tia.

"You say that, Liesha, but he is your better and someone my sister entrusted with the aster. A symbol we must recognize," Mother explained, pushing Aliesha out of the way. Aliesha fumed when Rob was called her better.

"But I beat him."

"You beat a man who had already fought two others, did not want to fight us, and held back on using his weapon." Aliesha gripped her fist, but Kya grabbed her arm before anything more. Tia started to undo the knives as Kya held onto Aliesha.

"No, *man,* is my better. But have it your way. We'll be in my room," Aliesha snarled as she stormed off. Kya stayed at her hip, and Tia followed the command despite rolling her eyes at the tantrum.

"Don't mind them. Aliesha leads our fighters with incredible skill and pride," she explained with a pause. "Anyways, let's talk about what brought you here."

Now free, he followed the quick-footed Mother to a more appropriate location. It was hard for him to believe this woman was related to Mother Althea. Althea had been kind and flirtatious, while this sister seemed cold and calculated. She led him past the operation, where none of the women would make eye contact with him.

He tried to see what they were typing, but each covered their work as he passed. Whatever it was they were creating, no one took it lightly. He would have asked Mother, but it was evident by the way she moved that she would not slow down before arriving at their destination. She led him up the staircase to an old wooden door leading to a dressing room closet.

The women in this part of the facility were less conservative than the ones in the basement. They hustled through the room with no care about Rob or his eyes. They bared it all, nearly pulling him away from Mother, but he remembered his second promise to Dani. Then, Mother grabbed Rob's ear as well. She pulled him along when his eyes drifted to her girls.

Once past the temptation room, he found himself in a hallway where women led men and other women into private rooms. He was now inside the wooden building he had seen before.

She opened another room and threw him inside. She locked the door behind them before taking her seat. Once seated, they stared at each other, waiting for the other to speak.

"So, what is your actual name?" Rob asked to break the standoff.

"You can call me Mother Kathleen, Mr. Doran." Rob's eyebrow raised. This was the second time she had used his name, and he did not understand how she knew.

"So how do you know…" he began before she raised her hand.

"Don't ask dumb questions. You know how my girls work. I know all about John's favorite plaything and your meeting with Mancio," she explained while pulling out a bottle from a nearby cabinet.

"If you know everything, then you don't need to ask anything," Rob smirked as Kathleen uncorked the bottle. She took a long pull from it.

"The good thing about living in New Orleans is that we can still access the best liquor. Bourbon aged in barrels scorched by the fires of war has plenty of flavor to deal with twerps like you," she commented, wiping her mouth.

"Hahaha. I might need to try some."

"Later," she said as they both paused to stare at one another again,

"Alright, I'll cut to the chase. I was hoping you could help me in the coming fight and smooth things with Mancio if you are connected."

She spit some of her whiskey out with his answer. "You're kidding, right?" she asked once she recovered her composure.

"Unfortunately not. I need his help in taking down John." She looked at him momentarily and could not believe her ears.

"My God, you are serious, but why would I help you die? More importantly, why would I lead my people to their death?"

"Because you know it is worth it. Life is worth taking the risk on, and our only chance is if we do it together."

"Well, you do have the whole young adult hero speech down, don't you," she mocked while taking another drink and rubbing her forehead.

"I need all of you, and you all need me. John has monsters. We need humans with hope and passion."

Kathleen sat for a moment, thinking about what he was saying. She bit her tongue before speaking. "Alright, if I do this, what can you bring?" She did not know why she was considering helping him, but there was something about his eyes.

"Pan of the revolutionary army is heading to our city. He awaits my word and will fight for this city if you do," he explained.

He hoped that invoking Pan's name would give him weight and credibility. Usually, he would be correct, but she did not have the normal reaction to Pan's name. She had her own plans, and the thought of throwing it all away stressed her out.

"Even if you and Mancio team up with Pan, this will end in disaster for all of us."

"It could, but it might not. I can tell you that the end is coming, and if we do not fight, we will die from apathy."

"Ugh, I hoped my sister gave you the tattoo for good sex, but no, you have that *something*."

"Something?"

"Yeah, that *something*. That thing that you can not name, but when you have it, people follow you despite their better judgment." She leaned back in her chair and placed her bottle on a nearby table while rubbing her face. "Fine...I will bring you to him, but I cannot make any promises."

While Rob and Kathleen discussed, the three ladies met in Aliesha's room. Kya stood on her hands, and Tia sharpened one of her knives while Aliesha tapped her finger against her cheek. The other two could see Aliesha's irritation, and they avoided the scowl of her scrunched face.

"She is going to give in to that *man*!" she snarled as her fist tightened again. Kya planted her feet back on the ground before walking over to Aliesha.

"Liesha, you know Mother only does what is best for all of us." Kya smiled, hoping that it would comfort Aliesha a little bit. Instead, Aliesha rolled her eyes and walked away from her touchy, feely friend.

"Don't you start, Kya. If Mother wanted to do what is best, she would let us do something other than sit here," Aliesha pointed out while pacing the room.

"Liesha…"

"Don't bother Kya. You won't win," Tia interrupted without stopping her sharpening.

"Mother knows we could do more important things for this city than guarding the print room. We should be taking our city back, and now she will entrust that to some man she calls my better!" she hissed again with more venom on her tongue.

"At least he is a cute man." Kya blushed, trying to make light of the situation. Aliesha scowled at her friend while Tia broke character and flashed a small smile at the comment.

"He may be *cute*. But he threatens all we stand for. Our Mother is giving another man the power to call the shots when we are capable."

"You don't know that she gave in to anything or even why he is here," Tia argued as her smile faded.

"You're right. I don't know why he is here, but couldn't you feel it, Tia? Something about him will make Mother agree just as Althea did," she conceded as she slammed her fist on her table.

While they discussed, a ringing came from the bed stand. Aliesha answered the intercom and started to say yes to everything said. All despite an enlarging vein across her forehead. She hung up and turned to the ladies.

"Mother wants us to escort her and Rob to Mancio's camp." She smiled with a head twitch.

"Remember, deep breaths, Liesha. It will be okay," Kya advised as she imitated deep breaths for her companion.

"Get out," Aliesha ordered as calmly as she could. Neither woman argued as they left the room. Once they were out, they heard a scream and the sound of a table being broken. They just walked away, knowing that it wasn't worth it.

Unfortunately, today's outburst was a common theme for her and had led to several conflicts with Mother, but no matter what, she always follows Mother's orders. She joined the convoy once she had broken enough furniture and calmed down. Every hair was back in place along with her smug grin as the group led Rob back to Mancio.

The five navigated the back alleys away from the Aster hideout. Kathleen had explained to Rob that there was no direct underground tunnel to the Sewer District and that their quickest option would be by foot. He was hesitant at first to travel in the open, but Kathleen assured him that the boas did not recognize the Asters.

"So, why are we heading to Monkey Brain and his clan of apes?" Aliesha asked once she was back with the group.

"I need his help to put John down for good," Rob replied without much thought.

"We don't need that imbecile. I could take care of him myself," Aliesha boasted.

"Aliesha, I've told you..." Mother began before Rob raised his own hand.

"Considering what you did to me, I think you could give John a run in a fair fight, but trust me, he doesn't play fair. Mancio will help both of us take back your city," Rob complimented. Mother smirked at his response. Even Aliesha was taken aback by the comment.

"I...I appreciate the confidence. I understand why I want to take him down, but what about you?" Aliesha asked as her venom was tempered for now.

"Well, he was my friend, and I failed to save him, so now I need to stop him," Rob answered as his eyes fell.

"Hmph, a bunch of dudes flexing egos." Tia sighed.

"Oh, be nice, Tia. You're being a Debbie Downer again," Kya commented in response to her friend as she returned to walking on her hands.

"I must say you three are an odd group. Who taught you all your moves?" Rob asked.

"Well, I was a gymnast when I was young, then Liesh found me during the War and helped me incorporate martial arts into it," Kya explained with a large grin as she looked toward Aliesha.

"I was trained to aim by my father, and then Liesh taught me how to throw knives when we met up," Tia replied with less excitement than her friend.

"Well, you seem to receive a lot of praise, Aliesha," Rob commented, while Aliesha just smirked as she walked faster.

She had no interest in talking like the others. She may hide her contempt for Mother, but her displeasure with Rob was evident. She enjoyed his early compliment, but it was not enough to overcome her deep-rooted feelings. This was not going to stop Rob. These three reminded him of Sam and Morgan, so he was hoping they could help them.

"Don't feel offended. She talks on her terms." Tia sighed as Kya planted her feet back on the ground.

"No offense taken. Most people don't like sharing at first, but I always ask questions when I meet exceptional people."

"Awh, he thinks we're exceptional Liesh," Kya gushed with a skip to her walk now that she was on her feet. Aliesha just ignored them both.

"Of course I do. Not many people can push me like the three of you did; of those that can they are sitting in a fortress waiting for me. But I also understand her not wanting to talk. We'll deal with Mancio first," Rob suggested as his compliments were not hitting home with Aliesha.

"Mancio will have to wait. We have another obstacle to deal with first," Aliesha stated. The ladies were not sure what Aliesha was talking about, but Rob instantly started to listen closely.

He could hear feet shuffling on the rooftops above them, and as every moment passed, more steps were heard. An ambush was coming, but he could not tell how many there were. Regardless, Aliesha shifted her feet into a ready stance while the other ladies moved to her shoulders, and Rob drew his staff.

A few moments later, a mixture of 25 men and women came crashing down around them. All of their ambushers wore black robes with a viper stitched on the shoulder. This would be Rob's first opportunity to test the strength of the vipers. Every battle was set to be five-on-one, with the Asters and Rob trapped like rats. However, they seemed hesitant to act. That was until ten boas and a flashy-looking guard appeared. The new guard had decorated armor that glowed with gold and silver plating.

"Asters, you are under arrest for treason against the great city of New Orleans!" the chief shouted as he pulled out a blade.

"I thought you said they did not care about you," Rob whispered to Mother Kathleen.

"They have never bothered us before. You would be the only change."

"Not necessarily, we just took that 'thing,'" Aliesha commented as Kathleen bit her lip.

"Feel like we need to discuss 'that thing' once we win," Rob stated as the guards crept closer.

"Stop your whispering and surrender! You four do not leave the fortress often; whoever this guy is shall be my bonus," the chief ordered. Rob was bewildered that this man had no idea who he was. John was playing the game close to the chest by the looks of it.

"I'd advise you to surrender or die slowly," Aliesha hissed back.

"I think you are out of your depth, girly."

"Then you die." Aliesha was the first to strike at one of the vipers, and the rest followed her without hesitation.

Rob flowed from one combatant to the next, creating space with his staff and prevented them from overpowering him. The boas initially went to help fight the Asters but were quickly drawn to Rob. He slid past one of the guards he had downed to put his back against the wall. It was not a position he wanted to be in, but it kept them from attacking him from behind. They attempted to act in unison, but Rob disrupted any plans they would make with a quick strike of his staff.

Mother was a unique fighter; she prided herself in using her legs. Her kicks were like shots from a steel pipe and cracked bones when they connected cleanly. She spun and moved like a woman fifteen years her junior with light movement that divided the forces.

The three younger ladies worked in unison. They were vicious huntresses who complimented each other. Tia worked from a distance, covering Kya and Aliesha as they moved in close. Kya was often a distraction who would flip and dance around as she landed her blows. Aliesha was the terminator cutting guards down. The opponents would lose the blur that was Kya and catch a blow from Aliesha. Unfortunately, all three groups faced the same problem. They could knock a guard down, but another would replace them. Then, by the time the second guard was down, the first was back.

The brawl dragged on for about ten minutes, with the five clearing out everyone but the chief. Reinforcements were on the way, and they needed to escape now, but Aliesha had her eyes set on the chief. She wanted to take her frustrations out on the man who had been taunting them from the sides. The ladies tried to pull Aliesha away, but nothing seemed to work.

"You three run. I'll stay with Liesh," Rob whispered to Kathleen and the other two. Kathleen hesitated to leave Rob with Aliesha but knew there was nothing more she could do.

Aliesha chased down the chief, who was using guards as shields. She knocked each one down while Rob covered her from behind. He wanted to pull her back, but he had seen the look in her eyes before. She had to work through her anger. Granted, she needed a better coping skill but now was not the time for him to be a preacher.

The chief was running scared as Aliesha approached him. He hoped his reinforcements would be enough, but Rob was an immovable force protecting her as she cornered the chief. She pinned him down at last. He tried to defend himself, but his pathetic swings were deflected as she kicked him in the face.

"I told you; you would die slowly," Aliesha hissed as the chief sniveled something inaudible. She continued to beat him. This was not the same fighter that Rob had seen before. She was calculated and focused on damage when they were a group. Now, she was a savage beast. He saw himself and John reflected in her actions. Her movements were reminiscent of an action John took in the War. It was a moment where he saw the demon emerge in John, but he would not let her follow the same path.

He pulled Aliesha off of the chief despite her kicking and screaming. She tried to fight Rob off, but he had learned from their last encounter. He held on tight, not letting her budge from his grasp. As he pulled her out, they both heard the footsteps of more guards.

She was twitching as he held her. Then, when he let her go, she turned and slapped him, "Who do you think you are!". He rubbed his cheek as he thought of the answer.

"I told you I failed to stop John before he became a monster, and I wasn't going to fail again." There was something about his stare that was powerful and commanding. She did not buy his answer, but that look pacified her for the moment.

"Just stay out of my way next time," she ordered as she tried to reclaim some of the power that his stare took from her. They moved quickly to avoid any more guards, with her guiding him to Mancio.

As they ran, he heard something sailing through the air. A whistling that pierced through the air. It was the last sound he wanted to hear, and once he recognized it, he threw himself in front of Aliesha. Two needles pierced his upper back just after he jumped in front of her. She was shocked to see his body hunch over after throwing it in front of her.

"What…What happened?" she asked as he dropped to his knee.

"Ex," was all that he mumbled as he turned to look down the alleyway. The Executioner had exited from the shadows to reveal themself. At first, the black-clad figure stood there as the rainwater dripped off their mask. Then, they threw a pair of knives from their waistband. This time, Rob deflected the blades with his staff, but still, the needles bothered him. They had just missed his spine and rested around each shoulder blade.

"So that's the Executioner," Aliesha said.

"Yeah, and they are not someone we want to mess with right now."

"Come now, Rob. I have seen you fight. We can take them," Aliesha encouraged as he removed the needles from his back. He just watched as Ex crept closer down the alley, thinking about the last two times they met. Both times he had collided with Ex, he had been left a broken man.

The first time in St. Louis, he was dismantled by Ex. Then Rob was left powerless as Ex blew up Memphis and shot two of Rob's old squad mates. Ex had lived up to the name and did not want to cross them now.

"No, this is an Executive, and we have guards bearing down on us," Rob insisted. His body shivered and tightened. Aliesha saw the fear in his eyes that was unlike anything she had seen from him.

"Fine," she sneered, unsure of what was happening. They started to run again, but Ex did not give chase.

They were able to lose their tails after a few minutes and caught up to the other three. Once they were caught up, Aliesha and Rob told their story, with Aliesha downplaying most of the tale.

"And they let you two go?" Kathleen asked.

"They did. John is planning something."

"Then we should hurry," Kathleen suggested.

"Before we do, what exactly did you take from them?" Kathleen had attempted to leave, but Rob would not move until he had some form of answer. Kathleen looked at the ladies, but none of them would help her.

Mother gritted her teeth and clenched her fist. There was no time for his delay nor her resistance, which forced her hand. "A key."

"A key to what?"

"A key for Prison Island."

"For the whole island?"

"Don't worry about it," Kathleen snapped as her eyes darted away from him.

"Well, now I am more worried."

"Don't be. She can't tell you because we don't know," Aliesha jumped in as Kathleen searched for words.

"Shush," Kathleen snapped back as Aliesha rolled her eyes.

"So, you stole a key. A key for an important facility. A key that causes you to risk capture, but you don't even know what it opens," Rob summarized with his jaw hanging open.

"Well, yes, but we had heard it was an important key, so we intercepted it. Regardless of whether or not we can use it, John can't," she defended.

"Well…this conversation is going nowhere, so let's find Mancio, and then we can worry about your key," Rob suggested as he heard the guards in the distance. Kathleen was relieved to hear the change in direction. With everything settled, they headed back out.

Chapter 16
Union

After they had put some distance between them and John's guards, Aliesha grew closer to Rob. It had taken her several steps to do it, but he had felt her drifting closer and closer the whole time until she was right alongside him. Though he noticed her encroachment, he tried to pay it no mind. She would speak when she wanted to, so he was determined not to push it. Kathleen kept her distance from them and watched Aliesha's behavior.

Several more steps passed before Aliesha finally whispered, "Thank you for taking the needles."

Rob chuckled a little as he saw the pain in Aliesha's face. She struggled with the thank you, "Of course. Kathleen trusted me, and I wouldn't let them hurt you now that you are my ally." Aliesha scoffed at the idea of being an 'ally.'

"What makes you think we are allies?"

"For starters, we share a common purpose and are helping each other."

"That makes you and Mother allies, but I only work for her. We don't have the same purpose." Aliesha was sharp and direct with her statement, but Rob could feel something else behind the words.

"Whatever you say, but I will call you an ally, and like all my allies, I will protect you with everything I have." Aliesha tightened her fist and turned her head away from Rob as he spoke. She was hiding from him, but he saw through it.

"Don't make promises you cannot keep," she snarled, still looking away. Before he could respond, she walked back to Kya and Tia. Kathleen joined Rob in her place.

"She's warming up to you," Kathleen stated, just loud enough for him to hear.

"Is that what that was?"

"Yes, it was. It took me two weeks to have a real conversation with her, and the last time I saw her talk to a male about something besides battle was months ago."

"Hmph, so what is the story? You say she is prideful, but this contempt for men. Why?"

Kathleen walked for a few moments as she calculated her following words. "To be honest, I don't know. Something terrible happened, and I don't think she has ever spoken about it."

"Something has happened to all of us."

"You are not wrong, but she has carried it extremely close." As Rob listened, he stared at Aliesha strutting in front of them. There was pride in every step, but something else: there was pain masked by strength and suffering he recognized from that look, that walk, and the defensiveness. He had seen it in her when she punched the guard, the same look John had during the War. Rob knew that the pain inside of John had led to what he was now. A pain John never spoke of, just like her. Some of him wanted to reach out, but he knew he could not force it with her.

"Well, maybe that is why she has opened up to me. Maybe she and I are not that different after all," he mumbled.

"And what do you mean by that?"

"Oh, nothing to discuss now. Just a lot of pain and tragedy."

"Maybe we aren't so different either."

"I agree with you, but I can smell the Sewer District. We must be close."

"Indeed, we should probably keep conversation to a minimum. Wouldn't want to give Mancio any more information than he needs," Mother Kathleen suggested as they crossed from the final alleyway to the open terrain of the Sewer District. Rob recognized the sights from before and the eyes staring at them. He was convinced that if it was not for the Asters, he would have been attacked by now.

They continued to cut through the district until a group of Mancio's men cut them off. Kathleen stepped between Mancio's forces and their group. Neither side said a word. They just stared until the men gave way. The men cleared out of the way for her as she led the group to Mancio's shed. There he sat by a campfire out front with his pipe bellowing smoke to match the fire.

"I will not do business with this man, Mother," Mancio stated as he let a long puff go.

"I merely want to talk to you, Mancio, without the omens," Rob explained as he sat at the fire. Mancio chuckled at the response as he released another puff of smoke toward the sky.

"So, that is why he brought you ladies," Mancio commented as he turned to the Asters.

"It would seem so," Mother Kathleen responded with a flirtatious smile.

"A mistake really, only her sister can entertain me…Or maybe you thought they'd watch your back?" Mancio started as he looked at Aliesha, ready to fight anyone around her. He did not let Rob reply before speaking again. "Regardless of your plan. I will give you a few more moments than last time." Mancio put his elbow against his knee and rested his face on his hand. Mother Kathleen scrunched her face as Mancio talked about her sister.

"I understand why you saw danger and destruction."

"You do? Well, please explain."

"You saw destruction because I will ask you to join me against John."

"And why would I do that?"

"Because in a few days, Pan and his revolutionaries will be at the doorstep of New Orleans, and we need people inside the city to give anyone a shot at taking John down," Rob explained. Though Mother Kathleen did not react, the news shocked the other three. Even Tia, who hid her emotions, took a step back. Meanwhile, Mancio stroked his chin as he took another draw from his pipe.

"When will they arrive?"

"From what intel I have. Just after the end of Peace Week."

"This will be too late. John plans to use the district for his firework display and has one of my boys," Mancio explained as he set his pipe down this time.

"Well, can't you just hide in your holes and enjoy the show?" Aliesha taunted as she turned a rock over in her hand multiple times.

"Eager for a fight, I see," Mancio commented, turning his eyes towards her.

"Not necessarily, but I hate wasting time. This man is offering an army, and you sit here looking the gift horse in the mouth."

Mancio chuckled at her assertions. She was boastful and arrogant, but in a way, he appreciated the directness. The group was a bit surprised that Aliesha was the one speaking for Rob, but he stayed silent throughout their brief encounter. When Mancio noticed Rob sitting and listening, he returned to the initial point of conversation.

"You are quiet there. Nothing like your reputation. I thought you would have shut her up by now since her arrogance could cost you a partnership," Mancio stated while Aliesha rolled her eyes. She waited for Rob's response, figuring it would be dismissive as she had grown accustomed to. Rob, in turn, sat momentarily as he made everyone wait for his words. His eyes turned to Mancio for a moment and then to the Asters. As he paused, the only sound to be heard was the crackling of the fire.

"Well, are you going to say anything, or have you finally learned that I am not the ally for you," Mancio grunted as he grew impatient.

"I want to ally with you, Mancio, but I do consider the opinions of the Asters after I saw them fight today. If Aliesha sees you as a waste of my time, then maybe you are. I hope she is wrong, though," Rob replied at last. He was steady and firm in his speech. Aliesha bit her lip, unsure how to respond to Rob's confidence in her.

Mancio smiled. "And what happens when we stand together?"

"We might accomplish our goal."

"And that goal is…"

"To remove John and Ascension from power with minimum bloodshed," Rob commanded with a voice that took control of the group. Even those who were mere onlookers now understood who was in charge of the meeting and its importance. Sensing the power in his words and the command Rob was taking with him, Mancio paused to take another puff of smoke.

"That is the goal, but the omens said you are not meant to kill John," Mancio pointed out.

Rob could feel Mancio peering into his soul with this question. The old man believed in his omens, but Rob could see that he hoped they were wrong this time. The fate of the city hung on the answer to that simple question. Could Rob kill John? At the start of his journey, he wanted revenge, but his heart had softened during it. John's letters reminded him of their brotherhood, and their fate was intertwined. The whole journey made him unsure whether he could kill John, but he knew he could stop him.

"I will stop him and protect the world from his tyranny," Rob replied, knowing it was noncommittal. Mancio understood this as well but could see in Rob's eyes that it was the only truthful response he could give.

"I understand…the conflict rages in your heart, but I do see the fire to stop John is there. However, I fear that conflict will bring destruction my way," Mancio replied after a moment of soul-searching.

"Destruction is coming either way," Rob replied without hesitation.

Mancio paused again as he looked at the camp surrounding them. He saw the children clinging to their parents and the fear in everyone's eyes. They were all his responsibility, and he had to act in their best interest, but there was no clear path. He had read the omens surrounding Rob but had seen the others as well. Death was coming, but when was the only unknown.

"What monsters did you see?"

"I saw a pit full of giants. Men enhanced by Leopard Skin and machinery. Each monster could rip a man in half and fight until it is dead."

"And how does one fight a monster like this?" Mancio asked as the group surrounding them pictured horrors from the brief description.

"You stab the eyes, but they can take on five or more of your soldiers at a time." Rob stared at Mancio as the old man looked at those around him. Omens are easier to see than understand. A foolish man ignores signs, but a dumb man will pretend to understand them fully.

"Then we will be outmatched and outnumbered if we fight alone."

"Without a doubt."

"I will make a deal with you," Mancio finally replied as a collective breath was taken.

"And what are the terms?" Rob asked.

"I will give you command of my forces when Pan's army arrives if you swear you and your allies to my command during the festival's final days. I need to protect my home until Pan arrives," Mancio bargained.

"I swear myself, but I command no one. The friends I travel with make their own decisions, and the Asters are their own force. I can ask, but promise nothing but myself," Rob informed Mancio as he thought about Dani's conditions.

"Well, then ask them. They are right there," Mancio suggested. Rob turned to Mother Kathleen and bowed to the Asters.

"You owe me nothing, but I beg for your assistance." Rob knelt down and placed his forehead against the ground.

"Groveling is a weakness," Aliesha commented as she tried to process the interaction. Kathleen chuckled at the response.

"Oh, Liesha, this is not groveling. This is submitting. He acts weak and places his fate in our hands, hoping we do not betray him. It takes more strength to trust than to fight," Kathleen explained as she rose from her seat, followed by the others. Rob did not move as he awaited the answer.

Mancio's men watched as the ladies began to make their exit. Rob could not comprehend their apparent denial as he did not understand the history that preceded him. He thought that he had failed until Aliesha stopped in her tracks. This shocked Mancio, Tia, and Kya, while Kathleen grinned at the sudden change.

"Mother, this is the chance I have been waiting for. I cannot leave with you," Aliesha stated as she turned back to the campfire.

"Really? I thought you despised Mancio's forces," Kathleen commented as she kept her back to the fire.

"Yeah, but this fool is different. I have seen his actions enough to know that there is something about him."

"Very well, then we shall join Mancio," Kathleen explained as the other three returned to the fire.

Mancio said nothing as he watched the ladies sit. He could not believe his eyes. He had planned to throw Rob out again, but now he was an ally with the Asters. Instead of throwing the man out, he was now trying to maintain composure with another puff of smoke.

"Thank you, Aliesha, Mother. And I will bring the ladies I travel with here so they can decide," Rob explained as he rose from his knees.

"Then I will await your return," Mancio said as a tall man leaned against Mancio's shack. Rob could not see the man's face, but the Asters grabbed Rob to escort him back.

Whoever this new man was, the Asters wanted no part of him, so they led Rob back to their facility. This was the most leisurely trip Rob had made across the city. No one jumped him, and he made the trip without any additional damage. However, it was growing dark, and he needed to return to the girls. Though he was not sure what he was going to say to them.

Before he reached them, he did have one final question for the Asters, "So why did you, out of everyone, come back?" Rob asked as he turned towards Aliesha.

"Like I said back there, this is my best chance to fight, and you have proven somewhat competent," Aliesha replied.

"Oh, I'm blushing." He smirked, "But thank you for agreeing to help. I owe you one."

"You already saved my life once."

"True, then I guess I'll owe you for a different favor I have to ask," Rob claimed while he rubbed the back of his head and smiled.

"What?" she asked as her eyes rolled. All this time, he had impressed her. He had shown her he might be different, but now he had what he wanted, so he would disappoint her. She was positive about this. She knew that this was the moment she had been waiting for.

"I was wondering if you three could help train my friends. I thought I could do it alone, but after seeing you all, I know I am not enough," he admitted.

Aliesha was taken aback by the confession. She was so confident in her assessment of the moment that she became flustered when he showed humbleness again. Kya giggled as she recognized how the usually collected Aliesha was completely off balance.

"I'll help," Kya spouted to break the silence left by Aliesha's shock.

"I'm intrigued, too." Tia grinned as they both turned to Aliesha.

"I...I...I guess I have to help. If I leave you with these two, your friends will only learn bad habits." Aliesha scoffed while collecting herself. Despite the insult, Kya clapped repeatedly as she roped everyone in for a group hug. Aliesha squirmed out of it quickly.

"Thank you, all of you. I will see everyone in the Sewer District tomorrow morning," Rob said as Kya let go of the hug. Aliesha rolled her eyes one last time as the group separated. The Asters returned to their hideout while Rob went to Clarissa's house.

Chapter 17
Fallout

The Asters arrived at their facility, and Aliesha separated herself from the group. She went straight to her room and locked the door before screaming into her pillow. Then, she pulled a small trunk out from underneath her bed. Inside was a collection of photographs and other papers that she flipped through until she found an old Polaroid of two men holding a young Aliesha. Her face had a giant smile despite missing her two front teeth.

"Dads, I think things are finally changing." She began to tear up as she held the photo. The man on her left was a tall, balding man who was slightly overweight and had rosy cheeks. The man on her right was extremely skinny and had a shaved head. The photo was held close to her chest as she shook. The other pictures in the box were of various men and women. Each image had a line through the face or a word written on the top, usually traitor, bastard, or cheat.

She sat in her room thinking about her fathers and the people who had hurt her over the years. Something about Rob and the kindness he had shown her created a conflict she did not know how to resolve. Earlier in the day, she knew everything she needed to, and she had no doubts, but he made her question this. Her doubts swirled as a sudden knock came at the door. She quickly wiped the tears and threw the photo in the trunk. Then, kicked it under the bed and headed to the door. When she opened it, Tia was standing there. She walked in and leaned against a dresser.

"What do you want, Tia?"

"I just wanted to check in on you."

"I'm fine; if you knew me, you would already know that," Aliesha asserted as she walked back to her bed.

"I knew that is what you would say, but I hoped you would be honest this time. My mistake." Tia shrugged as she walked back to the door.

Aliesha's head hung low as she searched for the right words. "I will be fine…is that better?" she said just as Tia was about to leave the room.

"It is for you," Tia smirked, turning back. "He is definitely different from Dan, Brad, Jose, and those others we met before Kya." Aliesha rolled her eyes this time as she started to laugh.

"Oh, I forgot about Dan. God, was he talented at disappointing someone no matter how low the expectation."

"Yeah, I'm still positive he puts his underwear on wrong daily."

"And still thought he could boss us around despite those marshmallow arms." They both laughed, thinking back to the man they once knew.

"But I told you that someone would come along that could be that friend you've always needed," Tia said.

"Oh, so just a friend. I figured you and Kya would try to set me up with him." Aliesha smirked.

"Never. He's too old for you, but I think he can help you find what you lost when your dads died," Tia stated as she sat next to Aliesha.

"I didn't lose anything. I just saw how cruel people could be, so I became what they wanted me to be," Aliesha snarled. She was talking with Tia, but her mind could see several men who had turned on her, used her, betrayed her, or left when she needed them.

"Not everyone is cruel, Liesha, and I hope Rob can show you that."

"My way has worked so far, but I will give him a puncher's chance. So far, he has been competent."

"Competent? He has brought the Asters and Mancio together. I didn't think that would ever happen."

"I didn't either, but they were right. Enrique and the others that fight for Mancio give us the best chance to win."

"Are you worried about us failing?"

"No." Tia just looked at Aliesha with a raised eyebrow.

"How?"

"Easy, if it fails, we are all dead, so why worry? I either avenge my fathers, or I join them." Aliesha's stare looked just over Tia's shoulder. Her mind was in another place at another time. One that Tia was not allowed to be in. Before Tia could speak again, Kya knocked on the door and woke Aliesha from whatever trance she was in.

"Come in," Aliesha called before, looking at Tia with a death stare. The conversation they were having was over. None of it would be spoken in front of Kya. All that came with her arrival was some jokes and tomfoolery. The old gymnast was quick to bring a grin from the other two and kept them from constant depressive conversations.

***

Rob finally arrived at Clarissa's after the long journey across the city. When he walked in, he was greeted with smiles from Sam and Morgan but a scowl from Dani. He could see bruises on the women from a day of intense training. After multiple days of work, they could barely stay up. Dani walked towards Rob and slapped him across the face. "You just had to keep us waiting again, didn't you!"

Rob stood with his face turned from the slap. "I know, but it took longer than expected."

"Did it at least work?" The worry had left her voice. Clarissa had also descended the stairs when she heard the commotion in her living room. She did not know what had happened but did hear Dani's question.

"It did. The Asters will help us fight, and Mancio will if we agree to his terms.

"And those are?" There was relief from most of the room, but Dani was still tense. She worried about what deal Rob had made.

"He will help us when Pan arrives if we help him defend the Sewer District on the festival's last day. I told him I could only promise my support and would consult you all for the rest."

Dani stood thinking for a moment. Now that he had told her he did not make a deal without him, Rob could see some relief on her face, but she was still unsure what to say. Instead, Clarissa spoke first, "I will help as I can, but they all know I am limited until it is time for me to leave the hospital for good."

"I thank you for this and all you have already done. This is far more than you bargained for when you brought us here."

179

"I'd say, but I thought you were just saving my life back then. Now I know you are trying to save my city, and for that, there is no paying you back."

"What do the rest of you say?" he asked.

"What's the point of training if we're unwilling to fight?" Sam smiled as she walked over to Rob.

"And I cannot let you two do this alone. Sam would drive you nuts without me," Morgan announced as she joined Sam next to Rob. All four turned to Dani.

"There is no other option, is there?" Dani finally asked.

"If there was, we would have found it by now."

"Then I might as well."

"Good, now can I speak to you alone outside Dani?" he asked as he opened the door behind him. She nodded and followed him outside. He explained the situation with the Asters and their willingness to help train the ladies, followed by the story behind the key and Ex.

"This is all a trap," she said as soon as he was done. He nodded in agreement.

"That was my thought. I started to understand as soon as Mancio told me about an attack coming his way. John is letting me operate because he knows I'll gather all his enemies together for one decisive defeat."

"Then, why are we still doing it?"

"Because we don't have another option. If Mancio does not help us, Pan will be cut down before entering the city. And the komodos will run wild if Pan doesn't come. Meanwhile, the Asters' sewer hideout will be a perfect base if the District is destroyed." Dani was shaking her head as he talked.

"I know you are right, but you know how risky this is."

"I do. Will Pan go for it?"

"Normally, no, but by the time he finds out he'll be here. Then, I will do what I need to."

"Alright, then, we prepare for the worst."

She sighed before speaking, "You just couldn't make things easy."

"Have I ever?"

"For Iris, maybe, me, never."

"Hahaha, well, you could always put up with the bullshit. Iris was too sweet for me to make her life hard."

"I appreciate your faith in me."

"Hey, look at the bright side. I won't leave you alone again. From now on, we're in the thick of it together."

"If that is the bright side, I don't want to hear the bad news." She chuckled.

***

Back in the Sewer District, Mancio dealt with concerned citizens who asked him what they should do with the sick, elderly, and children. He did his best to calm down the worries that had arisen after Rob's visit, but it was not until his top sons and daughter arrived that the area could be cleared. Sitting by the fire again, he talked with his generals.

"I cannot believe you agreed to help him after your omen, father!" A string bean of a man yelled. His voice was lined with agitation and quickly paced. The man was descended from Haitian heritage and had a scar that disfigured his chin. As he sat on Mancio's left, his foot constantly twitched.

"And you have no say, Hennrick. Father knows what is best and has a plan," the only daughter, Ava, the calmest of the siblings, responded. She was a robust and punitive woman with dark skin and Canadian heritage. Her tone was soft, and a flow to each of her words.

Hennrick turned to her, unappreciative of her response. The tension between them was evident and would have broken out into a quarrel if Mancio and the oldest brother were not seated there. The eldest just watched and waited for the moment to speak.

"She is right. I do have a plan that will be aided by Rob," Mancio assured as the fire crackled.

"Well, tell us, Father!" Hennrick ordered, irritated. Mancio ignored the order and continued his train of thought.

"You will know when you need to. For now, focus on freeing your younger brother," Mancio instructed.

"But…" Hennrick began before being interrupted.

"Enough, Brother," the eldest spoke at last. His tone was even, and his words soft, but his cold green eyes were enough to paralyze Hennrick.

The eldest son, Enrique, stood as the tallest member of the family, towering over them as his open leather jacket fluttered in the breeze. Under the jacket was a sculpted core and arms that could punch through walls. His legs were just as powerful as they nearly tore through the seams. Across his whole body, only one or two scars were on his front, while none were on his back. Enrique was the protector of the district and enforcer of Mancio's will.

Enrique rose from his seat and sauntered over to his brother. Who in turn shrunk at the approach of his brother. The area adored Enrique's bravery but feared his brutality.

"No, need to make him wet himself. Your brother knows his role," Mancio stated while Enrique grinned.

"I hope he does. That prison is impenetrable, and our brother is in danger. If John or the Shadow Six get their hands on him, we could be down a soldier," Enrique snarled when speaking about his enemies.

"I understand, brother. I have already started to formulate a way around the sea mines."

"Good. We need him back." Enrique walked back to the other side of Mancio.

"That is good to hear. Now, Ava, I want you to take a group to clear out buried tunnels. We need a path for the defenseless citizens."

"Yes, father. I will take a crew tonight."

"And Enrique, I want you to secure our borders. The battle is coming fast." Enrique nodded. "Good, Ava and Hennrick, leave Enrique and I."

Ava started to leave, but Hennrick had a final comment, "But don't you want to hear my plan? And shouldn't we talk about our defense?"

Mancio took a long drag from his pipe. "There is no plan for our defense until Rob returns. As for your plan, give me results, not words, for once."

"Yes, Father." Hennrick bowed as Ava pulled at his arm. Hennrick's eyes were twitching as his whole body grew tight. His sister did her best to pull him away before he said anything else.

Once they were gone, Mancio and Enrique entered Mancio's shed. The old man sat back down and took off his prosthetic leg as the other sat across from him.

"What did you find? Mancio asked as he massaged the rest of his bad leg.

"Nothing?"

"Nothing, how can that be?"

"He apparently was in that squad with John. The one that had all the information redacted."

"So, he did not lie about training with John. And to be in a squad that was that secretive speaks to his skills. What do you think of him?"

"I think he speaks with a pure heart and a toughness that few have."

"What makes you say that?"

"You had our people beat him the other day, and not only does he stroll in here with humility, but without fear or weakness. Most men that took the shots he did would have been in bed still."

Mancio sat staring at his son for a moment. "I agree. Do these komodos worry you?"

"I am cautious of them. I know that after I took down twenty of John's forces, I was declared a run-on sight threat unless an Executive or a komodo was present."

"I had forgotten that because we did not know what the komodos were like. Just that they served with Ken, that is troubling." Mancio stroked his chin as he thought. His eyes closed as he searched his thoughts and feelings about the situation. He had made the agreement so fast, seeing no alternative, but he still had doubts.

"It was a good deal, Father," Enrique said as he read through the worried look on Mancio's face.

"Indeed, but I fear that it won't be enough."

"It won't be."

Mancio was surprised by Enrique's words and taken aback more so by the calm body language he said the words with. "This is our home. How can you say that?"

"I understand the numbers. Even with Aliesha, myself, and Rob, we cannot stand against John's full forces. But if we hold off long enough, reinforcements will come. That is a chance we never thought we'd have."

"This is true, and maybe that was the omen I read. I have to sacrifice this home so that the city can survive." Enrique said nothing as Mancio sat and thought again. He had so much pride in the Sewer District and had seen it rise to stability; no part of him could imagine it burning, but he loved the city more. He realized that Enrique was correct in the assessment. No matter how hard his forces fought, John had too many soldiers to throw at the District. "So, our defense is a strategic loss. One that makes them believe we are finished. That will require sacrifices."

"It will, and I have some ideas of who it could be."

Chapter 18
A Why

Day six of the celebrations began with a mist that hung over the city. The drunks paid the damp mist little mind as they stumbled home or back to the celebrations, but rain two days in a row created an uneasy feeling in Rob's gut. He was celebrating several wins with the unification of the two sides and the knowledge that he had found better teachers for Sam and Morgan. Yet, the idea of it being a trap still hung heavy on his mind. Even if most of them survived the first battle, he understood that the losses could be severe.

That morning, Rob and the three women said their goodbyes to Clarissa. There would be no more need for her house now that Mancio was housing them, but they ensured she understood how much they appreciated the warm housing while it lasted. Once their goodbyes were completed, the group headed to the Sewer District. The group was uncharacteristically quiet during the walk to the District. The other three could feel the tension emitting from Rob, which put them all on edge. He tried to talk to them about their training with Dani, but the conversation was short. They merely informed him that her style was more enjoyable. This bothered him slightly, but he let the comments go the best he could.

When they finally arrived at the District, Sam commented about the smell, but instead of smiling at her jokes, Rob gently placed his hand on her shoulder before squeezing it. It was just enough for him to send a message. They continued their walk until they reached Mancio's campfire. Sitting outside the shed were Aliesha and the other Asters.

"So, who are we training?" Aliesha asked while playing with her nails. She seemed to stare through Morgan and Sam, Dani being the only one to catch her eye.

"What is she talking about? And who are they?" Morgan asked as she and Sam both looked at him.

"These three are the Asters' best fighters and people that could teach you a thing or two?"

"I'm in, but I've got to ask Rob. How do beauties like them and us keep ending up connected to your ugly mug?" Sam snickered. The comment made Kya chuckle, but the rest of the group rolled their eyes.

"Because I was cursed by a witch once," he replied as he turned his attention back to Aliesha's question. "So, I hope Sam and Kya will work well together. While Morgan would benefit from your teachings," he explained as he pushed them both towards their soon-to-be mentors. Kya clapped and went to hug the equally giddy Sam.

Meanwhile, Morgan and Aliesha just looked each other up and down. Both of them smirked at what they saw. Rob sighed when he saw the reactions. He wasn't sure if he was worried more about how training would go for the apparent goofballs or the two who looked like they'd beat each other up.

"Good, so I can go home," Tia stated as she returned to the facility with a long yawn.

"Actually, Rob was telling me about your long-distance specialty, and I was hoping you could help me prepare for Ex," Dani announced. He had only briefly mentioned this part of the plan when the girls slept, and Dani did not mention her intentions. Though he was happy to see her opening up to the Asters.

"Fine," Tia agreed as she returned to the group.

"Well, since you all have a partner, I'm going to discuss the plan with Mancio," Rob announced despite no one actually listening to him.

"So, where shall we train?" Dani asked once Rob had ducked into the shed.

"Here is fine. None of John's guards enter the territory, and this courtyard by his shed is the most open area," Aliesha replied.

"If you think this is wise."

"It will do. Let us begin, but be warned, we will not go easy on you," Aliesha proclaimed as she went straight for a leg sweep that Morgan barely dodged. Morgan was sent off-balance, and the training had begun. Aliesha was not messing around or going easy.

Neither were the other two, who started equally as ferociously, but unlike Aliesha, they talked their partners through the training. Aliesha just went into attack mode. She wanted to see what her pupil was capable of with no training. Then, she began to correct mistakes once she had pieced out the errors. However, the battle only grew more intense as she offered advice. There was no excuse for mistakes once addressed, and she pounded the points home.

Kya and Sam, on the other hand, looked like they were dancing in their fight. Their strikes were small but precise and allowed for user flexibility. They were like two flags intertwined in the wind. Kya was far superior, but Sam learned quickly with her help.

Tia was just as merciless as Aliesha, but she needed to be. Dani was the superior fighter; only her restraint kept the fight going long enough for her to learn. Tia threw everything at Dani, who was learning to better predict and see the tools. She could knock knives out of the air with her whip and avoid the smallest objects. She knocked one blade from the air at one point just to send it back to deflect two more.

After a while, Aliesha yelled to the group, "Alright, everyone switches!" When she said this, she released her locked horns with Morgan and moved to Sam. Kya shifted to Dani and Tia to Morgan.

"This wasn't the plan," Dani announced as she tried to land a blow on the slippery Kya.

"It was my plan. We only learn to fight if we can adapt to new fighters," Aliesha explained while struggling to hit Sam. She could land a few blows, but Kya had taught her to move with force and absorb strong hits. Meanwhile, Morgan could test her new moves on Tia, who was not ready for the melee that Morgan pushed for. This drew some side eyes from Tia, who was unaware of Aliesha's plan.

The second round lasted a few minutes when Aliesha called for another switch. Once again, the girls adapted to their new opponents, but the fight between Dani and Aliesha was the most intriguing. They collided like two gladiators fighting for survival, and their souls were fully displayed. Even though it was merely a sparring practice, people from across the district gathered to watch them fight. The other ladies stopped their practice rounds to observe the masters at work.

The fight continued to drag on longer than planned, but they both enjoyed it. There was fire behind the bout and stress. Had it not been for Rob catching Dani's arm and Enrique wrapping up Aliesha, the fight would have continued. Neither woman was happy with the interruption and pulled away instantly.

"Enough, what are you two doing?" Rob asked as he let go of Dani's arm.

"Training."

"Yes, the two best fighters giving high efforts while the young ones who need combat experience are left watching." Rob was dumbstruck by the display he saw.

"It was fine. They were learning from watching, and I was in control."

"I saw those last few punches. You weren't going to be for long."

"Hmph." She scoffed as Aliesha approached them.

"Come now, we were just practicing. It is clear neither of us have had someone like the other to practice with," she argued, moving her hair back into place.

"I understand that I do. Hell, I would have done the same thing back in my day, but we are short on time."

"Don't lecture me on my choices. You asked for my training, and this is how I operate." Rob turned and paced for a few minutes.

"You're right, but we are crunched by time. Mancio believes John will come tomorrow, but I wouldn't be surprised if he moves today."

"He won't. Today is the day of truce," she stated.

"What truce?" Rob asked, confused by the wording.

"The truce of the sixth day. John declares it a day of heartbreak and one where he does not allow for bloodshed. If he attacks, he would lose the city's support," Mancio explained as he approached the scene. Both Rob were even more confused. He had experienced numerous Peace Weeks before this and never had a day of truce.

"That's all good and nice, but what does that mean?" Rob asked.

"During New Orleans' first Peace Week with John, a man struck our leader. We all thought the man would be obliterated on the spot, but John left him alone and later made a statement:

"'On the sixth day, while the papers were being signed, young men and women died fighting for old bags. The young shot at each other, causing useless bloodshed. All a waste, and I will not do the same on that anniversary.'

"And ever since we accepted that today is a day where we honor a truce and do more than celebrate the end of the War," Mancio detailed with an eerily accurate John impersonation.

"Now, that would have been helpful information before now, but regardless, I need you two to focus on training those who do not fight like you," Rob instructed as he and Mancio re-entered the shed. Enrique stood outside for a moment and glared at Aliesha. Once she saw his glance, she flicked her wrist. He shook his head and joined his father.

"I'm sorry. I got a little carried away," Dani said once the men were back inside the tent.

"Don't apologize. It was fun." Aliesha smiled as they bowed to each other out of respect. Kya and Tia were shocked to see how genuine the smile was that Aliesha flashed. It was something they had not seen in a long time.

"With that settled, let's return to our training. But please lighten up on poor Morgan. She puts on a tough face but does appreciate the instruction," Dani said, whispering the second portion to Aliesha.

"Indeed, but may I ask one last question?" Aliesha asked.

"Sure."

"Why do you follow him?" Aliesha whispered as she only wanted Dani's answer.

"I wouldn't say I follow him. I fight alongside him," she corrected, though this was not what Aliesha was looking for.

"Okay, but why?"

"Duty for Pan would be the simple answer, but the real answer is more complicated."

"I've got time."

"Well, let me ask first, why did you agree to help him?" Aliesha was not sure how to respond. Her answer felt foolish, and did not want to say it out loud. "It was that *something*. That aura he walks with that makes you believe in yourself and him," Dani said after Aliesha was silent for a moment.

"Something like that."

"Then you know my answer. I fight with Rob because he has always had that aura for the 10-plus years I have known him. That feeling that makes you believe that things will work out no matter the odds. He is our best bet."

"This feeling makes you believe, but do things work out? Or is it all just a feeling?"

"Most of the time, they do. He is worth any bet you place on him. He will tear his body apart for us and make sure we survive and win," she explained as her own heart ached.

"So, you think we can beat the odds with him?"

"That is why I am out here training with you and not in there making the plan. We will either win with him, or he will die fighting until his last breath. There will be no scenario where he walks away from that battle alive without our victory," she vocalized, knowing Rob was likely going to die on that battlefield.

The thought of losing him was crushing as he was her last connection to her old life. She remembered that awkward man-child she had known, starting her first week of college. He was both the most awkward guy she had met and one of the wisest. On top of that, she thought of his heart of gold, which she had seen more of since joining forces with Sam and Morgan.

That heart is why she was so relieved when he and Iris began dating. Their hearts shined brighter than twin suns. It was magnificent to see, but there was still a reserved part of him. Old emotional scars kept even Iris at bay for most of their relationship, and then the War came. Something happened during those battles that he refused to talk about. Something changed that he hid from everyone, except maybe for John.

While Dani became lost in her thoughts, the others returned to their training. Aliesha had seen Dani fading out of the conversation. She was happy with the answer, though she did ask Morgan more about him as the training continued. As the others started, Tia was delighted to take a break while Dani reminisced.

***

North of where the group trained, Pan's forces were sailing down the river on their way to New Orleans. The storm had finally passed, but still, they were left making slow progress that would take time. Pan sat in his cabin scanning reports from across the country and Dani's notes. His ashtray was full of old cigars and cigarettes from the day, while his newest hung from his mouth. He was calculating every option he had and the truth became clearer and clearer. His odds were slim. Still, there was never going to be a better opportunity. He had people inside the city for the first time. Once the komodos were fully operational, there would be no victory for him.

Everything needed to be perfect, but he still worried about Rob's part. In Dani's notes, she had told him about his hesitation to kill John, which would put everything at risk. Pan's mind raced as he

190

thought through the upcoming battle. Then, a sturdy yet calm knock fell on his door.

"Come in," he ordered now that his train of thought was broken. The door slid open, and a tall blonde with broad shoulders and the kindest smile walked in. She glided across the floor as she made her way to the seat. Rob's friend from Despartian, Anna, now sat opposite of Pan. The renowned field surgeon and doctor who had taken control of the former Ascension headquarters in Despartian when John "died" had made her way to Pan's forces.

"It's Anna, correct?" he muttered as he took in the striking beauty of the famed surgeon before him. He was well aware that her experience and expertise were far beyond her years.

"That is correct, and I want to talk about your plans for the medics during the battle," she explained, leaning towards his desk.

"I enjoy the forwardness, but anything medical-related falls under Doc's domain," he said as he leaned back in his chair with a full stretch.

"Funny, he said you would be in charge, so that means there isn't a plan."

"Hmph, you are everything I was told…but you are right. There is no plan for them as we do not have enough to separate them."

"I can train enough for a full platoon if you give me control."

"Hahaha, bold you are. I told you Doc is in command, but I enjoy your ambition. He and Dani spoke highly of you, so you have my blessings," he authorized without much thought.

"Thank you. I just wanted to clear that up. I will be going now." She thanked him as she headed back to the door.

"Hold on for a moment. I have a question for you."

"What is it?"

"Why would Dani say that Rob is struggling over the thought of killing John? I know they saved each other in numerous battles and fought side-by-side, but John did kill Iris."

"Why does it matter?"

"Well, I'm worried that he will not pull the trigger, making all this pointless."

"I see, and you are right to be worried, but I need you to understand that they are both torn in this conflict. I'm not sure John will be capable of pulling that trigger either," she explained without too much detail.

"Hm, what would John be torn about? I thought he was just a psychopath," Pan asked as he grew more interested in the conversation.

"It is a long story, but to simplify it, they virtually share the same blood even though they are not related."

"Go on."

"Both men have A- blood, which is fairly rare and meant they could only receive transfusions from A- or O-, but unfortunately, no one on the squad matched them. This led to two instances where Rob and John desperately needed blood and had to donate to their partner. Had they not done so, neither man would be alive. More importantly, when donating, the donor was often low on blood from a battle and risking his life to help his brother," she explained as she gripped the back of a chair tight.

"So, they are a different type of blood brother."

"Yes, and that has always connected them. When Rob was in his spiral, I saw him glow when John took control of Ascension. He hated John at this point, but that was his brother. Then John hired Iris, who needed work because of her connection to Rob. He even asked me about Rob when we were all in Despartian."

"Then why would he kill her and do this to Rob after all that?" Pan asked as he attempted to make sense of what he was hearing.

"Honestly, I think it was the hardest decision John has made, and I partially think there is something wrong with John, something that he is hiding, and he wants to have one last fight. However, if he dies, I think he wants it to be at Rob's hand," she explained as she worked through thoughts she had been having for some time.

"Why would he want that?" Pan asked.

"I don't know the full story, but something happened before, during, and after that second transfusion. Something that Rob keeps buried deep down, and I'm sure John is the same way." She did not have the answer he sought, but she wished she did. Outside of Shadow Squad, no one knew them better than her.

"That does not quell my fears but gives me insight. I appreciate it. You can go now," Pan insisted as he shooed Anna out without any more discussion. She wondered what he would do with the information, but she let it go, as Pan was in charge and had already granted her her request.

Chapter 19
Day Dreams

ob, Iris, John, and Bunny sit together at a wooden booth in an old brick restaurant and eat dinner. The men are wearing jeans and polos while the ladies are wearing blouses with their jeans. The group is laughing as they work through their main courses.

"Oh, it is nice to have a night away from the kids." Bunny sighed before taking a sip from her glass of wine.

"Tell us about it. The baby has made sleep rare these last couple of weeks," Iris said. The dark spots under her eyes were obvious despite the make-up she had put on.

"Does your husband at least help with the diapers?"

"He does, though he struggles sometimes."

"Hey, I'm doing my best, but that kid is always squirming," Rob interjected after he had swallowed his last piece of steak.

"At least he helps you. This one here never cleaned up after Lawrence. It was always my job." Bunny scowled as she looked at John.

"I helped a few times."

"Oh, when you sprayed him down with the kitchen sink hose or the time you did it outside."

"See, I helped. I cleaned the kid up."

"That isn't how you do it."

"When there is that much poop, it is."

"You're impossible." John was the first to laugh at the comment and was soon joined by the rest of the table as his laugh bellowed.

"Well, if you would all excuse me, I'm going to run to the bathroom," Iris announced as she squeezed past Rob.

"I'll join you so these two can share baby secrets." Bunny giggled as she pushed past John and joined Iris. John watched his wife walking away from him. There was a large smile on his face as he turned back to Rob.

"We don't deserve them, do we?"

"Not after the hose story." Rob smiled. John gave him a side-eye.

"Everyone's a critic, the boy stank. I was not getting my hand anywhere near the source."

"Hahaha, well, it is good that Trisha was fully grown when you adopted her."

"Yes, a blessing, but I also missed the cute years. Now I just have an angsty teenage girl."

"Oh, she is a delight in practice, and Gerald says she is a great student."

"That's because you two don't always have to deal with her."

"True...very true." Rob momentarily swirled his glass of wine as he looked at the liquid inside. *"Have you heard from her mother recently?"* John's eyes dropped as he thought about the question.

"No, she hasn't called Trisha in three months but was getting her needed help."

"And Trisha?"

"The doctor Iris suggested has made a lot of progress. Trisha even called me father the other day." John smiled before he finished his glass. *"We actually operate like a family now."* As John said this, his vision started to blur. His world swirled, and he was at his front door laughing with the group. He opens the door, but as he walks in, he is not entering a house to see his son and Trisha. Instead, he sees a crescent table with a group of old, white-haired, balding men in military uniforms and suits.

As John stood in the room, his body shook. He turned to run back out, but the younger version of himself entered behind him. He was well-decorated but confused by what he saw.

"What did you need, sir?" the young John asked.

"There has been a change in plans. You have one more mission before heading north to become an instructor," one of the old men announced.

"But, sir, I am already packed." The older John just watched in silence as he remembered the interaction. The pain and confusion he felt, along with the powerlessness to do anything.

"It will be quick. Next week, Irons has a speech in New Orleans, and you have been cleared to kill him in a long-range assassination." The younger John was shocked by the

announcement, while the older reached out to his younger self. He tried to touch him, but he fazed through him.

"Sir, I cannot. It is not legal."

"It is. We have gone through multiple channels of clearance. Normally, someone else would do it, but it was agreed by the highest powers that you are the best and only one for this mission."

"Sir..."

"That is an order; if you disobey, you will face the consequences. Is that clear?"

John walked to his younger self, "Don't! Just walk away! None of it is worth it!" he shouted at his younger self. "We could have that back there. We could have a family, friends, and a life." The younger John stood silent as he thought of what to say. He weighed the consequences of each action.

"This is not a discussion. This is an order!" the old man shouted again.

"Yes, sir. I will prepare immediately," the younger John said. As he heard this, the older one ran out the door and found himself in an abandoned apartment. The only person in the room was the young John with a rifle pointed out the window. His sights rested on Jeremy Irons as he gave an anti-gun speech and preached for peace. The young John pulled a series of bullets out of his pocket.

"One bullet for him, one for each man who ordered this crime, and one for me as my final admission." John placed the first bullet in his rifle. On it, an "I" was carved. He fired the shot.

***

John jerked awake as he saw the shot fired from his rifle. His body was sweating heavily as his heart beat fast. He had fallen asleep in his chair, and now his body was near convulsion. His body started coughing ferociously, and a pit in his stomach formed. Blood leaked from his mouth, and specks flew out at each cough. He reached for a nearby trash can and started to throw up. Several dry heaves were needed before he finally let go of what was in his stomach, a mix of bile and blood that left him exhausted. He breathed heavily as his body remained hunched over the trash, hoping there would be no more.

John set the trash can down once his stomach and lungs had settled. He rose from his chair to walk around the room. His mind was still unsettled, but he was finding some peace again. The dream, mixed with a memory, had left his mind racing. Doubts about his plan had been swirling inside him the entire time he had constructed it, but his convictions had grown stronger as time progressed. Each time he visited his son's grave, he seemed more sure of himself. Yet, this dream had placed doubt in him again. His mind was set on the idea that he had no choice back then, and the disaster that struck was the fault of others. They needed to pay for what they had done.

However, the dream made him wonder what would have happened had he made a different choice. What would have been different? What would the world look like? He had told himself that they would have found someone else. They would have placed him in jail for a court-martial, and his family would still have died. It was an inevitable outcome because humans were destined to destroy each other. That was the story he told himself, and now he was just finishing that destiny. These thoughts kept him on his path, but the doubts crept as he looked towards the coming days.

As his mind tore, the door to his office opened. Trisha strolled into the room and stood before him. "Everything is set for tomorrow. And Rob has taken up residence in the District as you anticipated." John just sat as his niece informed him of the news. His silence dragged on longer than she anticipated. "Did you hear me?"

"I did."

"And what's your next order?" John paused again. He saw the boardroom and the men behind that desk as they ordered him to kill, knowing what would result. An order to kill an innocent civilian in New Orleans that started a war. As he pictured that table, he saw himself sitting there.

"Tomorrow, we burn the District down. Call up a squad of komodos and the Viper Weaponized Tanks. They will back up the boas and vipers in the attack." His eyes grew colder as they looked away.

"Understood, no survivors?" John turned his eyes to her. She had a smirk on her face as she waited for his response.

"Only Rob, no other survivors."

Chapter 20
Fireworks

The following day, the city was peaceful and quiet. The people began to sober up as they prepared for the last night of celebration and the day after when they would return to their daily lives. The talk of the city was the fireworks show that night. It is always the keynote event of the night.

While the majority of the city was excited, they could still feel the tension. Especially those who were on the border with the Sewer District. The people on the city's north side watched as the District raised walls to funnel people to a select few points. Members of the District posted on top of walls and roofs as they watched for any movement.

There were whispers around the city that the fireworks this year would be different. The people worried that all the celebrating would be caped with a disaster. Even as John spoke to the city in his final address, people could feel something was wrong. Rob, in particular, felt a chill run down his spine with every word. His voice had a conviction that told Rob that John was in complete control. He had still hoped that there was a chance that John would stop whatever he was planning, but now it was real. Rob would have to make his decision soon.

After John was finished, Rob headed to join Enrique and Aliesha, sitting on top of a roof watching the borders. "Is everything ready?" Rob asked as he took a seat by them.

"Yes, the spots are secure," Enrique answered as Aliesha sat watching the world around her and polishing some of her blades.

"Good. Has he started to evacuate any of those unable to fight?"

"No, that stubborn old man has refused to start. We secured the route, but he won't send anyone through it," Aliesha chimed in before Enrique could formulate a response. Enrique growled at the answer she gave.

"That does not surprise me. He was against the idea from the start." Rob just shook his head and bit his lip as he thought.

"Are we going to get any backups?" Aliesha asked as she rose from her seat and stretched with her hands held high.

"No, we will guard the main gate alone. The rest of the Asters will hold the escape tunnel. Dani, Morgan, and Sam have the West gate with a militia. At the same time, Mancio and the other siblings guard the east with soldiers.

"Hmph, that will be fun. I'm excited to see how we fight together." Aliesha grinned with her hands on her hips.

"Excited? This is my home," Enrique growled.

"Oh, I get that, but the battle is coming regardless. I'm just excited to fight with some competent people." Enrique just stared at her as she rolled her eyes and turned back to the city.

"I need to go check on the rest of the borders. I'll be back an hour before the fireworks are scheduled." Rob was convinced there was more between them and did not want to deal with it. They just nodded, and he left for a few hours.

Time passed with neither Enrique nor Aliesha saying a word outside of warning each other if they saw something suspicious. Enrique sat with a coin that he kept flipping in the air, and she sharpened her weapons, just waiting for any movement.

"Why is your old man so stubborn?" Aliesha asked, breaking the silence that had been in place for over an hour.

"It isn't stubbornness. He is just cautious."

"Ah, so it is stupidity."

"Cautious."

"No, that would be evacuating people that are in danger. This is prideful stupidity." Enrique stayed sitting and watching the world around him as Aliesha walked around during the conversation.

He didn't have much to say at first but did find a reply, "Why are you here? You hate this District."

"I don't hate it. It is just the stubbornness that bothers me. And I'm here because I am tired of doing nothing."

"If you are so tired of doing nothing, why not fight with us this whole time?"

Aliesha turned away from him momentarily before answering, "Because the last time I asked that old man for help, he abandoned my friends and me. Had Kathleen not arrived, Braden would have taken us."

"When was this?"

"Almost two years ago. Just after John consolidated Ascension to a few cities and put his Executives in charge here." As she spoke, there was a different tone in her voice that Enrique was not used to when speaking with her. He had few encounters over their time in the city but had grown used to her direct and rough speaking. This had pain in it.

He let her words hang for a moment to feel what she said, "That would have been at the start of the District."

"Yes, one of my friends had been captured, and I was fighting to get them back. I asked Mancio for help as he had the kernels of a rebellion starting even before John's takeover, but the soldiers he promised never arrived. I had to fight alone, and he never told me why."

"I cannot apologize for what I was not involved in, but I thank you for putting it aside to fight now."

"Whatever, just don't make the same mistake." She did not care about anything else he had to say, and Rob returned to the rooftop soon after. There, he sat and meditated until word arrived.

After hours of waiting, the District thought the attack would not come. They had seen drunks cross the city but never any guards. Then, just as dusk was upon them, a singular figure approached Mancio's position. The militia at the position told the figure to stop repeatedly, to no avail. They were ready to fire when Hennrick recognized the face.

"Hold your fire, it's brother!" he yelled in jubilation to see his brother free again. All the militia cheered as well, but Mancio stayed quiet.

"Why so gloomy, Father?" Ava asked as she noticed her father's lack of excitement.

"Because you are watching a dead man walk Ava," Mancio explained as his 3rd son approached.

"Oh, come now, Pops. He is right there, and miracles happen," Hennrick argued.

"Look closer, children. Look at his eyes and his movement. That is a man with a broken spirit and body!" Mancio yelled as everyone took a closer look. The normally proud Teche no longer marched with a chest puffed out or his customary swagger. This was just a corpse walking under the influence of other forces.

Once Hennrick finally understood his father's words, it was too late. It was too late to fire on him, and he could barely utter the words. Teche looked at them with his robotic eye and imploded next to the walls they prepared. In the confusion, boas and vipers rushed from their hiding spot to Mancio's and Dani's positions. While large, hefty vipers approached the three at the central position. The three of them jumped off the rooftop and stood in front of the vipers.

Rob extended his staff as the vipers came to a halt. To his right, Aliesha put a glove on her left hand with tiny daggers attached to the nails. On his left, Enrique stood with a sickle. His prominent leather-covered figure looked like the Grim Reaper as the sickle hung from his hand. Rob's eyebrows raised as he stood before the enemies he did not anticipate seeing.

"Why are these ones fat?" Rob asked, staring at the large sumo-sized vipers approaching them.

"They're the viper weaponized tanks, or VWTs for short. Vipers' with tummies, I call them," Aliesha responded as the largest of them approached. The man of Chinese descent was probably seven feet tall and north of 400 lbs with a crowned dragon across his chest.

"Xiaobo," Enrique snarled as the man laughed. Xiaobo had a robotic left arm, flowing blonde hair, and a loud, high-pitched laugh.

"He's already irritating me, and all he's done is laugh," Rob commented as the trio took up their position.

"He is irritating, but, along with the other Shadow Six, he is one of John's best fighters," Aliesha explained.

"Still excited?" Rob asked as he watched the rest of the VWTs move into position around Xiaobo.

"Something like that," Aliesha replied.

"YO!" Xiaobo yelled as he interrupted. "Why don't you stop your balking, and girl, stop your talking. I'm too much loving for you, and you just won't do. The VWTs are here to kill; now swallow that pill," Xiaobo sang. Rob's eye just twitched as he tried to take this guy seriously. He knew they were a threat, but still, it was getting more challenging by the minute.

"Hey, chunky, if your fighting is as bad as your signing, this will be done fast!" Rob yelled back. Enrique and Aliesha grinned while the VWTs looked at their leader, shocked by the disrespect. Xiaobo just stood momentarily before firing a canister from his robotic arm.

"No, one calls me chunky!" he yelled back as the smoke poured from the canister. The VWTs used the smoke to move into an attack position.

"Together, and do not let them separate us," Rob ordered as the three moved into a counter position at each other's back.

While Rob engaged Xiaobo and Mancio's forces cleared the debris from the explosion, Dani's group engaged a mix of boas and vipers. It quickly became evident that John's guards were not prepared for the three ladies in Dani's position. They were the only front that had the advantage. Dani took a moment to gaze towards the other battle points as they battled. She saw the smoke rising quickly from the different positions and stepped back for a moment.

"Sam, Morgan to me now!" she ordered as the other militia soldiers took the lead role. As soon as they heard Dani, the ladies moved to her.

"What's the call?" Morgan asked.

"We need to finish this quickly, so I want you two to take a group through the sewers and flank the guards from behind. I will drive forward at that point, and we will scatter them," Dani instructed. Without hesitation, Sam and Morgan grabbed a few fighters.

Dani glided through the enemy lines, taking minimal damage. A flick of the wrist sent her whip towards the enemies' weapons. Then, she glided and cut them down. While also pulling allies out of harm's way.

As she moved through the enemy lines, the boas started to retreat. "They're on their heels; push through and finish the fight!" she shouted to the militia fighting alongside her. They began to push hard as Sam and Morgan appeared behind the lines to strike from the rear. Pinching the forces between them, causing John's captains to lose control. Sam slithered through the vipers like a real snake, while Morgan showed her newfound ability with the sai. Brutal blows and counterstrikes kept the boas reeling. Each had refined their abilities since their fight in Memphis. In a short time, they had gone from street fighters to warriors.

A guard had gotten behind Dani, but Sam slithered to her and protected her from the blindside hit. "Watch your surroundings,"

Sam smirked as she kicked the guard back. Her eyes were filled with pride for protecting one of her mentors.

"You're doing better," she started and deflected a thrown weapon heading towards an unaware Sam. "But you can still be better. Gloat when the battle is over." The pair returned to their battle and kept pushing the forces away.

As Dani's front saw success, Mancio's position was less lucky. The explosion split them, and they lost several in the initial hit. Ava and Hennrick led the defense while their father assisted in putting out the fire that had started to spread from the explosion. Ava charged in with twin hammers that cracked skulls. At the same time, Hennrick used his blade to cut through the guards.

At one point, one of Ava's hammers lodged into an enemy's skull. The guards saw this moment to strike. Before they arrived, Hennrick jumped between them and her to buy her time. Once she was free, they sent the forces back.

"I told you those are uncivilized and ineffective," Hennrick sneered as they fought side-by-side, trying to reunite a unified line.

"Ineffective, tell that to the guy I had to pull this out of," she responded, knocking a blade down before sending the other hammer into a man's sternum.

"Just don't get yourself killed. I don't want to lose you too," he choked out, doing his best to hold back the tears for his lost brother. Ava knocked another guard back before placing a hand on his shoulder between his slices.

"I won't. We will avenge him. Now, let's go." The two charged back through the line of boas.

Mancio had started with the fires but was quickly drawn back into the battle. His age had diminished his abilities, but as the boas began to penetrate the lines, he drew his katana to defend his family. His movements were slow and controlled as he would stand waiting for the enemies to rush at him, and then he could cut them down in smooth strikes.

"Do not waste the sacrifices of those lost and protect your families!" he ordered over the yelling on the battlefield. He started to push with his troops. Once the District's defense line was reestablished, Mancio found his children.

"Father, we may win this," Hennrick said as the line took another step forward. Mancio did not respond at first. He stood listening, and he could hear something coming.

His silence and stillness were noticed by Ava. "What is it?"

"I don't know." Then they all heard it. There was a sudden roar that echoed in the air. They looked to the left side of their forces, and a pair of metal-plated tigers were tearing through the line. The team of beasts started to turn Mancio's militia backward as they tore men and women in half with their teeth. They were guided by a man covered in leather and wearing metal claws on his hands. The man had slicked-back raven hair and a large curled mustache popping on his brown Indian skin.

"It's Inesh and his tigers." Mancio grimaced as he looked at the new opponent. A beast tamer that commanded two twin tigers, Ade and Kali. Inesh was another member of Shadow Six known for being sweet to his beasts but cruel to all humans.

"Can we handle him and those two?" Ava asked. All three of them had started making their way over before the answer was given.

"We'll have to," Mancio replied as they approached Inesh.

"Isn't this a treat! Even the old man has come to play, kids!" Inesh taunted as he licked blood from his metal claws.

"Ava, Hennrick, take care of the tigers. I will focus on him. Everyone else to battle. We will finish with the fire after," Mancio ordered.

"Bold to assume you will see an after," Inesh taunted again as he whistled. Upon the whistle, the tigers attacked the children while he engaged the old man. Much like his beast, he struck with fury and fearlessness.

The children struck at the pair of beasts, but their plated armor was impenetrable. Ava's hammers could stagger Kali while Hennrick's blade collided with Ade's claws. Though they could strike, the beasts were overpowering.

Mancio and Inesh sliced at each other while their respected children fought. Inesh's claws were quick, but Mancio benefited from being a superior technician. The clanging of their blades echoed across their battlefield like chimes in the wind. Only drowned out by the occasional roar of a tiger. Inesh caught Mancio a few times but did nothing more than superficial damage. Some boas and militia tried to interfere as they fought but were dispatched quickly. The superior fighters would not be fazed by the flies that tried to fight.

Aliesha, Enrique, and Rob held their ground at the primary position despite their heavy breathing and the blood they had lost. Enrique had to wipe blood from his left eye to see constantly. Aliesha had taken a slice to her lower right abdomen and had to place pressure after that every few encounters. In contrast, Rob had kept the most severe blows away from his body.

"Aliesha, back up and take care of that." Rob stepped in front of her to block a VWT that had come at her.

"I'm fine and don't need you protecting me." She tried to charge after a VWT, but Rob cut her off.

"I'm not protecting. I'm buying you time. We need you at full strength if we are going to beat fatso over there." She looked at the other two, fighting hard to keep the soldiers from her. Her mind was torn by the display, but aware that there was only one thing to do. She ripped part of her pants leg and applied pressure by moving her belt up on her body. After securing it, she jumped in to strike a guard who had gotten close to Rob. Her dagger hand drove into the guards' flesh and sent them back.

"Thank you," he said as the three re-grouped. Despite their exhaustion, they were smiling while Xiaobo snarled.

The VWTs moved their fallen comrades out of the way and reengaged Enrique and Aliesha as Xiaobo attacked Rob. That metal arm was full of various gadgets that he employed, but Rob handled them all. Rob saw everything from a spinning blade to a dart gun and flares. Despite the tricks, he still wanted to grapple with Rob. He did his best, but it was a poor fit given the man's immense size advantage.

"Any more words, smart man, or you finally a big fan. Going to make you a Stan, ain't that a big ole' damn." Xiaobo laughed as he knocked Rob back.

"This is getting fun. I may even take the kid's gloves off," Rob told him as he spit some blood out. He cracked his neck and returned his staff to his belt. He turned his back on Xiaobo, which angered the man again. Xiaobo shot a cannon from his arm that Rob dodged without even turning around. The shot hit a VWT while Rob picked up a blade.

"I have not fought with a blade for quite some time, but I think it's time to be a warrior again," Rob said as he spun the blade in his hand.

He turned to Xiaobo, who had exposed his own. Rob struck at his opponent with a ferocity different than before. Something changed with the new weapon. Xiaobo could not keep up with the smaller foe who moved with a precision the large body could not counteract. Boas came to his aide, but Rob cut them down instantly. As the blood flew in the air, Rob looked at Xiaobo with those eyes that reminded him of Inesh's tigers. Xiaobo backed away from the man who had yet to bleed but was covered in blood. He called in reinforcements to overwhelm the trio.

He held his ground for some time and cut down several guards before he saw Aliesha and Enrique being driven backward.

"We need to retreat!" Rob shouted. They looked at him angrily but recognized he was the only one holding his ground.

"But we can't be the ones that fail. We have to hold this position," Enrique replied as he cut down another guard.

"This is not a failure. This is strategy."

"But."

"Trust me."

Enrique was going to say something again, but Aliesha tapped his arm. "We cannot die here. We are needed elsewhere." With both of them choosing to run, he finally caved. They started to run.

During the retreat, they ran into militia members spreading from Dani's position. Her team had driven John's forces away, moving to reinforce the other spots. Aliesha was the first to smile when she saw Sam leading the backup.

"Oh, good, we get the fun and spunky one," she commented. Sam tried to act natural but blushed almost instantly. With them, they turned back and drove at their enemies. There was a rejuvenation as the VWTs were driven away.

Unfortunately, Xiaobo used the retreat to infiltrate the district and release firebombs on the houses. Rob's team did not initially notice Xiaobo's absence. Still, as soon as the smoke rose, they realized how this had changed the situation. If they were to save the District, the fire had to be stopped, but they barely had enough to fight off the growing boa and viper numbers.

"We have to move in," Rob said more to himself than anyone in particular.

"Agreed, but what of the smoke from the old man's position?" Aliesha asked as she stuck down two more guards.

"We have to focus on us and hope Dani will reinforce them."

Mancio, Ava, and Hennrick were beaten back and on their last legs when Inesh pulled back. "Where are they going?" Hennrick asked, limping back into battle with the militia now gaining ground again.

"I don't know, but I don't like it. Grab the wounded and focus on the fires!" he shouted as Morgan arrived with backup.

"Did we win?" Morgan asked as she helped carry an injured man to a cart that was brought for the injured.

"I don't think so," Mancio said as he looked towards the other side. Smoke had started to blur the alleys and open area from which the guards were striking. Then he saw something enormous poking through the smoke. Without warning, the figure threw a body at Mancio's forces. It screamed as it flew through the air and cried out as it landed on Mancio's militia. Then another flew at him, but this time, a dead guard landed on them. Then, the figure and a group of others appeared from the smoke. Completed komodos standing between seven and eight feet tall with muscles like a gorilla and mechanical parts attached to their bodies entered the fight.

"Move, regroup in the center, and start the evacuations!" Mancio shouted, but his order came late. His militia were already running for their lives. Only a few, including his children and Morgan, stood tall when the beasts approached them.

Dani's team was the next to retreat. They had been tending to the wounded when chunks of buildings and large rocks were thrown at them. These sudden launches crushed several militia soldiers before anyone knew what was happening.

"I'll cover the rear, but we need to run," she ordered as six komodos, along with other boas, started to approach.

Sam's reinforcements had helped Rob push back to the starting position. Still, he saw what awaited them before they could handle the fires or Xiaobo. A line of ten komodos holding large weapons or dead bodies in their hands. They had a lifeless stare as they waited for Rob.

"Halt the counter. We need to head to the District center!" he yelled.

"No. Not when we are winning," Enrique argued as he cut down more boas.

"We may be winning, but I'm sure these beasts are at the other gates, and your father will not win without you. We need to regroup," Rob instructed as he signaled for the rest of the militia to turn around. Enrique stood and stared at the half-machine, half-man beast and knew Rob was right. He needed to protect his family. They turned and ran. They could hear the beasts tearing the district apart behind them as they ran. Friends or foes were launched into the air, and buildings were torn apart like cardboard. The small wooden sheds were broken to pieces with swipes of the komodos' hands.

Kathleen was evacuating forces at this point and began to have the injured carried away as the three fronts regrouped. All nine of the leaders were dripping blood and panting heavily. Kathleen just watched as Aliesha's hand shook from a fight. The blood from her abdomen started to seep out of the cloth she used. The unstoppable Enrique had a cut above his eye and a puncture through his oblique. Meanwhile, it was impossible to discern where Rob's blood started and his enemies began.

"So how do we beat them?" Mancio asked as he turned to Rob for the plan.

"Go for their mechanical eye. It is what John uses to tap into their minds' electrical field. It is our only chance now that they are juiced on Leopard Skin," Rob hurried to explain as he huffed from exhaustion.

It took only moments for the komodos to reach the evacuation point. Rob ordered all standard militia into the tunnel system. Only the twelve leads were allowed to fight the surrounding twenty komodos. Rob flew towards the largest one but was caught mid-air and tossed aside. He skidded across the ground, only stopping when he hit a wall. The pain from the previous fights was immense, and now he had these monsters to contend with. It was insanity, but he planted his blade in the ground and rose on his shaking legs. He took a breath to center himself again and charged. This time, he was a step faster and staggered one of them. His allies saw the opportunity to join in. They tried to attack in groups, but the komodos outnumbered them.

Sam wrapped around one while Morgan tried to go low and stagger the beast, but another ripped Sam off, tossing her onto the ground. Enrique freed her from its grip but was then sent flying with the kick of another. Dani's movements held one off on her own and used speed to stay away from another.

There was a light for a moment as Aliesha and Rob destroyed one eye. The beast fell, but another came after Aliesha. Rob and Dani partnered up back-to-back as they kept two more at bay. Rob looked at his comrades being beaten to a pulp. He watched his girls standing brave but unable to free themselves. He knew what had to be done.

"This was his plan, but he wants me alive. Lead them out of here," he whispered to Dani. Her eyes widened as she heard his order.

"You promised you wouldn't leave again," she responded as they leaped away from the swinging komodos. She knew his mind was set but hoped he would say something else. He said nothing and just put his hand on her shoulder with a tight squeeze.

She bit her lip and grinded her teeth as she found the words she didn't want to say. "Everyone, fall back. We need to live for another day!" she yelled with one last glance at Rob. She wondered if this would be the last time and held her gaze for an extra moment.

She saw the young kid she knew. The awful taste in fashion, the puny muscles, and that childish grin. Then she saw the new man he had become. The muscles that he had grown and the scars across his body. The years of fighting had twisted much of him, but he still flashed that childish grin one last time.

After the last look, Dani began the retreat. They all knew it was the right move as no one had much left in them. Only Enrique and Aliesha stayed at Rob's side for an extra moment.

"I need you two to run. John won't kill me yet, but I cannot promise your safety," he explained as they lashed at the komodos circling them.

"I don't run," Enrique snarled. He was tired of being on his heels.

"Don't let your pride ruin us. If anything happens, they are going to need you two to lead. I need you two to lead them," Rob pleaded as he was able to knock another komodo down.

"He's right, Enrique," Aliesha said at last. Her words shocked them both. They thought she would be on Enrique's side, yet she was giving up.

"Alright," he conceded after a moment of thought. Aliesha grabbed his arm as they ran to the escape tunnel. Rob jumped in front of the komodos that wanted to pursue the escapist. He shifted into position and raised his blade again. A lone cornered wolf, but a beast nonetheless.

"Come now, uglies," he taunted as he launched himself at the komodos again. They did not go easy on him as they tossed him around. He was confident when he told Enrique he'd survive, but the confidence was fleeting. On his last legs, Rob continued to rise and prepare for more. As he stood ready for the next blow, Aliesha flew in and dismantled a metal arm with her dagger nails.

"Why are you here?!?" Rob shouted at the sight of her.

"Don't worry. I threw Enrique in the tunnel and sealed the entrance." She smirked as they defended each other.

"That doesn't answer my question."

"I know, but what difference does it make?" The komodos cut off the rest of their conversation and subdued the pair. Both were forced to their knees while Xiaobo and Inesh approached.

"I have you now, so take a bow. The idiot must stand trial, but you'll be dead by a mile." Xiaobo laughed. Aliesha was content with the ending. To her and Xiaobo's surprise, a komodo raised its metal arm to finish her but stopped mid-swing.

"Take her to the island as well," Ex's voice commanded from a perch above them. They were all shocked by their appearance. Xiaobo was shaking at the sight.

"But..." he tried to argue, only to feel the gaze of Ex pierce through him. "Yeeesss...as you command."

"Good, now komodos will take the prisoners to the island, and Inesh will send word to John!" Ex ordered from their perch. The pair were dragged to the island, Xiaobo lit the fireworks, and Ex disappeared into the night.

In the tunnel, Dani stood exhausted. She looked at the others, who were all licking their wounds. Enrique leaned against the tunnel, barely able to stand. Then, he slammed his sickle into the wall multiple times. Hennrick and Ava collapsed on the ground, crying over Teche as Mancio sat to put pressure on a wound. Sam, Morgan, and Kya cried as they were sure their friends were gone.

"How many did we lose?" Dani asked, taking long breaths in between words.

"At least half of my fighters," Mancio replied with a distant look.

"And two of our best," Dani started looking at the others. "Kathleen, take them back to your hideout. I need to see if Pan has arrived yet," she ordered as she started to walk down the tunnel, only stopping to help Morgan and Sam to their feet. Each grabbed at their bodies as they felt the beating they had just taken.

Meanwhile, the komodos threw the dead into the fires and blood flooded the water. All while John stood at the window of his mansion with a grin as he watched the fireworks in the distance.

Chapter 21
Choices

After the battle, Rob passed out from exhaustion, and the next thing he knew, he was lying on a cold concrete floor. His hands and legs were chained to the ground. As he looked up, the metal bars of a prison cell were the first thing he saw when his eyes opened. On the other side of the cell door was an open space.

The next cell was thirty yards away and sat on its own. Each cell was like this: they were individual units just large enough for a person to inhabit, and they were isolated with a thirty-yard radius around them so that no prisoner could speak to the others. Outside the cell, Rob could barely see the ceiling to the floor he was on. Poor lighting made the twenty-foot ceiling look miles away.

He rose to a seated position, feeling every ache from the battle the night before. The wounds he had received were patched roughly, but he felt everything when he shivered in the cold basement. There was no warmth wherever he was, and he had to use all his mental willpower to keep himself under control. He took a minute to breath and listen. At first, there were the other prisoners' moans and water dripping from the ceiling into puddles on the floor. Then, there were footsteps traversing the floor. The steps grew closer and closer until he saw John in front of him.

"You've looked better," John's voice echoed through the darkness. He stood tall before the cell and looked down at the seated Rob, who never turned his head up.

"Yet, I still look better than you."

"Hmph, defiant as ever." Rob finally looked up at John, whose face had no emotion.

"So, why am I here? And where am I?"

John knelt down to Rob's level to speak, "Well, you are in my Hell. And you are here because we need to talk."

"Talk? Now, you want to talk? After you kill Iris, leave cryptic notes about your life, and fight beside me for years, never telling me about your wife or killing Irons. Now you want to talk."

"Maybe you are right. Talking has never been our thing. How about you answer my question through a demonstration?" John walked to the side of Rob's cell and pressed a button that released Rob's chains. Rob rose as John unlocked and entered the cell, closing the door behind him. "Come at me." John raised his guard.

Rob stood for a minute, waiting for John to move first, and John did the same. Eventually, John just rolled his eyes and struck first. He was quick and efficient with his movements. Rob was still tired from the fight twelve hours prior, but there was something else. Unlike the fight the night before, there was reservation in the strikes. John left himself open several times, but Rob did not act quickly. He would hesitate. After the last hesitation, John kicked Rob to the ground.

"What are you doing? Why aren't you trying to kill me? This is your chance for revenge, Rob, and you are doing nothing with it!" John yelled as he wiped his face in frustration. Rob sat on the ground, breathing heavily as he paced in the cell. "Don't you loathe and hate me?"

Rob breathed before looking up at John, whose eyes had grown large. "I did, but killing you won't bring her back. Don't get me wrong, I still want to stop you, but I love you like a brother, John, and I cannot kill you."

John sat down on the cot in Rob's cell. "But you have to. That is the only way to stop me. No one else can do it."

"Why? I've seen the others fight. Someone can match your blade."

"No, only you can do it because you are the only one I can't kill. The only one I won't kill, and I need you to kill me. I need you to hate me and kill me."

Rob sat staring at John, who looked off in the distance. Had he charged at John, he might have been able to get the key, but his legs were weak. "Why do you need to die, and why do I have to hate you?"

John looked up to the ceiling. "I'm going to die anyways, Rob."

Rob closed his eyes as everything started to make sense, "Cancer…that's why you brought in Clarissa."

"Yes, brain cancer that returned a little before I started this final move."

"So, why do I need to hate you if you were going to die anyway? You could have come to me. You could have died peacefully with our whole squad still alive. Iris could have been here to help you and Trisha. So, why, John?"

John rose from his chair and slammed the cell door as he left. Making sure that it was locked as he stood on the other side. "You weren't there, Rob, when they gave me the order. I didn't have a choice. You weren't there when I was stuck in this cell for the order they gave me. I didn't have a choice or an opportunity to protect my son who was lynched and a wife that was raped in front of him before her own death." John's voice quivered as he grew emotional. "Even now, I don't have a choice as I die from cancer. I was going to save this planet and rule it with Trisha and my komodos, but that was taken from me."

"John…"

"Don't you John me! You got to go be a drunk because you were afraid to face a choice you made. You got to choose your life before and after the War, so I took the choices away. I made it so you had to chase and kill me, yet here you are, trying to act like you have a say."

"What are you going to do, John?"

"I'm going to burn the world down because that is all I can do, but I still cannot kill you because you are all I have. Isn't that something?"

"John, you can still surrender. This doesn't have to end in bloodshed. You want a choice and I am giving it to you."

"No, there is no choice Rob. I thought I'd taken enough from you to see that there are no choices, but apparently I didn't take enough." John snapped his fingers, and a guard brought a thorned trap over that John placed the cell key in. "If you truly believe there is a choice, then you can sit in here. As deep as this prison is, you may survive the coming reckoning, or you can stick your hand into this box of thorns and open your cell. Just know that if you open this cell and come for me, the only way to stop me is to kill me." John placed the trap just within Rob's reach.

"How long do I have?"

"At midnight the day after tomorrow, I will end things. Just after Pan's forces arrive." John grinned with the devilish look Rob saw when John killed Iris.

John started to walk away, but Rob had a few more words. "Please, John, don't make me do this."

"Hmph, then don't. See if refusing the call works, it wouldn't have changed anything for me."

"John, we can stop this."

"My plan is in motion, make your choice."

Rob's fist tightened as he let out a long exhale, "I will stop you, John."

"We will see." John walked away and left Rob with the box.

As John and his guard left, Rob just stared at it. He sat thinking about John. During the whole conversation, he felt lost listening to John. There was so much pain in his old friend. He started to blame himself as he wondered what would have happened had he not dedicated his life to the drink, then he could have seen his friend faltering. Perhaps John wasn't given a choice. Sure, he could be blamed for what occurred, but what about everything that led to it. John lost everything, and the one person who could have been there for the dying man wasn't.

Whether he believed John had a choice or not, now he had one: kill John or not. If he engaged in that battle, there could be no "stopping." He thought there was another way, but there wasn't. He needed to make his call now. He looked at the trap. Next to the trap, he could picture Dani, Morgan, and Sam. He could see Philip, Anna, Pan, and Gerald in Despatian, all waiting for him to make a move. He could still see John on his cot at his most vulnerable, alone, and lost. Then he crawled to the edge of the cage and drove his hand into the trap. His left hand and forearm were ripped to shreds as he pulled the key out.

Once his bloody arm was free, he opened the door, tore at the cot's fabric, and wrapped the scraps around the cuts. He sat to apply pressure for several minutes to stop the bleeding. Once it had, he exited the cell, looking for the exit. The poor lighting made every direction look like a black abyss. The scattered cells were spaced out so far and facing in different directions to create a maze. He started to walk, looking for any sign that could help him. When he heard a whistle and a voice.

"You'll never make it out of here alone!" the voice hollered with a chirpiness to it.

"I won't be alone. I have a friend to free first," he replied as he walked towards the sound of their whistle.

"Friends are good to have. Especially when facing a madman. How would you like another?" the voice asked now that Rob was just outside the cell. He peered inside to see the shadow of a relatively petite figure that seemed strange.

"That depends on who the friend is."

"Who? Well, that is a brilliant question, and the answer is something that eluded me for years as I took many throughout my life." The figure rose from their seat and walked towards Rob. They were dressed in a black prison outfit, and half of their brown hair was longer than the rest. The figure had tattoos on both hands, a turtle on their neck, and another on the right side of their face.

"So, who are you, and why should I trust you?"

"Well, I was Laura, a proud daughter of the Oneida Nation, but then I was Anpu after I began to understand I was not only a daughter but a son as well. Most recently, I took the name Executioner," the figure stated while standing proud in front of Rob. He took a step back when he heard Executioner.

"Why is the Executioner here? You were just chasing me a day ago."

"Oh, I'm not your Ex. I was the old one. I fought other battles, and none against you, or at least I don't think I have. Had you fought Ex before January this year?"

"I had not."

"Well, good, then we have no reason to be enemies as I am back to being Anpu, a name from my father's side and one I enjoy the most." The figure bowed and then reached their hand out to shake. Rob just raised an eyebrow as they looked at the two-spirit. Anpu brought their hand back into their cell. "Still don't trust me?"

"Not particularly. I have fallen for enough of John's traps."

"Smart, but lend me your ear for a moment as I have a few truths to share." Rob kept his distance from the figure.

"Go on."

"The first is that you are badly beaten, and the next few floors of this prison will be brutal." Anpu paused to watch for a reaction that Rob did not provide. "Second, John threw me into a forgotten Hell because I am a threat, which makes me at least a temporary ally, does it not?"

"It can, but not necessarily."

"Well, if that is the case, how about this. I have information such as where the exit is and the location of the komodo control room on this floor." Anpu grinned as they leaned on the cell door. Their arms hung through the openings and reached for Rob, but now he sat to think. "Tik-tok little jailbird. You don't know what is happening to your friend above us."

"All excellent points, but why would you help me?" Rob stood staring at the figure whose eyes were much warmer than John's but still had a distance to them. They did not look at him. They looked through him.

"Because I enjoy freedom, and John took that from me when he had promised the world."

"He breaks that promise a lot…and I think that you could help us in the coming fight. I will let you out, but no funny business," Rob instructed as he started to fiddle with the lock.

"I'm all funny business, but I have no reason to stab you in the back…until you give me one," he agreed as Rob opened the door and pressed the button that undid the binds.

Anpu wrapped the chains around his hands and guided Rob through the maze of cells to the first stairs. The stairs were large and wide enough to carry an elephant through them. Just before they reached the stairs, they ran into the first set of guards that Anpu dispatched quickly. As Anpu cut through the guards, Rob could see the moves taught to the new Ex and the stylistic differences that proved him to be a different person.

Once Anpu had taken care of the guards, Rob was curious to know more about him. "So, how did you become the original Ex?"

"John had a help wanted sign in the paper."

"I guess he hasn't always been his suave self then."

"No, he has been, but more importantly, he was a man without prejudice towards me. Something that my own family cannot say."

"That is a trait of his. He will dehumanize his opponents through slur, but the only hate he holds is for those that did him wrong."

"Indeed, and when he hates you. Well, you are better off killing yourself," Anpu responded. Anpu was ready to run, but Rob's body could not keep up. Just before they climbed, they heard large footsteps approaching. Down the large winding stairs, a komodo approached. This one was different from what Rob had encountered before. It was larger and had more machine parts implanted, but it also appeared to be in more control of its movements.

"A komodo!" Rob yelled as it approached them.

"Worse, it is a guardian komodo. He and one other were the first successful komodos and the most loyal. Unlike the others under full mind control, these still have most of their mental capabilities, making them a dangerous opponent," Anpu explained. Unlike most people when they saw a komodo, Anpu had little fear for the beast of a man. The pair set themselves as the komodo's mechanical eye scanned the area.

Just by looking at the thing, Rob knew he could not fight it head-on. They needed another option. He took a deep breath to calm himself before scanning the area. Rob noticed holes in the floor, that fit a giant steel gate above them, used to seal off the floor. They could climb the stairs if they could trap the beast on the level side of the gate.

Rob nudged Anpu's arm and led his eyes to the gate in the ceiling. They did not need a single word to understand the plan. They each had to do whatever it took to lure the komodo to this side of the gate, and then they needed to close it rapidly. Anpu was the first to act. Given his healthier legs, he distracted the beast while Rob struck from behind. However, his hits only aggravated the beast. Anpu unfurled the chains and lashed them as if they were whips drawing it down the stairs. It caught the chains and threw Anpu up the stairs with a thud. Rob backed off as he waited for Anpu to rise. He had to dodge several strikes as it came after him, but as soon Anpu was on his feet again, he went to the gate controls. Seeing this, Rob dodged a swing and slid past the komodo, using all his strength to run to the stairs before the komodo could catch him. Anpu closed the gate and slammed it just before the komodo reached them.

Anpu and Rob stood looking at the beast and hoped the gate would hold, but before they could grow comfortable, the komodo started to lift the gate. It was a slow process, but it raised it inch by inch.

As they climbed, they could hear the gate below them. The gears were grinding, but the komodo was progressing. After enough distance was made, Rob turned to Anpu for one last question, "Who is the man behind the mask now?"

"Who? Does there have to be a who?"

"Generally."

"Well, the person under that mask lost their true self years ago. I would say they are the Executioner even when the mask is off."

"But there has to be someone under there."

"There was, but even when I trained them, they were lost, and knowing the identity will not help you stop them," Anpu said with a distant look. Unlike the confidence he showed versus, the komodo Anpu had fear in their voice.

Chapter 22
Taken From Me

Two floors above Rob and Anpu, a group of men were screaming bloody murder while others were unconscious in their cell. Their bodies surrounded Aliesha, who had just knocked down another prisoner. Aliesha walked to the cell door with them down, looking at the prison around her. While Rob's floor was built for isolation with small cells and distance between each one, her floor was packed like a traditional prison.

The cells were all attached to each other and were built to house twenty prisoners at once. They were stacked two high, and a large passageway separated her cell from those across her. As she looked to the left and right, the cells stretched as far as she could see, filled to the brim with prisoners. From the left, she saw Trisha approaching.

Trisha stopped as soon as she reached the cell and looked at all the bodies Aliesha had scattered with a grin, "Men are idiots, aren't they?" She chuckled.

"They are the worst, Mayland," Aliesha snarled. She leaned into the cell as if trying to reach out and strangle Trisha.

"Why the hostility, Liesha? I told Ex to save you. We are friends here." Trisha claimed as her hand moved over her heart. She feigned being offended, but her smirk told the real story.

"If you're a friend, let me out of here, princess." Trisha's eyes twitched at Aliesha's words.

"Don't call me princess, Ms. Mendoza, or I will let you rot," Trisha replied. The use of her last name surprised Aliesha. Neither Kya nor Tia knew her last name, and for good reason.

"How…" she trembled as Trisha saw the power return to her.

"I knew your cousin and met you at her birthday party before the War."

"Did I?... Which cousin?"

"Kelsey," Trisha replied with pain that Aliesha recognized. Trisha's hand gripped tight as her eyes closed for a moment.

"And I take it by the sound of your voice you stayed friends during the War. Even until…"

"Even until she killed herself, yes! And we were much more than friends, Liesha. She was my first everything." Trisha's eyes looked as if she would cry, yet no tear fell. Sadness and hatred filled her, but nothing escaped.

"I'm sorry to hear that, Trisha, but what does it matter," Aliesha replied, unsure why Trisha was sharing this information.

"Do you know why she killed herself?"

"No, I lost touch with them after my fathers were killed. I met her mother in a refugee camp afterward. Otherwise, I would not have known she killed herself."

"I wish I could say the same…I wish I didn't know, but it is a curse that I want to share with you," Trisha explained as she leaned against the cell with a devil's grin, much like her uncle's. Aliesha stepped back as Trisha approached.

"Why? Why are you telling me any of this?"

"Because just like the death of your fathers, Kelsey's death was because of a man, and once I tell you I am going to make you an offer, you won't want to refuse," Trisha replied as she fixed a hair that had fallen out of place.

"Go on then, I have nowhere else to be," Aliesha conceded.

"Your cousin was fourteen years old and lived alone with her widowed mother. I loved her, and she loved me. She would come over often, and I would go there as we hid in our small town that sustained life during the War. But without me knowing it, my father liked visiting your aunt when he was craving things my mother couldn't supply." Trisha gripped the cell tightly as if she wanted to rip it apart.

"But one night he went with cravings to the house, and Kelsey was home alone…she was fourteen and had hit puberty fast…" Trisha's eyes wanted to cry, but nothing was falling. Her hands gripped the cell tightly as if she would rip the metal apart.

"She never told me, but I found her journal after her suicide…That is when I gutted him. I stabbed my father with the same knife Kelsey had used on her wrist. I castrated the monster who had taken Kelsey from me. No, I castrated the man who took me from her, because, in those final days, she could not look at me…she could not look at the girl she loved without seeing her rapist." Trisha finished with a punch to the cell! Aliesha just sat as she absorbed the story that was told to her.

"And what am I supposed to do with that? He's dead," Aliesha asked as she tried to keep calm. She started pacing in the cell as her mind remembered her lovely cousin.

"You are supposed to join me," Trisha replied without hesitation. Aliesha's eyes grew big. She could have thought through a million replies, and that would never have been one of them.

"Join you?" Aliesha asked with her brow turned up.

"Yes, join me in building something new."

"You're nuts."

"No, no, I'm not. In two days, the men will wage another war led by John, Rob, and Pan. They will repeat history, but this time, they will eradicate each other for good. We will grab power and build the world anew when they do. I have already started preparing elsewhere," Trisha explained while pacing outside of the cell.

"It's madness…listening to you is madness. I can't trust you," Aliesha stuttered as she thought through what Trisha was saying. Trisha just exhaled as she leaned into the cell even more.

"I know overcoming what has happened is hard, but I promise you. My uncle is your enemy, not me. However, I also understand this has been a lot, so I will give you time to think. When the battle comes, we will fight as we are supposed to, but afterward, my offer will stand."

"And if I refuse it?"

"Then I will build a world in my likeness without you and eliminate you along with the others that have made this disaster of a world," Trisha explained as Aliesha approached slowly. Until they were nearly touching.

"Why wait then? And why rely on me?"

"Because I need to be here to ensure John is defeated, as he will burn us all if not. And I choose you and your friends because you are powerful, wise, beautiful, and perfect, Liesha," Trisha said as she touched Aliesha's cheek and caressed her face. Aliesha breathed heavily as the hand wiped blood from her that was leftover from her earlier fights. She did not understand what she was feeling. She had always heard stories of the evil Trisha was capable of, but there was this feeling as she spoke of this new world and held her face. Trisha smiled as she saw into Aliesha's soul.

"And what is next?" She quivered as Trisha withdrew her hand.

"I'm going to leave you a key so you can assist Rob and ensure his victory by leading the attack on the prison komodo control center. Finally, you will wait for me on my boat stationed at the prison after the final battle," Trisha instructed as she gently placed the key on the ground. As she turned to walk away, a pair of guards approached. They were about to question her, but she stabbed them in the throat.

As Trisha hedged her bets above, Rob and Anpu fought through the next floor. Rob was surprised when he saw the layout but understood where the leaks in the ceiling below were coming from. This floor was a giant indoor lake from wall to wall, with a single path heading from one stairwell to the next. Inside the water, gators acted as extra guards. The few prisoners on this level did not have cells but small islands that were slightly raised to keep the gators off of them, but they could swim away if they were brave enough.

As Rob and Anpu fought the guards approaching from the opposite end of the passageway, the gators tried to take bites at them. This was their main distraction as the guards caused little issue as Rob and Anpu knocked them into the water with the hungry beasts.

"This feels too easy. Shouldn't there be more guards?"

"I agree, this prison should have two to three times as many guards. I wonder, what is John thinking?"

"He could be testing us. I think he wants me to escape, but he wants me to be sure about what I will do."

Anpu knocked out another guard before he could follow up, "And why does he want to fight? He could just end it now with less fighting."

"Doubt."

"That is different for him. I don't know if I've ever seen him doubt anything," Anpu admitted as they reached the stairs.

"Neither have I, so let's not waste the opportunity, come on." Rob and Anpu were heading up to the next floor of the prison. During the fight on the previous floor, Anpu had picked up a mace that one of the guards carried while Rob had grabbed a blade. Now that they were armed, they hoped to find Aliesha with little issue.

As they reached the top floor, Rob could feel the floor's heat. Compared to the floor below, it was blazing. The pair also started to hear the sound of fighting in the distance. They could not see where the sound was coming from, but the commotion grew louder as they ran down the passageway, passing the two-high cells along the way. When they finally came into view of the fighting, they found Aliesha with a group of prisoners she had freed.

"Your friend, I assume?" Anpu stopped running before reaching the fight.

"Indeed, and I guess it wasn't a test. The guards were just preoccupied." The pair ran and started to drive the guards back. This burst of energy helped break the line that had stalled before the next stairwell. Fighting side-by-side, the two went to Aliesha, where the three became unstoppable.

As they fought through the guard's line, Rob could speak with Aliesha, "How did you escape?" he asked as he knocked out a guard behind Aliesha.

"Someone got too close to me? How about you?" she responded as they moved in unison. Her eyes noticed his wrapped arm and the blood staining the cloth.

"John, let me out," he admitted to her surprise.

"Is that why they haven't used guns yet? They are setting a trap."

"No, the lack of guns is due to his final protocol," Anpu interrupted as he joined the conversation.

"Final protocol?" Rob asked.

"And who are you?" Aliesha followed up with.

"This is Anpu. He helped me escape," Rob informed her. "Now, what is the final protocol?" he asked again as the prisoners overcame the guards and started to move up the stairs.

"In case of invasion, he has a transmitter, like the one he carries on himself, that deactivates guns activated within the city. That way, all his opponents would be disadvantaged when his guards strike with blades," Anpu explained. As he finished, they heard loud footsteps. They turned to look down the hall, and the komodo from below had escaped.

"Hold that, why does that one look bigger?" Aliesha asked as the komodo came close.

"Because it is, and smarter…we should probably run," Anpu replied as he started to head up the stairs, and the other two were quick to follow. Despite his prey running, the komodo just kept its slow and easy pace.

On the next floor, the rioting prisoners had already run into their next opponents. The guards had met them at the top of the stairs and pushed them back down until the three reached them. Aliesha, Rob, and Anpu were pushing hard, but their numbers were dwindling.

The current floor was open and built like a factory. Each prisoner was chained to machines that pumped out various building materials that John used to build his empire. The path to the next stairs was not as straight with the factory layout. It was designed like a maze with cages and machinery scattered across the floor.

"Anpu!" Rob called as the group battled through.

"Yes."

"Do you know the way out?" Anpu knocked a guard to the ground and pointed to the back left corner of the room. "Okay, you lead us…Aliesha, you and I will break chains as we can," he ordered as he freed a prisoner on that level. She nodded as she drove a guard into a machine press. The guard numbers thinned as the group pushed toward the exit led by Anpu.

Rob and Aliesha trailed the leading group but kept them in sight for most of the run through the factory floor. The exit was growing nearer when they heard an explosion coming from the direction they were headed, followed by screams. The pair ran to the front and saw their rioters being thrown aside by another monster komodo.

Anpu jumped in to engage the beast as other prisoners ran around and headed to the top floor. Anpu used the mace to knock the beast's hands to the side but could not land a good blow. Rob and Aliesha ran to engage as it swiped him to the side.

Anpu looked at the two running to help, holding his hand up. "Run with them! We need to clear a way out. If we get bogged down, the other will catch us. Now, go!" Anpu shouted as he jumped back in to engage the beast that had turned its attention to Rob.

For a moment, Rob hesitated, but in the distance, he could hear the footsteps of the other komodo. Anpu was right. A clear way out was more critical now if anyone was to escape. "Thank you!" he shouted back as Aliesha, and he ran to the steps. The komodo tried to stop them, but Anpu struck the beast to take the attention back. From there, he did all he could to distract and avoid while the others ran.

"Quite the ally," Aliesha said as they climbed the stairs.

Rob looked behind him briefly, answering, "Apparently, so let's not waste the opportunity."

The prisoners had already progressed to the floor at the top of the steps. With a mix of group and individual cells accompanied by the torture rooms, the first floor had the best lighting and was relatively straightforward. Even from the top of the steps, they could see the giant gate at the end of the passage.

About a quarter of the rioters were still alive, with the pair at the final obstacle. A giant solid metal gate with no sign of a lever to open. Rob and Aliesha searched for a way to open it as Anpu ran to them with the komodos in hot pursuit. Once Anpu reached them, another gate slammed behind them. All of them were trapped in a metal box.

With the gates secure, a speaker above them said, "I'm impressed you made it this far, but my poison will stop you for good!"

They all recognized Braden's annoying voice. Anpu found a gap in the gate and began to work on releasing the seal. As he did, the poison gas started to pour in.

Rob recognized it in a single sniff. He ordered the others to mask their faces and hold their breath as much as possible. Rob remembered the toxins he had encountered since Despartian and knew that their time was limited no matter what they did.

Anpu released the lock, but they had to pry the door the rest of the way. The clock ticked as they worked to open it slowly. The few prisoners that had made it that far joined in the effort until there was just enough room for the group to sneak out.

At last, they could breathe but not rest. They were on a deadly island with enemies in pursuit, and night was approaching fast. The darkness would help them hide on the other side of the island, but the guards would soon make it past the gas and sealed gates. And none of the prisoners knew what to expect in the darkness. After running to the island's other side, the group paused to think through their options.

"So what now?" Anpu sighed.

"I was really hoping you would know," Rob replied as he paced around. Aliesha just sat on the ground, smiling.

"Why are you so calm?" Anpu asked as he noticed her.

"Well, Rob and…Anpu, we Asters collected a lot of information and got a map. One that shows a method for transporting giants without boats," she replied as she knocked on the ground. The others looked at her as her knocks sounded like they were hitting metal.

They cleared the brush and opened a giant tunnel. It was a long, dark tunnel that eventually led to the bayou. Once out, they wandered around the swamp for a time. They kept their eyes on a swivel when Rob saw a young woman walking through the wetlands.

"Morgan, what are you doing here?" he called. She ran towards him with a flying hug.

"We were looking for a hidden tunnel, and who is this?" she asked as Anpu caught her eye.

"A friend…I think." Anpu was happy to hear Rob's answer but also understood the hesitation.

"That doesn't help," she replied.

"We'll talk more when we are away. These people all need a safe home." Rob motioned to the prisoners who had escaped with them. Morgan thought about asking more questions but knew it would be pointless now. She led them back to the sewers where the Asters had turned one of the old abandoned tunnels into a refugee camp.

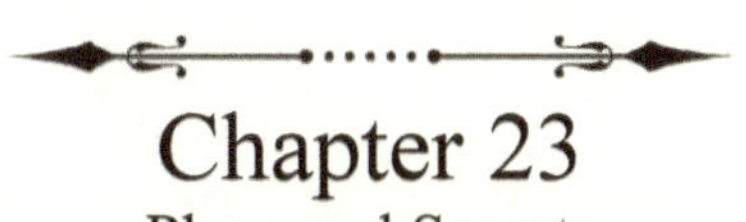

Chapter 23
Plans and Secrets

Once back, Aliesha headed to Kya and Tia to talk. While Anpu followed Rob and Morgan to a central office in the sewers. Past the open area with all the typewriters was a series of tunnels leading to a giant office. Inside, he first noticed Dani. Her hair was pulled in a ponytail as it glistened in the dim sewer lights. In his eyes, she commanded the room despite the others who stood there with her.

"How are you not dead yet?" She smirked while approaching him.

"I'm pretty sure I did die, but I got lost on my way to Hell." He smiled back with a great hug. A small tear of relief ran down her face as she pulled his tattered body tight. He gripped her as Sam flew in, and Morgan joined last.

As they let go, a familiar voice jumped in, "Just once I want to see you, not a bloody mess." Rob turned to see Anna shaking her head with hands on hips.

"Come now, your life would be boring without me. Now, why are you here?" he asked.

"This fight began in Despartian, and we wanted to finish it," Ponleak, Rob's ally back in Despartian, replied as he stepped out of the crowd. He had a new metal arm and grin that Rob hadn't seen in some time. His large frame was hard to miss as he stood taller than most people there. As he hugged them both, he noticed something he had not anticipated: a matching wedding ring on both hands.

"Happy for you two," Rob said, letting go of them both.

"Thank you, but let's get you stitched up properly now," Anna commanded as Pon handed her a medical kit added to his new arm. She then sent him to grab something from another room.

Anna began to stitch up his wounds from both fights and pulled shards of wood and metal from his body. She used a sponge to clean the wounds as Pon returned with a bag of plasma and a new shirt.

They set up a transfusion while Rob placed his new shirt on. He looked around at all his allies.

"Alright, now that you are in one piece, I have someone who wants to meet you," Dani instructed after the transfusion ended. She didn't need to say another word as Pan stepped towards him. He knew at that moment who it was. They each had an aura around them that captured the room. Pan had a fire of resistance that inspired people to fight on, while Rob's presence was a feeling of calmness. They each stood in silence. Just staring at one another with fierce eyes.

"I expected someone taller," Pan commented.

"I expected someone stronger," Rob replied as they continued to lock eyes.

Dani just shook her head. She could read both minds and understood what they were trying to do.

"So, whose dick is bigger?" Mother Kathleen asked as she and Mother Althea interrupted the stare-down.

"Come now, sister. You know as well as I do that size doesn't matter; it is about how they wield it, and Rob does that pretty well from my experience." Althea chuckled. All Rob could do was lower his head while his face turned bright red. It was not what he expected to hear during his stare-down. At the same time, Dani, Morgan, Sam, and Anna also started to turn colors. Pan and Pon both chuckled at the comment.

"So, *all* the stories are true," Pan said as he leaned against a large circular table in the center of the room. Pan pulled out his cigarettes and lit his first of the evening. "Want one?" he asked Rob. His forces that were present were surprised by the question.

"No. Smoking has never been my vice, and I take it by their expressions you do not offer often."

"I do not, but I understand. I heard you prefer your liquid vices much more anyway."

"Actually, I prefer my vices to have long legs and smooth skin, but usually, the liquor is easier," Rob commented softly. He could feel Pan digging for information but was trying not to give any more away. Pan just smiled as he stood at the main table. "Now, what have you all come up with since I have been in prison?" Rob asked once they were all at the table.

He leaned over the table, looking at the outline of New Orleans. The team had drawn out the wall and gate with rough estimates of guard numbers per position. They had placed Pan's forces west of the main gate. He added the prison and its fortifications with information from Anpu. While John's fortress was placed on the northeast corner.

"So these are the main points of interest: the main gate, the prison, and John's mansion. The gate is what stands between us and a full army. Your friend's intel says the komodo control center is in the prison. Then, naturally, John's mansion is where he will wait for us when the time comes. Our main issue is dividing our forces without crippling another front," Pan summarized as he talked through the points.

"How many do we have?" Rob asked as he started to calculate the different strategies to employ.

"Outside the city, I have just under 1,300 soldiers ready to fight and die for the cause. Inside, I have my division commanders. Mancio says there are 342 people still healthy enough to fight for him, and the Asters pledge 88, not including the Mothers or Aliesha's strike force," Pan explained with a puff of smoke.

"1600 fighters to lay siege to the enemy's capital. One with 3,000 in the wings, including the komodos, is not promising. Especially if the citizens of New Orleans rally to their leader," Rob acknowledged as he looked over the map.

"My forces are up for the task," Pan assured.

"They might be, but they still have to cross the entire city and do so without stopping. Meanwhile, John can throw people at them in waves," Rob explained as he continued to work through plans in his mind.

"This is all we have unless you can create fighters from sewage," Mancio commented as he grabbed a seat. His sons and daughter stood close to him. When Mancio talked about creating soldiers, the gears clicked for Rob at last, but he did have one last condition before sharing.

"Pan, clear your commanders out of here except for Dani," Rob ordered. Pan hesitated for a moment before waving them out of the room.

"Why did I do that?" he asked once the door was shut behind the last commander. Rob stood for a moment as he figured out how to phrase it.

"You have a spy in your organization," he said after a moment.

"Rob, I said play nice. Remember?" Dani butted in before Pan could speak. Pan raised his hand before she could say another word.

"Dani, I promise I am, but John knew when Pan's forces were supposed to be here."

"He did?" Pan asked with another puff of smoke.

"Yes, in the prison, he knew that your forces would be here before his plan went into motion. I didn't even know when you would be here. Which means he got that information from your forces," Rob explained as the rest of the room sat in silence. Even Dani was unsure of what to say. Anpu smirked from the corner as if he knew something that no one else did.

"And you don't want the plan leaking," Pan assessed as he paced the room.

"Correct."

"So, I was right. But nonetheless, the soldiers do not need the entire plan. If you have a good one," Pan acknowledged.

"Do you know who it is?"

"No, my commanders were supposed to be on the lookout, but nothing. One of my captains went missing before we left, and I saw a hawk that tipped me off, but still nothing. I fear it was one of my commanders then."

"I doubt it's Khalil or the others. All of them have saved our lives so many times. Why would they wait until now to act?" Dani said.

"It is natural. With the size of our organization, leaks occur, but we cannot worry about that now. We need a plan," Pan replied with no emotion in his face.

"That is troubling, but yes, we have to move ahead. Now, my thought is we turn this city against John," Rob explained to the rest of the room. A few eyebrows raised, but there were no comments at first.

"How so?" Enrique asked to break the silence.

"We use the Asters' information network to tell the people the truth."

"And what is the truth? He is a psychopath?" Kathleen asked now that her Asters were involved.

"They already know that, but they don't know that John is the one that shot Irons 10 years ago," he admitted as those who knew stood silently, watching the others reel momentarily.

"He what…" Anna muttered as her jaw hung open.

"He pulled that trigger," Rob repeated.

"And how do you know? More importantly, how do we convince the people?" Mother Althea asked this time.

"He spelled out his admission with a series of bullets he has used over the last few months. The first one used on Irons."

"And why would they believe it?" Pan asked now.

"Because the Asters will print it. And even if they don't believe it, the seed will be planted, and hopefully, his other deeds and the threat of you will push people to the edge when we begin our attack," Rob explained, knowing how far-fetched it sounded. The room looked ready to tear the plan apart, but Mancio raised his hand first.

"Before we speak our peace. What is the rest of your plan?" he asked from his chair.

"Well, we hit multiple fronts. First, Aliesha's crew, Sam and Morgan, strike the prison to start a riot and release those wrongfully imprisoned while using that battle to go after the komodo control center. Just after that attack begins, Enrique, some of Pan's officers, and I will start a battle over by the hospital. We will use it as a safe zone for innocents and a halfway point for our injured. Once guards are diverted to the hospital, I want Dani and Pan to secure the gate. Lastly, Mancio will lead a group far east of the mansion, using the sewers and back alleys to position as flankers for when the main battle occurs at the mansion," Rob explained using pens to trace the plan out on the map.

"Sounds like a lot of hopeful thinking," Mancio rebutted after he had the whole plan explained.

"All we have is hope," Rob reminded him.

"My sons and daughters lost much of that hope after our last failure," Mancio started with a coldness that Rob did not anticipate.

"Well, I did not know about the Shadow Six last time. A group you still haven't explained to me," Rob hissed. He was aware of how the night prior went but knew there was more to that story. Mancio just gripped the table, frustrated by Rob's tone. Enrique placed his hand on his father's shoulder.

"They are a mysterious group. No one knows who they are except for the two you met. Supposedly, they hit targets that are not worth John's or his Executives' time all across the country," Enrique explained while holding onto his father.

"Wow, you guys really don't know anything." Anpu chuckled from the corner.

"And who are you?" Mancio snapped as Anpu approached the table at last.

"This is Anpu. I freed him from the prison, and he is the…original Executioner," Rob explained as the dagger eyes shot at him instantly.

"The original," Dani stuttered as the rest of the room put their hands on their weapons.

"That is right, cutie. But that is ancient history. John betrayed me, and now I want payback," Anpu explained, but Dani still approached him, placing her knife against his throat.

"How many of my friends did you kill?" she asked with a look Rob had never seen in her eyes. He had anticipated this reaction from some of them, but she was the last one he expected.

As she stood with her knife to his throat, he looked through her with cold eyes. She was ready to finish him there, but Rob grabbed her wrist.

"Ah, so you are that girl, aren't you," Anpu said at last as he realized why she was so hostile. "Now please understand, that dam was always going to be blown. If it wasn't me, it would have been another. But for my part, I do apologize."

Dani stayed tense, and Rob could feel her resisting his restraint, but he would not let her proceed. Rob eventually pulled her back with Pan's help, but Dani would not fully relax until Pan spoke.

"So, you have intel to share about the Shadow Six," Pan added as he helped pull Dani off of Anpu.

"Indeed. I trained 5 of them. There is Inesh with his two kittens. There is Xiaobo, the inventor. A mad scientist with a belly bigger than his brain. Then you have Widow. Basically, any place that offers the services of respectable ladies without an Aster tattoo is under her command. She is the head of Ascension's communication network as well. Then you have the Twins. The calm Older Sister is an explosive expert, while the brash Younger Brother makes weapons. Then, the one I never met is the spy. The very one in Pan's organization, but they only ever communicated with John directly, so I do not know the face," Anpu explained as he confirmed Rob's suspicions.

"As I feared," Pan muttered, putting out the dying cigarette.

"Well, that helps a little. I can anticipate where John will use them now," Rob instructed as he stayed hunched over the map.

"We cannot wait. A traitor is a risk to all of us!" Mancio demanded, slamming his fist on the table.

"Don't worry, old man. I will figure out how to work around it. For now, let's focus on creating some civil unrest," Rob ordered despite Mancio's disdain.

"Your arrogance will doom us," Mancio commented.

"You've said that before, but most of your people lived to see today, didn't they? Plus, you said I would command your people if we survived," Rob snapped back as he grew tired of Mancio's comments. Mancio was ready to speak again when Enrique gripped his father's shoulder.

"So what is the move?" Pan asked once Mancio had settled down.

"We use the Asters' printing operation to create flyers to fill the city with news of John's actions and inform them that you are coming. No reason to keep that a secret if John already knows."

"The ladies and the machines will be ready," Mother Kathleen assured.

"Good, that is all for now. I will write the rest of the orders once I have thought it through. We have what is left of tonight and tomorrow to prepare," he said, scanning the room making eye contact with every person. Each of them looked at each other with various levels of trust, but not a single word needed to be said before the room scattered except for Pan, Rob, and Dani. "So, you let me make the plan. Does that mean I have full command?" Rob asked when they were alone.

Pan paused as he considered Rob's words. "This morning, when Dani came to check her hideout for us, she spoke highly of you."

"That isn't an answer."

"No, it isn't. I still don't trust you, but you have been in this city longer and have our other allies' trust."

"I see we are on the same page."

"Dani told me." Rob looked at Dani, who could not look at either of them as they spoke.

"That…that doesn't surprise me, but I only ask that you work with me."

"Until you give me a reason not to. For now, I have things to take care of." Pan left the room to meet with Dirk. Dani followed him as she made her way out of the room. Leaving Rob to think on his own.

"Search every captain's room. There is a traitor among us, and I want it handled quietly," Pan informed Dirk, who did not question his leader. He began a search while the others in the facility helped take pictures of the bullets and print the flyers for dispersal.

Mancio spoke with Enrique in another corridor, "These people do not love this city like we do. I refuse to involve innocents, so I want you to start the evacuation."

"But we need people," Enrique replied.

"Enrique, I will not do it this way. This city has suffered enough, and we will not put it through more," Mancio lectured. His son wanted to argue but knew nothing would change his mind. He bowed his head and left.

With people acting outside his control, Rob went to find out where Dani had run to. In the day since the attack, the Asters had taken in the Sewer District with most citizens in the basement, but Sam, Morgan, and Dani were given a spot inside the mansion. He had to ask around to find which room was hers until he finally arrived at her door.

He knocked a few times before her voice answered, "Go Away!"

"Come now, Dani. We both know I won't do that," he replied as he leaned against the door. After a few moments, he heard a sigh and a click of the lock.

"You will if it is convenient for you." She begrudgingly opened the door. As he entered, he noticed that she had started to wind down and was washing her face. While she cleaned up, he could see the scars on her shoulders from the lashings he had to give her back in St. Louis.

"That's not fair."

"It is, but I'm done with this conversation. We have had it so many times, and I don't think you'll really change that part of you, so I'll just have to accept it." She returned her washcloth to the bathroom as Rob thought about his following words.

"I didn't want to leave this time, but there really wasn't another choice."

"There is always a choice, Rob. But like I said, I don't want this conversation again. I'm done with it. Why did you come here? To lecture me about telling Pan you didn't trust him or something else?"

"No, I'm over what you share. I came here to see if you were alright," he admitted as she sat on her bed, leaving him standing by the door looking at her. His eyes were soft as he tried to empathize with whatever she was feeling.

"You are worried about that interaction with this Anpu person."

"Yes, it seemed very personal."

Dani placed her hands behind her and leaned back on her bed, using them as support. "It was. He blew up a dam that killed many soldiers under my command and flooded an innocent city." He could see tears forming in her eyes as they closed. Rob went to sit next to her.

"How do you know it was him?"

"Because I remember that face and that voice. Anpu had disguised themselves as a helpless woman on the dam, and when I went to help, he jumped me. He beat me and then blew the dam, flooding everything. Had it not been for Khalil and Dirk, I would have been dead too." Despite the quiver and hurt in her voice, she did not let the tears fall from her eyes. He could feel the pain as she returned to the day she last saw Anpu.

"Dani," he said as he placed his arm around her. She dropped her head against his body as he held her tight.

"I swear I still hear the screams sometimes." He said nothing in response but held her closer. Now he understood why he was taken aback when she acted so rashly. He had seen himself in her actions. Dani was a better version of him for so long, but she was just as broken as he was. "And the worst part was I wanted to be happy today. I had you and Anna together again but became blinded by him." By this point, he felt a pair of tears falling.

"Then let's be happy, Dani. I haven't tried it in a while." He smiled. She chuckled at his words and raised her head after clearing her eyes.

"You are back," she mumbled softly.

"And what does that mean?"

"When you were gone, I talked to Anna, and she confirmed what I saw when I stopped in Despartian. She told me how the *you* we both knew disappeared," she replied, putting her hand to his heart when she said you.

"I was a little lost, but I was still there," he rebutted.

"No, you weren't Rob. Your body was there satisfying basic needs, but your mind hadn't returned yet. Then, I saw something closer to John than Rob in St. Louis."

"That's not fair."

"No, it isn't, but it is true. But I've listened to and watched you since leaving the museum. I've seen the man I knew come back to us. Yes, you have flaws and jagged edges, but this is you," she explained, placing her hand on his heart again. He interlocked his hand in hers and squeezed it tight.

"I'm not just back. I'm better," he claimed.

"How so?"

"I finally understand what makes me different from John," he answered as he looked deep into her eyes and smiled.

"And what is that, besides not being psychotic?" she asked with a slight laugh.

"I learned how to live for the living and find people to call family. I learned to love while he has isolated himself. He has walled off the world and become bitter as he mourned for those he can never bring back," he replied as he assured her with another one of his childish grins. His calmness filled the room, and despite the turmoil engulfing the city, she thought, at least for that moment, everything was going to be alright. However, she still had one question that nagged her.

"Are you planning on dying when you face John?" she asked with a directness that he did not anticipate.

"I don't plan on dying, but it is the likeliest outcome," he replied with a dry honesty.

"That is what I am afraid of." Her head fell slightly again as her hands gripped her pant legs.

"But trust me, Dani. I am fighting to live, but I have to be willing to sacrifice to beat a man with nothing left to lose," he explained as he held her hand again.

"Just don't die, don't leave me alone with Sam and Morgan."

"I don't plan on it, but if I have to sacrifice for you three, Anna, Pon, Gerald, Philip, and Kendra, I will without hesitation," he said.

"Don't forget Alexandra," Dani remarked softly.

"And Alexandra, but how do you know about her?" he asked. He did not intend to forget the little girl he had grown close to in Despartian, but she was not his priority. At 10 years old, he was sure she would forget him anyway. On the other hand, Dani realized she had opened her mouth too soon.

"She never told you." She sighed in a barely audible tone.

"Who never told me what?" he asked with a slight raise in the tone of his voice.

"Rob..." she began as her mind searched for the right words, "When the War started, Iris was going to join Anna and me but...but she had to stay in Despartian...she had to stay because...she was pregnant." The moment the words left her mouth, she clasped her hand over it. She wanted to take the words back but knew it was too late.

"That's impossible," he whispered as he rose. His legs were unstable, and he shook his head a few times. He pictured Alex for a moment and saw those blue eyes of her. He saw the dirty blonde hair, and he saw Iris. It was right there all that time, but no one told him.

"I'm sorry you found out like this, but I thought Anna, Iris, or Philip would have said something," Dani pleaded as he staggered towards the door. He bolted out of the room for fresh air and passed Anna on his way. She was unsure of what was occurring and entered Dani's room to see her with her face in her hands.

"What happened?" Anna asked.

"Why didn't anyone tell him about Alex?"

Rob made his way outside, unsure about how he was feeling. All he knew was that there was a twisting inside of him that he had to rid himself of. He was angry, filled with joy, sick, and depressed. He found a small bridge overlooking a stream and leaned over the railing. His thoughts ran faster than the water below. He tried everything to calm himself, but the secret was overpowering. There was a feeling that he would throw up, but it never came.

Iris had died next to him, and no one said anything. She had sent him many letters during the War, but he had heard nothing about a child. He could not fathom why it was a secret as it was not like her.

"What's with ya?" Sam asked him from behind. Her voice helped him return to the present for a moment. He could not be away from their conversation. She was just too annoying for that.

"Just sorting things out," he replied with a fake smile.

"For figuring things out, you ran stupid fast."

"I did indeed. I got big news and needed some fresh air."

"Why? Are you going to puke? I hate watching people puke," Sam asked as she took a step away from him.

"No, I'm good. I can feel myself calming down."

"Phew, so what type of news?" she asked now that he was relaxing.

Rob paused for a moment to figure out his answer. He hadn't lied to the girls before but was unsure what she would say about his news. On top of that, it was the first time he would tell someone he was a dad.

"I just discovered that Iris had my kid during the War."

"Oh my God…You have a kid!" Sam yelled, giving Rob a giant hug. It was not the anticipated reaction, but as he leaned into the hug, he found the warmth and comfort he needed.

"You seem happy," he commented as she finally let go of him.

"Why wouldn't I be? You'll be a great father, and I will be an awesome aunt." She smiled without hesitation. Anointing herself as an aunt minutes after he discovered his child.

"I wouldn't say that yet. I have been absent for 10 years of the girl's life. That's not really 'best dad' worthy yet."

"Butthead, I may not know your kid, but based on how you treat Morgan and I. I know that you are a great father already." She smiled.

Rob held back a tear as he looked at his favorite airhead. She could play dumb easily but knew how to pull his heartstrings.

"I appreciate it, Sam, but I still wonder why Iris hid this from me."

"Does it matter?"

"Of course it does. That is my child."

"But haven't you been preaching that the past is the past? You get the present moment, and that is it. So why does it matter what happened back then? She made a decision when she was young, and now you can make a call as an old man," she replied, citing lessons that he taught her during their training sessions. He was unsure what made him happier, the words or knowing she listened to him.

"You know, for a ditz. You can be clever."

"I learned from the biggest idiot around." Sam laughed as he shook his head and called her over for a big hug again.

"You know you will make a good aunt."

Chapter 24
Admission of Truth

That following morning, John woke up early and completed his everyday routine, spending extra time at his son's grave, knowing it could be the last time. In one more day, fate would decide if he was right. Rob's refusal to go for the kill and decision to show forgiveness had troubled him greatly. The questions returned to his mind, but the fight had already begun. There would be no turning back after lighting the Sewer District ablaze.

Once he returned to the office, he wondered what Rob would do and thought through the many strategies they used during the War. They had destabilized many strongholds together when their squad tore through East Asia. Still, none presented the same difficulty as New Orleans. John peered out his window and stared at the wall he had built. It should be impenetrable without artillery, something Pan did not have. All high-powered weapons were useless within and near the city's boundaries, meaning manpower would be critical. Everything was set, and he could not see Rob's option. As he thought, a knock came at the door.

"Come in," he commanded. Braden slinked in through the tiniest opening he could make. His tail firmly between his legs like a dog.

"I have bad news, sir," he said softly with his head bowed.

"Yes, I know Rob escaped," John claimed dismissively.

"Why yes, he did, but it wasn't just him," Braden responded with a more timid voice. John's brow twitched at the lack of directness Braden was using.

"And who else escaped?"

"Aliesha and…and…" Braden stuttered in terror.

"Spit it out, or I will gut you!" John yelled with a slamming of his fist.

"Anpu assisted him," Braden squeaked out at last. John was intrigued by the news. He went to sit in his chair with pyramided fingers.

"Now, that is a move I did not see coming. Anpu must have heard me talking to him. Still, he will not be well received given his former spot in our organization, so I am curious to see what happens."

"And what do you want us to do about the berdache?" Braden asked with restored confidence.

"Nothing. Anpu is a constant wild card that not even I can account for…But use that derogatory word again, and I cut out your tongue," John replied with a terrifying grin. Braden stepped back, realizing his mistake while the wheels turned in John's head.

"My apologies, sir. It was a term I grew up on, my mistake." Braden bowed as he spoke. "But what is our next order?"

"We wait."

"But, sir."

"You may leave Braden. And take several units back to the prison. If Anpu left with them, they know where the komodo command center is."

"As you command." Braden exited the room as swiftly as he could. Leaving John sitting in his chair.

"I wonder what you will do? And I wonder if your new friend will stay loyal," he said to himself as his foot tapped on the ground. As he sat with his thoughts, his eyes noticed a crowd outside his mansion's gate. These were not the soldiers, so he went to investigate.

At the front door of his mansion, he was met by a guard. "Sir, the people are demanding answers," the guard informed him as she handed him a piece of paper. On it was a picture of his bullets and a story about them, along with word that Pan, the Revolutionary, was at the gates waiting for action within.

"So, this is the plan. Quite interesting," he mumbled as he crumpled the sheet and threw it to the side.

"What shall we do?" the guard asked.

"Nothing. I will speak to them," he insisted as he exited his mansion to see the horde gathering in front. They were shouting over one another as he climbed a nearby stump. A few people tried to throw things at him, but he knocked them all out of the way.

"Citizens! I understand how this piece of paper can confuse you! Especially when it is printed by such a reliable source as the Asters, but I ask that you all disperse for the time being! Shouting in this crowd accomplishes nothing, and I will address these stories at 3 o'clock! I give you my word that you will have the full truth!" he shouted louder than those in the crowd. The crowd began to quiet down after he spoke, but none wanted to leave until he motioned for the guards to join him. Whispers were spread throughout, and slowly, people started to leave.

Once the crowd was gone, John returned to his offices and mapped out his strategy. He had not anticipated Rob using the bullets in this manner. Still, John had a response that would send the opposition into their own turmoil. Then, his messenger bird returned with sparse intel. The spy could only give him the target locations and the anticipated numbers of all groups. As John looked over his city map, he thought through the combinations Rob would use and sketched out his plan.

As John worked through the different plans, he remembered the day Rob and John were taught how to play shogi by a pair of monks their squad had saved. At first, they did not understand how it differed from chess. Still, as they practiced with one another, they truly began to see the complexity in the drops and using your opponent's pieces.

To John, this was one last game for them to play, and it had started back in Despartian, but without John's knowledge, Rob had already moved into the middle game by taking Anpu and the people of New Orleans. Now, he had to take and flip pieces as well. This time, the victor would determine the future rather than who had the overnight lookout shift.

John wrote down the information from his spy and created counters to Rob's plan. Though Rob had taken a few pieces, John still had the advantage in numbers and flexibility. John did not worry about how many pawns were sacrificed while he knew Rob would play it safe to safe to save as many lives as possible. This meant Rob would be in the heart of the action, easy to access and confront. Rob's compassion would pin him to only a few strategies that John could anticipate and counter. He wrote instructions, returned his note to the spy's bird, and then pressed a button.

Soon after the button was pressed, Ex entered the room. "I hear my predecessor has chosen the losing side."

"They have, but that is not why I called you here."

"What do you need?"

"Tomorrow, I want you to stay by the mansion. Rob will split the forces to the gate and prison, so I need you here to help me clean up the scraps. Meanwhile, the Shadow Six will be spread to the different battle points."

"Understood, and what will we do about the rumor circling the city. Apparently, it has created a lot of unrest."

"Yes, it was an interesting strategy." He paused for a moment. "I want the Widow to activate the emergency broadcast. I will give a speech to turn the city back in our favor."

"The broadcast room will be prepared for you."

"Good, and have the vipers clean up the loudest voices however you deem necessary. Some will respect my admissions, but those who do not will fear our power."

"Threats will be eliminated," Ex spoke coldly before exiting the room to follow the commands.

The following hours passed like seconds to John as he wrote out his final commands and distributed them to the forces as needed. Time continued to pass, and he left his office when his clock rang quarter to three. He marched through his mansion with boas and vipers lining the halls as he made his way to a room in the basement. Then, a pair of vipers led him to a broadcast booth, where he sat in an old leather chair. The vipers finished turning on the equipment and alerted him when it was time.

Right at three, he flicked a switch that turned on his microphone and warmed up speakers spread across the city. The static of the speakers echoed to every corner of the city, including the sewers where the rebels waited to hear John's answer.

Rob took a deep breath as he worried about John's reply. The static hummed in the system as his breath came through the speakers. John said nothing for a moment and let the silence fill the city. Parents hushed their children as the anticipation gripped them all. Then, at last, he spoke words that could never be withdrawn:

"People of New Orleans and those who have visited our lovely city. This morning, the Asters released a flyer that claimed I started the War by killing Jeffrey Irons, and they used a couple of old shell casings as proof. They spelled an admission that came with a story attached to each one. This story and this rumor…is all true.

"All those years ago, I was a soldier in the US military, with some of the highest clearance due to my ability to complete missions that others could not. One of these missions was to kill Irons because the government feared him. Years of corruption at the top and a collapsing economic system bred by greed, race riots, and disease had made them all paranoid. They saw this black man collecting guns to stop the violence as a threat. He was doing what they could not, and they twisted his mission, so they sent me to kill him. A group of old men gave me that order and threatened my imprisonment if I did not complete it. So, I followed my order like a good soldier, as it was just one person, and I never imagined what would come of this. And for that, I was jailed in the very prison that still exists southwest of here. I was detained as I was too dangerous to them. With me in prison, they let my wife and young child get raped and murdered for being black while I was rotting. Then, when the War grew into an international affair, I was released to save them. I did this by completing missions with a group that others could never imagine.

"I am a killer, but since I was freed from their grasp, I have brought a reckoning to all those who caused this disaster. I hunted down and killed the men who gave me the orders. I took Ascension from the greedy elites who created the turmoil and bribed the men who ordered me. Then, I used Ascension to rebuild this world. Did I do it peacefully? No, not all the time. I had guards eradicate gangs and mafias that tore cities apart for power. I had rebels killed in their sleep to stop the bombings of your places of business. I have shed blood for all of you. I shed blood because none of you should face what we did before. I created an empire to ensure peace across this world and have been working to unify everyone.

"It was not until Pan arrived that conflicts arose again on a large scale. But I understand his qualms. He believes that I have limited freedom. He says I have turned the gun on whoever I choose if they refuse my message, but he airs my sins while ignoring the good I have done. He ignores the railroads and electrical grids that I restored. He ignores me eradicating crime rates. And he ignores my push for inclusion. My guard forces in every Ascension city represent the people they serve, as any race, sexuality, or religious background is welcome. I did what no US government or other world government policy ever did. Economically, every Ascension city is equitable, as everyone can afford to eat and live. Those who cannot refuse Ascension but still stay within the walls. And that is the truth.

"However, it is not the only truth you need to know. Those who stand against me have truths of their own. So, let's start with Pan. He pretended to be a man who saves and shows mercy, but that was not his role in the War. He was part of the "clean-up" crew, as we called them. Yes, he buried bodies, but their most important duty was to sit with the enemies, civilians or soldiers, and collect intel as he pretended to save their lives. Then, when they told him what he needed, he executed them. Wives who were barely alive were interrogated while they bled out just so we knew where their husbands' base was. Then killed in cold blood. Even now he uses the deaths of his soldiers to build a world in his own image not theirs.

"Then there is Mancio, the man who loves New Orleans. He would do anything for his citizens. But it is not out of love, but guilt. For me to kill Irons in this city, the mayor had to sign off on it. That way, the police would not intervene with the mission. That mayor was Mancio. He signed the piece of paper that made Irons' killing possible. The last line of common sense and defense that doomed Irons that day.

"And finally, there is a third man that this city might not know, but the forces know. His name is Rob Doran. He was my brother-in-arms, and I used my blood to save his life, and he used his to save mine as we turned the tide of the War. However, his hands were stained before I ever met him. They were stained, and he could never wash the blood off.

"You see, Minneapolis was the last northern stronghold of the Reverter faction, and it was impenetrable. However, Rob knew they were arrogant and wanted to take Despartian to gain access to the Mississippi River again.

"Unity would not surrender the city, but the city's favorite son had other plans. He had Unity leak information that the city would be unguarded to draw them out. Then Unity marched north and left the city unguarded. The Reverters took the bait and attacked their prize. At the same time, Unity flanked and took Minneapolis before attacking the Reverter forces in the less fortified Despartian. It was a move that may have saved millions, but he did it by sacrificing the city where his friends and his fiance lived. If he will sacrifice his fiance for victory, ask yourself why he is turning you all against me.

"You who have lived in harmony and peace. He is not your protector. He is a man who is sacrificing you to stop me," John monologued while the city sat in silence for the speech. John spoke with conviction but softness. He took a moment to breathe as the city absorbed what had already been said. The forces in the sewer could not believe what was happening, and Rob's heart had completely sunk. Then John spoke one final line:

"Tomorrow, New Orleans will be a battlefield, and you have a choice: join them, stay with me, or leave." And with that, John turned off the speakers. His eyes closed as he imagined what his opponents were doing now. He grinned as he headed back to his office. At the same time, Ex had the vipers listening to the word on the streets, and those who still dissented were marked for elimination.

The three men that John called out stood in shock. The main sewer office had been cleared of all the typewriters and filled with rebels who listened to every word. None of them expected John to be so open and honest. Nor did they know he knew everything. The three men were silent as the rebels behind them started to whisper and appear disgruntled. On top of their forces, a few city citizens had been invited to discuss what would happen, but now they looked unsure. Everything was blowing up in their faces.

"Did you know about this, Father?" Enrique asked as the first person brave enough to speak. Mancio just hung his head.

"And you. You lied about what you did," Dirk stated while his fist tightened. Pan just lit a cigarette and thought.

"So, that was your secret," Anna pointed out. Rob just turned to look at the hundreds around them. He ignored Anna for a moment and grabbed a chair to stand on top of.

"Everyone! Please, I need a moment. Before you allow John to sway your mind, let me speak," Rob called. The room grew quiet to give him time. Some had started to leave the room before he spoke, but others wanted to hear his rebuttal. "As John did, I will come clean as well. It was my idea to sacrifice Despartian during the War. It was my call to pull our forces out to put an end to the northern fight, one that had cost millions their lives. But he did not tell you everything. He did not tell you about the forces that were supposed to come from Madison to support the city but were delayed by another general's orders. He did not tell you about me abandoning the fight before it was finished so I could return to the city to save who I could. And he did not tell you about the years I've spent avoiding that truth and seeing the faces of all those I knew who died.

"He told you a part of the truth, but he knew the rest and didn't tell you. And he didn't tell you because that does not fit his narrative. I need you all to remember this important part of John's game. He may tell you the truth, but pieces are always missing, which is why you are here now. You are here because he burned the Sewer District and claimed it was to squash rebellion but does not mention the women and children who died. You are here because this city or the cities you came from were given pieces of freedom, but he did not tell you what you had to sacrifice.

"He says those who are not fed are those who reject him, and that is only partially true because some of them are just those who spoke against his name once. He had you turn on your own before he turned on you, so you came to stand with us. You stand with us not because of that note sent today but because you already had the seeds of rebellion in you. Those letters were just the nourishment your seed needed to grow. Do not lose sight of the crimes he has committed, as he blinds you with our sins and uses smoke to make his accomplishments look better. With that said, I give you the same options as John. You can stay with me, fight for him, or leave the city. But you must know he told me there would be nowhere to run before I escaped the prison. The world will burn if he wins. So please fight with me as I stand in the front and protect as many of you as possible. And if that isn't enough, I have one last thing to show you!" he announced as he stepped down and grabbed a bag he had kept in the office as backup. He pulled a group of letters from his bag and started to hand them out to whoever was closest. Then, he stood on the chair again.

"I found these when I was in the hospital. These are handwritten letters from the komodos before they were weaponized. They did it for their families or they were kidnapped, and none of them want to be there anymore. That is why he has to control them. So, when we take the control room, they will fight for us instead. Now find the families and give them out. Make the people understand what is still in the shadows," Rob explained as the letters were passed to the elected representatives. As people recognized names and read stories, their wavering wills solidified again. The representatives were the first to leave with several of the letters as other soldiers spread out to find the families of the komodos.

The room seemed to calm back down after Rob spoke, and now he hoped the city would respond similarly. Even if they did not join, he hoped they would evacuate. Meanwhile, Pan and Mancio stood speechless. Each of them had questions, but when the moment came, he took control of the forces and united them.

The room cleared except for Rob, Pan, Mancio, Anna, and Dani. Mancio approached Rob first. "I have kept many secrets from you, and time after time, you show me that you love this city despite only arriving a week ago. I will send my people to recruit as many as I can. You have our blades." Mancio shook Rob's hand and headed out to handle things with his family. He went to Enrique first to undo his order from the day prior and was surprised his orders had been ignored already.

Rob then approached Pan. "Tell me about the different commanders and why we should trust them. I need to know before I hand out the new orders." Pan's cigarette continued to burn as he thought about the order.

"Dirk was a bandit and mercenary running attacks when I found him in a southern prison. Gina was a founding member with me. She and her daughter have often prided themselves as humanitarians running into cities starved by Ascension rule. Dani, you know better than I. Catori is my stealth commander. She runs the attacks on John's supply chains and keeps her ear to the ground to rout out any Ascension cells that appear on the West Coast or internationally. Finally, Tank is my loud mouth. He is an extremely charismatic leader who has done much to recruit our people in the East. He has also handled our battles in old New York and Miami, where we fought with John and criminal organizations to control the coasts." Pan laid out in quick succession.

"There was one more person, wasn't there?"

"That is Khalil. He is a mute but an outstanding captain. He has saved my life numerous times," Dani explained.

"So a mercenary, old woman, a stealth operative, loud mouth, and a mute. Who do you think the spy is?"

"It is Dirk."

"Why him? Isn't he your right hand?" Rob asked as Dani started to process the thought as well.

"Yes, but before the speech, I went to his room to search it as I told him to search everyone else last night and found this," Pan explained, pulling out an engraved knife that was covered in blood.

"What is this?"

"It is the blade of the captain that went missing before we left, and it was in Dirk's stuff."

"So, what should we do?" Rob asked as he paced around the room.

"I have a poison that I will slip into his drink. It will not kill him but weaken him. That way, if he is not the traitor, he can still fight the grunts but will not be able to stop me."

"Then he will stay close to you tomorrow."

"Indeed, I will watch him; if he makes a move, I will kill him. And if he dies in battle because of the poison, he gets the end he desired." Pan pulled out another cigarette before leaving the room as well.

"If it is Dirk, Pan will be crushed," Dani said once her leader had left the room.

"Yes, but we need to be ready for it to be whoever," Rob replied as Anna approached them.

"Can we talk about Despartian?" Anna asked as she pulled their attention away from the spy.

"So, no more secrets, I guess," he said softly as he bit his lip. The man who had just commanded the rule had fallen submissive to the two of them. He awaited their judgment despite his own anger about Alex. Both said nothing at first and merely approached him. He waited to hear their disapproval, but instead, they hugged him.

"Promise us no more secrets," Dani whispered while they gripped him.

"Why are you hugging me? I put everyone in danger. Hell, apparently, my daughter was at risk that day," Rob replied as his eyes teared at the realization that his fiancé and a daughter he did not know about were almost killed that day.

"Rob…stop it!" Anna commanded as she let go. "Stop blaming yourself for that. They would have landed on that plan regardless, but they burdened you. And because of it, we lost you."

"Lost me?" he asked as he wiped his eyes.

"Yeah, I now understand what happened to the boy we knew. You had to kill him that day to be the fall guy, just like John was," Anna explained to him.

"I…I don't understand. How can you forgive me so easily?" Rob asked this time.

"We forgive you because you chose to shoulder all the blame after that day and waited for forgiveness for something only you can forgive." Dani put her hand on his heart again. "So, forgive yourself because we were never angry." Rob briefly sat with that reply as he thought about the past few years. He had blamed himself and carried that guilt for so long, but she was right.

"And Rob, I'm sorry for not telling you the truth, but Iris already knew you carried too much on your shoulders," Anna admitted after giving him a moment.

"But she is my daughter."

"She is, but were you ready for a daughter? And would you have come back alive if you were thinking about her?" Anna asked. He just shook his head, knowing she was right. His mind was overwhelmed in just that brief moment when he thought about her during the Despartian attack. Had he known before, the guilt would have destroyed him entirely.

"We love you, Rob, but you need to stop carrying the demons on your own. Let us help, and let Iris help," Dani said as she went to grab a case out of her room. When she returned, she handed it to him. Inside, he found his old military vest and a dagger Iris gave him before basic training.

"I thought I pawned this for whiskey." Rob smiled as he flashed the weapon that still had traces of blood embedded in it.

"You did, but Philip went to retrieve it after he found out. He told me that it was from Iris," Anna explained. Rob began to tear up as he looked at the hilt Iris had engraved with the words 'Mo Shíorghrá.'

"What does that mean?" Dani asked when she saw his eyes tearing.

"It's an old Irish phrase. Iris always knew how I enjoyed my Gaelic heritage, but the message is between her and me." He smirked while wiping his eyes.

"Fine, but let me clean this mothball up," Dani said as she picked the vest up with two fingers and held it far from her.

Afterward, they all retired to their rooms. Most were training as Rob wrote out the orders he would hand out the following day. He already knew where he wanted some people, but as he wrote the plans, he had to think through all of John's counters. He had to plan for one of Pan's people to betray them. While Dirk had rubbed him wrong earlier in his journey, he doubted the assessment. His heart beat fast as he recalled the day he ordered Unity forces out of Despartian. His thoughts were heavy as he grew aware that these new orders would send hundreds to their death. Sitting in his room, he leaned back to breathe. He meditated on the orders for an hour before finalizing them. There was no going back.

Part 3
The Calamity

Chapter 25
Day of Reckoning

*R*ob saw himself walking on the misty beach. He moved slowly but in peace, as he walked into the void. Then he heard a scream in front of him. He rushed ahead and found it was not mist but smoke that filled the air. The city in front of him was burning as bodies littered the street. His hands were now covered in blood, and his body was torn to pieces.

"Rob, why didn't you make it in time?" Carly's voice called as she walked towards him. He looked at his dead friend, the first to die by the Eye's hand. Her body slouched to the ground and turned to ash. While he passed hundreds of bodies.

"Why are you two still alive?" Gene, Jackson, Rick, Chen, and Dave's voices said as their bodies lay burnt and torn. The five men who fought with him on Shadow Squad were all gone, with just John and Rob remaining.

Another scream echoed in the air. He ran this time, passing the bodies of the De Luca family, the Cairo Butcher, Braden, and Kenneth. He could not find the source as the fire raged across the landscape. The bodies of Pan's commanders and captains covered the ground as komodos lay next to them.

"Did we win?" Pon asked Rob as he emerged from the smoke. He grabbed Rob and fell to the dirt, where he died next to Anna. This time, he heard a different wail as he stumbled across Aliesha, who knelt over her friends.

"They were all I had left," she said as she turned to him. Littered with stab wounds that should have killed her already. Only anger kept her up before burning up with the Asters. He continued to pass the bodies of Pan, Kathleen, Althea, and Mancio's family. All turned to ash in front of him.

"Rob, we weren't ready," Morgan and Sam called as both girls fell into his arms. Both smiled at him until they vanished before they could touch his face again.

"Die!" Dani's voice screamed in the distance as Rob heard the sound of metal against metal. Rob ran and found Dani fighting John as Iris lay in the dirt, barely breathing.

"She was my friend!" Dani yelled as she struck ferociously at John, who said nothing. He took her swings and deflected them before placing his blade into her gut. She fell back and landed next to Iris. Rob ran to them both and kissed their foreheads as they disintegrated.

"And here we are, alone again. Just as we are meant to be," John proclaimed as he raised his arms to show Rob the destruction around them. Nothing was left alive or standing except for them. Rob knelt defeated, as all that he loved was nothing more than ash.

"Don't listen to him. You are never alone if your heart stays open to love," Mark whispered from the ashes as a gust blew the fire and ash around. It twisted around as John laughed at his defeated opponent. Ex soon appeared next to their boss to do what John would not.

They lunged at him, but the wind consumed the Executioner and threw them to the sea before they could strike. While the ash began to take shape around a tiny light stolen from the flames. It was not a large figure, but it reached its hand out to Rob.

"Daddy?" Alex's young voice said as her dirty blonde hair took shape and her sky blue eyes looked deep into his. He grabbed her hand as he rose to the shock of John. He took another look at Alex and saw the ghosts of everyone and heard them all say one at a time, "Finish it."

Rob grabbed his knife and lunged at John.

***

And as he made contact, he woke up. It was about four in the morning, and only a few night guards remained awake. To calm his mind, Rob walked the empty streets. Climbing a nearby building to look over the city again. Wondering how many people had abandoned the city and how many would stand with him. John's speech was convincing even to Rob. He had joined this fight so late that he hoped he was on the right side. Ascension and John had done a lot of good for the world, and he had no idea what Pan would actually do. Especially, after hearing John's warning on a "world built in his image."

When he returned to the base, his first stop was the room of Morgan and Sam. It took them several knocks for them to finally wake up.

"Why are you here so early?" Sam yawned while Morgan rubbed her eyes.

"Get dressed. Your team moves out first," Rob ordered as he handed them their orders. Then he leaned in to hug them each. No one said another word. There was no need to. He then gave a similar instruction to Aliesha and her team. Team A was organized in the main sewer room before heading out.

Rob's next stop was Enrique's room. He passed him the orders and the names of the other people who would be a part of Team B, with them acting as a distraction. He let Enrique gather strong soldiers to fight with them as Rob passed along the rest of his orders.

Next, Rob stopped at Mancio's room. The only one that was awake and waiting for him. Mancio told Rob to come in while he took a final drag from his pipe. Rob handed him the note and left. His journey would be the longest and most important, requiring most soldiers.

The last stop was Dani's room. He knocked twice, and she opened the door with his vest in her hands. She hand-cleaned it and repaired the few holes made by bullets and knives during the War. She also recolored it black with maroon patches on the shoulders.

"What are those?"

"The wings of your angel." She smiled.

"You can't draw," he joked as she punched him in the arm. Once their laugh was exchanged, he passed her the orders that she read promptly.

"Good luck."

"We'll need more than that. But promise you will meet me at the compound at the end. I no longer want to do this without you," he told her with a slight grin.

"I promise. Just don't do anything stupid before I get there," she countered with her own grin.

"Would I ever?" He shrugged as he headed back down the hall. It was time for him to get ready now as well.

"That's what I was afraid of," she whispered as she watched him leave. The teams all said their goodbyes and left in the silence of the morning.

Team A was the first to arrive at the prison. They used the tunnel Aliesha, and Rob escaped the other day to avoid detection. John had placed a few guards inside that Aliesha and Tia quickly eliminated. Their main objective was to reach the komodo command center and shut it down. Morgan was entrusted with the Asters' stolen key during Peace Week, and they all hoped it would open the door. Aliesha had the watch synchronized with all the other teams, and when the hour struck, the forces exited the tunnel.

Aliesha led the way early as they hugged the prison walls and snuck around the large diameter. They first saw a group of vipers guarding the main gate with two long-ranged fighters up top. Aliesha sent Tia first to take out the long-ranged fighters and alarm system with her throwing knives. She was quickly followed by the others, who dispatched the vipers efficiently.

They quickly pushed through the gate and entered the facility without much noise. The five moved in unison past the first gate. It took two more guard checkpoints before the alarm was finally rung, and everything was set into motion. While the other four battled, Kya snuck into a guard room. There, she grabbed the keys to the first-floor jail cells. The ladies fought through guards as they opened up the cells and handed the prisoners weapons seized from the guards' bodies. The hopeless men and women were quick to join the riot. Though a few did run as soon as their cell opened. With the prisoners at their back, the ladies overwhelmed the unprepared guards and quickly pushed through the first floor.

"Things are going well," Kya stated as she kicked the teeth out of a guard's mouth.

"So far, but we have bigger foes still ahead," Aliesha replied as she sent her dagger nails through a pair of guards.

When they hit the second floor, the team ran into the first guardian komodo and a pair of captains that reorganized the troops behind it. The five and the prisoners that joined them stood at the bottom of the steps as they waited for the guards to charge in. The counter came quick, with the komodo joining in the fight. His hits sent the prisoners flying and fleeing. Kya worked to open more shackles, but the factory floor was more problematic to maneuver for her and forced her farther away from her allies. All the while, the komodo tossed the equipment and bodies at the rioters.

While the prison team moved through the first floor and reached their first roadblock, Team B arrived at the hospital. Enrique, Anpu, and two officers of Pan's army, Khalil and Catori, surveyed the space around them. At the same time, Rob snuck in to find Clarissa. He found Thomas and Jackie first, and they led him to the office where Maki and she were working.

Maki was the first to see him. "What is this?" he asked with a snarl. Clarissa turned to see Rob with the siblings.

"Rob, why are you here?" She tried to escort him out, but he stood his ground.

"Clarissa, I need you to prepare a cure for the komodos and this hospital for the wounded or helpless," he explained with no care of Maki's presence.

Maki started to put the pieces together. "Rob…cure for komodos…you're him! I must report this to…" he began before Clarissa dropped him with a single punch.

"Thomas, tie him up in the back closet," Clarissa ordered. The siblings dragged Maki to a broom closet in the office. "Now, what is going on? I heard you had been imprisoned."

"I was, but now we are making our move. Dr. Hakimi is supposed to join you upon entering the city. Once that is done, we will need a place for the injured and a jump-start on the komodo cure," Rob instructed.

"I understand. Most doctors here will treat anyone, and the guards cleared out since the command center moved," she assured. "And Rob."

"Yes."

"Will you kill him?"

"I don't want to, but I will stop him."

"Then you will have to kill him. I have not known him for as long as you, but we grew close for a while, and I know he will drag us all down if you don't finish this," she explained as she spoke from her heart. He could hear the pain in her voice, finally realizing the deeper connection between them. He placed his hand on her shoulder and nodded before he left.

As Rob exited the building, Enrique and a few soldiers ambushed a guard unit. At the same time, the other officers did the same. The team intentionally left a single unit untouched so that they could call for reinforcements. Then they cleared the few civilians out of the hospital courtyard and hunkered down until they heard the gate was secured.

It took only moments for a horde of guards to consume the square with several komodos. Enrique and Rob each went for a komodo as the others attacked the guards that outnumbered them.

As Team B hunkered down and awaited more forces, the prison five fought as if they were fifty and only had an issue with the guardian komodo until Tia stepped up.

"You four need to go. I'll take care of him," she volunteered as she sent small explosives at the komodo to draw its attention.

"Don't be a fool!" Aliesha yelled as she stabbed a guard.

"This is the price, Liesh. If we stay here, everyone else will be overwhelmed by komodos," she insisted as the komodo's attention was directly on her now. She ran and drew the beast away from her friends. Clearing the path to the next floor.

"Alright, let's move," Aliesha commanded as she led the charge to the next floor. She turned back once to see her friend fighting off the beast. Tia used the machinery and surroundings to her advantage in the long-distance fight while the others pushed on, and their riot grew, drawing more vipers and boas to the prison. With two battles raging, guard forces grew thin across the city.

Once a division exited the guard tower at the gate, Team C saw their opportunity. Pan whistled, and a fire bomb was heaved from the outside, drawing the guards' attention. They turned to fight the approaching forces. While they did this, Dani led an assault on the gate from the inside. Pan and Dani led a few soldiers into the guard's quarters while Pon and Dirk distracted guards from outside the wall. The pair had been snuck back to communicate the plan with Gina, who led the outside forces from a distance.

Pan and Dani met heavy resistance inside the gate's guard tower, but he showed why he led the revolutionaries, and she earned her position as second commander. They marched through the guard tower using the tables and beds inside to create environmental advantages to compensate for their low numbers.

Pan distracted five guards while Dani reached the gate control. She took out two more and cranked the gate switch. The gate flung open, and yells of a thousand soldiers rang in the sky. They charged at the gate as arrows and spears filled the air from the wall and Pan's forces. The guards at the gate were quickly cleared out.

Once the forces controlled the gate, Anna's medics rushed to treat those who could be saved. However, they only had a moment to breathe before a siren filled the air. John's reinforcements would arrive quickly, and they had to push into the city.

Kenneth, Inesh, and a legion arrived at the gate minutes after it had been taken. Kenneth cut down three revolutionaries with a single swing of his blade, and his diamond-covered gloves broke skulls as he punched through the opposition. His armor was large and so heavy that the weight would crush an ordinary man. All while his komodos tossed bodies out of their way. The regular soldiers started to fall back as the commanders stood their ground. Pan assessed the situation before giving orders.

"Alright, I need everyone to listen carefully. Dirk, Pon, and Tank will stay with me to draw attention while Dani leads everyone else to the capital. Rob needs you for the final battle," Pan ordered as the group began to divide.

"But Pan, we need you too," Dani stated as Kenneth grew closer.

"He does not need me as much as he needs you, and you know it," Pan assured. She gritted her teeth for a moment before conceding at last.

"Alright, everyone else, follow me!" she yelled. Inesh called for his tigers to go after Dani, but Tank engaged them first.

"Now, now stay here, kitties." Tank grinned as he held off the beasts with his spear and blade. Meanwhile, Inesh was sent flying by Pon.

"Attack!" Kenneth shouted. The shoulders went to fight the komodos and other guards while Dirk and Pan went for Ken. Dirk led the way to the Executive by cutting down any force in their way. During this, Pan kept an eye on Dirk, who was notably slower from the water he drank earlier, poisoned by Pan. Seeing that his back was covered, Pan engaged Ken blade-to-blade.

While Pan locked horns with Ken, the actual traitor was making their move. Rob and Catori were holding the west side of the hospital courtyard together, and their line was pushing John's forces back. Then, out of nowhere, an explosion ignited in the middle of them all.

"Hold the line! We need to sure up the hole," Rob shouted as he ran to support those affected by the explosion. As he ran, he turned to Catori. "That looked like it came from behind the line."

"It did, but who?" They searched the battlefield, looking for where the explosive came from. Neither had seen anything thrown, and no one called it out. As they fought, Catori saw Khalil out of the corner of her eye. He approached the commander and Rob swiftly with his blade drawn. He dove for Rob, but she jumped in the way before he managed to strike, costing her her right hand. Rob was still engaging another guard when Khalil went to strike again, barely halted by Enrique and his sickle. Rob disengaged and pulled Catori to the hospital's doors.

"I need to stop him," she cried out as Rob wrapped her hand.

"No, we need to stop the bleeding. Enrique can handle it," Rob told her as Thomas came out of the hospital with supplies for the fighters. "Take care of her," he ordered as he took some of the supplies to the others on the battlefield.

He saw the smoke coming from the gate and checked a watch he had stored in his pocket. It was time for them to move. He went after the komodo in the group and stabbed the eye, dropping the modified guard and clearing a path. He jumped on the komodo's fallen body and ordered his troops, "Everyone! It is time for us to move! Push towards the capital!" He raised his blade and pointed north to the mansion.

Those not engaged at the moment shifted into attack positions. No longer were they just hunkering down to survive. Now, they would be attacking. Khalil wanted Rob's head, but Enrique would not let him pass. He protected Rob's back as the forces moved.

"Make sure you catch up when you wipe the floor with him," Rob told Enrique as they headed out. Enrique never looked back or responded. He just charged at Khalil.

Chapter 26
The Surge

Only the guardian komodo and Tia remained on the prison's second floor. The komodo launched bodies, machinery, and anything else at her as it tried to approach her, growing angrier as its hard skin started to bleed from her barrage of knives. Unfortunately, her supply of knives was depleting. All while her own body was growing tired. None of the komodo's boulders had landed flush yet, but enough of them had grazed her to do damage.

As Tia labored on the second floor, the group ran into the second komodo on the floor below. With the tighter corridor from the prison cells, the beast had created a choke point. This time, Kya jumped in to distract the komodo.

"You can't waste any more time," she declared as she jumped over the komodo's swing. She snuck behind it and struck the back of the neck, distracting it enough to draw it down one of the few side corridors on the floor.

"Kya…" Sam whispered as she watched the one who had trained her the past few days take on an opponent not meant for her. Kya's style did not fit the fight, but she was willing to do anything for Aliesha, who pushed on without hesitation.

They hoped it would be smooth sailing to the control room now that the guardians were gone and the prisoners outnumbered the guards within. At this point, those who had tried to escape were running into the guards arriving from the mainland and forced to fight.

Everything was progressing as planned when Rob and Dani reunited in front of the mansion. Both of them had fought through the city to reach the mansion. Most of the streets had been abandoned, but John had positioned guards at several spots to brutalize the forces. Still, the run was relatively smooth as they exited the city streets and rebuilt buildings to reach the large grass field that was once part of the city before the War.

The gates to the mansion were open as the field in front of them was filled with hundreds of guards and several komodos led by the Twins and Widow. Rob and Dani looked at the forces in front of them and the tired bodies emerging from the city streets behind them. No soldier seemed to waver as they looked at what awaited them.

Rob walked ahead and stood between both sides as thousands of eyes looked at him. His staff on his back the wind whipped the ash from the burning buildings in the air around him. He stood just outside the buildings and looked at what was ahead. They were outnumbered heavily and he could feel the fear from his side as they looked ahead. John's forces were yelling and hollering as they saw their advantage. That was until a sound came from the east and Mancio appeared with his soldiers and hundreds of citizens, from young to old, all ready to fight. Rob's body ached as blood dripped from several points, but he pointed his staff towards the mansion window overlooking the field. Anticipating John to be waiting for him there but saw a figure exit the mansion. John strolled out and stood on the slightly elevated steps, staring at Rob. They could not truly lock eyes, but both could feel the other staring. Rob stood in his blood-stained black vest with his knife at his side, while John stood proud with a shiny silver vest and his dual broadswords drawn. A red sash hung from his shoulder as he flashed his ruthless grin again.

"Shall we," John mouthed from the steps. Rob lowered his staff, and both sides charged in. The Aster Mothers went after Widow, while the Twins locked horns with Hennrick and Ava. Leaving the komodos to the other leaders of the rebellion.

John and Rob had sights only for one another, but first, they had to cross the battlefield. Rob had the more difficult task as he had komodos to deal with, but Dani did her best to stay by his side and guide him through. Rob made a quick mockery of the boas that tried to step in front of him. While John played with his opponents. He danced around without swinging and then would drive in, cutting three or four at a time. It was clear that both of them were on different tiers compared to anyone else on the battlefield.

As Rob, Dani, and Mancio engaged John in front of the mansion, the battle at the gate was coming near its end as only the best on both sides remained. Most of Pan's people had abandoned the area for the mansion, leaving the few still there exhausted. Dirk did his best to keep most guards off of Pan, but he was on an island, and fatigue was mounting. Pan had started to trust him again but worried that the traitor was still at his back.

This gave Ken an advantage he did not need. He was already an overpowering monster whose blows sent Pan flying back even when they were successfully blocked. Pan was barely able to stand, but Ken just kept charging.

While Pan and Dirk worked to handle Ken, Tank had issues dealing with both of the tigers. They worked in unison to keep him on the retreat. Forcing him to rely on Pon, who was colliding with Inesh. Inesh was breathing heavily as he discovered the metal-armed man was not a pushover.

"Why fight?" Inesh panted as Pon calculated his next move.

"Because I am strong enough to save the people I love this time," he replied.

"And what will that accomplish? If you win, someone will oppose you just as you rose to oppose John! Conflict only breeds more!"

"Maybe, but we plan on being different."

"Oh, I hate idealists. They always think they are different."

"We have to believe that there is something better out there. Now fight me." Pon jumped at Inesh, who barely got away from the hit.

The gate crew was faltering while the prison team reached the final level. The three remaining used Anpu's intel to reach the control room. Just outside of it, Xiaobo and VWTs waited for them.

"It's the end of the road. Now, you three pay the blood owed. For taking out so many men, wearing them out like a dried pen," he attempted to rhyme at the distaste of the ladies.

"This idiot is mine!" Aliesha exclaimed. She charged at the large man, only to be intercepted by VWTs and their heavy armor. Xiaobo laughed at her futile attempts. As Aliesha scowled at Xiaobo, Sam leaped in dand used her quick movements to strike at the armored VWTs, finding any opening she could and taking them out methodically. The nunchaku she used allowed her to hit angles that the VWT's armor could not defend against.

"I'll hold them off," Sam told Aliesha as her gaze turned to Xiaobo again. His eyes grew large as he realized he would have to fight her alone. She charged in and went straight for the large man who could barely keep up with Aliesha's speed and ferocity.

Using the opportunity, Morgan ran to the control center. She was this close to turning the tide of the battle, and only one man stood in her way. However, the one man was Braden, who stared at her in confusion.

"And who are you?" he asked with his back to the control panel.

"You!" she hissed as she grabbed her sai. Her eyes filled with rage and intent to kill that he could see instantly.

"Do I know you?"

"You killed the love of my life and tried to take me!" she yelled as she charged at the small man. He deflected her sai with his dagger.

"That does not narrow it down," he insulted with a fake grin that antagonized her more.

"No matter, because I remember you!" she screamed as she went to attack again. He deflected her attack and then blasted her with gas from his cufflinks. The gas dazed her immediately and dropped her to her knees.

"Unfortunately, I can't let you go any further. John would kill me for sure." He smiled as he kicked her in the gut. Her body dropped to the floor as he paced around her. "You know that ass does look familiar," he taunted as he wiped his boot across her face.

Chapter 27
Shadow Six

The revolutionaries were taking heavy losses in front of the mansion, and Rob could not reach John. The komodos were overpowering in every sector as the revolutionaries were driven back towards the city. Mancio's reinforcements tried to bring life to the situation, but even Mancio was pinned by a pair of komodos when the tragedy occurred.

The Twins were toying with Hennrick and Ava, who were unprepared for the skill level. Younger Brother was a master of every weapon type and countered whatever his opponents used. This consumed Hennrick and Ava's attention, blinding them from the Older Sister who had set a trap. Younger Brother led both of his opponents meticulously toward his sister's trap.

"Come now. Compared to your brother, you two are like preschoolers," Brother insulted as he danced away from Ava's attack. His body was built like a brick house, but he moved like a deer in the forest. His ponytail whipped in the wind as he grabbed the weapons of fallen soldiers and pulled out his own when needed.

"We are just as capable!" Hennrick yelled as his temper was at a boiling point. Brother disarmed him and sent him stumbling forward with a quick sidestep. He then threw a dagger at Hennrick's knee, that crippled him. Ava reacted quickly and engaged the Younger Brother, who laughed at the futile attempts.

"Oh, come now. You really can't be this pathetic…hohahaha." He swept her legs and swung at her, but she rolled to Hennrick before he made contact. "Bad move." He sneered as a flash of light blinded Hennrick and Ava before an explosion erupted around them. The Twins laughed as Mancio cried out.

He sidestepped the swing of a komodo and drove his blade into its eye before running towards his children. The komodo fell with a thud, but Anpu stopped Mancio from charging the Twins.

"Stop," he commanded as he held the angered Mancio.

"Those are my children!" he cried out as the Twin's laughter filled the air.

"I understand, but knowing her, there is a trap waiting for you," Anpu insisted.

"Oh, Master, why would you spoil our fun?" the Older Sister asked as the Brother's laughter finally died down.

"You two have grown even more twisted since I left," Anpu stated as he turned to face his two former pupils.

"That hurts, Master. We loved you; you turned your back on us like a coward!" Sister yelled.

"Is that what he told you? Hmph, I never thought you were that dumb, Sister...I knew he was, but I didn't think you were," Anpu replied as he gripped his weapon. Younger Brother was enraged when Anpu insulted him and attacked.

"How dare you insult me!" Brother yelled as he engaged Anpu. "Now you will die like the bitch God intended you to be!" He sneered as he attacked recklessly, trying to crawl under the skin of his former master.

"Shishishi, well, that leaves you to me old bag." Older Sister laughed as she stared at the frustrated old man. Unlike her younger brother, Sister was a petite thing that glided through the air but landed with devastation. Her armor contained hundreds of small explosives, the size of marbles, that she released on command. Though they were small, they could eliminate areas a thousand times larger.

As his father engaged, Sister and his siblings perished, Enrique was fully committed to Khalil. John personally trained Khalil and was the strongest of the Shadow Six. He moved without sound as he drove his body into Enrique. Both men were like rams headbutting into one another without thought or retreat. Enrique took a swing with his sickle, but Khalil caught the blade with his bear-like hands and delivered a punch that cracked Enrique's sternum. Then, another that caused internal bleeding.

Despite the damage Khalil had inflicted, Enrique had done work as well. The most recent blow had exposed bone in Khalil's left hand, while others had drawn blood from his legs and core. Enrique caught his breath momentarily while Khalil picked up the blade of a fallen soldier.

"That's right, only steel will stop me," Enrique commented as the silent man charged.

Enrique saw the desperation in Khalil's eyes that none of John's other soldiers had. Something drove this man to fight for John, and he would serve his master faithfully until the end.

As they separated, Enrique spun Khalil and thought he had an opening. Yet, Khalil countered by twisting down and slicing Enrique's quad. Enrique fell to his knee and was then kicked in his injured sternum. He landed on his back, barely able to breathe.

Khalil knelt over the fallen man and began to punch his face. The mighty first son was being pummeled. Enrique only had a moment but used his left hand to grab a nearby dagger and drive it into Khalil's neck.

Khalil fell off to the side, but Enrique could not move. Between the cracked sternum limiting his air intake and the new gash in his leg, his body had quit on him. Once the battle was complete, the doctors rushed from the hospital. Jackie was the one who found Enrique and signed for her brother. Enrique looked at the young girl and chuckled. The innocence in her silence spoke volumes compared to Khalil's.

The Widow was taking on both Aster Mothers. The Widow was of average height with Jamaican fire in her blood as she repped a black widow symbol on the back of her armor and poison-dipped blades. She struck with ferocity but rarely went for significant blows. Instead, she tried to deliver as many minor cuts as possible to spread the toxin that covered her blade.

"Time for the old hags to die!" she taunted as she cut the throat of a soldier who attempted to interfere.

"Cocky bitch aren't you," Althea responded as she tried to catch her breath. Widow lunged at Althea, avoiding one of Kathleen's blows, and got behind them. She delivered a long slice along Althea's back and dropped her. The paralysis would hit soon enough, and Kathleen was left one-on-one.

"Sister!" Kathleen yelled as Althea's body began to shiver.

"Don't worry about her. You'll join soon enough."

While, Kathleen was left one-on-one a hundred meters away, one of Pan's captains, a man named Andy, went to engage John, who stood surrounded by a plethora of dead bodies and was plastered with their blood. He stood licking his lips as he awaited the next challenger. His venomous green eyes pierced Andy with fear.

John then charged in with murderous intent. His blades were ready to cut through anything in his path. Andy attempted to raise his weapon to defend himself, but John was too quick. He lopped off Andy's arms and, in the same motion, sheathed his own weapon just so he could use his hands to drive Andy's skull into the ground. Crushing Andy's head against the concrete with a devilish laugh and smile that caught the attention of many. He then charged back into the retreating revolutionaries as the komodos cleared the way with their swings.

A couple miles from the mansion and hospital, the final guards at the gate were cleared, leaving no one but Ken, Inesh, and the tigers to fight Pan, Pon, Dirk, and Tank. With the others gone, Dirk went to assist Pan. Dirk was exhausted from his battles, and the poison was taking its toll when Ken caught him with a left hand. The swipe sent him flying into the city's wall. Breaking the young commanders back on impact.

"Dirk!" Pan yelled as he avoided the giant swing of Ken once again. Dirk made a few grumbling noises to signify he was alive, but Pan could tell he could not get up again.

"Well, well, Pan. Looks like you are going to have to do this all alone," Ken taunted as his next strike sent Pan skidding. Pan drove his blade into the ground to settle himself as he took in the battlefield. Tank was near his limit, and Pon was the last hope.

Inesh was swinging wildly as Pon deflected his attacker's claws. He blasted smoke in Inesh's face before delivering a crushing blow to the man's gut. One that sent the beast trainer flying. But Pon did not relent; he charged again, delivering a blow that crushed Inesh's right femur.

The beast trainer let out a yelp as he dropped to the ground. He was bloodied and bruised as Pon knelt on his chest.

"So, why did you fight?" Pon asked as he pressed his hand into Inesh's leg.

"Gaaahhh!" he yelled, and Pon released the pressure.

"I answered you so you can at least return the courtesy." Inesh's beasts were too distracted by Tank to help their trainer. They had the man pinned with a giant gash across his chest. Inesh looked at his tigers, knowing this would be the end for him.

"I fought because John was the only one who promised them shelter after the War. I could not leave those cubs behind, and he promised they would be safe," Inesh admitted as he reached for his bad leg and stared into the sky. "When I die, they will stop attacking, so can you promise me that they'll be safe as he did?"

"I will not let any harm come to them." Pon nodded as he withdrew a blade from his metal arm.

"That's good, at least…" Inesh smiled as Pon drove his blade into the beast trainer's heart. During their battle, Pon saw Inesh's lunacy, but he also earned Pon's respect. Pon was on the offensive numerous times and saw Inesh peer over at his beast. He was more concerned for them than his own well-being.

As Pon finished Inesh, one of the tigers pierced Tank's jugular and killed the commander, but then it saw their fallen master. It roared, and both beasts ran to Inesh. They lay next to him, and Pon could feel their hearts break.

"No, harm will come to you both," he whispered as another komodo approached the area.

Chapter 28
The Prison

The second floor of the prison was near collapse as Tia's explosive long-range weapons had pierced holes in several columns that hid behind the machinery and kept the roof up while the guardian komodo had knocked down many others in his attack. The komodo's breath was labored as it limped on. Tia could not see out of her left eye and had broken her left collarbone, leaving that arm limp. She could barely move, more or less throw anything else at her attacker as the beast continued to approach her, driven by the mechanical eye's programming that overrode its every desire to stop. As she watched it limp closer, an explosive went off on the floor above. With the weakened supports, the ceiling fell on them. The komodo was pinned by a large rock segment while she was unconscious and barely breathing under the rubble and bodies.

Kya could hear the commotion above her as pieces of that floor fell on her and the guardian. It was not much, but more chaos that she had to avoid as the komodo lunged at her. Her adrenaline was wearing off while the komodo had no stop. She avoided its attack again, but only by inches this time. The komodo broke a steel prison gate with its punch and was honing in on her movements.

On the bottom floor, Aliesha was giving Xiaobo all he could handle. She drove him into a corner and prepared for the kill.

"Yo, yo. Chill, Ms. Kitty, there is room in the city," he begged as she lunged. He appeared scared until the last moment. Then he smiled while pressing a button on his trick arm. As she flew at him, a beanbag shotgun activated, placing a shot right in her ribs. The blow was non-fatal, but Xiaobo broke several ribs using her momentum and caused internal bleeding.

"Oops, that wasn't the kill, but I told you to chill. Next one will be correct, you're about to be decked." He smirked as his arm turned into a mallet, this time that struck her in the damaged ribs. She was sent sliding and writhed in pain as blood started to fill her throat. She spit it out, but he was on the offensive again, placing her in a sleeper hold.

"Liesha!" Sam yelled as she tried to fight through the VWTs, but there were too many. She was trapped in their circle without a way out. If Aliesha were to fall, she would soon follow.

Xiaobo continued to tighten his grip but underestimated her will. She drove her dagger claws into his gut. Causing him to jerk just enough for her to slip out. She then went for his face and caught it just enough to leave marks along his cheek and neck. His yell caught the VWTs' attention, allowing Sam to strike the distracted forces and regain her advantage.

Both thought they were gaining the advantage until Xiaobo turned his arm into a small cannon. He pointed it at Aliesha but could barely control it as it fired everywhere. If it connected, she would be dead. However, with how he fired it, the whole place would collapse if he continued. She needed to get close. She took a step, but he saw it and fired. Barely missing her. It collided with a VWT instead, who was blown away with the man next to him.

"You're going to kill us all!" Aliesha yelled as he continued to fire and blanket the area in smoke and fire.

"And John still wins because the komodos only stop if the system is deactivated, not if I destroy it," Xiaobo claimed as his shots grew more sporadic. As she caught her breath, she felt the water starting to drip from the walls and ceiling.

She spun around multiple shots and went in for the kill, but one hit the ground next to her and sent her rolling to the side. He began to line up and prepared to fire. But before he could, Sam stuck him from behind with her nunchuka. He fell to a knee as she struck him again. Then she went for a third, but he swung his arm wide, sending her flying.

With her out of the way, he lined up his shot again, but just as he was about to fire, Aliesha rolled and threw a dagger at the opening. It collided with the shot as he fired, blowing his arm on impact. Aliesha hopped to her feet and lunged at him. This time, she sent her claws into his fat neck. He hit the ground with a thud, and she ran to Sam.

"Hey, idiot. Rob is going to kill me if you die," she stated as she felt for a pulse.

"Go, help Morgan," Sam grunted as she coughed up some blood. Aliesha set Sam down gently and headed to the door, but it had locked behind Morgan.

Inside, Braden kicked the girl while she was down and taunted her endlessly.

"You know you both would be alive had he just let me have you." He snickered. "But no, people always need to be the hero, and look at what that got you…the same result." He started to undo his belt as he approached her.

He knelt near her and grabbed her face in his hands, "I'm going to enjoy this…and while I do it, you will watch those monitors to see all your friends dying," he stated as he turned her face towards the monitors that showed what the komodos were seeing across the city.

However, he had played with his food for too long. She had regained some feeling from his numbing agent and could grab one of the sai while he taunted her. As he let go of her head, she raised the sai into his genitals. He screamed as he fell over. Grabbing the region as it squirted blood. He writhed in pain as she thrust the sai into his neck.

"His name was Mason," she cried in a whispered tone while he fell to the floor. She crawled up the computers and pressed every button she could until the system's alarm went off, and the shutdown began. Then she hobbled out of the room to help Aliesha carry Sam up the stairs before the lower floor flooded.

The komodo's eye began to shut down across the city, and several komodos collapsed instantly from pain while others spoke and surrendered to their attackers. The boas were immediately disheartened by the events.

Chapter 29
The Gate

Ken stood in shock as he watched his komodo legions turn on him or fall. "How?" Ken asked as he looked around him. His giant blade was at his side, as his jaw dropped.

"Wish I could tell you. But that man is something special." Pan grinned from his knees.

"It doesn't matter. I will end you two still," Ken yelled as he stared down Pon and Pan. Ken raised his mighty weapon as he readied to cut through both men in one swoop.

"You got this?" Pon asked, never withdrawing his weapon.

"Of course." Pan smiled as he twirled his weapon a few times.

"How arrogant." Ken charged with a giant swing of his blade. Pan dove to the side and used the nearby wall to push off. Ken disengaged and sent Pan flying into the building. The force of the impact dropped part of the wooden building on Pan.

Ken smiled as he walked away from the wreckage. He marched towards Pon, who didn't blink as the giant approached.

"Don't you have a fight to finish?" Pon asked the approaching man.

"Hmph, he is dead like you will be soon enough."

"And you called him arrogant," Pon replied as the rubbage shifted, allowing Pan to climb out of it. He brushed the dirt off of his shoulder and spun his blade again. Ken turned to see the fool rising to face him.

This time, he would make sure he died. He charged and swung, splitting Earth when he made contact with the ground. The blade was stuck in the earth momentarily and opened Ken up for a blow, but Pan's sword barely pierced his armor. The weight and density were unreal. Pan had to find a weak spot along with an opening. Ken was angered by the slice and lashed out with his blade. It hit a body on the ground, cutting it in half instantly. As Pan watched Ken remove his sword, he noticed the heavy breaths that Ken had hidden.

Pan did not notice it before, but he wondered how the giant man could swing such a large blade without consequences. The truth was he couldn't. Pan lunged and kept attacking as Ken swung his enormous sword.

He chipped away a little bit at a time while avoiding the blade. It took time, but Pan could feel it weakening just as Ken could. The large man ditched his blade. He threw an elbow that caught Pan in the jaw. Then, he used his diamond gloves to swing more rapidly, breaking Pan's blade and nose as they made contact. He continued to rise as each blow sent him back.

Pan's face was bloodied as he stood barely conscious after the blow. Not only did it shatter his nose, but the edges of the diamonds cut his face up.

"Move to your left!" Pon yelled while Ken charged. Pan did not hesitate as he followed directions. Ken's right hook missed, and Pon moved in, using his metal arm to strike Ken's armor breastplate. Shattering it on impact and causing the giant to stumble backward. Pan jumped forward and drove his broken blade into the man's heart.

"I told you I had it," Pan said as he coughed up the blood draining from his nose. While Pan looked at Pon, he felt his left hand shatter. Ken had taken one last swing before falling to the ground for good.

With the end of the komodos, the courtyard turned in Rob's favor. The guards who had been driving were now pushed back. Allowing Rob to push toward John. Dani was close behind as she stayed close to his back, never letting a guard land a cheap blow from behind. As they pushed, John retreated to his mansion.

Meanwhile, Kathleen and the Widow were still exchanging blows.

"Just die, you hag!" the Widow cried as they fought.

"Age is what makes us strong, you punk."

"Until you become brittle!" The Widow was ferocious with her attack, but Kathleen could see she was not used to an extended fight. The blows became uncoordinated and telegraphed, easy for her to reflect and parry. This frustrated the young Widow more. She swung and grazed Kathleen's left arm when she tried to dodge. But in the process, her momentum carried her too far forward. Kathleen swung fast and sliced Widower's back. She tumbled as the blood oozed from the wound.

"You bitch…" she snarled while she tried to regain her footing.

"Just surrender. A wound like that does not have to be life-threatening, but if you attack again, it will open up more," Kathleen warned.

"Just die!" Widower yelled as she ignored Kathleen's advice and charged in.

"Fine, have it your way," Kathleen mumbled as the Widow tried to slice at her again, but the wound tore more open on her back as she swung forward. Killing her momentum instantly. Kathleen wanted to warn her again, but it was to no avail. Widow went in again, and Kathleen dodged her blow, letting the young woman stumble in pain. This time, she fell over and hit the floor with heavy breathing. Her body started to enter shock as she fainted on the ground.

Kathleen walked over and stabbed the Widow through the heart, "No need to suffer anymore," she whispered as she withdrew her blade. With the fight over, she ran to her sister and tried to sit her up. Calling for any available field medic.

While Kathleen called for the medics, Anpu sat beside the Younger Brother, who had giant slashes across his chest. His body was barely hanging on and breathing with extreme difficulty as Anpu watched Older Sister battle Mancio.

She had led him into numerous explosions that littered his body with burns, but revenge kept him moving. He had cut one of her hands off, and now he kept chasing her. Both of them were waiting for the other to drop.

"I never understood why John blamed himself for Trisha...but now I understand," Anpu said as he watched Mancio battle Older Sister, who was doing her best to blow him away. Younger Brother couldn't respond. All he could do was breathe laboriously as his body started to die.

"You two had seen war already when I found you imprisoned by some gang bosses. I could have shown you something different. I could have shown you what it means to be loved in this new era, but I taught you about death."

Younger Brother coughed up blood and moaned as his only response.

"I failed to give you better, and...and failed you again," Anpu cried as Mancio finally grabbed Older Sister and stabbed her through her gut. "I can't even show mercy by killing you now...I'm not strong enough." He teared, trying to wipe his eyes as he watched Older Sister slide off Mancio's blade and his body collapse beside her. Exhausted and half-dead, he could no longer stand. Younger Brother coughed out blood again as his heart finally gave way. His eyes closed as Anpu cried for his fallen students.

Chapter 30
The Executioner

Rob and Dani chased John up the stairs to the second floor. He had a step on them, but he was leading them where he wanted to go, at last running into his office. Before they could reach the door, Dani jumped in front of him, absorbing a pair of thrown blades. Rob stopped as blood dripped from her wounds.

"Dani!" he called as he ran to her. Looking up, he saw Ex in the shadows juggling a blade. Dani took a few breaths as her eyes turned to the black-cloaked figure.

"I'll take care of them. You go finish the fight," she ordered as she pulled out both her blade and whip to fight.

"Alright."

"And don't do anything stupid."

"Never." He ran into the room where John waited for him. Ex approached Dani with daggers drawn.

"You have terrible aim. Those daggers wouldn't have been fatal," she taunted as they circled each other.

"Do I really? I seem to have hit my target," Ex replied, tossing a blade in Dani's direction. It was not meant to hit her but to see how she would respond. Ex's eyes peered through the mask into Dani's heart. Her body was exhausted from battling at the gate, through the city, and in front of the mansion. Meanwhile, Ex had stayed behind waiting for them.

"So, you knew I would jump in front of the blades," she said with a crack of her whip. The whip hit the air just in front of Ex's face without a single reaction.

"Of course, I needed you to stay with me so they could settle this alone."

"And why would you want that?"

"Because if John dies. Then I can rule it all," Ex claimed. At that moment, the lightbulb clicked in Dani. The voice had been deepened, but Rob had told her everything he had learned in Memphis.

"Trisha…" Dani stuttered as she stopped walking.

"Trisha died years ago. The Executioner rules this body!" Ex yelled as she moved into her battle stance.

"Let's end this."

Ex twitched first as she skipped to the side, throwing a pair of needles Dani deflected while cracking her whip. They moved toward each other, allowing blades to collide. Several quick strikes as each turned their defense into offense just to defend again. Dani ducked under a swing and went for a swipe but was met with a kick as Ex did a flip backward. Tossing needles that caught Dani in the shoulder this time.

"Nice move." She pulled the needles out and went in again. This time, a step quicker, she knocked the blade away from Ex. Who then slid side-to-side, avoiding the blows until she grabbed Dani's arm. Twisting it and disarming her as well. Without their weapons, they caught one another's blows with their free hands and locked horns for a moment, trying to overpower each other. Dani was stronger and started to lean over Ex, who rolled back using their momentum and then launched Dani with a kick. She rolled onto her feet as Ex kiped up.

Their next swings met similar results, but this time, they disengaged and swung through with matching elbows that caught each other in the chin, cracking Ex's mask ever so slightly. Neither backed down as their opponent drove their elbows. They were mirror images of each other as they danced in front of the large oak doors separating them from John and Rob. The battle was near even, but Dani's exhaustion started to show as her following kicks were just a bit slower.

"Are you tired?" Ex mocked with a smile that Dani could feel coming from under the now chipped mask.

"Nah, princess. I'm just warming up."

"Don't call me that!" Ex yelled as she lunged at Dani with her needles drawn. Dani avoided the rapid blows and landed a knee to Ex's ribs. As Ex folded from the impact, she drove her fist into Dani's hip, sticking it with needles. As Ex stumbled back, her hand readjusted the padding on the armor that protected her gut.

"I'm surprised that the world's darling princess hates such a simple word." Dani pulled the needles from her hip and threw them to the side. Something in Ex's body language was changing. Her shoulders tightened each time Dani said, princess.

"Never repeat it!" She pulled out more of her needles and threw them in quick succession. Only to be avoided or deflected by the whip. Even these throws were more erratic and easier to avoid than before.

Dani twisted her wrist and hurled the whip at Ex as the last needle fell. The whip caught her in the mask, knocking her off her feet. She rolled for a few feet before swirling back to her knees. The crack growing in her mask.

"Can I ask you something?" Dani asked in an attempt to catch her breath.

"Sure," Ex responded as she tried to figure out her next move.

"Why fight us if you want John dead as well?"

"Because Rob will not let me rule this world. I need all of you to die for me to take my seat on the throne," she answered while grabbing her blade off of the ground. Dani saw the action and lunged at her own when Ex approached her.

Ex was pushing her to her limit with the speed behind the bladework. As they struggled, their grips slid, sending both blades into the nearby wall. It was back to their hands as they traversed the room, but now Ex landed a few body blows before Dani hit the mask again. The crack covered the entire left side now and only hung on by a prayer.

"So, you are fighting for you then?" Dani started wincing from the pain.

"No! No, I fight for all the women forced to suffer in this world constructed by those idiots! I do it to build a world for people like you and me!" Ex claimed as she began to pace again.

"Sure, we are both women, but there is no you and I. There is no you and I because I would not have put up with a rapist like Braden or hid my face behind a mask so that I could be more like them. All while acting like this cruel yet innocent princess the whole time." Dani's words enraged Ex. She threw her needles again, but this time with no aim. Dani barely had to deflect the misguided attack.

"Don't you dare make assumptions. If it were not for John, I would have castrated that Pig! As for the mask, I wear it because the original owner made it a symbol of fear. She was strong until she chose to become the weak male she is now! I had to reclaim it because Trisha was weak...Ex is strong." Ex moved even faster now, but the blows were increasingly erratic. She had left herself open for counters.

After one of Dani's counters, Ex grabbed the whip from Dani's side and spun around her opponent. She started to choke Dani, who fought it off the best she could. She tried to put space between it and her neck, but Ex would not budge. At last, Dani went for it. She threw the back of her head into Ex's mask, shattering it. The whip dropped to the floor as Ex hobbled back while her mask fell to the floor. Trisha's devil eyes looked at her now.

Trisha grabbed a needle and began to swing it wildly like a knife. Dani sidestepped the swing, grabbing her arm in the process. With a twist, the needle was dropped. Dani grabbed it and sent it through the palm of Trisha's hand, then grabbed the other hand. Doing the same thing before bending the edges. Trisha's hands were bound together behind her back as a bent needle pinned them. She separated from Dani before beginning to writhe in pain. She dropped to her knees when she realized she was trapped.

Dani looked at the young girl who was younger than Dani was when the War started. She looked at her and remembered something Rob had said after Trisha had talked to him again.

"She is a vile wretch just like her uncle," Dani said to Rob as they sat alone in Clarissa's house. He paused before answering. His gaze rested outside of the window.

"But she is also a child, Dani. A child I held in my arms when John faked his own death."

"Sure, but she is also the same child that led you and Iris to John's trap. Being a child doesn't change being psychotic."

"That's the thing...she is psychotic, but she would have been treated back before the War."

"Treated? Really, after all this, you want to get her treatment." Dani was shocked but could hear Iris in his voice as well.

"Dani, you haven't seen that look in her eyes. Looking into them, you see the eighteen-year-old who has suffered some tragedy. You see the innocence lost and the child that needs help. Not a jury-judge-executioner."

And now she was looking in those eyes for the first time. She was looking at her as she writhed in pain, still trying to fight with no way of doing it. She was looking at her and saw her.

"Come on, kill me!" Trisha yelled as she finally surrendered on the ground. Dani picked up her knife and looked at it. Seeing Trisha's face just past the edge. She saw Trisha's dead eyes, dyed black hair, and a youth corrupted by pain.

"No."

"No?" Trisha's eyes grew large.

"No, I won't kill you. Rob was right. You need help, not death," Dani replied softly. Trisha just screamed before Dani knocked her out with a kick. Shaking her head, she wondered if it was the right move, but she could not do it after seeing who was behind Ex.

Chapter 31
Together

As Dani and Trisha began their fight, Rob entered John's office. John stood by the window with his messenger bird. He gave it another mouse before sending it away, his blades at his sides as he watched the creature soar away.

"Thank you for your patience. Just wanted to set him free," John said as he turned to face Rob, withdrawing his blades. Both men stared at each other, just waiting to make their moves.

Then they lunged at each other simultaneously, John the master of dual-wielded blades and Rob the master of his two-handed staff. The fluidity of their movements was unlike anyone else on the battlefield. John would go high, and Rob would shift the right side of the staff to block while twisting the left side to go low. John matched the low attack with his second blade. This pattern, or various versions, continued for several minutes as they barely moved a foot.

Their styles were so precise that they could have been fighting in a room that was 10x10, and they would never have struck a wall. Even as they changed attacks, they would find themselves in a stalemate. There was no advantage, so they jumped away to reset and rethink their strategy.

Neither said a word as they circled each other. Their eyes spoke more than words ever could. John's venom green eyes were filled with rage, which he used for strength, while Rob's sea blues were calm and collected. One man used the storm's power to fuel him, while the other lived in the center of it.

John spun his blades and stepped quickly at Rob, who responded similarly. This time, their focus was on speed. The metal scraped and sparked as their movements could barely be tracked. Just missing one another by fractions. No energy was saved, nor was it wasted in the fight. These masters of battle went full force with passion in every swing.

They separated again to reevaluate the fight, "So, a straight-up fight is not going to end this," John stated as he took in his surroundings.

"It would appear not," Rob replied as he did the same.

They engaged, this time, using their feet to change the flow of the battle, doing whatever they could to draw their opponent out of a battle position. Rob used John's momentum to flow around him like Sam and Kya. However, Rob's attacks resulted in the same results. Either John would deflect the staff or dodge, leaving Rob to stumble into a chair.

John gained a slight advantage when he used his blades to separate Rob from his staff. It slid across the ground, stopping in front of a grandfather clock in the corner. Then, one of John's swings left him open. Rob locked onto it and twisted it while avoiding a swing from the other hand. He separated John from the blade and grabbed it for himself.

Each man had a blade now, and their battle continued. Each strike would lead to the next as they twisted and maneuvered around the room. Rob jumped over the large meeting table as John slid across it to catch him. Their combat continued without a missed step. They were flawless in technique, knowing a single falter could be the difference, but also knowing they knew each other too well.

"You've gotten better," John complimented as they separated again. His breaths were shallow but steady.

"And despite being sick, you're still pretty good," Rob replied as he tried to plan his next move. John had seen most of his skill set before, and the old ways would not work. He had to take a lesson from Mark and the girls. He took a deep breath to center his mind and become fully present.

"Ready for the next round?" John positioned himself to be more aggressive.

"I have a few more left in me." Rob smiled as he set himself, but his position differed from what John had seen.

Rob started to move like water as he flowed around John's strikes without delivering any of his own. His movements used John's aggression to destabilize him. Meanwhile, Rob analyzed each moment as its own, waiting for the right moment. John's next swing went a hair long, leaving him overstretched without a solid base below him. Rob acted fast, separating John from his blade, but John was not to be outdone by the sudden move. He used his speed to get close to Rob to negate the blade. Then, he grabbed the hand with the sword and knocked it away as he headbutted Rob.

The two proud warriors' battle turned from an elegant duel to a bloody fistfight. Blows landed more frequently as the bare-knuckle brawl grew sloppy. Each man grew desperate as it continued, grabbing lamps, books, and chairs they could swing or throw.

With their bodies growing tired, they went after each other's weak spots. John swung a chair leg at Rob's ribs and went for the leg Rob damaged during their first mission. Rob responded by focusing on John's right shoulder. An injury sustained during the War's final days had left it prone to being separated, but rarely did anyone get close enough to worsen it. Then Rob went after John's previously damaged left oblique.

The fight grew uglier and uglier. Limbs hung long, and blood was dripping at dangerous paces. Neither man could breathe easily while their movement speed plummeted. There was no style when Rob caught John and drove him back first into the large desk. John was laid out in the wreckage of the desk as Rob rolled away to catch a few breaths.

"Now…Now I understand…why…you were mad…at me…tables hurt." John panted as he crawled to his knees.

"Yeah…they do…jack…ass. Now yield," Rob pleaded as he rose to his feet, shaking.

"You wish. But I am death…the old lady told us…So you have to stop me…I told you…you have no choice."

"Mancio explained…that she didn't tell us…everything."

"What?" John's eyesight had grown blurry from the blood that dripped around him.

"Yeah…apparently we are driven by it…I…I am driven by life and the love of it…while you are driven by those that are dead or fear of death." He panted with a slight step towards John that sent a painful shiver up his body.

"Hmph, well…Maybe there was a choice…but not now…now you need to kill me," John taunted.

"Oh, I will stop you," Rob boasted as he stood ready for John.

"Then enough talk!" John yelled as they grappled again. Each man threw haymakers as it was all they had left. Their fight had turned into two men just punching each other one at a time. Waiting to see who would fall first. Then, they both stopped throwing punches as they leaned against each other. Only standing thanks to the others' mass. John bit Rob on the shoulder, which caused Rob's body to push John down, only for him to fall as well.

Both men lay on the ground, fighting the urge to pass out. Driven by the need to win the fight regardless of what that meant. As Rob's conscience slipped away, he heard something.

"Get up," the voice of Iris whispered in his ear. The sound kept his mind awake, *"Get up and save Alex. Save Dani and the girls."* Rob felt around his jacket and found the knife she had given him.

He rolled to his stomach and began to crawl an inch at a time towards John. John looked at his approaching brother and tried to move, but his body was exhausted. All he could do was grab a shard of glass from a lamp broken during the fight. Once Rob was within reach, John thrusted the glass shard into Rob's oblique while Rob sent his knife into John's Achilles Tendon, slicing it in half. Both yelped with the last bit of energy they had.

"Just yield," Rob begged as he tried to pull the glass shard from his side.

"Never…my son would have been celebrating his…cele…his birth…today…I can't dis…disappoint." John wheezed as his body convulsed.

"I'm sorry…but they wouldn't want it…they wouldn't want this…" Rob pleaded as he tried to find John's humanity. "And…I don…I don't think you do either."

"You don't know anything."

"But I do…I do because Iris didn't…she didn't want me to chase you…and I know…know you didn't have to wait for me…this could have ended months ago."

John stayed quiet for a moment, and Rob hoped he had passed out, but then saw the tears, "I miss them…"

"Mo Shíorghrá," Rob whispered as he looked at the knife.

"What?"

"It's Gaelic…it means my eternal love…We can always miss them, John…but if your love was true, they are always there…that flame is eternal…so, what would they want?" Rob asked.

"They'd…they would…to move on…to forgive, but I can't…this world just breeds suffering and deserves to die…I was not able to save it...I had...no choice...I needed to make sure others didn't suffer..." John cried as his tears and blood mixed on the floor.

"So you doom my child...my daughter...to death," Rob muttered; John just looked at him with shock.

"Wha...what...what daughter?"

"Apparently, I have a ten-year-old daughter." Rob teared, looking at his friend.

"10...so Iris...wow. She'll be trouble."

"And I'll love her no matter what." John just lay in silence again. The only sound that could be heard was that of their breath.

"I wonder if...my son would be 15 today...he would have made a good brother."

"He would have...so please...please give my daughter the chance he never did," Rob pleaded.

John lay on the ground momentarily as he thought about his son and imagined what Rob's daughter was like. His eyes turned to the window that overlooked the field, and something stirred in him.

He crawled to a bookcase by the window while Rob tried to pursue him. Each man struggled through the pain. John reached the bookcase and used it to climb up to stand on one foot. Knowing he could not do the same, Rob rolled to a seat and prepared for anything, but John just looked at the battle below. He stood saying nothing and grabbed a button from the bookshelf.

"What is that, John?"

"A detonator...I collected all...all the...nukes left...and this activates them...under each Ascen...Ascension."

"Don't...please..." Rob coughed as he tried to regain his breath and strength.

"I...don't have...no...choice." John looked up to the sky. Clouds that had filled the air were clearing, and the sun was piercing through the smoke.

"Yes, you do," Rob pleaded as he tried to stand, using anything for support.

"No...if I surrender...They will drag me...I...don't let me...be their prize...And you...you can't kill me!" He turned his eyes to the sky again and could see their faces for a moment. He saw Bunny and Lawrence.

"John..."

"Rob..."

"You have a choice…"

John closed his eyes as his convictions steadied. "I do…but its not the one…save Trisha…There is good somewhere…Then find Sweets and Pops…let them attend the funeral."

"John…"

"And I loved you…Hold your daughter tight…" John smashed the window.

"John…" As his brother looked at him, Rob said, "You were the brother I needed." John placed the detonator down and leaned back, allowing his unstable body to fall out the window.

Rob fell back down and gripped the ground, struggling to keep his tears away. He was barely conscious or alive when Dani finally knocked down the door. She ran to Rob's side and held him in her arms. Her eyes scanned the room for John, but all she saw was the blood by the open window. She pulled Rob tight to her as he passed out in her arms.

Chapter 32
After the End

Over the next week, Rob passed in and out of consciousness, along with many of the fighters being treated in the main hospital and makeshift ones. As civilians returned to the city, the bodies from both sides were buried, and people helped to clear the wreckage. An estimated 2,500 people were killed between the two sides, with over a thousand more dealing with injuries. Outside of Trisha, John's higher-ranking officials were dead, and the city attempted to move on.

Those who still wished to inhabit the city helped to tear down the wall and were led by Mancio and Enrique in all reconstruction efforts. With John's fall, those who worked for Ascension in other services feared that they would be outcasted, but many who were willing to work were still welcome. Clarissa even ensured that Maki kept a job as they developed a cure for the komodos.

As Mancio and Clarissa worked to stabilize the city, Pan worked to ensure global peace. Once his left hand had been amputated, he sent messages to Brooke informing her of the victory. He emphasized the urgency for her to enact any plans she had drawn up while he was gone. The news of John's fall would quickly spread to Berlin and Tokyo Ascension headquarters and non-Ascension assets, creating power struggles that could create even more chaos even if they did not move fast.

After about a week, Rob finally awoke. Looking around his room, he saw Sam, Morgan, Anna, Pon, Clarissa, and Dani surrounding him. Each hugged him as they informed him about the final outcomes and the lives lost.

"And what now?" he asked.

"We celebrate!" Mancio proclaimed as he hobbled into the room with Enrique.

"Celebrate?"

"Yes, the people need something. There is a lot of darkness right now, and some light can help them with the transfer." Mancio grinned as he sat at the foot of Rob's bed.

"He can barely move," Clarissa objected with hands on hips. Anna just put her hand on Clarissa's shoulder and shook her head.

"That won't stop any of them," Anna conceded as Rob began to smile under his bandages.

The following morning, a few hours before the celebration, Rob, Dani, Sam, Morgan, and Clarissa joined Sweets and Pops to cremate John. Rob had instructed a group of civilians to place a mound of debris from the wall's wood and make a pyre. Then he had John's body wrapped in cloth and placed on the wood.

Pops was the first to step forward, "To my confused son-in-law. I wish we could have helped you walk a different path, but no matter what you did, I will love you for the happiness you brought my daughter." Pops placed his torch in the pyre.

Sweets followed him, "The one comfort I've always had in my daughter's and grandson's death is that for as long as you were in their lives, they were the happiest. When my daughter told me about you, I thought you would be trouble, but you became a son, and no matter what you did, I will always be thankful for our time." Sweets threw her torch in and instantly turned around to cry.

"Though you started as my boss, I grew to love you. I saw the sweetness and kind eyes you hid from everyone else. I miss the days you made me laugh and smile like no one else. We may not have had what you and Bunny did, but I think we were happy for a time. You made me happy." Clarissa knelt down to place her torch in.

Rob paused for a moment as he watched the fire start to build. He could not find the words to say until Dani gripped his arm. He took one final breath before speaking. "During the War, we never thought we would get an actual funeral. We both figured we would be alone in the woods, known only to maggots. We were brothers and, at times, fought like it, but there was always love there. We saved each other's lives so, so many times…In truth, I wouldn't have made it home without you.

"Despite it all, you never told me the truth. You always held back and hurt because of it. You were my brother, and I was never there for your pain." Rob held back tears as he bit his lip so he could continue. "I wasn't there, and I am sorry. I will never forgive you,

John, but I will always love you. I hope you are finally at peace." Rob added his torch to the pyre, and Dani gave him a small bag filled with the letters and engraved shell casing from Rob's journey that he threw in. Sam and Morgan grabbed one of his hands as the fire grew. The two of them wept for him as he refused to cry as the other three did.

The body and pyre turned to ash over a few hours. Then they placed some ashes inside an urn and took them to where Bunny and Lawrence were buried. The urn was placed in the dirt between them, and they all said their final goodbyes.

That night, barrels of liquor and food were rolled to the mansion's field. The estate had been gutted of all usable goods before turning into a bonfire. Injured soldiers danced and cheered as they drank more than they had in years. New Orleans lived up to its reputation to entertain all within its borders. With songs being sung in many tongues, filling the air with merriness.

As the soldiers partied, Pon was responsible for calming Anna down. Despite the orders to enjoy themselves, she constantly worried about her patients as they pushed their limits, dancing and drinking. He laughed as she scolded those who opened their stitches. Eventually, he had to pour her several drinks. Once she had enough, she threw her hands to the sky and turned her attention to her husband.

Anpu and Catori stayed off to the side to discuss their own business.

"So, you were from the Oneida tribe originally," Catori stated while Anpu drank from his cup.

"I was, but my mother was unhappy that her only daughter considered herself more male than female. But I do miss them now," Anpu replied with a long stare into his drink.

"I can imagine. I know it's true for many cultures across the globe, but losing so many tribes…again, was devastating. Eons of stories and tales lost for good."

"It was indeed, but not much can be done."

"No, there is something," she said as her eyes turned to the stars shining bright above them. The smoke from the mansion fire danced across the skyline.

"And that is?" Anpu asked as he looked to see what she was staring at.

"Now that John is gone, I want to restore Native people. There is land for us again, but this time, I want us all to be a united tribe."

"A united tribe?"

"Yes, one that accepts all wanders like us who lost our people. That way, we can be strong and hold onto our cultures. As something united."

"And where would this be?"

"Well, I'm stationed in old Colorado, so that would be a good start." She smiled. It was the first time she could recall discussing a future focused on unity instead of fighting. It was refreshing.

"A start indeed." As their conversation shifted, they started to dance the dances of their own cultures. Several soldiers and civilians who hailed from tribes of their own gravitated to the pair.

As Catori and Anpu discussed their futures, Mother Althea tried pushing some of her Asters on Rob, but he declined so he could celebrate with his friends. Mother Althea was a bit disappointed in Rob for not joining her in the celebrations, and some of her Asters were just as sad, but Rob gave Mother Althea a kiss on the cheek and left for his friends.

By the fire pit, a dance floor had opened up, putting Sam and Morgan in their element as they became the life of the party. Dancing and singing at every opportunity. They engaged with everyone they could. Dani was much more reserved until Rob convinced her to take a few shots with him. Soon after, they were in the circle's center via his influence. Sam and Morgan cheered them on as Rob broke out every dance move his body could handle, and a few tugged at the stitches. Luckily, Anna was too far gone at that point to care. She just rolled her eyes and kissed Pon.

When Rob grew tired, he sat by Pon and Anna, who had taken a position on a log that had been rolled to the field. "I'm glad you two came."

"I helped you start this, so it's only right we finished it together," Pon replied.

"Yeah, and someone had to...had to keep you alive." Anna hiccupped through her words as she tried to collect herself. Both of the men chuckled at her out-of-character struggles.

"Thank you for that, Anna, and I promise you won't need to stitch me up again anytime soon." Anna threw her hands in the air, celebrating. The action almost caused her to fall backward had Pon not caught her. "So, what will you two do now?"

Anna looked at Pon briefly with a pouty lip before kissing his cheek. "We'll head back. She has been doing a phenomenal job leading the Ascension workers in Despartian, and I have made a few technical advancements that will make Pan's life easier as he unites the world," Pon replied as he pulled Anna tight. He kissed her again passionately.

"I'm happy to hear it and happy for both of you." As Rob spoke, he saw a civilian growing too close to Sam, and by her tightened fist, she was not happy about it. "I'll talk to you later. I have to handle something."

While Rob ran to keep Sam from knocking the man out, Dani exited from the dance floor towards Enrique and Mancio. The two sat in the back of the celebration, avoiding much of the antics despite it being Mancio's idea.

"So, why are you two back here?" she asked, sitting on the ground near them.

"Not much of a dancer," Mancio replied as he tapped his prosthetic foot.

"No excuse; this was your idea, old man. The city's people want a leader willing to have fun." Enrique chuckled at the comments while his father groaned.

"She is right, father. You should get in there."

"No, I am staying here. Now, we will change topics." Mancio looked through his son with the reply. "So, what will you do now that the fight is over?"

"I'm not sure." Dani looked at the giant fireball that was once the mansion as she spoke.

"Hm, based on what I hear about you, that is most uncommon, so why the indecision?" Dani said nothing and just stared at the fire again. "I wonder if an adopted family or a general that you have sworn yourself to tear you in two different ways."

Dani dropped her head, "Something like that."

"Well, I would advise you to think about this. Pan told me he has grand plans, and I fear we may find ourselves in trouble again without capable people like you."

"Then why are you leading New Orleans for him if you are worried?"

"Because he needs capable people," Mancio started, pausing to smoke. "And I abandoned my city once. I will not do it again, so please think about what you will do, but in the meantime, it looks like your friend needs help," Mancio pointed to Dirk, who had fallen out of his new wheelchair. When Dani saw this, she ran to help him instantly, stopping for a quick goodbye.

At first, he dismissed her attempts to help, but when he could not crawl back in, he finally relented.

"Don't worry, you'll get a hang of it," she told him as she stood by him.

"Aye, I will, but what does it matter? I no longer know what I will do with my life. All that sacrifice, and in the end, I heard that Pan did not trust me. He thought I was the spy," Dirk hollered as he reached for a glass of liquor that was nearby.

"Dirk, he was under a lot of stress. Can you really blame him?"

"Of course I can, especially now. I gave everything for him, and now…now he is going to leave me."

"Leave you? What do you mean?"

Dirk took a drink and cleared a tear from his eye. "He told me this morning that I will no longer be a commander given my circumstances. He said I will be an 'ambassador' in New Orleans…bah…he just wants to place me somewhere that I can feel useful without doing anything. I've heard his talks with Brooke. He always planned on rooting out the old heads for ones that know 'peaceful things,'" he said, putting air quotes around the last words.

"Come now, Dirk, Pan has always been loyal to us. He is just trying to take care of and reward us now that the fighting is over." Dani was confused by Dirk's words, and as she spoke, she tried to comprehend what he was saying.

"Trust me, Dani, once Catori has united the tribes, when Mancio hands over this city, and the Asters swear their allegiance, he will eliminate us all. It's his idea of peace, not ours."

"Dirk."

"Don't…just leave me be. He'll probably keep you if you're cute and useful," he said as he started to roll away before she could reply. Unsure of what to do, Dani returned to Rob and the girls talking to Clarissa close to the fire.

"Oh, Dani, there you are. I was just telling these three how much I appreciate you all, and I wanted to thank you for bringing Pan. This city needed that and him." She smiled as the two embraced for a quick hug.

"You're welcome…but I also…" Dani was cut off before she could finish. A voice from around the fire had called for Clarissa.

"Hold that thought. I will be right back." Clarissa stumbled her way to the voice and left the others alone. Dani sat with a long look on her face from the conversations she had, and this instantly caught the attention of Sam.

"What's wrong, Dani? We should be having fun." She grinned.

"Oh, just a few things on my mind now."

"Well, let them go and come dance with us. Rob told us you were a dancer when you were younger." Sam started to pull Dani's arm to the dance floor with the help of Morgan. Dani just looked at Rob, who was laughing.

"It's your turn, Dani. They just wore me out a few minutes ago," Rob hollered as they pulled on her. It took some time, but Morgan and Sam could finally distract Dani and bring a smile back to her face.

The party lasted until the first glimmers of light. The mansion turned into nothing but embers, with only a few awake in the morning to hear Kathleen playing one final song on a piano pulled out of the estate. It was a somber melody that those awake could sing along to. Rob and Dani sang as they watched over the other two who'd passed out. Pon sang it softly like a lullaby while Anna rested on his lap. Even Mancio joined in the harmony for a while.

As the piano notes echoed in the air, the last few singers passed out, and the celebration ended. Most did not wake up until late morning or the afternoon. Even Rob finally found peace while sleeping in that open field with the others.

He was still the first to wake up from his group, and he found himself wandering around the field, smiling at the happiness they all shared. He sat looking out at the water's edge and took a moment to breathe. That breath was the longest, deepest, and greatest he had taken in years. A weight on his chest finally lifted itself as a pure calm filled his every fiber.

While meditating, Pan approached him from behind. "What do you see when you look out across the water?"

"I see a peace that has been avoiding me for over a decade. And you?"

Pan paused to honestly look at the water, "I see possibilities. We have defeated the man who oppressed us, and now we have an opportunity to unite the world as one."

"We?"

"Yes, we. I want you by my side, Rob. This world needs its heroes and strong people like you and me who can fight for a better world." Rob shook his head as he sat in silence. "Why not? I need you so we can build this republic."

"No, Pan, I am done fighting. I will support you as you build this world, and if you need counsel to avoid becoming John, I will be there, but I am going home."

Pan paced behind Rob, thinking about the reply, "But why? You saw what happened last time you did nothing. I need strong people to be ready. I need you and Dani by my side."

"Pan, I cannot speak for Dani, but I told her I would not fight another man's battles. I'll be in Despartian with my daughter if you need me."

"Would you change your mind if I told you that Aliesha broke Trisha out of custody? Or would telling you that one of the criminals that John had locked up escaped with a group of others, and they have already started to cause issues in the region this week."

Rob shook his head again, "No, I will handle Trisha if the time comes, but this other prisoner is not my concern. As my first counsel, I warn you that taking the world by force will create issues."

"Hmph, apathy, yet you give advice. I will unite the world however I see fit, and when we are one, then democracy can rule again." Rob's head just shook as he avoided making eye contact with Pan.

"Pan, I will be in Despartian. And I will not fight your battles, especially if this is your route, but know this: I will stop you if you become a tyrant."

Pan wiped his face with his hand and started to walk away, "Fine, tell Dani I will await her answer then."

Rob sat meditating until his friends awoke and stumbled over to him hungover. From there, he led Dani, Sam, and Morgan to the fallen monument dedicated to those lost during the War and since. Each prayed and talked to those they had lost while counting their blessings to have the people next to them.

Dani and Rob walked a little behind the other two on their walk back to Clarissa's house. Dani asked Rob first, "So, what will you do?"

"I'm going home to take care of my daughter and show these two lives not plagued by war," he replied with the purest smile she had ever seen from him, and then he asked her the question, "And you?"

Sam and Morgan both turned to hear her answer and input their thoughts, "Please come with us." Dani pulled them in close as she thought.

"I'll be there occasionally, but I need to ensure Pan does this right," she replied half-heartedly.

"No, please stay," they both begged again, holding her tighter. Their eyes grew bigger as Dani thought about her answer more. Deep down, she knew she wanted the same peace, but it was not these two that needed to ask her to stay.

"Only if he asks," she said at last. The ladies all turned to Rob, who was still grinning from his answer. He looked at them and held his tongue for a moment, letting the moment hang in the air before finally speaking.

"Please come to Despartian. I can't deal with these two and raise a 10-year-old without your help. I need you." They all smiled, and Rob pulled them in tight and held them all as he looked to the sky and saw a group of mourning doves flying above them. "It's finally time to go home."

www.ingramcontent.com/pod-product-compliance
Lightning Source LLC
Chambersburg PA
CBHW031437200726
48289CB00002BA/428